A Boy made of Blocks

reader love

A Boy made of Blocks

Keith Stuart

sphere

SPHERE

First published by Sphere in 2016
This paperback edition published by Sphere in 2016

7 9 10 8

A CIP catalogue record for this book
is available from the British Library.

ISBN 978-0-7515-6329-0

Typeset in Electra by M Rules
Printed and bound in Great Britain by
Clays Ltd, St Ives plc

Papers used by Sphere are from well-managed forests
and other responsible sources.

MIX
Paper from
responsible sources
FSC® C104740

Sphere
An imprint of
Little, Brown Book Group
Carmelite House
50 Victoria Embankment
London EC4Y 0DZ

An Hachette UK Company
www.hachette.co.uk

www.littlebrown.co.uk

To Morag, Zac and Albie, for everything

Chapter 1

I am estranged.

This is the first thought that hits me as I leave the house, cross the road and climb into our battered old estate car. I guess the correct term is *we* are estranged, but then mostly, I suppose, this is my fault. I look back through the rear-view mirror and see my wife, Jody, in the doorway, her long hair dishevelled and knotted. Burying his head into her side is our eight-year-old son, Sam. He is trying to simultaneously cover his eyes and his ears, but I know it's not because he doesn't want to see me go. He is anticipating the sound of the engine, which will be too loud for him.

I raise my hand in a dumb apologetic gesture, the sort you make when you accidentally pull out in front of someone at a junction. Then I turn the key and start to pull slowly away. The next thing I know, Jody is at the driver-side window, knocking gently. I wind it down.

'Take care of yourself, Alex,' she says. 'Please figure things out – like you should have done years ago, when we were happy. Perhaps if you had ... I don't know. Perhaps we'd be happy now.'

1

Her eyes are moist and she angrily wipes away a tear with the back of her hand. Then she is looking at me, and it seems the expression on my face, of sorrow, of guilt, suddenly impacts on her anger. Her glistening stare becomes something softer.

'Remember that camping holiday we went on in Cumbria?' she says. 'The one where those goats ate our tent and you got trench foot? Whatever's happening here, it's not as bad as that, OK?'

I nod silently, put the car into gear and start heading up the road. When I check the mirror again, I see that Jody and Sam have already gone back in. The front door is closed.

That's it. Ten years together and it could all be over. And now I'm in our crappy car, driving away, and I have no idea where I'm going.

Sam was a beautiful baby. He was always beautiful. He was born with thick brown hair and these big sultry lips – like a tiny incontinent Mick Jagger.

Right from the start he was difficult. He wouldn't feed, he wouldn't sleep. He cried and cried; he cried when Jody held him and he cried when he was taken away. He seemed livid to be in the world. It was over a day before he finally managed to take in some milk. Shattered and desperate, Jody held him to her breast and bawled with relief. I looked on haggard and confused, clutching a Sainsbury's bag full of chocolate bars and magazines; useless treats for the new mum. I realised very quickly there was nothing I could give her to make this easier. This was it. This was life now.

It was such a rush.

'You can stay for as long as you like, dude,' says Dan, when I inevitably turn up at his flat twenty-three minutes later. I knew Dan would be there for me – or at least I knew he'd actually be home on a Sunday afternoon because he is usually recovering from something – a club opening, a casual sexual encounter, or some exciting combination of those two.

'You can stay in the spare room,' he says as we get into the lift. 'I've got an inflatable mattress somewhere. I think it may have a leak, though. Actually, they all leak, don't they? Have you ever slept on an inflatable mattress that didn't leak? Am I right? Sorry, man, you're not ready to think about this now. Got it.'

Then I'm standing in his doorway, feeling dumbfounded, still holding my Nike sports bag, which contains all my clothes, my laptop, some CDs (why?), a washbag and a photo I took of Jody and Sam on holiday in Devon four years ago. They are sitting on a beach smiling, but it is a terrible charade. The whole week was a complete nightmare because Sam couldn't sleep in the weird new bed with its heavy unfamiliar blanket, and also he was completely terrified of seagulls. So he slept with us, fidgeting and waking all night – every night – until we were so tired we could barely leave the caravan. We didn't go on holidays much after that.

'Do you want to go out and get drunk?' offers Dan.

'I . . . is it OK if I put my stuff in the room and sort of sit down for a bit?'

'Sure, yes. I'll put the kettle on. I think I have biscuits. I'm pretty sure I have biscuits.'

Dan heads off toward the kitchen and I trudge into the spare room, chuck my bag on the floor and slump into the office chair next to his computer. For a moment, I consider firing it up and emailing Jody, but instead I gaze out of the window. I mean, what would I write? 'Hey, Jody, sorry about fucking up our marriage. Any chance we could forget the last five years? ROFL.'

Truth is, I don't even know how to talk to her any more, let alone write to her. We've basically spent our whole marriage worrying about Sam – his outbursts, his silence, the days he'd scream at us, the days he'd hide in his bed and shrink from any contact at all. Days and days, stretching out to months, trying to anticipate the next breakdown. And while we were coping with all that, the things that Jody and I had together somehow faded away. Now, being away from Sam, even for only a few hours, is weird; the pressure is gone, but in its place a sorrow is already flooding. Nature abhors an emotional vacuum.

From Dan's seventh-floor flat in a smart new complex on the edge of the city, you can see the whole of Bristol stretching toward the horizon: a cobbled panorama of Victorian terraces, church spires and sixties office blocks, all shoving at each other like impatient commuters. There are thousands of homes out there filled with families – families that haven't this minute split apart.

I start to think that maybe a drink would be a good idea. But even as I'm contemplating it, my eyes become blurry and it takes me a few seconds to catch on to what is happening. Oh. Oh right, I'm crying. And then there are these giant tears running down my face, leaving hot moist streaks, and my nose is bubbling with snot, and I'm shaking.

'Tea's up!' says Dan from the hallway. 'I thought I had chocolate Hobnobs but all I could find was this packet of Rich Teas. I'm not sure if that's going to do the trick?'

He appears in the doorway, looks down and sees me cross-legged on the floor by the chair, head in hands, sobbing madly.

'Right, OK,' he says, gently putting the tea down on the desk. 'I'll have another look for those Hobnobs.'

We decide not to get drunk.

Later that night, I dream that I'm sinking into a terrible black swamp from which there is no escape. When I wake up gasping for air, I'm convinced this must be some desperate manifestation of my emotional state – but then I realise the mattress is rapidly deflating and I am literally sinking. So much for the subconscious.

'How did I get here?' I ask myself as the escaping air makes intermittent rasping sounds like a flatulent puppy. You know what it's like, weighing up your life at 3 a.m.: everything contracts around the mistakes you've made, the fissures of failure running back through time, like cracks in a badly plastered wall – even in the darkness you can trace them all the way to the source. Or at least you think you can. It usually turns out that the source is evasive and endlessly shifting – like the puncture on an inflatable mattress. The Ancient Greek philosophers had this phrase, 'know thyself'. I remember studying Oedipus at university – his big crime was to not know that he had been separated from his parents at birth and therefore he should be extra careful about killing strange men on the road and then shagging women twice his age. But who really knows themselves? I mean, I'm not saying we're all going to make the lifestyle errors that Oedipus made – that's fucked up. But who genuinely knows why we do the things we do? I am stuck in a job I hate, working long hours, trudging home in the dark, and I tell myself this is because we need the money, we need security. Sam is having speech therapy, and Jody can't work because he needs her constantly; it's her he runs to when his own behaviour terrifies him. I stand awkwardly in the background, worrying, offering help that isn't helpful. How can I connect everything again?

Somehow, at around 4 a.m., I fall into a state of semi-consciousness that I'll be generous and call sleep. In what seems like minutes, though, light is flooding in through the blinds and it is Monday morning and Dan is at the door in a tight pair of black Calvin Klein boxer shorts, scoffing hungrily from a bowl of Frosties.

'Are you going to work?' he asks. 'I can leave a key. I've got to go in, like, ten minutes. I'm helping Craig with a website he's building ... for this music label in Stokes Croft. You can help yourself to cereal and coffee. Are you OK? You look a bit better. I mean, you look like shit, but at least you're not crying.'

He disappears into the shower. I check my phone; there are two text messages, but neither of them are from Jody. They are from Daryl at work. One says, Get yr ass into work, I've got two new victims for you. The follow up says, Sorry, I mean 'clients'. I delete them both.

Then I'm dressed and outside and trudging toward town. The sun is low and bright over the apartment buildings, its light reflecting off the glass and glaring concrete. Twenty years ago, this area was all crumbling factories and empty lots, strewn with rubbish and buried under crawling weeds. Then the economy stirred, and suddenly it's prime real estate. Before you know it, the whole area is futuristic residential zone, a giant circuit board of faux-Brutalist apartment blocks, jammed with capsule flats for young professionals on the make.

I've met a lot of these people. I helped them live here. I am, for my many sins, a mortgage adviser. My job is to measure the hopes and dreams of our clients against both the property market and the savings they have accumulated. In other words I get people to swap everything they're ever going to earn for a studio flat in which you couldn't even swing a photo of a cat that you've downloaded on to your smartphone. This is a strangely parental job – let's work out what you have and what you can afford; let's not over-stretch, we have to be sensible. What assets do you have? Do you have any wealthy relatives? We work through budgets together. Young couples who have recently married, or have a baby on the way, pooling their meagre resources. They look at me with pathetic hope. Is this enough? Often it isn't. The only answer is to rent for a few more years, save up. I go through these routines every day. The system is busted; I'm seeing whole neighbourhoods where youngsters don't stand a chance of buying. Instead they're moving far away from their families. I don't know where.

I've been here eight years, all through the boom and the recession and the nascent recovery. It was meant to be a stopgap. An office job to pay the bills until something better cropped up. But I slipped on to a career path and couldn't get up. Turns out I'm good at it – sympathetic with the poor, helpful to the rich. I am very patient with clients who don't understand what they're talking about – a skill learned from spending three years debating philosophy with people who thought Nietzsche had a point. When the finances align, I can close the deal; when they don't, I let the customer down gently. Whatever is happening at home, though, I can't fix *that* with a computer and access to the national mortgage market.

I can't fix it at all.

A short walk over the Avon, and along the harbour front, and I'm at the office, a small independent estate agent named Stonewicks, tucked between a pub and a sandwich shop in a dense, unfashionable quarter of the city centre. Daryl is here, sitting nearest the window, his cheap Top Man suit radiating static, his spiky hair damp and wilting in the reflected sunlight.

'Oright, mate?' he says from his desk, without looking up from the computer. Daryl is in his early twenties and gives off an air of studied determination while still managing to remain nightmarishly chirpy at all times. This guy literally could not have done any other job than estate agent. There is a spreadsheet on his computer somewhere that maps out his sales targets for the next thirty years.

He honks a fucking bicycle horn when a property deal completes. It's almost tragic that Daryl was born in the nineties and not the late sixties. He should have been a young Thatcherite. He deserves a bulging Filofax and a Golf GTI. Instead he has a smartphone and a Corsa. I feel for him.

I mumble a reply and head up the creaky wooden stairs to my office. And then I call Jody.

'Hi, it's me.'

'Hi.'

'How are things? How is Sam?'

'He's fine. He's at school. He cried all the way there – even after I did all the *Toy Story* impressions. He punched me in the mouth during Buzz Lightyear. To be fair, it's not my best. Mrs Anson said she'd look after him.'

'Are *you* OK?' I ask.

There's a long pause. Jeanette, the secretary, pops her head in and mimes drinking from a mug. I nod and make a thumbs up.

The office is bare. A worn claret carpet, a grubby window overlooking the small car park to the rear of our building. There used to be a painting of Victorian Bristol on the wall, but I took it down and hung a photo of Corbusier's Villa Savoye to make myself feel clever and piss everyone off. There is a filing cabinet and on top of that, a dozen thank you cards from young couples setting out in the world with their enormous debts.

'So what are we doing?' Jody says.

'I don't know. I've never run away from home before. Look, I'm sorry, I've got to go – there's another couple coming in.'

As I slam the phone down, Jeanette arrives with the tea. She quietly puts the drink down on the desk, shoots me a sympathetic look and leaves. She's heard everything. The rest of the office will know within ten minutes. I left my wife and my autistic son.

I think I've escaped from the domestic torment for a while, but I'm wrong. An hour later I head into town for lunch, and pop into a little sandwich place Jody and I used to bring Sam to. Amid the midday hustle, I spot Jody sitting at a table with her friend Clare. They are conspiratorially hunched over two medium lattes. I approach, nudging my way through the young mums and students. They haven't seen me.

'He's become so distant,' Jody is saying. 'I can't depend on him at all at home. There's always something else.'

'Has he looked into counselling?' asks Clare. 'I mean, has he ever dealt with what happened to him?'

Of course, Jody and Clare talk about *everything*. Of course, they are here at lunchtime dissecting our relationship. They have that effortless unguarded frankness that most men are incapable of. You know: 'Have some of this lemon cake, it's lovely, and also, tell me more about the emotionally apocalyptic disintegration of your nine-year marriage.'

'Hi,' I say pathetically.

They both look up, slightly shocked.

'Oh, hi, Alex,' says Clare. 'We were just talking about you.'

'I heard,' I say. 'Can I have a quick word with Jody?'

'Sure, I was heading off anyway. Jody, I'll see you later, OK?'

Jody nods silently. I sit down. She plays with the empty sugar sachet by her cup.

'I guess Clare knows everything then?' I say.

'Yes, I was upset, and I need to talk to my friends, Alex. We don't talk. We can't live like that any more. I'm so tired. I'm so very tired of it all.'

'I know, I know. I've been needed a lot at work, that's all; we're under so much pressure. I'm sorry I've not been there for you and Sam; I'm sorry I'm backing out of looking after him. It's all so ...'

'Hard?' Jody finishes. 'Damn right it is, Alex. It's fucking hard. But he needs you.'

'You know how sometimes we go through weeks and he's fine? He's adorable. Then for no reason it goes back. That's the worst thing. I always think we've turned a corner. It's all that going on, and work—'

'Oh, Alex, it's not work, it's you.'

'I know.'

'This is why, Alex. This is why I need some time. Sam can't cope with us shouting at each other. Mum has offered to stay for a bit if I need help, and Clare is around. You have to sort yourself out.'

'What about Sam and his school? We've only got a few months to decide if we're going to try and move him.'

What about Sam? Oh, how those words have echoed around our lives. Sam is the planet of concern and confusion that we have been orbiting for most of our relationship. Last year the paediatrician told us, after interminable months of tests and interviews, that he is on the upper end of the autism spectrum. The higher-functioning end. The easy end. The shallow end. He has trouble with language, he fears social situations, he hates noise, he obsesses over certain things, and gets physical when situations confuse or frighten him. But the underlying message seemed to be: you've got it easy compared to other parents.

And yes, the diagnosis was a relief. At last, a label! When he's screaming and fighting on the way to school; when he hides under the table at restaurants; when he refuses to hug or acknowledge relatives or friends or anyone but Jody, it's autism. Autism did it. I started to see autism as a sort of malevolent spirit, a poltergeist, a demon. Sometimes it really is like living in *The Exorcist*. There are days it wouldn't surprise me if his head started spinning in 360-degree revolutions while he vomited green slime across the room.

10

At least I could say, 'It's OK, it's autism – and that green slime comes off in a hot wash.' But labels only get you so far. They don't help you sleep, they don't stop you from getting angry and frustrated when something gets thrown at you, or broken. They don't stop you fretting about your child and their life; what will happen to them in ten years, or twenty, or thirty. Because of autism, there is no Jody and I, there is Jody, me and the problem of Sam. That's how it feels. But I can't say that. I can barely think it.

'With Sam and everything . . .' I can't finish, but it's enough.

'I know. But *you* need some help. Or you need to start dealing with things. Why don't you come over on Saturday and see him? Come and take him out.'

I fumble with my phone, turning it over in my hand. I see Sam at the park, crying, running away. Running through the gate. Running into the road.

'It could be tricky, I may be needed at work.'

But I see the steel in her eyes, a flash of fury obvious even amid the clatter of the café.

'Yes, sure,' I say.

'We can talk about schools then.'

'Yes. Let's do that.'

'Goodbye, Alex. Take care.'

'You too. I'm sorry. I'm so sorry.'

Chapter 2

I wake up with a start. I have been dreaming about my brother George – again. I'm covered in a sheen of sweat and I'm breathing heavily. I try to reach out for Jody, but the mattress has deflated, lowering me on to my arm, which is now completely numb. I sit up in a panic and wildly fling it around, smacking the useless limb against the wall and the leg of Dan's desk. It takes several moments for the feeling to return – and for me to realise that I am not at home, I'm at Dan's and I'm in the spare room alone. The mattress makes a pathetic 'phfffffft' noise as if quietly mocking me.

It's Friday morning. Dan is singing the Taylor Swift song 'Shake It Off' in the bathroom and I dread to think what action is accompanying this performance. I sit up, scrabble through my bag for clothes, and head for the sitting room, with its French windows leading to a tiny balcony on to which Dan has managed to wedge two deckchairs. In the corner there is a miniature kitchen area with a cooker, a fridge, a washing machine and a sink – all of them are pristine white. Dan doesn't use them much. The rest of the room is a chaotic ballet of Ikea furniture, comic books, video game controllers and audio equipment. There is a fifty-two-inch LED TV that takes up most of one wall. *Grand Theft Auto V* is paused on screen, mid shoot-out. If the people who designed this apartment block could see Dan and how he lives they would probably high-five each other. This is exactly the sort of stylish young dude they had in mind. The sort of stylish dude who doesn't care that you physically can't open the fridge and the oven doors at the same time. You also can't fit a washing-up bowl in the sink. Dan has a large margarine container. It's fine because he doesn't wash anything up except for mugs. He eats out or has his cool Japanese pot noodles or soup. I don't really understand what the fuck he does to earn this dream bachelor pad. It is sort of terrifying to watch how he lives, drifting aimlessly between projects, leapfrogging over the precipice of the modern economy. I couldn't do that. Not now. After George – after what happened to George – I lost sight of my own ambitions. Everything darkened, the possibilities closed in on me like prison walls. I sleepwalked to university, then lurched between safe, mundane jobs. Meanwhile, Dan always had mates at various creative agencies who would call on him to help with some website launch or club opening or new shop interior. But I don't know exactly how he helps. He is such a charming bastard, though, they keep calling. Bristol is the sort of city where there's always some new development, some new arts centre or pop-up artisan shopping arcade made out of shipping containers. Dan seems to know everyone involved; he's in the thick of it all.

I am, of course, massively jealous of him, but then, I always have been – ever since I was seven and his family moved in next to mine, rolling into the driveway in their cobalt blue 5-series BMW. Dan tumbled out, a bright and precocious five-year-old in red jeans and a yellow Lacoste polo shirt. Emma, George and I were watching our glamorous new neighbours from the front garden and he sauntered over.

'Hi, I'm Dan, what are you playing? Can I play?' he drawled.

And we fell for him, the same way everyone else has fallen for him throughout his life. But me, who do I know? I know Jody's friend Clare and her husband, Matt, who have four children and that's pretty much all they do. I know estate agents and mortgage advisers. I know Jody and Sam. That's about it. Why haven't I been able to manage more than that? What the hell happened?

Sam. Sam happened.

When I get to work, I check my emails and discover that the whole office is going for a mandatory pub lunch at 1 p.m. Me, Daryl, Jeanette, the other agents Paul and Katie, and the manager, Charles. Paul and Katie are in their late thirties and act like they've been married for about three hundred years. They are an insep- arable unit. They don't have kids. Houses are their kids. They may even have said that at one point, I don't remember. They speak to each other as though their relationship is one long real estate transaction – in clipped businesslike tones. Sometimes, I acciden- tally imagine them having sex, and Paul is on top shouting, 'We're gonna exchange, we're gonna exchange . . . we've EXCHANGED!' I can't look at them any more. Charles is in his forties; he's some- thing of an also-ran on the local estate agency scene. By now he should be regional manager at some massive national chain, or at least co-director of our piddling operation. But he's still in-branch, slogging through sales; his hair thinning, his skin slackening. He keeps a small bottle of whisky in his second desk drawer – Jeanette told us all. Sale falls through? Have a little chug, take the edge off. Please God, don't let me end up like that.

Our venue of choice is the King's Head, a beautiful Tudor inn on a cobbled street near the harbour. Inside, though, it is like any British pub. A warped wooden bar damp with spilled booze, a gambling machine flickering in the corner, the pervasive stench of the men's bathroom, its long porcelain troughs scattered with urinal cakes. If some cosmetics company wanted to bottle the archetypal fragrance of the British night out, this would be it: urine cake. Though I'm not sure L'Eau de Gateau D'Urine would be a top seller. Still, it's something to think about while I count down the seconds until Daryl starts talking shop.

The tables are mostly empty, so we choose the one by the window, and pick up the laminated menus offering classic British pub grub, i.e. thawed processed food that someone in the kitchen has microwaved and slopped out on to a plate, perhaps with a sprig of parsley if they're feeling fancy. Sometimes it seems like everything in Britain happens this way, automatically and without care. This isn't a real pub, and this isn't real pub food, it's a weird simulation of what people think they want.

Christ, no wonder I've been chucked out of my home.

'I'm having the fish and chips,' announces Daryl. 'Got to eat fast, though, got a buyer for that Clifton place coming in at two.'

Oh God, we're off already. I bury my face in the menu and try to decide between ordering the rich authentic lasagne with lashings of mozzarella cheese or throwing myself into the river. The Avon might taste fresher.

That night, I get back to Dan's place exhausted and on edge. All I can think is that I have to take Sam out tomorrow, probably to the park and then a café. And I'm dreading it. Don't get me wrong, I love Sam with every molecule of my being, but he is so difficult. And I'm useless at managing him. The times I can see him starting to get upset – if he's not allowed to watch television, or if he wakes up and realises it's a school day, or if he gets confused about what we're planning for the weekend – I get wound up too. My stomach clenches, the frustration rises, and suddenly it's about who is going to explode first. Only Jody can take him and calm him down. Only Jody.

This afternoon a couple came in to see about a mortgage on a small terraced house in Totterdown; they had their toddler with them. 'He's so *talkative*,' they yelp. 'He will not shut up.' And it's such a humblebrag, because really they're telling me how clever he is, how advanced – this chubby little boy going through my wastepaper basket and singing the words to Disney songs. I stop short of telling them that when my son was his age, he could say maybe three words, four if you included 'schlur' which he said a lot and which, to this day, we remain unable to interpret. Back then, friends would say, 'Oh, children all develop in their own ways, he'll get there.' And we'd nod sagely and pretend not to care. But later we'd be on the internet, riffling through parenting sites. 'It says here he should have a vocabulary of fifty words by the time he's two!' He didn't. Nowhere near. I'm not even sure he has that now, and he's eight.

Poor Sam. My poor boy.

Dan is going out.

'Do you want to come? It's a new club night at Creation. My mate is running it.'

He is always going to a club night and his mate is always running it. Not for the first time I wonder: how does he do it? He's two years younger than me, but that's not all. His life has sort of ambled along on cruise control; good things happen to him whether he wants them to or not. When his long-lost uncle died three years ago, it turned out he'd left Dan his car: a vintage Porsche 911

Carrera in gulf blue. Dan barely uses it, it's sat in the underground car park beneath his building, gaining value. He doesn't seem to have any concerns, he has no real responsibilities, apart from the many start-up record labels in the Stokes Croft area that he appears to be assisting. Dan is Dan. As we grew up together, going to the same schools, meeting the same friends, the same girls, the same bullies, Dan was always Dan. He'd get me out of fights, he'd protect Emma from clumsy and unwanted advances at youth club discos. Whatever else was happening to me – parenthood, the spectre of grief, the realisation that I have to do this crappy job because I need to support my quietly dysfunctional family – Dan was grooving along, being cool.

I was cool too, for several years. Well, maybe four. At university I somehow ended up running an alternative music society called Oblivion, where we played post-rock and weird electronic dance music to tiny roomfuls of chin-stroking musos. Sometimes we put on live events in rubbish local pubs, and I once organised a music festival on a disused industrial estate, which the local paper attended and described as 'almost unlistenable'. That quote appeared on all our flyers for the next two years. Dan would come up and stay while he was on his design course in Bristol; he'd make our posters and even built a website for us. He's still doing all that, but it faded for me. Life got in the way.

'I think I'll stay in. Thanks, though. Thanks, Dan.'

'No worries, buddy.'

I am staring at the blank television screen – even though Dan's house is not short of screened entertainment options. He has four hundred channels on cable and a hard drive packed with movies and television shows, more than any one person could experience in a lifetime. But I find the choice bewildering and stultifying. How do you decide what to watch these days? What if you commit to the wrong series and there's a better one, but you've already invested hours of your life? This is the sort of thing that certain people like to call 'First World problems'. You know the people – they pop up gleefully under your Facebook and Twitter posts, thoughtlessly shaming you for worrying about everyday stuff. One super-fun lesson you learn very quickly as the parent of a sometimes disruptive child: people love to judge. They like to sneer at you from their apparently perfect lives. Anyway, let's not go there. I need to find something to take my mind off Sam, and off tomorrow, but nothing feels right. I don't want to concentrate on anything. I can't. Jody says I need help; perhaps I do. Everything swirls around in my head, my brain is a whirlpool of fears and worries, I can't catch hold of anything.

OK, deep breath. Right. Here it is: I have had to leave Jody and Sam. I left because we were arguing and stressed all the time. I need to work out how to stop that. I need to cope with the pressure. I need to find the pinprick of light that will lead me out of here.

This doesn't feel like the right frame of mind to finally make a start on *Breaking Bad*.

Chapter 3

Sam is ready for me at the door when I arrive the next morning. He has his hoodie on with the hood up, and underneath that is one of his special T-shirts with all the linings and stitching masked so he doesn't feel it on his skin. There are whole websites for this sort of clothing; this is something you discover as you go along, battling each inexplicable foible and phobia. There are entire businesses based around catering for children who are uncomfortable in our world.

'Daddy, are we going to the park? Are we going to the café? Daddy, are you coming in?'

'I'll come in for a moment.'

The living room is an achingly familiar bomb site of clothes, books and toys, all strewn like shrapnel across the floor. Every surface is piled with stuff – wipes, unopened mail, newspapers. The worn settee is a map of breakfast cereal stains; the television screen is smudged with fingerprints; the bookshelves explode with the detritus of parenthood. Half-built Lego models, Playmobile motorbikes, action figures with limbs missing. My CDs and DVDs are piled carelessly in a corner, the curtain rail is half hanging off the wall, the curtain itself flapping uselessly in the breeze of an open window.

This is home, I think. And suddenly I can't shift the lump in my throat.

Jody comes downstairs, her long auburn hair wet and wrapped in a towel, the stray curls tumbling around her face. She's wearing jeans and a saggy sweatshirt. She looks tired and cautious.

'Hi, Alex.'

'Hi. How ... how is everything?'

'Daddy, are we going to the park? Can I bring my ball? Daddy, do I need a bag for my ball?'

'I'm not sure we can bring the ball, we're going to the café afterwards and ...'

'OHHHHH,' says Sam and straight away he is crying.

'We've had a few *challenges* this morning,' says Jody, through a forced smile. She strides over and takes Sam in her arms. Her eyes say everything. He's probably been up since five, maybe earlier. He will have tried to put the TV on, and then broken down when Jody staggered in and turned it off. He will have tried to make breakfast and spilt milk everywhere, then cried about that. He will have woken Jody up again asking to watch television, crying until she said yes. The familiar patterns.

'What happened?' I ask uselessly.

'Well, the *X-Men* cartoon wasn't on so he threw the remote control at my head,' she says. And sure enough, there is a dark bruise. When he was three, he hit me in the face with a Duplo bucket and knocked my front tooth out. He was like Joe Pesci in *Goodfellas* – small, funny, but at the flick of a mental switch, easily capable of extreme and demented violence.

I can feel my anxiety levels rising. Sam in a good mood is a challenge, Sam in a bad mood is unpredictable and frightening.

20

There's a ball of fear in my gut. What if he runs away? What if something happens and I can't protect him? I'm flooded with images of what could happen if he storms off. I can feel sweat prickling beneath my forehead.

'Maybe we should do something else? If he's not in a great mood . . . ' I suggest meekly.

Jody glares at me accusingly. A look I am familiar with.

'We agreed, Alex,' she says through gritted teeth. 'And I've written it on his timetable.' Every morning, Jody draws a cartoon guide to Sam's day, so he can see when he has to get dressed, when he'll eat, and what he'll be doing until bedtime. At weekends, he carries it around with him, consulting it regularly. If it's on the timetable, it *has* to happen. As though to emphasise the point, Jody's eyes move toward Sam, who's struggling to tighten the Velcro straps on his trainers. That's another thing: he doesn't do laces. Plus, the straps have to be so tight I worry about them cutting off the circulation to his feet. Everything has to be tight. There can be no give.

'I know,' I say with similarly restrained aggression. 'But if he's not in the mood. The roads are very busy around the park. I'm a little concerned—'

'Nothing is going to happen,' cuts in Jody. 'You cannot keep backing away from these things – and you definitely can't keep backing away from your own son. This is the problem, Alex; I shouldn't have to stand here trying to persuade you to take him out for the morning – to take responsibility for him for three bloody hours!'

I'm about to say something but she cuts me off again.

'And I don't want to hear about how tough work is,' she rages. 'Try being at home, waiting for the next phone call from the school telling us that Sam has kicked someone, or he's been punched, or that he's been screaming out for me the whole morning. Try making his dinner then keeping it at exactly the right temperature for the hour it takes him to eat it. Try that! I'm exhausted. And you give me nothing! This is exactly why we are where we are right now.'

There is a moment of silence, a sort of emotional Mexican stand-off.

'Daddy, I'm ready,' says Sam. 'I'm ready for the park. Are we taking the ball?'

'OK,' I say, trying to breathe steadily. 'Let's take the ball and let's leave Mummy here. She needs some time to herself.'

'Are we going to the park?'

'Yes.'

'Then the café?'

'Yes, Sam.'

'Can I have frothy milk?'

'Yes.'

'But we're going to the park first?'

'Yes, the park first, and then the café.'

I nod toward Jody, but I can barely look her in the eye. Momentarily, I am grateful for the chance to escape.

'Daddy, are we taking the ball?'

The park is on a hill between Bedminster and Totterdown, a dollop of green space amid rows of Victorian terraces, the roads spreading out in all directions like the threads of a giant spiderweb. Around the edges are the crumbling pathways where joggers huff and stumble, wordlessly criss-crossing each other's routes like sweaty robots. There's a small area with swings and slides that was erected sometime in the early nineties and then abandoned to its fate. The swings have no seats any more, so it's just a rusted metal frame with a row of chains dangling uselessly, like some sort of open-air sex dungeon. The slide is covered in graffiti and X-rated anatomical drawings. I don't know whether the council should dismantle it or enter it for the Turner Prize.

Sam has the ball clutched to his chest. Sometimes we kick it between us, sometimes he doesn't put it down. I look around and try to anticipate what is going to upset him.

Playground meltdown: odds

Passing adult attempting to make conversation: 10/1
Noisy dog: 8/1
Other children showing interest in football: 5/2
Stinging nettles: 5/1
Wasps: 8/3
Pregnancy workshop meditating behind goal posts (this actually happened once and Sam found it horrifying): 100/1
Ice cream van not being here: evens

Today, there's only a small group of children and they appear to be totally engrossed in playing on the sex dungeon, so that should be fine. The only dog walkers are in the far distance, which gives me time to warn Sam. The ice cream van is there in its usual spot, looking to take full advantage of a rare sunny day. This might go OK. I breathe an inward sigh of relief.

Here is an important lesson I learned fairly early on about autism. The 1988 movie *Rain Man* starring Tom Cruise and Dustin Hoffman is NOT a documentary. Autistic children do not all have special powers. If I took Sam to the casino in Bristol, he would not be able to count cards and earn us a small fortune. Instead the noise would terrify him, and he'd end up cowering under the roulette table until security removed me for bringing a child into a casino.

He does have an interesting way of looking at the world, though, which I try very hard to remember whenever the stress levels explode, perhaps when I am making him put on the wrong coat, or because the plate of spaghetti that Jody has made for him is two degrees too warm. To Sam, the world is a gigantic engine that needs to function in a certain way, with predictable actions, in order to ensure his safety. Before he can relax, he needs to know the timings and movements of everything around him and he must have one finger on the off button at all times.

I watch him run toward an arrangement of fallen tree trunks that he likes to play on, and I know exactly how this interaction will work. He will climb on to one specific tree, he will walk along it, he will check that I am watching when he gets to the end. He will consider jumping to the next log, but will instead climb down and then step up on to it. If another child is playing on the logs, he will push them out of the way – not because he's a bully, but because this is the machine of the fallen tree trunks and it has to work in a certain way. To him, another child is a fault in the system; pushing them off is his equivalent of running an anti-virus program: 'CHILD DETECTED. PUSHING SEQUENCE ACTIVATED. CHILD DELETED. WARNING: CHILD RUNNING OFF CRYING TO PARENTS.'

I could be on there climbing over the sodden bark with him, but I'm not. I never do. I'll push the swings, I'll kick a ball back, but I'm not what you'd call hands-on when it comes to messing around. I'm not one of *those* dads. You know the ones – the dads in Converse trainers and Batman T-shirts, seemingly desperate to prove that they are fun and childlike and great pals with their children. They lark about, telegraphing their playful exuberance as though starring in a live performance of the Tom Hanks film *Big*. They eye me up suspiciously as I stand back surveying the area for potential hazards. Play doesn't come easily to me. Play is hard. Getting myself in that frame of mind. To let go enough.

Watching Sam clamber over the soggy tree trunks takes me

soaring back, back to me and George as kids in the park near where we lived, daring each other to get to the very top of the climbing frame. George was two years older, braver, less cautious than me. 'Come to the top. Come on, Alex.' But this makes me realise that I'm beginning to forget what his voice sounds like. Suddenly, I want to scoop Sam up and hold him, and then take him home to Jody. I want to say, Take care of him, Jody, take care.

And as I'm thinking that, I see it: a large dog, a Labrador maybe, charging toward us from behind a clump of bushes. It's around fifty metres away, but it has spotted Sam's football in the grass. It wants to play. Fuck. I start to walk toward Sam, slowly at first but then I pick up pace. I need to be careful.

'Sam, don't worry, a dog is coming, do you want to give me the ball?'

Sam turns around and in doing so, almost slips off the trunk, then he gasps in horror. The dog is very near now, wheeling and barking. Sam turns to me, terrified, then jumps down off the fallen tree and runs in my direction. The worst thing he could do. The dog can't decide whether to go for the ball or the boy running away. Its tail is wagging furiously. It decides that the boy looks like more fun.

'Sam, Sam, he only wants to play.'

I break into a jog and I grab him, hurling him around, so that I am between the dog and his body. He is shaking with terror and sobbing. 'No, no, no, no,' he is saying.

'It's OK,' I repeat.

Then the dog is at us, barking and jumping. I push it away, looking for its owner. A middle-aged woman appears around the bushes, holding a lead and a ball. She's smiling. It's that dog-owner smile. The smile that seems to say, 'I like dogs, everyone likes dogs, who could possibly begrudge my dog anything?'

'He only wants to play! He loves children,' she says.

'Can you call it away?' I ask as politely as I can, but with an edge of contained fury.

Her tone changes. 'He's a friendly dog, he wouldn't hurt anyone.'

Sam is burrowing into my arms, yelping and sobbing, struggling to get away. The woman audibly tuts, grabs the dog's collar and hauls it back.

'Come on, Timmy, we'll play over here.'

I watch her walk off, utterly oblivious to the terror her wretched mutt has caused, oblivious to the possibility this may be about more than a kid who doesn't like dogs.

'Hey!' I shout. 'It's supposed to be on a lead. Can't you read the fucking signs?'

She looks back, clearly surprised by my ferocity.

'Come on,' I say quietly to Sam, smoothing his hair away from his face. He is whimpering quietly and his arms are clutched around himself so tightly his knuckles are white. 'Come on, son, let's go to the café.'

As we leave, I look back and see a group of kids playing with a frisbee. They are happy and comfortable with each other; their parents sit on a bench nearby, talking, relaxing. I feel a momentary stab of envy for these people. How easy their lives must be.

'Daddy, is it the café now?'

'Yes, we're going to the café.'

'Can I have frothy milk?'

'Yes.'

'The dog was scary. I didn't like the dog.'

'I know.'

And that was our trip to the park.

Chapter 4

The café is comparatively serene. Situated amid a small row of shops, it's one of the quasi-hipster joints that's been springing up in this area, laser-targeted at middle-class mums who grew up watching *Friends* and yearning for Central Perk. The decor is Bohemian coffee shop 101. There's an old Rowe AMI jukebox in the corner and the walls are lined with kitsch sixties prints of sultry women and sad, wide-eyed boys. Sam is fascinated by them. We sit in our usual seats at the back – a big sofa in front of a large wooden coffee table covered in old comics and magazines.

'Daddy, why does that woman have a green face?'

'Daddy, why did they draw children with big massive heads?'

I tell him I don't know, the sixties was a hell of a time.

I order a cappuccino – The Best in the West according to a chalkboard outside, which also features the T. S. Eliot quote, 'I have measured out my life with coffee spoons', written in an annoyingly loopy font. The barista, who – of course – has a moustache like a 1920s movie villain and a tight vintage T-shirt that shows off his ribcage, brings it over and makes a big play of serving Sam his warm milk. 'Here you go, sir, our best frothy milk, from the finest frothy milk cows in all of Somerset.'

Sam giggles adoringly. The barista is his hero. For some reason, despite Sam's social awkwardness, he's fascinated by charismatic and confident young people. He doesn't fear them at all, and even makes eye contact – which is rare, even with me. When he was a toddler, Jody used to take him to the university canteen for lunch – he was so transfixed by the students, she'd get a few moments of quiet to herself. It's weird but cute. I don't care that I'm paying £4 for a thimble of hot caffeine, it's worth it for this.

Now we are settled, it would be great if I could chat to Sam – ask him about school, about home, about his mum – but that's not how he works. He doesn't do chat. At best he would nod or shake his head at direct questions, more likely he would shrink away from me and become upset. These moments between us are fragile – I don't know how to make more of them without breaking everything. Instead, I wordlessly hand Sam my iPhone and pick up a newspaper off the table. Relaxed, he goes straight to his favourite app, Flight Track, which shows the current position of commercial aircraft as they fly across the globe. When you touch one of the little plane icons, a fact box pops up telling you where it took off from and where it's going. This information obsesses him. He has gradually learned all the main airlines, the key routes, the distances between major cities. I suppose this is his most *Rain Man*-like quirk. The outside world scares him a lot of the time – or at least it's a challenge for him to cope with this endless array of unpredictable sensory inputs – so I guess Flight Track is his way of safely exploring. He loves to sit and prod at the screen, getting me to read all the stats that pop up. Sometimes I show him where his Aunt Emma is this month. That's my sister. The globetrotter. She got on a plane two days after her eighteenth birthday and never came back. Sam's not really interested, but it's my attempt to humanise the whole procedure. I point out Toronto on the screen. Emma uploaded several photos of the city on to Facebook last week. She is pictured with two other women who I don't recognise, larking about on a tourist boat, the needle-like CN Tower looming in the background. She looks like she does in all her Facebook photos: joyously happy, carefree, living in the moment. But I don't fully buy it. Her eyes hide something that I recognise from long ago.

'If she wanted to fly to London Heathrow, it would take her seven hours and fifteen minutes,' says Sam. 'She could fly from Toronto Pearson International Airport. She could fly on a British Airways plane or an Air Canada plane. Why doesn't she come back?'

'She's happy travelling,' I say. 'She likes to see new things.'

Obviously, it's more complicated than that. She's either happy travelling or scared to come home. More of the latter, I'm guessing. But her infrequent emails give little away.

'I can see new things on here. And we've got Google Maps. I can see new things on Google Maps.'

'I know, but it's not quite the same, is it? You don't get all the people, the sounds, the smells . . .'

'I don't like any of those things. I have autism,' he says.

We both laugh at Sam's moment of self-awareness. As much as I view the condition as some sort of malevolent phantom, Sam is happy to acknowledge it – usually for comic effect or to get out of trouble. Other kids blame their young siblings for a broken plate, or felt-tip pen all over the sofa, or if all the cookies in the tin strangely disappear. Sam says, 'It's autism,' and nonchalantly waves away the blame. Looking back, we probably shouldn't have tried explaining autism to him by comparing it to the Incredible Hulk ('You see, Sam, David Banner can't help it because of *gamma rays*!').

We sit in silence for a few minutes, and then:

'Mummy has bought me an Xbox!' he says.

'Oh,' I say. 'Oh. OK.'

Instantly, I'm not sure about this. Sam is reserved enough already – does he need another excuse to spend time alone? He plays by himself almost all the time, even at school – it's part of the disorder, or condition, or whatever we're supposed to call it. He *can* play with other kids, as long as they're not interfering with what he wants to do and don't try to talk to him too much. His definition of friendship seems to be 'people I can just about tolerate'. Which I guess isn't so weird. We all have relationships like that. When you begin to strip social systems back, you see how habitual a lot of it is. You go through the motions of interaction: asking about someone's day, laughing at their crappy jokes, saying, 'We must meet up more often'. But underneath, very often, is the complicit understanding that this is all bullshit. It's a dance, a series of repetitive social tics. No wonder Sam finds it all so confusing. Autism, as far as I understand it, is about not being given the rule book at birth. To Sam, everyone else is playing this huge game and he's got to try to figure it out as he goes along. It's exhausting for him, and for Jody and me – because we're his rule book. We have to explain everything, over and over again, and some of the rules will never make sense to him. Like the one about not necessarily saying the first thing that comes into his head. In the past month alone we've had these excruciating conversational gambits:

(To Jody's mum on her varicose veins) 'Why do your legs have pipes?'

(To our rather rotund neighbour) 'Your face is like jelly.'

(To his head teacher during a parent/child evening) 'Daddy says this school is a shithole.'

So I'm thinking that giving him a games console to escape into is maybe not the best idea. I mean, I let him play on my phone, but that's different: he likes flight apps and Google Earth; at least there's some sort of connection to the real world. But in games, the player is at the centre of the universe and every action is about them. This feels like the opposite of what Sam needs to know about life. I'm not angry with Jody, I'm guessing she needs some respite from his never-ending questions – or his explosive tantrums.

'Well, let's talk to Mummy about the Xbox,' I say.

'Flight VO 226 from London to New York is travelling at thirty-seven thousand feet,' he replies.

We get home – to *their* home (I don't know if it is still mine) – shortly after 3 p.m. Jody has tidied up and she looks refreshed and almost relaxed. She has fought her wild curly hair into a sort of bun and she's lounging on the sofa reading a newspaper.

'There's my boy! I missed you!' She leaps out of the chair to hug Sam.

'He's been good,' I say. 'A little problem with a dog in the park, but he's been good.'

'The dog ran after me,' says Sam. 'We had frothy milk in the café. I played on Flight Track. Daddy said "fuck" to the lady with the dog. I'm hungry.'

That's another thing: you can never swear near Sam. He always remembers, and he always tells.

After I've explained what happened, Jody makes him a sandwich – the only sandwich he'll eat: cheese and piccalilli. Then he rushes off to play on his new Xbox.

Here are the rules governing Sam and food. He has a rota of four acceptable meals. They are:

Cheddar cheese and piccalilli sandwiches (white bread, no crusts, no yellow piccalilli stains on the edges of the bread).

Fish fingers and skinny chips (has to be Birds Eye or Marks and Spencer fish fingers. Holy shit, do not give him the Lidl ones).

Spaghetti hoops on toast (spaghetti letters are sometimes acceptable, although it's never clear exactly when they're acceptable so it's really not worth the risk).

Macaroni cheese (but only the exact recipe Jody makes. If I do it, it ends up decorating the kitchen wall. Although, to be honest, that's a fair assessment of my cooking abilities).

This is augmented with breakfast cereals, yogurt and carefully cubed fruit. CAREFULLY CUBED fruit. Have you ever cut apples into exact one-centimetre cubes at five in the morning? It's tough – especially when the recipient makes Gordon Ramsay look laid back and amenable.

'So ... he's got a games console?'

'Yes, a friend's son was getting rid of it. It's the old model, apparently. I thought it would be better than television, once in a while.'

'But isn't it going to encourage him to be alone more? I mean, we're trying to get him to be more social.'

'I'm sorry, *we're* trying?'

'You know what I mean.'

'Yes, I know what you mean. But maybe having something in common with the other kids isn't such a bad thing. Everyone in his school has a games console.'

'Fine, OK, I'm sorry. But no *Grand Theft Auto*, OK?'

'Oh no, that's only for Mummy. I've discovered that driving around a city smashing into things is pretty good therapy.'

There is a brittle moment of peace. Jody starts absent-mindedly clearing magazines and colouring books off the table and floor.

'How are you?' she asks.

'I'm OK. I miss you.'

She freezes for a moment in her tidying.

'I miss you too,' she says quietly, before resuming, as if shaking the moment off. 'What have you been up to?'

'Oh, you know: work, watching Dan's massive television.'

'Don't go anywhere near the new season of *Homeland*, it's total bullshit.'

'Dammit, I can't believe you're watching it without me!'

'I'm doing you a *huge* favour.'

'Maybe when I'm back we can start on one of those Scandinavian crime dramas everyone else was into five years ago?'

Awkward silence. Maybe that was a bit soon.

'I don't know when that's going to be, Alex,' she says. 'I can't cope with you being here at the moment.'

'I know. I'm sorry. I will sort it out. It would be, you know, great to come back. If only to stop you watching crappy television.'

Jody forces a smile.

'You're too distracted and unreachable,' she says. 'And when we talk, we fight. It's making everything worse. Remember that time we drove up to your mum's, when Sam was still a toddler? The car broke down and he was crying and wailing in the back seat, and it was dark and pouring with rain. But we—'

'We sang all the songs from *The Little Mermaid*, in the correct order. I did "Under the Sea" while changing the tyre.'

'We coped, right? We coped. We made it funny. It's not fun any more. It's so far from fun.'

'I'm exhausted. The work, no sleep, and . . .'

Immediately, I realise that was the wrong thing to say.

'Oh God, here we are again!' says Jody. 'You keep saying the work will get easier, but it never happens. You come home stressed, you're stressed all weekend, you go back stressed. I can't cope with that *and* Sam. You've got to deal with it.'

'I know. I know, but . . .'

'No, Alex, no buts. You've got to *do* something or you can't come back. I mean it!' She is trying not to cry, but I can hear it in her voice and see it in her eyes, those big brown eyes that drew me in a decade ago. They don't hide anything, the pupils as big and dark as galaxies. And I can't face it. I can't face what I know is coming.

'You have to do something about work, you have to do something about YOU, but you really, really have to do something about George. Do you understand?'

Then I know I am going to cry too. Because this is the wrenching awful pain that, although weaker than it once was, still rumbles beneath the surface like a vast tectonic plate. And suddenly I am glad that Sam has an Xbox to play on, so that he doesn't have to see this again.

Later, I'm with Dan in the Old Ship Inn, the little local pub around the corner from his apartment building. It is a lonely relic of the area's industrial past, the crumbling red-brick façade an affront to the glass, steel and concrete structures that now surround it. Inside, a few old geezers huddle around, dogs sleeping at the feet of their stools. We've got to know some of them. Frank and Tony worked on the docks in the sixties, hauling cargo from the ships to the vast warehouses – they like to perch at the bar jovially telling stories about horrendous industrial accidents. There's Alfie who runs the rock 'n' roll disco every other Sunday, still wearing the blue suede shoes he bought in 1957 (they're now as bald as he is). There's old Sid in the corner, playing chess against himself, a half-pint of Guinness by his elbow. Many an unwary patron has sauntered over, slapped Sid on the shoulder and asked for a game, only to be loudly sworn at or pushed away. 'Christ,' the barman always says. 'Don't interrupt Sid when he's on the chess.' Legend has it, he's playing against the ghost of his dead wife. Maybe he just wants some peace and quiet.

Like its inhabitants, the pub itself is a shabby remnant, but unlike the rows of houses that it was originally constructed to serve, it's probably a listed building. Now it stands alone, its only regulars a dwindling population of pensioners who remember when all this was terraces. And me and Dan. We come here because the beer is cheap and they sell actual packets of crisps. You don't get crisps in the massive chain-brand wine bars and bistros lining the harbour side. You get tiny bowls of olives for a fiver. Thanks a lot, Europe, that's your fault.

'So what have you been up to today?' I ask, slurping the dregs of my pint.

'Messing around on the Mac,' says Dan. Dan has the very latest Apple Mac with a gigantic monitor. I guess it's for his website design work or music production, or . . . oh God, I don't know.

'Are you seeing anyone at the moment?' I ask.

'Nah, not really, mate. I was with Nikki for a while, but it was all a bit awkward.'

Nikki works at a small design studio that Dan sometimes freelances for. It's populated almost entirely by men in their early twenties who buy all their clothes in Hollister and Urban Outfitters – apart from the ironic vintage T-shirts they pay huge amounts of money for on eBay. They are all in love with Nikki, because she's three years older, beautiful and an amazing Photoshop designer. They were secretly competing to see who would ask her out, but then they made the mistake of getting Dan in to design part of a social media advertising campaign. Those poor bastards didn't stand a chance.

Dan is sort of handsome. He has cropped dark hair and a tanned doe-eyed face; he has a natural sense of style that extends beyond the skinny jeans, skinny shirts, skinny hats uniform of his work-mates. He's sitting here in a cable-knit jumper, button-down shirt and black chinos. The colours, fabric and fit are all so perfect, he could be in a fashion shoot. But it's his charm that goes off the scale; he exudes it. It hums like a dangerously overloaded electrical outlet.

'Dan, thanks for helping me out. It's all a bit ... heavy.'

'No worries. We're mates. I like having you around. It reminds me of good times. I was helping Luke with a podcast today. Reminded me of when we used to record our own radio shows on my dad's old PC.'

'Radio Shogun – Somerset's finest West Coast hip-hop radio station.'

'Bringing Wu-Tang to Weston-super-Mare.'

'Yeah, slight confession, I never much liked West Coast hip-hop.'

'I know, Alex. I know.'

We leave that thought hanging for a few moments.

'So ... How is Sam?' asks Dan.

'He's fine. You know. He's Sam.'

'Are you guys still thinking of moving him out of that school?'

I'm surprised Dan has remembered, but it feels unnatural, talk-ing to him about this. In all the years I've known him, through everything, we've only ever talked about movies and music. Everything has been filtered through that. It's painful when some-thing darker bobs to the surface.

'I don't know, we're talking about it. Are you OK? I mean, is work OK and everything?' I ask.

'Yeah, I mean, it's a bit haphazard at times, but you do the right bits for the right people and it adds up. They tend to bring me in when things have gone pear-shaped, when there's some big client somewhere yelling at them every day. But you know me, I'm like, OK, go.'

36

OK, go is Dan's motivational phrase. Whenever he has to psyche himself up for something, he mutters it under his breath and then he does it – whether it's taking on the design of a multimillion-pound product rebranding or jumping into the sea off Clevedon Pier. Once he's said it, he's got to do it.

'Jesus, Dan, I have no idea how you live like this.' I say it with a little more bitterness than I expected. 'I feel like there's a chasm beneath me all the time, but you … How do you not care? Why aren't you constantly scared shitless?'

He smiles and stares into his pint. From the pub's crackling sound system, Otis Redding is singing 'These Arms of Mine'. Sid is moving pieces across the board. Car headlights flash through the moth-eaten curtains, sending jagged lights across the tobacco-stained wallpaper.

'I don't have to deal with … well, what you have to deal with – real things, real people,' says Dan finally. He looks away. It seems for a second that there is something he wants to say; he is on the verge, but it slips away from him. Then he says, 'Can you imagine *me* selling a mortgage?'

'No! But then I couldn't imagine myself selling a mortgage a few years ago. Now look at me.'

We laugh, consciously trying to shift the mood.

'If you hate it, you *have* to get out.'

'I can't, I have my own mortgage to pay. Sam is having speech therapy, which is unbelievably expensive. Jody isn't working …'

'Alex, listen to me. If you hate it, you've got to get out.'

I sigh and finish my pint. 'Everyone knows what's best for me.'

'Hold that thought,' he says. He gets up and ruffles my hair in a way that would aggravate the hell out of me from anyone else. Then he heads to the bar, orders another couple of pints and comes back.

'Right, time for another flashback. Remember when we watched *Battlestar Galactica* – the new series not the old one,' he says. This is a tangent I wasn't expecting.

'Yeeeeees.'

'I told you it's not about killer space robots, it's about the Iraq War.'

'Yeeeees.'

'And what did you say?'

'I said, Dan, for God's sake, this is clearly a programme about killer space robots.'

'That's the problem!' says Dan, splashing his pint down on the table for effect. 'You are the deepest thinker I know, you analyse everything, you have theories about everything. But once you've made up your mind, you hang on for dear life. What if you're looking at things the wrong way?'

I take a long, thoughtful sip from my pint and set it down gently.

'Dan. I appreciate what you're trying to say, honestly I do. But this is a complicated situation, and it's not one that I can escape by, like, letting go. Also, *Battlestar Galactica is* a programme about killer space robots – it's just that a lot of people in their twenties projected meaning on to it in order to ease the guilt of watching a programme about killer space robots, instead of actually watching the news about the war in Iraq.'

'Perception is reality,' says Dan, and he pulls that ridiculously lovable smile – the one I am sure has helped snare a dozen lucrative freelance contracts.

'Oh Jesus, Dan, we are not doing this tonight,' I moan. 'Now get me some more crisps and let's change the subject. I don't want to talk about work or my life or space robots any more.'

An hour later, I'm back at Dan's and alone, because true to form Dan has gone to a club night called Wicked Glitch, which plays only distorted soundtracks from eighties arcade games. It's the sort of thing I'd have listened to at university, that three-year oasis of unguarded, uncomplicated pleasure. Jesus, even Kant was fun. Sometimes I wonder: was that the real Alex, or an imposter?

I go through the ritual of inflating the mattress, then check my email on Dan's gigantic Mac. There are two messages. One is from Jody, forwarding an appointment to visit a local school, which has a good reputation for helping children on the autism spectrum. The other is from Emma. She's thinking about heading back to the UK. I'll believe that when I see it.

I'm awoken at 4 a.m. by Dan staggering back into the flat with a woman. They are giggling and shhh-ing each other, then there is silence, then an almighty crash. When I go to investigate I find them wedged low down against opposite walls of his narrow hall-way, tanned limbs jutting out everywhere, like the aftermath of some sort of sexy car crash.

'We're stuck,' slurs Dan. 'We were kissing and now we're stuck.'

'Hi, I'm Donna,' says Donna. 'I was named after Donna from Elastica. Can you help us up?'

Eventually I stop trying to work out Donna's age based on her parents' music tastes and switch the light on. Donna's back is against one wall, Dan is suspended over her, his knees jammed against each other, his hands on the floor, either side of Donna's head, balancing himself in mid-air. One of Donna's legs is between Dan's, the other is sort of flailing. She's wearing a very short sequinned silver dress that would look amazing and sophisticated in almost any other situation but this one.

'OK,' I say. 'I think I know what to do here. Dan, I'm going to have to lift you up and then sort of throw you to the side.'

'All right,' he says. 'Give me a second to prepare. *OK, go.*'

I take his hips between my hands and haul him up, dragging her leg until it frees itself, a shiny kitten-heel shoe popping off in the process. With his help, I manage to push Dan forward until he collapses laughing next to Donna, who now manages to shimmy up the wall.

'I've got pins and needles in my head,' she says.

'Drinks, anyone?' asks Dan. 'I think you'll all agree this is going splendidly well so far.'

'I'd better get back to bed,' I say. 'Oh God, it's 5.30 a.m. You idiots have fun. But remember, single file in the corridor.'

And as Dan switches on his hi-fi and quietly plays a Hot Chip track, I think about him, my old friend, and the things we've done, and how he has such a spark of life in him – like my sister Emma. How do they do it?

I lie in bed listening to the low rumble of a jet plane as it passes through the lightening sky toward Bristol Airport. The sound merges hypnotically with the wheeze of the deflated mattress as my backside completes its own descent on to the hard floor.

Chapter 5

When we got Sam home the day after he was born, we were drunk on a heady cocktail of happiness, adrenalin and sleep deprivation. Sam, for his part, simply cried. He yelled and gnashed and screamed, his tiny limbs writhing furiously. Most nights, I took him on long walks in his pushchair through the empty suburban streets. I'd sing to him and tell him stories until he calmed down; then I'd get him home for a feed. And he was always hungry. We tried him with a bottle, to give Jody some respite once in a while, but, oh my God, he was not having any of that – even then he was a fussy eater. I remember one time trying to squirt the milk into his mouth, and he seemed to be OK with it – but then, lying in my arms, he vomited reams of semi-digested formula into his own eyes. That's a fun memory of parental guilt that won't go away.

Later, when he started on solids, he was quick to develop very specific eating preferences. There was one flavour of one particular brand of organic baby food that he would willingly eat and we were so terrified they'd discontinue it that we stockpiled two hundred jars in the garden shed. Meanwhile, we were inundated with well-meaning but endlessly aggravating advice:

'Have you tried cutting the vegetables into little batons?'

'Have you tried serving his lunch in a bowl rather than on a plate?'

'Have you tried making the food look *fun*?'

We would smile and thank them for their amazing advice, which we'd invariably tried many times before – like that time I fashioned a slice of ham, two olives and a red pepper into a startlingly accurate facsimile of Peppa Pig (sadly, Peppa ended up taking a dramatic unplanned flight across the kitchen). Perhaps these formative experiences should have given us a hint that something was different about Sam. But then, me and Jody barely talked, let alone discussed Sam's psychological development. Instead we steadfastly divided up chores. We became business partners and our business was trying to get through the day without falling asleep on the toilet or in the nappy aisle at Waitrose. But we were together and we were determined, and we knew we could get through it because, my God, there was so much love between us.

I'm thinking of all this as I sit with Jody outside the secretary's office at St Peter's Primary School in a quiet suburb at the fringes of the city. This is the third one we've looked at since deciding to get Sam out of his current hell pit. It's got an 'outstanding' Ofsted report, we're millimetres within its catchment area, and best of all Sam already knows someone here. Olivia went to the same nursery school apparently, and Jody stayed in touch with her mum – a canny piece of social manoeuvring as the family live in a giant grade-II-listed townhouse in Southville, with five floors, including a soundproofed media room in the cellar. Somehow the two children have always got on, despite the fact that Sam once tried to bury her in a sandpit.

This morning, with a precious four hours off work, I drove over to pick up Jody and we barely spoke as we chugged through Bristol's suburban sprawl. We both know the score. Sam is struggling at school – not academically. Well, *obviously* academically, but that isn't the main problem. The main problem is that he can't get on with the other children. Not in the way he needs to be able to. He can't join in with playground games without crying or stealing the football or kicking someone – and this has made him a loner. Worse, it's made him a target. The kids know they can get an instant reaction out of him, and so they do. They are like piranhas: they sense blood in the water and there's a feeding frenzy. They don't know this is bullying, it's just the way it is. Perhaps it is instinctive: single out and ostracise the runt of the litter for the safety of the group. All I know is, Sam doesn't play with the other kids. We think that perhaps in a more gentle school, away from city boys in crowded classrooms all struggling to be the alpha male, he'll fit in more. It's worth a shot. It has to be worth a shot.

'You can go in now,' says the secretary, a kindly woman who looks so ancient she could conceivably have been a pupil at the school when it was opened in the early 1800s. I'm so busy imagining her in a frilly bonnet, writing the three times table on to a piece of slate, that Jody has to jab me into action. We're shown into a small office, dominated by a vast wooden desk, overflowing with papers and lever-arch files. At the back, there's an old sash window held slightly open by a mug that actually features the phrase, 'Keep calm and carry on teaching'. That's the first black mark against this place, I decide. The walls are a maze of cracked plaster, hidden behind dozens of children's paintings and drawings. Some of them are lovely colourful depictions of simple square houses and happy families, although one appears to have two men dressed in black cloaks slaughtering a cow.

43

'Hi, I'm Miss Denton, it's good to meet you,' says a soft, friendly voice from behind a cheap PC monitor on the desk, lopsidedly angled downward by a pile of textbooks. Miss Denton stands up and offers her hand. She's maybe in her early thirties and tiny, though her bright floral dress amplifies her presence. Her short blonde hair is held back by a single plastic grip, her lipstick is pillar-box red. She looks friendly and effervescent, a stark contrast to the bleak rabble of guarded career teachers who dutifully reassured us through Sam's opening years of crappy education.

'I'm Jody, this is Sam's dad, Alex.'

I am not 'my husband Alex'; I am relegated to biological parent.

I shake Miss Denton's hand and try not to betray anything other than enthusiasm. I feel like this is an interview, a test maybe. I don't know. All I know is, I don't want to fail.

'I hear Sam's having trouble fitting in?' she says. 'He was diagnosed on the autism spectrum last year, is that right?'

'Yes,' says Jody. 'He's . . .'

She pauses, obviously thinking. How do you contain eight years of struggle into one sentence without sounding like you're pitching one of those misery memoirs to a book publisher?

'He was always a little behind in terms of speech,' she continues. 'He was always very anxious about things. We thought it was maybe his hearing or something at first, but we had it checked and it was fine. We kept going to the GP, but all they would say was "keep an eye on it". I mean, keep an eye on *what*? Anyway, when Sam went to nursery, they knew something was wrong, but they couldn't help much. The first person to mention autism was the special educational needs coordinator at his infant school, but . . . what did they say, Alex?'

'They said he wasn't "bad" enough to get individual support. They wouldn't get the funding they needed. But he was so distraught every morning I had to carry him to school. You know, that's how every day started. Fight him into his clothes, get him to school, then worry about him all day. It's been a bit better at the junior school. But ...'

'He's still not happy,' says Jody. 'Whatever that means.' She glances at me, and then quickly looks away. 'He's all alone.'

Jody takes a tissue out of her coat pocket and dabs gently at her eyes.

Miss Denton smiles sympathetically, and then in a bright tone, starts to tell us about her school. There are four hundred children, so it's big, but she insists it has a homely feel. She talks about an 'emphasis on fostering a supportive, caring environment'. A couple of the teachers have experience with autism. It's all very well rehearsed but genuine. Quietly, I feel a growing sense of hope – I sense it from Jody too. The school is usually oversubscribed, but a new Steiner Academy has opened nearby and several children have been withdrawn to go there. There's a space for Sam. If we need it.

'Have a think over the summer,' says Miss Denton. 'It'll mean a longer drive for you in the mornings, a bit more preparation. But we'd do our best with him. Maybe bring him in to have a look around? He can meet the children and staff. Obviously, I can't promise him lots of specialist support, but, well, we're a happy school.'

A *happy* school. Strange that this should be a selling point. Shouldn't all schools aspire to make children happy? But it is reassuring she is willing to concede that this is not the case. Instead, happiness is an elusive commodity. It cannot be written on to any education or business plan – or any spreadsheet, for that matter. It cannot be distributed via government grants. It is not available on Sky for one low monthly cost (which reminds me, they're testing super-fast broadband in Bristol right now, 200MB, fibre-optic, right to the door ... oh shit, I'm getting off track here).

If happiness was like this, we'd all get it. We'd sign up for happiness online. We'd download and install the happiness app. The price wouldn't matter. We'd pay anything for it.

The secretary shows us out. We head to the small car park in silence. There are birds singing in the hawthorn trees surrounding the playground. We get into the car and sit there for a long time.

'I like it,' says Jody.

'So do I.'

We can't help it. Despite everything, despite all the dark clouds gathering over our relationship, we sit together and smile. It's like when we found out Jody was pregnant. It was so early – far too early – in our relationship. We were kids – well, I was twenty-four, but this is the twenty-first century, that's practically adolescent these days. We looked at that test kit, the little blue lines spelling out 'positive', and after the initial shock we grinned drunkenly for hours.

'Shall we bring Sam?' I say.

'Can you take more time off work?'

'I'm sure I can. This is important.'

'Good. Thank you. Are you staying with that idiot Dan?'

'Yeah.'

'Have you figured out what he actually does for a living yet?'

'I'm afraid not. It has something to do with design, maybe? I don't think anyone is completely certain.'

'In ten years' time he'll be the CEO of some weird social media start-up. Honestly, we'll see him on the cover of *Wired* in a white turtle-neck pullover, talking about how he spent his first billion.'

I start the engine, and the car crawls out of the school grounds and back toward the centre of Bristol. Back to our actual real lives. The lives that have come apart. And when Jody gets out of the car and heads toward our front door, despite the positivity of the morning, I've never felt further away from her.

Chapter 6

I get into work at two. Daryl is out doing a couple of evaluations, standing in someone's home in his pinstripe suit, scratching his chin over a clipboard and a laser tape measure; Paul and Katie are idly playing footsie under their desks while checking paperwork. I have two mortgage meetings: a wannabe property developer buying an old church near the Gloucester Road and an elderly couple downsizing from a vast family home to a neat flat in Clifton. The last of their three children has left home, that place is too big for them now, they explain. They want to release some equity, get out and see the world together. 'The house is so empty,' the wife says with a sort of matter-of-fact forlornness. I look at her husband, who is nodding sympathetically. But what I see in his eyes – and I am somehow quite sure about this – is relief.

Three hours later, I'm back at the house to collect some clothes and books. I miss the books. When we moved in here eight years ago, I had the upstairs hallway converted into a miniature study/library, with a row of bookshelves stuffed with paperbacks, graphic novels and all my old university set texts. In the mornings, toddler Sam used to go along and systematically take out as many books as he could, then pile them up against our bedroom door. I'd get up bleary-eyed to find out what all the rustling was about, then trip over a pile of Penguin Classics. Eventually we got bored and put a lot of the books into boxes and shoved those in the attic.

Jody lets me in and I traipse across the living room carpet, which is littered with ripped comics and Pokémon trading cards. 'Jesus, Jody, you've got to start putting your stuff away properly,' I joke, half-heartedly. And then I take a proper look around, and this isn't the usual mess of books and newspapers and Sam any more. There are several dirty plates, on the floor and on top of our hi-fi speakers. There's a dark patch on the rug where something has been spilled. Sam's homework is lying crumpled on the sofa, covered in crumbs and smudged with piccalilli. I look back at her. The flickering light from the television casts shadows over her face. She smiles thinly, but she looks exhausted.

'Go and grab your stuff, Sam is in his room playing on the Xbox.'

I stand silently for a second, glancing around the room again. It feels like things are caving in.

'I was thinking, maybe I should creep up and not disturb him? I don't want to upset him.'

Jody shrugs and sighs heavily. I had meant to communicate concern for her, but of course, she reads through every artifice I attempt, as she has always done.

'Whatever, Alex.'

I go upstairs and from Sam's room I can hear the familiar sound of a joypad in use, the little plasticky button clicks echoing down the hall. Surprisingly, I can also hear piano music – delicate, slow, slightly maudlin, coming from whatever he's playing. At least it's definitely not *Call of Duty*. I knock on the door and push it open. Inside, Sam is sitting cross-legged on his bed, a small LCD screen and the Xbox 360 jammed on a little Ikea desk opposite. Above that there is a huge map of the world, which I bought last year and eventually had to nail to the wall because it kept falling down in the night and scaring the shit out of him. Then there is the usual kid stuff – discarded clothes and toys, sweet wrappers, action figures with their limbs hanging off.

'Hey, Sam, what are you playing?' I say, realising I have the fundaments of a *Casablanca* joke here, that would be utterly wasted on an eight-year-old child.

'*Minecraft, Minecraft,*' he says, without looking away from the television.

I've heard of *Minecraft*, of course, but I've never played it. On screen, I see a vast blocky landscape of grass and rock, dotted with chunky trees – Sam appears to be chopping one of them down with a clumsily drawn axe. In the background, the doleful piano music creates a weirdly benign atmosphere. It is almost hypnotic.

'Is it fun?' I ask airily.

'I'm making a hut. A big hut with two floors and a bedroom. Sit down, Daddy. Sit down and watch.'

'Did you have a good day at school?'

'I've got to chop down the trees to make this hut.'

'That's great. But at school, was it a happy day or a sad day? Sam?'

'Yes. Daddy, look at the pigs, they're funny.'

I stare at the screen. The pigs are interconnected pink blocks, like something from a weird children's cartoon. I don't know what I'm supposed to say, or what role they perform in the game. There's a long silence as Sam keeps playing, chopping at trees and running around. I fiddle with the door handle, half in the room, half out, utterly unsure of how to communicate. After a minute of this, it's getting awkward. I go through the pantomime of checking my watch – even though Sam's not watching and all that's waiting for me at the flat is Dan playing video games in his pants.

'Sam, I've got to get back.'

'No! Watch, Daddy, I can build things.'

But what's the point, I ask myself. When I was a kid these games had baddies to shoot at and high scores to beat. There were considerably fewer cardboard-box-shaped pigs to herd up.

'It's not for grown-ups,' I mumble at last. 'Daddies don't play computer games.'

'Oooh,' he says, 'I want you to watch me!' It's the whiny tone that can often proceed a breakdown, and I tense up accordingly. But this time he looks up from the game and straight at me with something like disappointment in his eyes. By now I'm anxious and impatient – I know that later I'll feel bad about abandoning him, but I tell myself I need to go before I get something wrong and set him off. In truth, though, I want to go. I'm desperate to go.

'I've got to get back,' I repeat.

He thumps the bed with his free hand and for a second I'm worried he's going to throw the controller.

'Not fair!' he shouts. But then after this flash, he is absorbed into the game again.

I slowly withdraw, watching his face, his slightly quizzical expression, the colours reflecting off his soft skin. He is sitting quite close to the screen and concentrating so hard on what he's doing that, for a split second, it looks as though he is within the landscape.

I pull the door closed behind me, and go into our bedroom. The bed is unmade, the sheets piled up in the middle of the mattress along with several hopelessly creased dresses. The laundry basket, as ever, is overflowing on to the floor. Without thinking too much, without hovering, without taking in every last heart-bursting detail of this room, I open the bottom drawer of our huge oak wardrobe and cram underwear and shirts into my holdall. I feel like I'm committing a robbery. I grab some books from beside the bed – a biography of Isambard Kingdom Brunel (I live in Bristol, a Brunel anecdote is always useful), a Raymond Carver short story collection, a couple of crime novels – and then I'm out, bounding down the stairs like a child terrified of imaginary ghosts.

Chapter 7

It's Tuesday night, and I'm heading across town to Matt and Clare's leviathan-like house in an upmarket development on the north-eastern fringe of the city. This is classic middle-class, middle-manager territory – a carefully planned scattering of mega-homes, all designed to look ever-so-slightly different in their beige uniformity. Some are three-storey town houses, some are smaller and have bay windows, a deranged nod to classic thirties semis. The ambition is to simulate the multi-architectural feel of a classic British suburb, but here, every reconstituted stone surface, every two-car garage, every high wooden fence, is brand new and gleaming. It is a town for people who are scared of towns.

Matt has invited me over to watch a Champions League match between Barcelona and Juventus. Well, he didn't ask, he begged. I know exactly what's going on. He wants to watch the football in peace, but wouldn't usually be allowed, because they have four children between the ages of one and eight so every evening is a gruelling production line of nappies, baths and bedtime stories. However, Clare wants to know how I'm doing – perhaps in a spying capacity for Jody – so he's managed to barter some time out involving him, me and twenty-two world-class football players.

Clare grew up with Jody. When they were kids, they were like sisters. Then somehow they both ended up moving to Bristol at roughly the same time. Jody was struggling with Sam while most of her friends were still out partying, but Clare had Tabitha a year later. They joked about being irresponsible teenage mums. Then Clare had Archie, quit her job as a restaurant manager, and the two friends became a miniature parental support network. Very quickly, they realised that it was important to engineer a friendly relationship between me and Matt, because that way they'd get to see each other more often – such are the psychodynamics of adult friendships. So we got a lot of quality pub time together while Sam was small, and Matt only had the two kids. We'd sit in a pub almost too tired to move, furtively trying to sound each other out about our comparative domestic traumas – mostly through the universal language of 'blokey bullshit'.

For example:

'I think Liverpool have blown it again this season.'

'Yeah, they need at least two new defenders and a midfield playmaker.'

'Talking about midfield playmakers, I haven't slept for three nights and I can't remember where I live.'

'That . . . that sentence doesn't quite make sense.'

'Hold me.'

Stuff like that. Matt and I are quite different, though. He is chubby and lovable with a big hearty laugh, and he completely unselfconsciously wears football shirts all the time. He's a business software consultant and makes a ton of money, which all goes on the children. In the early days it was organic baby food and the kind of high-end prams that television stars wheel through the pages of celebrity magazines. Now it's piano lessons, top-of-the-range Lego sets and Disneyland Paris every year. He is middle-class dad man. Ultra dad. He'll put on a papoose without even thinking twice about it. In fact, I'm not even sure what he thinks about. He and Clare never read papers, never watch the news, rarely go out. To them, the real world is something that happens to other people. They exist in a hermetically sealed parental bubble, a prism into which all other experiences are sucked and obliterated. A black hole of domesticity. But they are bloody good at it. Matt can change two nappies simultaneously while on a Skype conference call to a software developer in Bangalore.

The reassuring thing is, their house is as messy as ours. Worse, even. Matt lets me in and already the entrance hall is a Toyland demilitarised zone. There are semi-clad Barbie and Ken dolls strewn across the floor, their teeny clothes everywhere, like the morning after a particularly debauched party at the Fisher-Price Playboy Mansion. There is a Lego *Star Wars* AT-AT collapsed on the stairs, vomiting bricks on to a bright pink Barbie sports car. There are hundreds of little plastic soldiers, forming platoons of agonising barefoot hazards. Inside the living room, a massive Habitat sofa is tragically lost beneath an attack force of Beanie Babies. The bookcases are a chaotic holding area for an immigratory mass of Disney DVDs. There is a play kitchen on its side, surrounded by little metal pots and pans, and plastic vegetables, as though – in the midst of this crazed battle – some Michelin-star chef has had an apocalyptic shit-fit over a pretend *côte de boeuf.*

'I see you've tidied up for me,' I say.

'Well, you've got to make the effort,' shrugs Matt.

I'm fascinated by mess, I think it tells us so much. To paraphrase Tolstoy (sorry), tidy homes are all alike, but every messy home is messy in its own way. Our home was always about Jody and me being disorganised and cluttered, it was our stuff spilling out everywhere, with Sam's adding a dash of colour. Here, it's a land-grab by the children. A hostile takeover bid.

As I'm thinking about this and trying to find somewhere to sit that isn't covered in toys or jam, Matt's daughter, Tabitha, bursts in surrounded by at least four friends, all screaming and laughing and dressed as characters from *Frozen*. Closely tailing them is Matt's son Archie, in an impressively detailed stormtrooper outfit, brandishing a gun that makes an exciting range of incredibly loud and obnoxious laser noises. He cycles through them with psychopathic abandon, whipping his prey into a frenzy of bloodcurdling yelps. Then they are up on to the sofa screaming and bouncing, and next they leap down and gallop through to the breakfast room, and on into the kitchen, a howling dervish of man-made materials and synthetic gunfire.

'Holy shit!' I say. 'What the hell was that?'

'Yeah,' says Matt. 'That's my life, all right.' And he smiles broadly. He's so unequivocally happy with his lot it makes me want to hug him for ever.

We somehow clear a space on the sofa, remove the Batman costume that's draped over the TV, and sit down. Clare appears in the doorway. She's wearing a neat checked shirt and jeans, which is essentially her uniform. She cut her hair short two years ago because she was fed up with their eighteen-month-old twins swinging on it. She is, blessedly, carrying two cans of Stella Artois.

'Hi, Alex,' she says warmly. I get up and we do an awkward polite middle-class no-actual-touching-God-forbid embrace. 'How are you?'

'I'm OK, you know. OK.'

'Have a beer,' she says. 'Are you staying at Dan's?'

'Yes, for now, I guess. I don't know.'

'For now?'

'I don't know, Clare. Has Jody said anything?'

Clare hands the other beer to Matt and their eyes meet for a fleeting second. Long enough for me to understand that I'm not going to get anywhere near the whole story.

'Not much, Alex. She's upset, but . . . she needs some time and space.'

'Right.'

'But you're OK?'

'Yeah. I mean, I'm not great, but I'm carrying on. I'll figure something out.'

I want to ask if there's any chance of going back home soon. I want to find out if there's an endgame here, if there's something I definitely have to do, so that I can go home. But somehow, I can't ask that question. Too much is riding on the answer.

'Well, OK,' she says. 'Enjoy the match, I'll put the twins to bed.'

And she sort of glares at Matt, an encouraging glare, a 'YOU talk to him' glare. But I'm safe, because I know he won't. Not in so many words.

'So,' he says. 'How is Sam?' It's a brave conversational gambit from Matt. I'm momentarily taken aback.

'He's OK. I'm never sure how much he takes in. It's very difficult to tell what he thinks about things. I know when I've given him the wrong dinner, or the wrong jumper, or I've fastened his trainers up too loosely. But I don't know if he misses me. I don't know if he understands about . . . ' I break off.

There's a pause as we stare at the TV and pretend to mull over the pre-match analysis.

'Barcelona are unstoppable right now,' Matt says finally.

'You're right,' I say. 'Unstoppable.'

'I mean, Juventus have a good defence, but I'm not sure they have the strength to counter-attack.'

I take a swig of beer. Matt taps away on his phone, grimacing in concentration. When I try to look at the screen, he very subtly angles it away from me. Uninterested in his secrets, I go back to considering the Juventus back line.

'Sometimes, there's no escape,' I say. 'Sometimes you have to bear the pressure and hope for a miracle.'

'Well, miracles do happen in football,' says Matt.

'Yes. Yes, they do happen in football.'

Barcelona win 3–0.

Chapter 8

The next morning at work, Charles calls a meeting. His face is expressionless, his eyes bloodshot and beady. Either he's drunk or he has bad news. We gather in the centre of the office, Daryl turns his chair around and leans on the backrest, checking his phone as though he's in a sixth-form common room.

'As you know, we've had trouble this year meeting our quotas, despite the uplift in the market,' Charles slurs. Ah, so he's drunk *and* he has bad news. 'This is not isolated to our branch, the others have been struggling a little too.' He lets this sink in for a few seconds. 'Now, don't be alarmed, we all know this business, sometimes there are troughs that you can't explain. We're out there, getting good properties and doing a good job for our clients, but we're up against some very aggressive and innovative competitors.' Another dramatic pause. Is he going for an Oscar – or is he going to be sick? 'And actually, we're currently talking to one of those competitors. Urban Chic. They are interested in acquiring our business.'

There's an audible gasp from someone in the room. Daryl finally looks up from his phone.

'Now, it's very early days, so again, don't panic,' Charles continues, waving his arms in a motion that I think is meant to be calming, but actually looks like he is losing his balance at the edge of a precipice. 'However, I need to warn you. There may be some changes.'

Changes. Management-speak for job losses. It's the humane alternative to 'downsizing'. Or 'culling'. No one looks surprised. We're busy, but not busy enough, considering how bullish the property market is right now. Everyone slinks back to their desks. I head into my office and shut the door. I'm about to boot up the PC when a text message comes through. It's from Jody.

> Can you come over and look after Sam tonight?
> Clare wants to meet me. Can't get babysitter.

I hesitate for a moment, that familiar worry rising up in me. I start typing out an excuse, but I delete it. I start another one, and delete that too.

Finally, I send:

> Yes, sure, that's fine. I'll head over straight after
> work.

At 6.37 p.m. I'm standing outside the front door with a handful of comics, a new colouring book, a Lego minifigure and some football stickers. Jody mentioned Sam's class had been doing a project on London too, so I picked up a book full of photographs of the city. I'm not going in without backup. Mingled in with the usual concern and trepidation, though, is something else. I realise that I miss him. Jody answers the door and she looks amazing. She's wearing a flowing light blue dress I don't recognise and perfume

I haven't smelled before; her make-up is subtle and perfectly applied; her hair cascades around her shoulders in glossy curls. I am breathless, rooted to the spot. I stare at her stupidly. It's strange how, when someone stops being a habitual presence in your life, they revert back to being a human being again – mysterious and largely unknowable.

'Hey, come in,' she says. Her tone is friendly and relaxed. 'Sam, Daddy is here! I'm sorry I've got to go, I promised to meet Clare at seven thirty. I won't be long. There's wine in the fridge if you want it. Thank you, Alex. Thank you!'

And she's gone. Cautiously, I peer into the living room, thinking, What version of Sam am I going to get? He is in his pyjamas watching a cartoon on the television; several of his favourite action figures are placed around him, all carefully positioned so they can see the screen too. I breathe an almost audible sigh of relief. As I sit down beside him, I wonder how long he's supposed to be watching when I get a text message. Only let him watch until the end of this episode, it says. At least we still have that empathic parental bond around bedtime rules. I wait until it's over before making an attempt at conversation.

'So, how did you get on today?'

'Good. Daddy, you are sitting on Spider-Man.'

'Oh, right.'

I remove the large plastic figure from beneath me and pop him next to Batman on the cushion. Most of these were charity shop purchases a few years ago – he'd started to show interest in superheroes, so we totally went with it, forking out for comic books, figures, DVDs. Anything to feed his imagination. He liked to set them up, and carry them around with him, but he couldn't seem to play with them alone, he didn't create the wild imaginative scenarios that Matt's kids do with their toys – it was another sign that something was different about him. For the next half hour, I try to entertain him with the stuff I've brought. He makes a few splodges of green pen in the colouring book, then he rips open the stickers and scatters them on the floor before assembling the minifigure – a few moments of intense concentration. Then he's bored again. We read the comics together, him making stuttering attempts at one or two speech bubbles on the first few pages before getting cross with me for pushing him to try more. The school says he's progressing. That's a word we hear a lot. Progression. Forward momentum, however slow, is the best we can hope for, it seems. But his reading is stilted and laboured, while Matt's oldest – who's a year younger than Sam – is zipping through the Harry Potter novels. We know we ought to ask the school if he'll ever catch up, but I think we're both terrified of the answer. And the school doesn't seem enormously interested. Finally, I show him the London photos book and read some of the captions. We flick through the glossy images of Big Ben, the Gherkin, the Lloyds Building, he stops on the Tower of London and looks interested so I read to him about its history, but he doesn't seem to be listening – he turns the page before I've finished the caption.

'OK, we've read the comic, we got the minifigure, we've opened the stickers, we've visited London, what shall we do now?' I ask him.

'Have you brought anything else?'

'No, not tonight. Shall we play with the action figures?'

I sit down on the floor and beckon Sam down too. Then, improvising madly, I grab Batman and Spider-Man, and put them in an Action Man tank, handily lying under the coffee table. Next, I find an empty cardboard box and place the Joker inside with Sam's cuddly kitten toy, which he has predictably called Kitty.

'Oh no, the Joker has kidnapped Kitty the kitten,' I shout, summoning the clipped drama of an old cartoon narrator. 'Only the unlikely partnership of the Dark Knight and Spider-Man can save the day – and the cat!'

I move Batman's head around to make it look as though he's speaking. 'Come on, Spider-Man! Although we are figureheads of two rival comic book companies we must work together to save Kitty.'

'You're right, and this alliance will doubtless prove incredibly lucrative!'

I look up and realise that Sam has backed slowly away and is now curled up on the sofa, fascinated.

'I'm watching,' he says.

'I'm not a cartoon, Sam!' I protest.

Chuckling, he grabs the television controller and presses the off button. I drop the figures and slump lifeless on to the floor. He laughs, delightedly, and hits the button again. I jolt back into life. We repeat this twenty-seven times until, somehow, it is no longer funny. Then we're not exactly sure what to do. I get back on to the sofa. The silence descends again. These are the moments I dread the most: transitions. Transitions are bad news. Turning off the TV is usually a big one, getting ready to go out, finishing a meal, getting out of the bath – any switch in gear is a potential breaking point. I suppose transition can be scary for all of us, right? Getting a new job, starting a relationship, ending a relationship. But for Sam, it seems any change, however small, churns up the same emotions of fear and dread. In short, silence is terrifying.

'Can I show you something?' he asks finally. 'It's on the Xbox, though!'

His excitement is so intense and surprising that, before I even think, I'm nodding, and then he has me by the hand, hauling me off the sofa and toward the stairs. We're tumbling upward, avoiding the toys and clothes strewn on each step, and he is breathlessly explaining:

'It has a front door. No, not a front door, it has a side door and a back door. They open and close. There are eight windows, four small ones and four big ones.'

He bashes open his bedroom door, and there on the table is the Xbox and the controller. There is a game paused on the screen.

'Does Mummy know you have the game on?' I ask. And as I'm thinking about what a bad idea it is to let him have a console in his room, the TV flickers into life.

It is *Minecraft*.

We appear to be standing on a plateau, overlooking a long valley. The squares that make up the game's landscape lend it a rugged, craggy look, and everywhere there are areas of rock peeking through the pixelated grass. Sam's character is not visible on screen; instead the camera portrays what he sees, as though we're looking through his eyes. When Sam pushes the controller stick, the camera points up toward the great chunks of white cloud suspended in the bright blue sky. Then he looks straight ahead and begins to move toward the cliff edge.

'It's down here,' he says.

And a few hundred metres before us, down a step-like ravine, is a large building, its exterior constructed partly from what looks like wood, and partly from grey, freckled rock. It is almost rectangular, except for a tall tower built into its flat roof, and several odd clumps of block jutting out of the sides. There is a wooden fence running most of the way round, and within that a sort of garden messily dotted with gaudy flowers. The effect is strangely incongruous – a weird little detached property in the middle of this digital wilderness.

'This is a home,' says Sam. 'I built it.'

'You built this?' I ask. 'By yourself?'

He approaches a door to the side of the house and goes in.

'You can build things on this craft table, and here is a furnace which melts things. I made all my things in this room.'

I stare quietly at the screen for a while, trying to take it in. Finally I say:

'OK, it's very impressive, Sam, but you've got to go to bed now.'

'Can I show you something else?'

'Next time, Sam, come on.'

'I can show you very quick. There is a ladder up to—'

But I want to get him into bed, go downstairs and relax. I feel like I've done enough. I cut in:

'No, Sam, it's time for bed now, you need to switch it off.'

'But I don't want bedtime!' he cries. And suddenly we're in the familiar stand-off. He hates going to sleep. He hates the loss of control it represents. But he especially hates going to sleep on a week night, because that means waking up and going to school. It's always been like this – refusing to get into bed is his way of wrangling some autonomy for himself, putting off the inevitable – and all the time the tension mounts up. As ever, I see it coming, my brain flashes forward down the inevitable path to screaming and crying. And as ever, I'm in a rush to get there first.

'Sam, switch it off!' I shout.

He turns away from me, the controller in his fists, and stares determinedly at the screen. Furious now, the nuance of the situation gone, I snap and jam my finger on the Xbox power button and the screen goes black. Sam screams and smashes the joypad down.

'I didn't save it, I didn't save it!' he's yelling, and then he slides on to the floor, his head in his hands, kicking at me to stay away, his body convulsing with anger and sorrow. Instantly, I feel guilty – or at least a tiny part of my brain does, the part still awake enough not to switch into autopilot when these flashpoints start. But I'm too worked up to listen to it; I can't deviate from the path I'm on, I've been down it so many times before.

'Sam, I don't care, I told you to switch it off, now get into bed!'

I storm out into the hallway, fetch his toothbrush from the bathroom and jab it towards him as he bawls. He looks pitiful, skinny and bereft on the floor, his gangly arms wrapped around his face, his superhero pyjamas ridden up around his chest. I haul him up on to the bed, motivated solely by this blank determination to get away. The adrenalin of exhaustion and fear.

'I didn't save my house,' he's still saying, through the low moans and snotty tears.

'What's going on?' says Jody.

Suddenly she's right behind us in the hall. I didn't hear her come in. The anger quickly switches to embarrassment. I feel like I've been caught.

'He wouldn't switch the console off, so I did it. Now he's crying.'

'He switched it off, Mummy, and I hadn't saved. The pigs will get away.'

She looks at me accusingly.

'Oh, you sort it out,' I say.

Then I barge out of the room and clatter down the dangerously booby-trapped staircase. I hear Jody talking upstairs for a few minutes as I pace the living room, pumped with adrenalin and shame. Then she appears.

'Why didn't you let him save the game?' she half whispers, half yells.

'You weren't there. I asked him over and over again.'

'You could have taken the controller and done it yourself.'

'I don't know how! And anyway, he should switch it off if I ask him!'

'Oh, give him a break! It's the only bloody thing that makes him happy at the moment.'

'Ah right, and that's my fault?'

'Jesus, Alex, don't start on *me* now! I've had a nice night, I don't want to come home to another shouting match.'

Her words hang in the air for a few seconds, and we both realise what she's saying. This is why I'm living at Dan's. This is exactly why everything broke down. But acknowledging something is so much easier than changing it. Behind the stress, the exhaustion, I know I'm doing everything wrong, I just can't seem to change it. I can't stop. So I keep going.

'I thought if I could get him to switch off the console, then he'd get into bed without a fuss. But obviously I lost it. I fucked up again. I'm sorry.'

'This isn't about you, it's about Sam and what he needs!' she says. 'You have this idea about how everything should be in our lives, but you can't control *everything*! Somehow, you've got to learn to live with that. I am so fucking tired of it, Alex. Please, go up and say goodnight to him and be nice. Let him talk about that silly game if he wants. Then go.'

Numbed by this sudden outburst and the very unambiguous directive at the end, I have nothing left to do but nod and head up the stairs once again. I find him already asleep, curled up and still, his duvet in a pile on the floor. When I pick it up to cover him, I see the London book I bought him, discarded under a pile of colouring books and empty Lego boxes. I gently tuck the duvet around him. His eyes flicker open briefly and his head jerks from the pillow, but he lies down again without fully waking. I remember when he was younger, after a day of battles and breakdowns, we would often creep into his room at night and drink in the peace of it. We'd talk about how we would cope better tomorrow, about all the things we'd do differently. We would put our arms around each other and agree not to lose our tempers, because look at this beautiful boy, so perfect and sweet. Then we'd do it all again the same way.

When I get back down, Jody is coming out of the kitchen with a glass of water. She looks radiant, the smell of summer air all around her still. I find myself yearning for her to say 'come back'. But that's so far away now. Maybe I can at least patch things up a little, or I'll lie awake all night going over everything.

'How was Clare?' I manage.

'OK. She's worried about Matt. I'm not sure why – he seems a bit distant, apparently. Have you noticed anything?'

I shake my head. We don't know what to say now.

'Has Sam shown you what he's been doing in *Minecraft*?' I try.

With the subject moved back to Sam, Jody suddenly seems brighter.

'Have I! "Mummy I've built a house, Mummy I've built a fence, Mummy there's a wolf eating my cows" . . . '

'I'm a bit worried about the console being in his room, though.'

She sighs and I immediately know that's a contentious topic and this is not the time to be broaching it. Our relationship is like walking over eggshells at the moment – and I'm wearing steel-toed Doc Martens.

'Well, maybe one day you can help me clear out the dining room area and we can put it down here? At least that way I won't have to keep going upstairs every time he builds an extension.'

'He seems OK, though, doesn't he?' I say.

'Well, let's see what he's like tomorrow morning when he has to go to school,' says Jody. Then she realises that I won't be here. And it's awkward again.

'I'd better go,' I say, and she makes no effort to stop me.

When I turn to leave, I accidentally kick the Batman figure under the sofa. His fleeting partnership with Spider-Man is over.

Chapter 9

The rain is coming. I'm walking along a quiet Baldwin Street at eight in the morning, the shops shut, the gargantuan superbars closed and bolted. Huge bags of rubbish line the road, giving off a putrid hum, and the pavements are a slippy smorgasbord of abandoned kebabs. Above me it looks like a vast dirty grey blanket has been suspended from the tips of the city's office blocks. Already there are droplets of rain in the air. Soon it will be a torrent.

I make it into the office seconds before the storm breaks, the downpour battering the windows behind me. It's over a week since Charles mentioned the takeover plans, and the Stonewicks workforce has returned to a slightly edgy kind of normality. However, when I close the door and turn to say hello to everyone, I am greeted by a wall of ashen faces, as bleak and endless as the sky outside. Uh-oh. Daryl can barely look at me; Paul and Katie fidget nervously. I scan slowly toward Charles, who holds my gaze, his eyes sunken and beady in his corpulent face, like pebbles disappearing into muddy sand. It doesn't take a genius to work out what is going on. These are challenging times; the dead weight has to be jettisoned. And as it turns out, I'm the deadest weight here.

'Can we have a quick chat, Alex?' says Charles. The attempt at casual bonhomie fails miserably thanks to his strangulated voice and a nuclear blush response that turns the whole room crimson.

'Sure,' I say.

We walk slowly into my office and Charles shuts the door behind us. I sit in my worn swivel chair, he on the other side of the desk, where my clients usually perch clutching their bank statements. The rain is streaking down my small window; I can hear it cascading into the rusting metal gutters outside. Charles clears his throat, and then his deposition begins.

'Now, as you know, Urban Chic are looking to purchase us. They're offering a good deal, it's a lifeline. But I'm afraid they don't need a mortgage adviser. They use an independent broker, you see. It's the way most agencies work. So, I'm afraid we will have to let you go.'

Although I expected this, I still experience a sudden, sickening explosion of fear. Sam. Sam's speech therapy. The house. The mortgage. Jody. My responsibilities flash before me like the whirling symbols on a fruit machine. I open my mouth to speak but find that I cannot. Charles carries on:

'It's no reflection on you or your work. You've been an asset to this company since the day you started. But it's the way the market is. I'm so very sorry.'

And he is, bless him. His shoulders are hunched, his hands darting from my desktop to his lap, to the desktop again. I think maybe his eyes have moistened a little.

'I can tell you that we're providing a generous redundancy package. Three months' full pay, then three months' half. You take your pension fund with you. There's no notice to work. Things are moving quite fast.'

'They certainly are,' I say.

'I'm sorry. We all are.'

'So I can go?'

'There's some paperwork, of course, and we'll need to let your current clients know, but Jeanette will help with all that. We've got to tie up the loose ends, as it were.'

So that's what I am now. A loose end.

The next two hours are a solemn procession of phone calls and form-signing. I process everything in a dream-like state. Everyone comes in to say how sorry they are, and then they awkwardly drift away, back to their desks – the desks they all still work behind. Jeanette keeps making me cups of tea like Mrs Doyle in *Father Ted*, expressing her sorrow and embarrassment in the only way we Brits truly understand at times like this: through the medium of hot beverages. The mugs pile up on my desk unwashed. I take down my Corbusier print and slowly empty eight years' worth of useless office knick-knacks into a plastic bag. I have two framed photos on my desk – one is of Jody and Sam at Dyrham Park in Bath, eating a picnic on the hillside; the other is of me as a ten-year-old, standing next to George outside a café in London. I put both of them in the bag, then log out of the PC and shut it down. The screen flickers and goes black.

I walk out of the office and mumble a few awkward goodbyes. Daryl gets up, seemingly to hug me, but he guardedly offers a hand instead, as though closing a slightly disappointing property deal. Charles pats me on the back at the door:

'Obviously we'll provide references. If I hear of any opportunities, I'll let you know. You'll be in a new job in no time. Come back any time if you need anything, Alex. Any time.'

'I will, thanks, Charles.'

And then I'm gone. The door shuts behind me and when I look back I can barely see my old workmates past the carousels of houses for sale. The rain is softer now, but there is still a little river trickling down the edge of the road toward the drain covers. A couple on the other side of the street are holding hands as they stroll into a restaurant; a mother and her toddler stamp in the puddles; two men in suits laugh loudly as they pass, both gripping paper bags from the expensive deli up the road. Everything is normal.

But everything isn't.

For the second time in a month I've been cast out. I feel weightless. I feel like I am circling helplessly toward a whirlpool. I never wanted this job, I took it because we needed stability, we needed money, and we had a baby on the way. And then I stayed because I had no idea what I actually wanted to do. I still don't. The job provided something fixed and unerring, something sure. But there is no certainty. I should have known that, I studied philosophy at university, for Christ's sake. Fat lot of good *that* did me. No one stands outside their old office, jobless and terrified, and asks: what would Karl Popper do? I consider calling Dan and getting smashed, but then I remember he's in Bath working on some design project. And there is only one person I want to speak to at a time like this. So I take out my phone and I tap the number on to the screen.

I fell for Jody within thirty-five seconds of meeting her. I'd left university with the same career plan as most humanities graduates – i.e. none whatsoever, apart from maybe interning at the *New Statesman*. Therefore, I pursued the same short-term financial solution as any young man who finds himself bored, alone and broke in Somerset: apple picking. A farm near our old family home, where I'd been doing odd jobs (badly) since I was a teenager, was happy to take me back for a few months. When I turned up that warm September morning ten years ago, Jody was standing in the yard amid a small group of other unenthusiastic workers, holding a basket. We were assigned to the same row of trees. It was a beautiful day and the orchard shimmered in the late summer heat.

'Shall we work together on the same tree, or do we alternate?' I asked.

She looked at me quizzically.

'I didn't realise we'd have to develop a strategy. You're clearly the expert here. How shall we handle this?'

She was beautiful, confident and intimidating; her brown hair tumbled about her shoulders in great wild curls. She was wearing a Nirvana T-shirt and a pair of straggly jean shorts cut so high you could see her bottom. I tried not to stare as we stripped the trees of their fruit. 'Stop staring at my arse,' she continually demanded from the top of the ladder.

That autumn, Jody and I spent six weeks together, picking apples during the day and drinking cider in the local pub every night, a perfectly circular existence. We talked endlessly. I found out she'd attended the girls' school five miles away from where I grew up, that she'd studied Industrial Design at university, that she was killing time before starting an MA in Arts Management. She'd recently returned from an archaeological dig in Kazakhstan; I'd spent two weeks in a static caravan in Brean with Dan and two friends I don't remember. 'We are so alike,' we joked. She told me all about how smartphones are designed. I told her about my useless degree and about my family, and the terrible thing that happened to us a decade ago. Some nights we took a train into the city centre and watched bizarre experimental movies at the

Watershed, or we'd get drunk and stagger around the Arnolfini, loudly discussing an array of incomprehensible art exhibitions. At the weekends we'd buy a day ticket and ride the river taxi back and forth from Temple Meads station to the SS *Great Britain*, lounging on the plastic seats as the boat chugged asthmatically through Bristol's swampy river network. When we passed the huge cranes still standing uselessly along the old docks, I told her that the AT-ATs in *The Empire Strikes Back* were inspired by similar structures in the port of San Francisco. In fact, I think I told her that every time we saw them. She would nod indulgently.

One night, after two weeks of this, we cycled back to her parents' house, our sweaty faces illuminated under the milky moon.

'Good night then,' I said awkwardly.

'Aren't you going to kiss me?' she asked.

And I summoned the courage to wordlessly lean across from my bike to hers, take her face in my hands, and kiss her on the mouth for a very long time. I am not a man prone to romantic hyperbole, but as we finally parted, I wouldn't have been surprised to see the warm night sky filled with fireworks.

Then Jody answers the phone, and I'm snapped back to the Bristol of now. The city where everything's going wrong.

'Hi, Alex. Is everything OK?'

'No, not really. Jody, I've been made redundant.'

'What? Oh shit! Did they give you any notice?'

'It's been brewing for weeks; the company's been taken over. They don't need a mortgage adviser ... I'm sorry.'

'What are you sorry for?'

'The house, Sam ... I'm responsible.'

The line goes silent for a few seconds. I wonder if the enormity of this is sinking in on the other end.

'Look, don't think about all that now,' says Jody. 'Is Dan around? Can you go and see him?'

'He's working. Are you . . .'

'Alex, I'm so sorry, I've got an appointment I need to get to.'

'I know. I understand.'

'I'll see you later in the week, we can talk then, OK?'

'OK.'

'Alex, take care. It's only a job. That's what we always said. You'll get another one.'

Cast adrift.

'OK. Bye.'

Later on, Dan gets home to his flat and finds me slumped in front of the TV, playing *Grand Theft Auto V*, shooting wildly at pedestrians from a severely dented muscle car while hurtling through the crowded city streets.

'What the hell, am I in the wrong flat?' he says. 'Wait, has something happened – why are you playing video games?'

'I got made redundant,' I sigh. 'How do I unlock the rocket launcher?'

'Put the controller down. We are going out and we are getting shit-faced.'

For once, I don't argue with him.

All security in life is an illusion. This is the fun thought that goes through my head at 2 a.m. as I collapse on to the inflatable mattress in the spare room without even bothering with the charade of inflating it. Tonight, we trawled the hip bars lining the Gloucester and Cheltenham roads, before hitting a Caribbean takeaway – a classic Bristol piss-up. We didn't discuss the events of this past month, we didn't go over my options or my emotions. We downed our drinks and talked about music and movies and all that safe, neutral stuff everyone retreats to when life gets too shitty to deal with head-on. But now I'm drunk and alone, and in the screaming silence of the flat, everything surfaces again. What am I going to do? How will I take care of Jody and Sam? How can I figure out a way to help my little boy, himself so lost in his own world? And then somehow I start to think, well, maybe autism isn't a weakness or a medical condition – maybe it's an evolutionary stage; a self-protective distancing from the universe and the cruel uncertainty it represents. Then I think, maybe I shouldn't have had that last Jägerbomb.

The next week is a blur of sleeping, moping about in Dan's flat, and then sleeping some more. I joylessly work my way through several television box sets, eat a lot of pot noodles and drink several gallons of tea. I go online and half-heartedly search a few job sites with no idea what I'm looking for. I lie on the sofa staring at the ceiling. I help Dan rearrange his vinyl record collection, I tidy his kitchen, I do all our clothes washing. In a weird asynchronous process, the flat gets tidier as I become more of a mess. One night Jody texts to ask if I can look after Sam, but racked with guilt, I make an excuse. I can't face him like this – I can't answer to his needs, I don't have the strength or patience. Fortunately for me, the two of them are going away to stay with Jody's parents in Gloucester for the last two weeks of Sam's summer holiday, rescuing me from a series of Saturday mornings in the park. Matt invites me over to watch the football a couple of times, but I turn him down too. I think his chaotic house, with its standing army of marauding children, would scare the crap out of me right now. I only leave the flat once in seven days to stock up on snacks and milk. The woman behind the counter at the local shop gives me a look that manages to combine both sympathy and fear; when I get home I realise I'm wearing tartan pyjama bottoms, a crumpled Marks and Spencer shirt and two trainers that don't match. Add in the fact that I haven't shaved for five days and I look like what I am – a pathetic shuffling husk of a man.

Dan is brilliant, though. Every night he comes home and sort of pretends everything is fine – not in an awkward, male 'I can't face this emotional crisis' way, but in a way that says, 'You need time, mate, and you're welcome to fall apart in my flat.' He doesn't pry, he doesn't ask what I'm doing or why I look like Jack Nicholson at the end of *The Shining*. He just gets on with it – although I've noticed he hasn't brought any women home in several days. Oh God, I'm the mad woman in the attic. Or, more accurately, the sad man in the spare room wearing mismatched trainers and a shirt stained with beef-and-tomato Super Noodles.

One night he suggests we try to skype Emma, for a laugh he says, so I have a quick, tear-inducingly painful shave and we sit together in front of his Mac and dial her up – but there's no answer. He seems more disappointed than me. I dimly recall that they dated briefly when we all lived next door to each other, but, well, whatever was going on, it came to an abrupt end when she got on a plane to New Zealand one day and never came back. Right now that sounds like an appealing idea. Not for the first time, I envy her freedom; later that night I go on a travel website and idly look up flights to distant locations. 'I'm sorry, Jody, I can't look after Sam this evening, I'm in Kuala Lumpur.'

Then one Tuesday afternoon, while I'm lying on the sofa watching my seventh episode of *Arrested Development*, Jody calls.

'Hey, Alex, how are you?'

'Ah, I'm OK. Well, I've kind of lost it a bit. Temporarily.'

'Do you know what you're going to do?'

'No. No, not yet. It's all sinking in. Everything is still sinking in. How about you? How are things at your parents'? How's Sam?'

'Fine, all fine.' She pauses for a second. 'Something has come up, actually. One of the mums at Sam's school works at a gallery in town and they need an assistant curator. Mum drove me down to chat to them, and they've offered me the job. They want me to start as soon as the school holidays are over. It's only two days a week, but, Alex, I really want to do it. I know, I'm sorry, the timing is pretty horrible, it's—'

'You've got to do it,' I say with barely a pause. 'It's what you always wanted to do.'

'But, Sam ...'

'We'll sort it.'

'Alex, it would mean you'd have to collect him from school.'

With that, time suddenly distorts and slows. There's a sudden horrible pressure in my chest, the edges of my vision fade like an old TV screen, and I can feel pinpricks of sweat on my forehead. I'm frozen in time and space, a sort of excruciating limbo.

And then I'm back twenty years.

My older brother George and I, running out of school and toward the gates, messing about, scrapping and chasing. It's Monday afternoon, classes are over, and all we want is to get home and collapse in front of the TV. I'm trying to trip him up, thrusting my leg out to catch his as we jog. 'Stop it,' he yells. 'Stop it, Alex.' But I'm having fun baiting my brother, because usually it's the other way around. Ahead, there are kids milling about at the gates, and some parents waiting for the younger children. It's late February and the sky is darkening already. A chill is coming in. He's speeding up, and I accelerate too, laughing and swinging my bag at him.

'Alex, leave me alone now!' he shouts.

And now, he's sprinting; he reaches the gates and zips through them, zig-zagging past the crowd of parents, on to the pavement, and then over the road toward the alley on the other side that leads to home. But he doesn't make it.

I can't see properly through the bustle of waiting mums and dads, but I hear the screech of tyres. For a second, I glimpse a body spinning. I know it is George, and almost laugh because the sight of him cartwheeling through the air is so ridiculous. I keep running, expecting him to get up, to cry or to shout at me, but as I reach the crowd, I hear a scream and then another. One mum recognises me. 'Stay here, Alex, stay here, honey.' Her hands, as they clasp around my face, smell of washing-up liquid. I hear a car door.

'Oh fucking hell, oh no.'

'You were driving too bloody fast!'

'Call an ambulance, Lindsay!'

'Where is Alex? Where is his brother?'

'Mum,' I repeat, softly at first, but then louder. 'My mum. My mummy.'

There is noise and shouting, the adults seem to push and wrestle with each other as they crowd around the road. I feel my legs give way, and the woman scoops me up. From a great distance comes the whine of a siren, merging with the sound of sobbing strangers. I close my eyes as tight as I can and try to put my hands over my ears. The world closes in around me.

'Don't let him see. Don't let him see.'

George was rushed to hospital but pronounced dead soon after arrival. Catastrophic head injuries. When I started back at school a week later, I walked the long way around and went in via the sports hall entrance at the rear of the building. I never used the front gates again.

'I know it's hard,' says Jody. I've no idea how long it's been since anyone said anything. 'I can ask someone else maybe? My mum? Alex, are you OK? Are you still there?'

'No. No, it's OK. I can do it. It's a different school. It's fine. It's fine.' But Jody knows that I always cross the road, I even walk for many minutes out of my way to avoid passing the school gates. Any school gates.

'It's fine,' I repeat again. We say goodbye to each other and I put the phone down and sit with my head in my hands, breathing slowly and deliberately. And it's obvious that I am nowhere near fine and haven't been for a long time.

Chapter 10

It's 'the big quiz night' at the Old Ship Inn, which means there are ten customers here instead of four. Dan and I have been roped into taking part, though as most of the questions are about seventies music and television we don't fancy our chances. Amid the unusual bustle and chatter, old Sid sits alone, mumbling over his chessboard, a half-pint of stout barely touched beside him. As people pass, his elbow flicks up protectively, forming a defensive perimeter around his table.

'So,' says Dan. 'Are things any better this week?'

'Well . . .' I begin. 'I've completed my first two school pick-ups.'

'How did it go?'

'Oh, fine. Absolutely fine.'

Here's how it actually went. On Thursday, I chickened out and waited a little way along the street from the school gates, so I had to shout for Sam as he emerged amid the crowds, carrying his battered backpack and two paintings.

'Where's Mummy?' he asked.

'She's at work. She's told you about work, hasn't she?'

'When is she back?'

'She'll be back at five thirty, which is two hours. I'm taking you home.'

'Is Mummy at home, though?'

'No, she's at work.'

'Why is she at work?'

'Let's get home, shall we?'

'But is Mummy there?'

This was pretty much our walk back to the house. I tried to ask about his day, but it was the familiar rota of responses: he ignored me, said 'good', or asked a question of his own. I tried to tell him about my day ('Daddy watched fifteen episodes of *The Simpsons*') but the cogs in his head whirred back to his overriding concern.

'But where's Mummy?'

Back home he rushed upstairs to the games console. Jody had said he was allowed an hour, so I sat and idly flicked through channels on the TV. An hour later, I headed up to his room to tell him his time was up, and he threw the controller on the floor.

'Where's Mummy?!'

The next day, I sidled toward the gates, gripping the fence as though making my way along a treacherous mountain pass. A couple of the mums seemed to eye me suspiciously; I thought one was a friend of Jody's but I wasn't sure. I smiled at her anyway and she turned away quickly and chatted to someone else. A bell sounded within the school building and gradually the children filed out, some of them laughing and joking, others quickly pacing toward their parents, heads down, determined.

Sam was with a teacher at first, a young man in a cheap suit who gently nudged my son toward the gates. Sam started off, and I was about to wave, but then another boy rushed up and slapped him over the back of his head. Sam shrank away. Angered, I made a move toward the gates, but then stopped, torn between protective fury and the spectre of George rushing past, through the crowds, into the road. Sam spotted me and walked slowly over. I tried to gather myself.

'Who was that boy? Why did he hit you? What's going on?'

He looked at me, baffled, unable to comprehend my barrage of questions.

'I don't know. Where's Mummy?'

'Do you want me to speak to the teacher?'

'No, Daddy, no.'

'Why did he hit you?'

'I want to go home! Where's Mummy? I want to play *Minecraft*.'

And then he was crying, properly crying with great shoulder-heaving sobs. I tried to hold him close, but he wriggled away. As ever, I had no idea how to calm him. I let him run ahead, and when he got home he was up into his room again before I had a chance to say anything. I traipsed up and down the living room, unable to sit down, wired with anger and fear. I thought about ringing the school and reporting the incident, but decided I'd better talk it over with Jody, who would doubtless know more than me. From upstairs came the increasingly familiar sounds of *Minecraft*. The gentle piano music, the almost hypnotic electronic effects.

'It's gone about as well as I thought it would go,' I say to Dan.

'That bad?' he replies.

We perform surprisingly well in the quiz. Dan reveals a hitherto unknown expertise in prog rock music, and I've been spending so much time watching retro TV channels, I manage to answer two questions about *The Sweeney* and correctly identify actor Fulton

Mackay in the picture round. We finish second, which earns us a bottle of British sherry.

'What even *is* sherry?' asks Dan.

Four pints in, we start actually talking. Surprisingly, it is Dan who kicks things off.

'So, dude, what's your plan?'

'My what?'

'Your *plan*, your goal. What's next?'

'I don't know. I'm looking at jobs, but nothing is springing out at me. It would help if I knew what I wanted to do, or what I'm good at. Do you need me out of the flat? I totally understand.'

'No!' says Dan. 'But you need to start thinking about the future, man. You've spent way too long stuck in the past.'

'I don't know what the future is. I have this crushing history and this unending present, and there's not much room for anything else. Things just happen *to* me. Do you know what I mean?'

'So do something! Turn it around. Take control.'

But I'm getting irritated. I don't want another lecture on where I'm going wrong, especially not from Dan.

'You mean take control like you have?' I'm not sure where this is coming from, but here it comes anyway.

'What do you mean?'

'I mean you drift from one vague freelance gig to the next, there's no plan, no ambition, and I don't think you've ever had a relationship that's lasted longer than a month. How do you live like that? You're as bad as me.'

'No,' says Dan. His voice is quiet and controlled. 'I'm different because I'm not making everyone else miserable.'

There is a moment's silence between us, punctuated by the jukebox starting up, playing the Everly Brothers. I don't know whether to be furious with Dan or impressed that he's being so bloody direct and incisive. So I decide to do the intelligent, mature thing and storm off.

'Well, thanks for the pep talk, I'll take my downer somewhere else.'

I get up, but Dan grabs my arm and thrusts me back into the chair.

'Alex, listen to me, man. I love you – like a brother, I mean – and that's not the beer talking. There is a funny, brilliant, wise Alex in that fucking annoying head of yours and you need to get that back.'

I'm momentarily dazed, partly because Dan has never physically assaulted me before, so that's new, and partly because we've never operated at this level of honesty. This is uncharted territory.

'I don't know how,' I say at last. 'I mean, maybe if I find a job, start something new ...'

'No, listen, you *have* a job now,' says Dan. 'It's an extremely important job. Alex, your job is to get to know your son. Forget everything else, forget work, forget George for a little while. This is what you've got to do. I mean, it's so bloody obvious. You've got to find Sam.'

I take a sip of beer and glance over at old Sid, alone in the corner, hiding some sort of miserable history of his own – a history far too long, now, to grasp and change.

'Can you tell me where to start looking?' I say. 'Because I am completely out of ideas.'

'Sheesh, mate,' says Dan. 'I'm done. This is the deepest conversation I've had in about ten years – I've got nothing left. We need to go home, drink some British sherry, whatever the fuck that is, and talk about the new Chvrches album.'

Chapter 11

The following week I'm in Blackwell's bookshop on Park Street, browsing the health section until I get to a small collection of books on autism. I have resolved to read one. Actually read it. We've got a few at home – most of them desperate online purchases made after a long day of exhausting meltdowns. Some are overly officious and instructional, treating the condition like a challenging DIY job; some are more like hippy lifestyle manuals so you end up feeling like *you're* the problem for ever viewing autism negatively in the first place. In any case, I've never managed more than a couple of chapters before getting sidetracked or giving up. For me, the books merged into the general miasma of condescending advice that has become part of our daily lives since Sam was a toddler. Maybe it's the same for everyone with kids, I don't know, but if there are three words the parents of autistic children especially dread hearing, it's 'Have you tried ...?' I mean, it's one thing to hear it from friends (that whole Peppa Pig incident pops into my head again) but it's even more fun to get it from passing strangers. For example:

'Have you tried going a different way around town?'

In response to Sam having a tantrum on the pavement outside the toyshop because we won't take him in.

'Have you tried letting him discover the food with his fingers?'

In a restaurant when Sam started to retch because we'd accidentally tried to poison him with a stray kernel of sweetcorn.

'Have you tried listening to him? Kids tell us more than we think.'

When he'd spent the whole day sobbing on the beach and we couldn't work out what was wrong or what we'd done.

The last one, on an ill-fated day trip to Salcombe, was my absolute favourite. Jody had to restrain me from picking Sam up, handing him over to the concerned woman on the deckchair next to us and saying, 'Here, honestly, you take him.' (We still have no idea what was wrong, but the smart money is probably on 'sand in his pants'.)

With all that in mind, I select a couple of books that look like they sit somewhere between the 'you can fix your broken child' and the 'hey, man, it's *society* that needs to be fixed' schools of thought and then head to the till. On the way, I spot a huge display of *Minecraft* books, stacked high around a cardboard cut-out of a blocky figure carrying a pickaxe. On a whim, I pick up something that promises a complete guide to the game.

'Are your kids *Minecraft* nuts as well, then?' says the sales assistant when I get to the counter. He stares at me intently while wrestling the books into a plastic bag.

'My son only just started playing recently. But yeah, he seems to like it.'

'Ah, mine don't talk about anything else. *Minecraft* this, *Minecraft* that. My daughter spent the whole of last weekend building the Taj Mahal.'

'Right . . .'

'And my lad's started Old Trafford. Two hours I spent last night, looking up pictures of the Stretford End on Google and printing them out. Why couldn't he have made Ashton Gate? We can see that from our house.'

'OK, well, that's something to look forward to.'

'Still, it's better than some of what they could be getting up to on that console, shooting people in the face, chopping their heads off with swords, bludgeoning prostitutes and all that.'

'I'm sure it is. Thank you.'

Unperturbed by this slightly unsettling exchange, I drop into a video game store on the way back to Dan's to actually buy a copy of *Minecraft*. It's the first time I've been into one of these shops since purchasing *FIFA Football* on the Sega Mega Drive about a hundred and fifty years ago. I feel strangely liberated. It's not that I'm a complete technophobe. I have a smartphone, I know how to use a computer, but the idea of actually playing something on a screen, just for the sake of it, seems alien to me. There are always movies to watch and books I should read – I'm still making my way through the required reading list they handed us at the start of my university degree. Now, whenever I want to try something new, I'm unconsciously comparing it to Dickens or Derrida. Here, there are no such pretensions. The shelves are stacked with bright boxes displaying muscular space marines and furious soldiers; a huge LCD display on the wall shows a rolling stream of graphically astonishing games footage. Eventually, I find *Minecraft* and grab the box. I'm now the sort of guy who buys video games, I think. I mean, I'll probably need to get Dan to load it up, but still. As I walk out of the shop I am hit by an unfamiliar wave of optimism. I don't know what to do about me and Jody, I really don't. But I am going to understand Sam; I am going to crack either autism or *Minecraft*, one of the two.

When Dan gets home later, he finds me sitting cross-legged in front of his TV, Xbox controller in one hand, *Minecraft* guide in the other.

'Video games *again*?' he asks. 'What are you – fifteen?'

On screen is the increasingly familiar blocky landscape, its jagged pastures dotted with cube-like flora. I have discovered that each time you start a new game, it generates a fresh landscape, just for you. It's like your own personal version of Genesis – except there's no forbidden tree of knowledge (and if there was, you could probably chop it down and make a shed with it). The experience would be sort of beautiful and exciting if I had any idea what I was supposed to be doing. I've chosen Survival mode, which seems to mean that if I don't make a shelter by nightfall I will be attacked by zombies and giant spiders. Somehow I am terrified. Following the guide, I manage to chop up some wood to make blocks, which I then drop on to a flat piece of land to build a very rudimentary house. It looks like an Ikea scout hut. As night falls, and the pixel sky turns dark, I realise I haven't built a door so can't get in. Very quickly I bash a hole in one wall, open the crafting menu to select a door, then chuck it into the gap. It opens and then closes behind me with a pleasing snap. I am safe. Is this what Sam has been doing for weeks?

'Do you know what I'm supposed to do now?' I ask Dan.

'Where are the guns?' he says.

'I don't think it has guns.'

'Then you're on your own, dude.'

I bring up the pause menu and hit Save so that my world is not obliterated for ever, then switch the console off.

'I don't understand the twenty-first century,' I say.

That night, I check my emails, concerned that I haven't heard from Emma for a couple of weeks. Nothing. I look at Facebook and Instagram – no updates there either. I settle down on the mattress with the *Minecraft* and autism books, flicking between them, reading chunks here and there. I fall asleep worrying about skeleton warriors and social barriers.

*

My phone alarm wakes me early on Saturday morning, Sam day, and there's that familiar feeling of trepidation. It's been raining heavily and now there's this endless British drizzle, so we can maybe skip the park. I think about taking him swimming, but that's a whole different nightmare – will I bring the right towel, will we get the correct changing cubicle, will another child splash him in the pool, kicking off a complete breakdown? Will I have to explain it all to a lifeguard who bounds over thinking Sam is drowning? Maybe I can get him into Bristol on the bus. We can do a café crawl, eat cake all day, watch planes on the Flight Track app. But then I'll be sending him home to Jody on a massive sugar and additives high, which probably isn't fair.

When I reach the house I park up and see Jody busy tidying inside. I put up the hood on my anorak and sprint up the path. She sees me outside and waves.

'Hello, Daddy, I've made a castle,' says Sam as he opens the front door.

'Ah, OK, *Minecraft*, right?'

But then he's off upstairs. I'm left with Jody and nothing to say.

'Hey.'

'Hey there.'

There is a CD playing that I don't recognise, something with choppy, distorted guitars and strangulated vocals. Jody is wearing skinny jeans and a tight black Joy Division T-shirt. She looks ten years younger than me.

'You look great,' I say.

'I've actually been sleeping,' she says.

'How's the job?'

'It's amazing! It's weird, getting back into it, but we have some interesting exhibitions coming up – new artists, lots of new stuff to learn.'

Suddenly she seems to realise how effusive she's being, and turns to look at me, her expression is guilty. Something has changed, I don't know what, but there is a gap between us and for the first time, with a thudding sense of horror, I suspect that it cannot be closed.

'Anyway, how are you? Do you want a cup of coffee? I've made some fresh.'

I hear laughter coming from upstairs, and with a slight shock I realise it's Sam, on his own and happy. We sit and drink coffee while we listen to our son, who usually requires near-constant contact with Jody, amusing himself far away from us, in another world. Our conversation is awkward and light, she talks about her job a little more, I tell her about the new books on autism, about my plan to finally, honestly, *genuinely* figure out Sam.

'Well, there may be a chance to put that into practice,' says Jody.

'What do you mean?'

'Ah, well, next month, my university friend Gemma is getting married in Norfolk. I was wondering if you would take Sam for the whole weekend, from Saturday morning to Sunday evening. It's the second weekend in October. Can you do it?'

I'm not prepared for this, but I walked straight into it. A whole weekend. My mind goes into a sort of jumbled panic. I've never had him that long – not even when Jody and I were together. The thought of keeping him happy, keeping him safe, for two days, the possibilities for things to go wrong. Running into the road, through the crowds of parents, cartwheeling into the air.

'Damn, I think I have a sort of goodbye work do that Saturday,' I blurt out. 'You know, see everyone, say a final farewell, get drunk and beg for my job back, that sort of thing. I'm sorry.'

Jody stares at me for a few seconds.

'OK, whatever, Alex. I thought this would be good for both of you, but obviously not.'

Backed into a corner, I manage to refocus my fear into anger.

'Jody, what are we doing? It's been almost two months. I don't know what the plan is. I don't know what I've got to do.'

It's a desperate gambit, mistimed and awkward. I know immediately that it's a mistake. She sighs and looks out of the window.

'I don't know, Alex. I don't know either. I'm trying to figure things out too. For eight years I feel like it's been all about Sam – dealing with Sam, worrying about Sam. And, Alex, honestly, I never felt like you were completely there with me. I know you were working, I know that. But it wasn't only the work, you were absent from *everything*. I can't do that any more. We're going round in circles.'

'I was doing what I needed to do, to keep you both safe.'

'We *were* safe! We didn't need you to be working all the time.'

There's a long silence, broken only by the low rumble of a plane passing overhead. It has the ominous sound of thunder. I look around and feel as though I am standing in someone else's front room.

'Sam is fine today,' Jody says, her voice calm and measured. 'He's playing upstairs and he's happy. So I think you should go.'

'We need to talk about this,' I say.

'No, not today. Not now. We've got an appointment to show Sam St Peter's school on Monday morning. Can you at least make that?'

'Yes, of course.'

'Well, we'll see you then.'

I turn to leave, and as I reach for the door latch, she says:

'Oh, your mum rang. I haven't told her what's going on. You should call her back.'

I pause and nod.

'And look,' she says. 'I appreciate you collecting Sam from school. Believe me, I know how hard it must be. But you need to get some help, Alex. You're sleepwalking through life. It's time to wake up.'

Chapter 12

When George died, everything closed in around us. Mum, Emma and I existed in a tiny speck of light. For a while, relatives, friends and neighbours gathered in, fussing, trying to help – and they succeeded at first. People came to cook and clean, I don't remember who. Some neighbours sent their children over with toys and sweets, which we accepted greedily. But we were alone in the centre of it all, cut off, isolated by shock and incomprehension. Then the generosity and support began to wane. Relatives we hadn't seen in years drifted back to their own lives; Mum's friends became frustrated that she was not grieving in the way they thought she should. She's a tough, proud woman who grew up with four brothers in a tiny terraced house in Redruth, during the last years of the tin-mining industry. There wasn't much room for sentiment or sorrow then, and she saw through those weeks after George's death with a resolve that many misread as iciness. Like tourists of grief, they stood about, waiting for her to break down, but she never did; robbed of their show, they turned on her or turned away. So then it was the three of us again, huddling together like the survivors of some great earthquake.

But Mum herded us back into life. She had to. Dad was long gone – although 'dad' is far from the right word for this man that none of us remember. My uncles called him a feckless bastard, they thought he was useless and inconsequential, yet he somehow convinced Mum, desperate for escape I guess, to follow him up to Somerset, to a job at the Bath printing press that he soon lost. He left before Emma was born, and Mum never saw him or spoke of him again. We knew not to ask, just as we knew that, when she told us to get back to school a week after George's death, it was something we would have to do. I was old enough to understand that what had happened was final, and that George was not coming back, but Emma had to be convinced. That was my job, it seemed. And within me, anchored firmly and unshifting, despite protestations from everyone I told, there was an agonising guilt.

'Stop it, Alex, leave me *alone!*'

Those words haunted me; they hung above me like a low black cloud.

Gradually, though, I taught myself to recall something else. Something from the day before he died. Mum had taken us on a trip to London to see the Science and Natural History Museums. It was a strangely hot day, the first sign of the coming spring. We spent the morning racing from one exhibit to another, pushing buttons, exploring dinosaur skeletons and the *Apollo* landing craft, and afterwards we went to an old café up the road with a bright red awning and small wooden tables outside. We sat and ate ice cream in the sun, chatting and laughing, comparing the souvenirs we'd bought: chunks of crystal, postcards, a bouncing ball that Emma threw across the road and thought she had lost, but George fetched it. On the way back to the tube station, he put his arm around my shoulder and I put mine around his, and Mum laughed at us. 'Look at you two,' she said. 'My little men.'

I used that memory against the darkness. Every night for many months, I forced myself to remember every detail so that it wouldn't be lost. Now I have the photo of George and me, standing outside the café – Mum found it and gave it to me a few years ago. I have several copies as well as digital versions on a hard drive. When you lose someone, the grief comes back at you like a flash flood, tearing through all your carefully constructed defences. You have to do what you can; you use whatever is available to get through.

It's a crisp, clear morning as I pull up once again outside our home, in its little street of identical Victorian terraced houses. We're taking Sam to see St Peter's school. Jody says she has been preparing him for days – he needs forewarning of events like this: being taken out of his own school for a day to see another is a big deal. It's disruptive and confusing. This is not going to be fun. Jody emerges from the house looking severe, wearing a smart shirt haphazardly tucked into her skirt. She is gripping a forlorn-looking Sam by his wrist as she shuts the door and heads toward the car.

'Hi,' she says wearily.

'Hi, is it going well?'

'Don't ask.'

Sam gets into the back, puts on his seat belt and sits with his head buried in his hands.

'Hi, Sam,' I say brightly.

'Shut up!'

'OK,' I reply, and glance at Jody.

'No Crunchy Nut Cornflakes,' she whispers. 'And his trousers are too long.'

I nod grimly.

We don't talk much on the way. I begin to tell Sam about the school – its tree-lined front drive, the little classrooms, the friendly teachers – but he puts his fingers in his ears.

'I don't want to go to the school!'

He starts to kick the back of my seat, with increasing savagery. I quietly move it forward.

'See what you're missing?' says Jody.

'That's not *my* choice,' I reply.

The atmosphere in the car is thick with resentment. When we reach the school and park up, none of us move, as though we're all frozen in this state of mutual hostility. Sam has sunk low on to the back seat, Jody is staring into the middle distance.

'OK,' I say at last. 'Let's go and meet the head.'

I get out of the car, and Jody follows, but when I try to open Sam's door, he swings round and holds it shut.

'NO!' he screams. 'No new school!'

'Sam,' I say. 'Sam, come on, you'll like it.'

'No!'

I open the door a little, but he manages to slam it shut again, then lies across the seat and kicks at the window.

'Sam, stop it, you're going to break the glass,' says Jody.

In a sudden flurry of movement, she drags open the door, grabs him by the ankle and starts to drag him out. Shocked, I stand back for a second, not sure how to intervene, and the memories of a hundred similar instances flood back: Sam as a toddler refusing to get out of a shopping trolley seat; Sam at playgroup, hiding under the crafting table, kicking at the other children, scaring them so much we had to bring him home; carrying Sam to school while he's crying and thrashing so much that he's physically sick. Sometimes it feels like this is what we've spent the last eight years doing – yanking our beautiful little boy from one drama to the next.

'Can you help?' yells Jody as Sam claws at the car seat, kicking her hands and arms.

I'm suddenly aware that we're right outside the school, in view of a classroom and the reception office.

'You're going to *hurt* him!' I say.

I spit it out with unexpected fury, surveying the school windows for teachers. Jody looks at me, distraught, and I immediately feel guilty for accusing her. There was a time we faced this sort of thing together, struggling to get him into a school uniform or fighting with him over food. Now we're apart and it's so easy to turn on each other.

'Look, this isn't going to work,' I say. 'We can't take him in like this.'

'Oh, fuck it!' shouts Jody. She lets go of Sam's leg and he crawls back into the car sobbing. Now she's crying too.

I'm desperately trying to think how to defuse the situation when my mobile starts buzzing in my pocket. Worried it's someone in the school wondering what the hell is going on in their car park, I take it out and check the screen.

'Oh shit,' I say when I see the name.

Momentarily distracted from the chaos around me, I hit the accept button.

'Hello?'

'Hi, Alex, it's me!' Her voice sounds bright and clear; the contrast to everything else that's happened this morning is shocking.

'Where are you?'

Jody is wiping her eyes with a tissue. She gets back into the car and slams the door shut behind her. Sam puts his seat belt straight and sits up, instantly brighter now that it appears the visit is over.

'I'm fine! I'm back, Alex!'

'What?'

'I'm back in Britain!'

'What? When?'

'Now, I'm here now! I'm on my way to Bristol! Sorry, can I stay with you guys for a few days?'

It feels like my life has suddenly been put into fast-forward, and now everything is flying at me with incomprehensible speed.

'You're what?' I manage.

And then we're cut off. I stand there stupidly looking at the phone for a few seconds, then climb slowly into the car.

'Emma's back,' I say.

'I heard,' replies Jody.

'I'm sorry. I'm sorry I wasn't more help. We'll bring him again next week. When he's in a better mood.'

Jody nods and looks away.

We drive into Bristol, the silence punctuated only by Sam, now in a much brighter mood, asking questions about the city as we pass through. 'Is that a church? What is a church? Why is that building so tall? How many people live in that house? I am going to make that building in *Minecraft*. Daddy, do you know that you can make steps in *Minecraft*? And fences? I have made a ladder that goes all the way up.'

I turn the radio on.

When we get to the house there is a taxi parked outside. Clambering out of it, with a backpack so gigantic it could conceivably contain another person, is Emma. Her blonde hair is cut short, almost cropped, and her skin is tanned to a shade of warm honey. She stuffs some money into the driver's hand, says something to him, then drags another massive backpack out of the boot. We all sit in the car, dumbly watching her.

'What the . . .' says Jody.

'Typical Emma,' I respond.

I get out of the car.

'Do you need some help with those?' I ask.

'Alex!' she screams and throws her arms around me. I return the hug, still dazed and vacant, still unable to process this radical turnaround. I haven't seen her for over a year – she was back briefly for a friend's lavish birthday party at Babington House, but I only saw her for a couple of hours. That's how it's been for almost ten years – snatched moments here and there.

'Are you OK? Has something happened?'

'Typical Alex!' she laughs, looking at Jody, who has finally emerged from the car. Sam has stepped out too, eyeing Emma with cautious interest.

'Is this Sam?' yells Emma. 'Oh my God, he's enormous!'

She goes over to him, but with good sense, instead of cuddling him, she offers him her hand. He doesn't look at her, but he does take it for an instant before squirming away.

'Good to meet you, Sam. I'm Emma! Aunt Emma if you have to. But not *Auntie* Emma, for God's sake. I hear you like planes. I have been on so many planes!'

She turns to Jody. The two of them have barely met. Emma missed us getting together, she missed our low-key wedding, though she sent a video message from Vietnam; she missed Sam being born. They've spoken on Skype calls, but that's it. They hug somewhat cautiously.

'I hope you don't mind me turning up like this!' says Emma.

'Jody,' I say. 'Do you want to take Sam in? Maybe I should have a quick word with Emma?'

Jody stares at me, attempting to communicate something, but I've no idea what it is. She takes Sam's hand and they head toward the house.

'What's up?' says Emma.

'It's complicated. Why didn't you tell me you were coming home?'

'It was a snap decision. What's going on?'

'Look, we've ... we're having a bit of a trial separation – that's what it's called, right? Things have been very tense. Sam and everything. Work ...'

'Shit. Do you want me to go?'

'No,' I say almost reluctantly, before instantly correcting myself. 'No! Absolutely not. But, oh God, this is a lot to deal with. Did you not think it would be a good idea to call in advance? Jesus. I haven't seen you in over a year.'

She shrugs, then starts checking her phone.

'OK, I think let's go to Dan's and maybe drop your stuff there?'

'You're staying at Dan's?'

'Yeah, he's got a new flat in Redcliffe.'

'Cool. Whatever.'

I try to explain what's going on to Jody, but unsure of what is going on myself, it ends up as gibberish. Jody waves me away, and closes the door.

'So,' says Emma, 'that was awkward.'

I think about filling Emma in on the last few months: the arguments and stress over Sam, my endlessly long working hours, the terrible Sunday afternoon when Jody said, 'We need some time without you', the redundancy. But I'm still in shock and that's a lot to offload on someone who's only this moment arrived from the other side of the planet.

'Jesus, Emma,' I say, shaking my head.

'Do you want me to go?' Her tone has a familiar petulance that takes me crashing back a decade.

'There's quite a lot to unpack here.'

'Tell me about it, I've got two more cases in storage at the station.'

She looks at me, clearly expecting me to laugh, and when I don't, she humphs and turns back to her phone. We get into the car for the quick drive to Dan's and don't speak at all, Emma totally engrossed in her phone. It's only when we pull up at the apartment block, and have to wait as the security gate slowly opens, that I break the silence.

'I'll call Dan, I'm sure it'll be fine for you to stay.'

'It's only for a while. I've got other friends in Bristol. I'll be gone soon.'

'Yeah,' I say. 'I don't doubt that at all.'

It is barbed, but she doesn't seem to take it in. I can't figure out how much she's changed in the last ten years. When I get through to Dan, he seems strangely delighted that Emma is back and is more than happy for her to stay. We agree that she gets the guest room for a few days to reacclimatise and I'll take the sofa in the living room. This feels familiar to me: making way for Emma. As a teenager, she was a little spoiled and self-centred, but also bright, outgoing and popular – my exact opposite. Her friends called her ditzy, but they did it with warmth and affection. While the rest of her peers slunk into the emo scene, with their black T-shirts and sullen faces and great streaks of dark eyeliner, she was a supernova of luminous dresses and shocking pink Doc Martens. Sometimes I thought she was over-compensating, putting on a performance for everyone – especially for Mum. If that was the case, she never let her guard slip. And then she left.

'Are *you* OK?' I ask finally, as we get out of the car.

'Yeah, I'm fine,' she says. 'I just got to the point where I wanted to come home and see everyone.'

'Are you staying?'

'I don't know.'

I sigh.

'Alex, I'm so fucking jet-lagged, can we not do this right now?'

When we get up to the flat, she practically barges past Dan into the bedroom and collapses on to the air mattress with considerable drama.

'Ugh, this thing is shit,' she says.

And with that she kicks the door shut. I put her backpack down in the hall. Feeling tense and bewildered, I head through to the living room and slump on the sofa.

'What the hell was that?' says Dan.

'Get used to it,' I reply.

Later, Dan heads out and I decide that playing some *Minecraft* will be a good way to unwind from my bizarrely disintegrating life. I've had a few experimental sessions with the game, mostly roaming the landscape, building little shelters when the night draws in. Now I want to actually construct something – something that resembles a piece of architecture rather than the sort of rickety wooden shack you'd find in an American horror movie about a chainsaw-wielding redneck psychopath menacing horny teenagers. I figure I've got to get better at this if I'm going to spend a whole weekend with Sam. So I go through my cardboard box from work and find the photograph of Corbusier's Villa Savoye that I'd hung on the office wall. The building is a white rectangle on a series of square columns – it seems like an achievable project. Two hours later, however, I have something that looks like a giant shoebox suspended on a collection of stubby brick posts. The dimensions are all totally wrong. It is effectively a three-dimensional child's painting of a Corbusier building.

As I'm studying the guidebook, Dan gets back, clutching a bottle of wine and three tubes of Pringles.

'Where is she then?' he asks.

'Oh, hi to you too,' I respond. 'She's still asleep.'

She doesn't surface until 1 p.m. the following day.

That evening I take Emma around to see Jody and Sam. I've realised, amid everything that's going on, that I miss him, that the weeks are stretching out into months, and that this little person that Jody and I created is beginning to grow up without me. I'm aware of that feeling again: that I need to get to know him before it's too late.

He is shy of Emma at first, hiding awkwardly behind his mum, clutching hold of her skirt, but then Emma gives him a whole bag full of little toy planes that she has collected from almost every airline she's flown on for the last five years. He is so delighted he forgets all about his apprehension and takes them from her.

'Give me a hug then!' she demands. And he does.

'Why don't you take Daddy upstairs to show him what you've been doing in your game,' says Jody.

'I suppose,' says Sam. 'It's not very good.'

So as my wife and sister eke out a stuttering but amiable conversation in the lounge, Sam takes me upstairs, switches on the Xbox and runs *Minecraft*. We're sitting together, but he moves slightly away from me, shifting toward the LCD display. He clicks quickly through the menus and loads a saved file titled 'Sams cassel'.

When the game loads, we're outside a building made mostly out of grey- and black-flecked cobblestone. There are stumpy towers at each corner, and irregularly sized battlements running along the rooftop. It looks like a sort of Victorian public toilet that's gone to ruin. I don't tell him this.

'Here is my castle. I made it out of stones. There was going to be ...'

But he breaks off, caught up suddenly in his own navigation

of the world. He walks into the building through a set of double doors. Inside, he has made wooden floors and a stone staircase to the roof level.

'I might do a bedroom, there should be a bedroom,' he says. 'I might do a book room, but I haven't made books yet. It's just in case . . .'

He talks as though to himself, quietly, in clipped, stilted sentences, but there are new words dotted about – enchantment, biome, portal – and I suddenly realise he's using the sort of imaginative language that his speech therapist told us to look out for. It's progress. Actual progress. I know I need to encourage him, to join in, to turn it into a conversation, but I don't know enough about the game, I'm stumped. Then I see a book beside him – open to a photo of the Tower of London. I realise with a slight jolt of surprise that it's the book I bought him, the one I thought he'd discarded with barely a thought.

'Oh, are you making a castle like this one?' I ask, pointing to the photo.

'I tried,' he sighs. 'I can't do it. It's too tall. I tried but I got cross.'

'I'm not surprised. It's very tall and has those towers on the corners – that must be hard.'

He perks up, shifting the screen around so I have a better view.

'Look, I tried the towers,' he says. 'I tried, but the blocks are square. I made a tall tower but then I fell off and died. So I have four small towers. One, two, three, four.'

'Well, I think it's a very good start, but we need to switch the game off now. Sam, can you show me how to save it? I don't know how.'

'It's easy,' he says. And to my surprise, he happily takes the controller, hits pause and brings up the save menu. He clicks on it slowly, showing me the buttons on the joypad. 'And *now* it's safe to switch off,' he says in a sort of gently mocking parental tone.

I help him get ready for bed, then take him downstairs to say goodnight to everyone. Emma and Jody are getting on OK. They each have a large glass of white wine, which has probably helped. Jody is talking about her job at the gallery – apparently they're showing the work of a local digital artist, and this has meant installing huge LCD displays around the space. The logistics sound complicated. Jody is loving it. But it hits me again that I don't live in this house any more. I'm a guest as much as my sister is.

An hour later, we're saying our goodbyes and heading out. It's a cool, clear night – there may even be frost on the windscreens tomorrow morning. Autumn is well and truly here. As we walk toward the car, Emma draws her cardigan around her and shivers dramatically.

'So what's going on, Alex? What are you going to do?'

'I don't know. Did she say anything?'

'Not exactly. She thinks you need some help – with George and everything.'

'I'm not sure what that means.'

When we get to the car, Emma stops before getting in.

'Jody still loves you, that's obvious,' she says. 'God knows why, you're a miserable bastard.'

Dan is at home when we arrive back at the flat. As I open the door, he's waiting in the hall beside it.

'Emma, you bitch!'

'Dan, you dickhead!'

They hug and she seems utterly relieved to finally be with someone who is separate from the gloom hanging over our family – someone who'll gladly play that popular British parlour game, 'Let's pretend everything isn't completely fucked'.

'I think we should go to the pub immediately!' says Dan. Ah, that *other* popular British game for avoiding difficult situations.

'You haven't changed,' replies Emma.

So we end up at the Old Ship, where it's fish and chips night, which means it's the same four regular punters, except now they're all eating fish and chips.

'Where's Sid?' I ask when I go up to order the drinks.

'He never comes in on fish and chips night,' says Maureen the barmaid, who has LOVE tattooed across the knuckles of her left hand and tonight is wearing a black T-shirt with a painting of a dolphin on the front. 'Fred always has a pickled egg with his fish, and Sid can't stand the smell, apparently. Don't blame him.'

I nod grimly as Fred, sitting on the stool next to me, takes a bite out of the giant vinegary monster on his plate, filling the bar area with an eye-watering sulphurous odour. When I take the drinks over to our table, Emma and Dan are talking and laughing and playfully smacking at each other. This is how the evening plays out. She tells him about her globetrotting adventures, he regales her with tales of Bristol club nights and music festivals. I sit quietly drinking and laughing in what I think are the appropriate places, unable to attune with them. After a few pints, I get up to go to the toilet and when I return, Dan is jokily interrogating Emma.

'No, but why *did* you go away?' he implores.

'Yeah, I'd like to hear this,' I say, trying to affect the same nonchalance.

'Oh God, the big question!' she says. She takes a swig of her pint, wiping her mouth with the back of her hand in a dramatic flourish. 'I needed *space*! It was so claustrophobic at home, and my friends always treated me like I was this broken ... thing. Then Alex was moping around and Mum was pretending nothing had happened. And I mean, Dan, you were lovely, but you were all over the place, and you had this fan club of girls following you everywhere, like Bristol's answer to Justin Timberlake. I couldn't take you seriously. Ugh, sorry!'

Dan shrugs and laughs, but I notice something in his manner, an infinitesimal flinch. Emma watches him too. There's a long silence, during which I gulp down almost half a pint.

'Here's what I think,' I say, emboldened by the first heady rush of drunkenness. 'Before George died, you were the baby of the family, everyone spoiled you. You were centre stage. But then, after the accident, we all had to change, and the dynamics shifted. You felt lost in that. There's that Philip Larkin poem about the young mums in the park: "Something is pushing them to the side of their own lives." That's how you felt for all those years until you left – like you'd been pushed to the side by grief and everything. You felt hard done by.'

I lift my glass and finish the last mouthful. 'Maybe you left because you wanted a new stage to stand on and be adored.'

Emma lets out a short bitter laugh, then stands up.

'Fuck you,' she says. Then my little sister, who I've barely seen in years, walks out of the pub, slamming its old wooden door behind her.

Dan looks at me, but I cannot read the emotion behind his eyes.

'Closing time!' shouts Maureen from the bar. 'And I hope the rest of you leave as quickly as her.'

Outside, the cold sobers me up a little. Dan gets a text from Emma to say she's staying with a friend tonight.

'Where did all *that* come from?' says Dan.

I shrug and we walk the rest of the way in silence. I'm thinking about Jody, and how she has been left behind, as I once was – how *she* has nowhere to escape to. When I met her she was a brilliant student, she was going to do an MA, then leave university and curate the most amazing art exhibitions, but her plans were derailed. A year after we met, during a cheap package holiday in Spain, there was one drunken night and no precautions, and nine months later, there was Sam. He was loved, but he was not planned. Whatever I've had to sacrifice along this route, she's lost more.

'Shit,' I say at last. 'I haven't been great to Jody.'

'Jody?' says Dan. 'What about Emma?'

'Oh, *she'll* be OK.'

When we get back into the flat, I collapse on the sofa and take out my phone. For a second, I dither over two names on my contact list, then I make my decision. I text Jody and explain that I will be free that weekend after all, if she wants to go away. I tell her she *must* go. We'll be fine, I write, Sam and I will be fine.

And I know I must be drunk because I almost believe it.

The next morning, I'm awoken by Dan noisily getting ready for work. I sit up on the mattress and check my phone. Jody has left a message: Thank you! I'll take you up on that. Oh shit, I think, I've done it now. Then I hear the door buzzer sounding. Dan walks out into the hall and checks out our visitor on the little LCD screen next to the intercom.

'Hi, Emma,' he says in a teasing drawl.

'Can I come in?' Her voice is playful but tinged with caution.

'Sure, dude.'

I get up and wander through to the lounge in a pair of jogging bottoms and one of Dan's old Massive Attack T-shirts.

'Your sister's on the way up.'

'I know.'

'This is my flat, so be nice, you twat.'

'I know.'

There's a knock on the door and Dan opens it, ushering Emma in. She appears in the lounge doorway, and her expression takes me right back to when we were teenagers and she'd arrive home early in the morning, after some date or party, a sort of defiance in her eyes, mingling with the guilt. She has obviously raided her friend's wardrobe – she's wearing a huge purple mohair jumper and a stonewashed denim skirt.

'Christ,' I say. 'Who did you stay with last night, the eighties?'

Dan gives me a piercing look, so I continue:

'Look, I'm sorry for what I said. I mean, what I said last night, not what I said about your clothes. It was out of order.'

'OK, whatever,' she tuts. 'I do want to make things right.'

'So do I. But also, you do look ridiculous.'

We all sit around Dan's breakfast table and eat cereal together, the fragile air of reconciliation extending only to stilted small talk. As we're finishing, a plane flies over and Emma's eyes dart up to the window – she watches until it has disappeared into the distant clouds. When she turns back, she sees me looking at her.

'Itchy feet already?' I ask.

She scowls and flicks a wet cornflake at me with her spoon.

As I'm wiping my face I get another text from Jody. We have an appointment in a week's time to visit a school for children on the autism spectrum. It's a forty-minute drive away, which is going to make for a hell of a commute, but we figured it was worth checking out. It was one of the last things we managed to agree on before I was ejected from the house. Then Dan and Emma leave, him to work, her to bum around in Bristol with some of her travelling friends. I'm alone again.

*

I spend a series of forlorn days checking employment sites and updating my threadbare CV. Turns out there isn't a whole lot available in Bristol for frustrated philosophy graduates who have unwanted experience in mortgage advice. Instead, I lie on the sofa leafing through my growing library of autism books (boredom, crippling anxiety and the availability of 'one-click-buy' internet shopping are a dangerous combination). September turns to October. Dan splits his time between playing a new dragon-slaying video game and designing a record label logo. Emma buzzes aimlessly in and out of our lives.

One afternoon I'm killing time before collecting Sam from school, reading a chapter on meltdowns and how to understand what triggers them, when my phone rings. It's Sam's teacher.

'Don't worry,' he says, bizarrely unaware that the words 'don't worry' when voiced by a teacher calling unexpectedly during the day will inevitably provoke that exact reaction. 'We had to exclude Sam this morning for hitting another boy. We put him in the library with a teaching assistant, but he has become a bit difficult to manage. Could you come and fetch him?'

It's not the first time this has happened. Jody has regularly been called to the school – sometimes because Sam is hiding under a desk or in the Wendy house and his shouting and crying is frightening the other kids, but more often because he's been 'fighting'. We're never sure how these scuffles start, because Sam can't tell us and the teacher is always vague, possibly because there are thirty-five other children in each classroom. Usually, Jody will drag Sam away, apologising, and we dutifully accept that he is at fault. But having seen that incident at the school gate, the boy running up and whacking Sam, I'm feeling decidedly less certain. Today I feel very different indeed. I grab the car keys and practically jog out of the flat.

It's quiet outside the school as I pull up a little way along from the entrance. The usual scrum of parents has yet to arrive and inside the drab seventies building I can see the children in their classrooms, still earnestly writing and drawing. I pause as I reach the gates and steel myself as the familiar image plays out.

Leave me alone, Alex.

Sometimes I manage to edit elements out, but the grim conclusion is never censored.

I stride past, up the pathway and through the doors to reception. The secretary is behind a glass panel, like a bank cashier – a weirdly incongruous security measure for a primary school.

'Hi, I'm Sam Rowe's dad, I think I need to collect him.'

'Oh yes, wait here, we'll bring him through.'

I sit down on a small plastic chair and glance along the empty corridor, its walls festooned with garish finger paintings. When I try to recall my own school, the memories are unfocused and fleeting, as though I have borrowed them from someone else. I guess they are too closely tied in with what happened later – the colour has drained from them like cheap clothes.

Then I see Sam being led from a doorway by his teacher, Mr Strachan, a bent, thin, slightly shrivelled figure in red-framed glasses who looks older than his fifty-something years. He has been at the school since the eighties, according to Matt, whose brother was a pupil here at the time. Back then, apparently, Mr Strachan would attempt to project the air of a trendy, playful children's TV presenter. Now he looks like a suspicious minor character in a cop drama.

'Hello, Mr Rowe,' he says with forced brightness. I look down at Sam, who is focusing on the floor, bereft and beaten. 'Sam has had quite an afternoon.'

'Hi, Sam, what's happened?' I say, but I know there will be no response, and sure enough he jerks his head away from me. So I turn to Mr Strachan for clarification.

'Well, he got into a bit of a fight with the boy he sits next to, and we had to get him out of the classroom. We usually give them some time out in the library, but Sam couldn't seem to calm down, and as we're running classes in there while the extension is being repaired, we thought it best if he came home.'

'What about the other boy?' I say.

'Pardon?'

'The other boy he was fighting with? Is he in the library?'

'No, we didn't think that was necessary. Sam had also been in a situation with another group of boys during playtime. He seems to have had one of his bad days.'

'But who started it? Are you clear on that?'

'It's all fifty-fifty with these boys, isn't it?'

I can feel myself losing it a little – that primal shift in mental gears that quietly guides us from 'awkward social interaction' to 'potential threat'. When you're young, the flight or fight mechanism is purely about personal safety, but when you're a parent it extends outward to your own children. Whether you're being threatened by a thug in a kebab shop at closing time, or discussing your son's behaviour in a school corridor, the result, it seems, is the same.

'Fifty-fifty?' I find myself saying with rising incredulity. 'A group of boys against one? That's fifty-fifty? Christ, I hope you're not teaching maths.'

'Now, Mr Rowe—'

'I thought the arrangement was that Sam would be getting class-room assistance? You've seen the diagnosis, he is on the autistic spectrum. He specifically cannot cope in certain social situations – like gangs of boys in the playground.'

'We're aware of Sam's condition, certainly.'

'And yet you resort to clichés about how boys get into these little fights and, you know, it's six of one, half a dozen of the other – except, the six on one side is a boy who finds school bloody terrifying.'

'Mr Rowe—'

'No, listen to me. I want a review of how the school is dealing with Sam. I want to talk to the headmaster and not to you. I want to see the education programme the school has prepared, and I want to know that my son is being protected. I do not want to hear anyone describing what looks like systematic bullying as a fifty-fifty incident. Come on, Sam.'

I take his hand, turn around and walk out of the building. As we're heading toward the car, I make the usual half-hearted attempt to extract Sam's side of the story.

'Sam, what happened? What happened today?'

He looks down at his feet while he walks.

'Sam?'

'I don't know. Where's Mummy?'

'Mummy's at work. What happened, Sam?'

'I don't know! I don't know!' he yells, and he's in tears now.

When we get to the car, I try to hug him, but he pushes me away.

'Sam, I need to find out . . .'

But he has his hands over his ears, and then he is banging his head softly on the car window, crying.

'I want to help, Sam,' I say again. When I unlock the door, he scrambles in and slams it behind him.

'No, Daddy,' he shouts from inside. 'No help!'

Having exhausted the meagre avenues of discussion, we drive to the house in silence. I let him watch TV as I fix his dinner, and when Jody gets in, I explain what's happened.

'You shouted at Mr Strachan?' she says.

'I didn't exactly shout at him . . .'

'For fuck's sake, Alex, I'm trying to get the school to take more

112

care of Sam, and then you barge in and accuse Mr Strachan of being incompetent!'

'He *was* being incompetent. I'm sick of that school. I'm sick of it. The sooner we get him out the better.'

She sits down at the kitchen table, her head in her hands. I'm inches away but it feels like it would take me a century to reach her.

'Just go,' she says. And suddenly I have a flashback to the times we've dealt with these things in the past: the time Sam pushed a girl off a tricycle at the church toddler group; the time at school when he emptied a pot of paint into the hamster cage because he was told it wasn't his turn to feed Minty and Monty – Jody had to help wash them in Fairy Liquid, like the victims of the world's tiniest oil slick. We laughed about that. Now there is no united front to draw those salvative moments of humour from.

Before I go, I ask, 'We're still OK for the wedding weekend?'

'Yes,' she sighs. 'I've made all the arrangements now.'

I back out of the front door, and look up to Sam's room. He is staring out of the window at me. He lifts the latch and opens it.

'You shouted at Mr Strachan,' he says, teasingly. And with an unmistakable sense of defiance, he does a thumbs-up sign. Despite myself, I return the gesture. Perhaps with the benefit of some reflective distance and shared guilt, we could now find a way to talk about the school situation. But that's not possible because I have to go. The spaces in which we're able to communicate are narrowing – I need to ensure they don't close for ever.

Chapter 13

The days slip by, hazy and unmarked, and then suddenly, it's the wedding weekend – the weekend of judgement. I have Sam for forty-eight hours. I leave Dan's at eight in the morning, throw my holdall into the back seat of the car and head off toward home. On the drive, I go over everything in my head – the need to be patient, to spot the warning signs of a tantrum early, to back off when he starts getting irritable, to make his lunch and dinner in exactly the right way. I have memorised three possible timetables based on his disposition: Good Mood, Indifferent Mood, and God Help Us All, It's The Apocalypse. The latter involves letting him watch television until he passes out. When I park up and walk to the house, I discover that the front door is already open. After the whole Mr Strachan argument, I'm expecting a frosty reception and Jody duly delivers. When I sheepishly poke my head into the room, she's there on the sofa, wearing an expression that quickly shifts from surprise that I've actually turned up to a sort of simmering disdain.

'Oh, it's you,' she says. 'I'm making a list of things to remember.

Luckily, he's not at school so I can leave off "don't threaten Sam's teachers".'

'I *am* really sorry about that.'

She is clutching several sheets of A4 paper, all with neatly written, numbered instructions. Clearly, the assumption is that I won't manage, although I stop myself from saying this out loud because I don't want to start an exciting new battle as she's leaving. There is a large suitcase near the doorway as I walk further in, and the front room has been tidied. It actually looks like a living space rather than a junk shop that's been hit by a tornado and then a missile. Sam is kneeling at the coffee table reluctantly scrawling out the two times table on to a piece of graph paper. He barely acknowledges me.

'He's cross because he has to do his homework,' says Jody, partially to me, but mostly to Sam as she writes the last few words of her 'how to look after your own son' manual. 'Then you can play with Daddy.'

She's being brisk and officious, which is partly to do with the argument, but it's also clear that she's anxious – I don't know whether she's worried about being away from Sam, or worried that she's leaving him with me. Whatever, I just want her to go so we can get this started.

'OK,' she says finally. 'This is everything you need – meal times, rules, refreshed bedtime routine, everything. Call me if you need me.'

'It'll be fine, but thank you.'

'Are you sure about this?'

'I'm sure. Go on. Have a good time.'

Somehow this exchange shifts the mood – one of those little micro-changes that long-term couples can pick up on, even when everything else is deteriorating between them.

'I haven't seen this lot for ages, it's going to be incredibly awkward,' she says with a nervous laugh.

'No, it isn't – they'll love you.'

We stand in silence for a few seconds. The awkwardness crackles like static – so many unresolved tensions.

'Come here, baby,' she says to Sam, and she bends down to hug him. He accepts her embrace passively. 'I'm going to miss you so much! Be a good boy. Look after Daddy.'

She's waiting for a response, but there's nothing. He has the pen in his mouth, lost in thought, or simply not processing what's going on.

'Say goodbye to Mummy,' I say.

'Goodbye, Mummy,' he says without looking up.

I shrug awkwardly. She glances between us – the two men in her life, equally bewildering to her, I realise.

'Go on,' I say, trying to show concern rather than the rising impatience I'm feeling. 'It'll be fine.'

I pick the suitcase up and take it out and she follows slowly. We don't say anything else. We don't hug – and the absence of that physical contact, the sheer impossibility of it, is crushing. She gets into the car, glances out at me very quickly, then starts the engine and she's away, down the street, and I am alone with Sam. For forty-eight hours.

When I go back in the house, his response is inevitable:

'Where's Mummy?'

'She's gone,' I reply simply. 'It's just us for the whole weekend.'

I mean it to sound like a treat, but when it comes out it sounds more like I'm sending him down for a ten-stretch in Wormwood Scrubs.

'I want Mummy,' he whimpers.

Already I feel a tinge of panic, a sense that the slightest slip could see the situation sliding out of control. I know that I have to instil some sort of order to the day.

'OK, let's get this homework finished, then we can do something fun,' I say.

'I want Mummy,' he repeats, getting up and slumping into the sofa.

'Well, like I said ... ' I plan to move slowly through the explanation, to make it obvious to him that Mummy is a long way away and can't come back straight away. But very quickly it's clear that isn't going to work.

'NO, SHUT UP. WHERE'S MUMMY?!'

He throws his pencil, it clatters across the room. I pick it up and slam it on the coffee table.

'Sam, calm down, she's gone away for the weekend.'

'I want Mummy *now*!' he says, and then he's crying, and I see the day stretching out like this; all the plans forgotten and useless.

'There's nothing we can do, we're both stuck with this,' I say.

It is an intentionally cruel way of putting it, making it sound like a chore for me. But that's how it goes: you fall into this cycle – out of exhaustion, out of fear – and without realising it you're not preventing a tantrum, you're laying out the red carpet for it and forming a guard of honour.

'Go away,' he says. 'You don't even live here!'

He leaps out of the sofa and charges at me, flailing with his fists. I put my own arms out to stop him and try to grab at his hands, desperately thinking of a way I can now manage the battle I've started. Ending it is not on the list of outcomes, it's all about damage limitation.

'Come on,' I say as calmly as I can manage. 'Come on, it's OK. Maybe we can play *Minecraft* ... '

'*Minecraft!*' he shouts.

And before I can think it through, he is bounding up the stairs, straight into his room, and I can hear the console being turned on.

OK, I think, I was going to say we could play later, after homework, after a trip to the park. I look through the sheets of paper that Jody left – there are no instructions that specifically state 'Do not start playing *Minecraft* two minutes after I leave the house'. I consider going up and telling him we have to go out first, but that would be apocalyptic. At least at home we are less likely to be attacked by wild dogs. Maybe this is what I need to do to get through the weekend. Then I hear his feet on the landing again, and he is at the top of the stairs.

'Come on, Daddy!' he shouts. And all my uncertainties are momentarily blitzed by his excitement, not only at the game, but at wanting to share it with me.

So I trudge up the stairs and step gingerly into Sam's room. He has some new *Minecraft* posters on his wall: a picture of the lead character, Steve, merrily brandishing a pickaxe, another showing all the types of block that you can find in the game. There are *Minecraft* magazines, well-read and tattered at the edges. They litter the bed where Sam is now sitting, bolt upright, zoned in on the TV screen.

'So, what are we going to build?' I ask.

'A castle! This castle!' he says, grabbing the London book and pointing to the picture of the Tower of London.

The familiar title screen comes up, and though I tell him I've played a little bit already, he wants to explain everything. He wants to take control.

'You can play in Survival mode or Creative mode. Survival mode has monsters and you have to be inside at night or they get you. They make scary noises and I don't like it. But I know something. If you change the settings to Peaceful, the monsters don't come. You can dig and find gold and diamonds and iron. Then you can make things and everything is OK.'

I think it's the longest sentence I've ever heard him say. It pours out unselfconsciously. No stutters, no breaks. I try not to betray any sort of reaction, but it feels revelatory. And this is also the weird thing about autism: it's a completely stomach-churning swoop between lows and highs. One minute he's attacking me in the living room, the next he's talking to me with more eloquence than I've ever heard. There is rarely a middle ground – it's like parenthood with the volume turned up to eleven – Parenthood MAX.

'Why did you decide to build the Tower of London?' I ask as the game loads, determined to keep the conversation flowing.

'Mummy says kings and queens live there. They catch naughty people and chop their heads off. Is that true?'

'Yes, but that was a long time ago. They're not allowed to chop people's heads off any more. Even if they're very naughty people like robbers or estate agents.'

'Can I go and see it?'

'The Tower of London? Maybe one day.'

'Is it near?'

'It's about two hours away on the train.'

'Can I go on the train?!'

'Trains are pretty loud, Sam, and London is a very big, loud city.'

'I have my headphones now.'

He scrabbles around on his floor, moving broken Lego models and comics out of the way, until he eventually finds a chunky pair of ear protectors – the sort a construction worker would wear while operating a pneumatic drill, except bright blue and covered in robot stickers. Jody must have bought them recently, perhaps in response to another noise-related breakdown. He puts them on.

'Mummy says I look like a spaceman,' he says.

'OK, well maybe you *can* go to London on the train then. We'll see.'

119

'Will you take me?'

'We'll see, Sam. So what shall we call our new world?'

'Sam and Daddy's World! Then you always have to play it with me.'

And the words make my heart sink with guilt. Daddy. The daddy who was shouting at you and telling you what a chore this all was.

'It's perfect,' I say.

Together we type the words in and select the Easy setting. After a few seconds a new landscape appears on the screen. Our first view is of a staggered curve of green pasture, leading down toward a long wide beach. On the right, we can see a range of choppy mountains, with several large cave openings. It is sort of beautiful, even though the graphics look so basic compared to Dan's *Grand Theft Auto* games. A majestic panorama, rendered into existence for our amusement. The only sound comes from the sedate piano music and the gentle mooing of several rectangular cows, hobbling about nearby.

Sam hands me another controller and when I enter the game, the screen divides in two, so that we both get our own view of the world. We turn to face each other. Sam's character is the standard version of Steve, with his blue T-shirt, jeans and massive square head, but for some reason mine is Steve in a tight white tennis outfit, complete with headband. It's a strong look.

We waste some time making our characters nod at each other, then we run around and jump up and down, enjoying the sense of co-inhabiting this strange space. I still haven't properly mastered the controls, however, so almost immediately I manage to jump off the edge of a small precipice, taking a huge chunk off my health bar.

'I meant to do that,' I say, scrambling back up the hillside. 'I wanted to see what was down there.'

'Let's start the castle!' says Sam, seemingly oblivious to my pratfall.

'We need to find flat land,' I announce, feeling like I should take charge.

Soon we discover a level area surrounded by trees, and looking out over the ocean. Perfect castle territory. We start chopping down timber, collecting wooden blocks as we go. We build a crafting table and convert the wood into pickaxes. Sam narrates quietly as he goes: 'We need wood, now we need stone, Sam and Daddy have pickaxes, we go to the mountains, Daddy has fallen down another hole, Sam is chopping the stone ...'

I join Sam at the cliff face, mining dozens of blocks of cobblestone. At one point I notice an odd creature sidling up behind me. It looks like a pile of chequered green boxes placed on top of each other.

'Hey, Sam, what's this guy's problem?' I ask as it approaches with what should be obvious menace.

'Daddy! It's a Creeper! If it gets too close it will ...'

There's the sound of a fuse and then a loud bang. And then I am standing alone in an enormous crater.

' ... explode,' finishes Sam. 'Creepers are so naughty.'

We collect all the loose blocks inadvertently quarried by our detonating friend and get back to our task. While he neatly works the mountain surface, systematically taking the blocks in rows, my chopping technique is more haphazard, randomly and violently hacking at everything within axe range.

When we have enough, the building project begins.

'Let's start with a big entrance hall,' I say. Sam nods.

He clearly has a system: each wall is twenty blocks wide and eight blocks high – he counts them under his breath. He builds quickly and elegantly, throwing blocks on to the landscape, methodically constructing the identical walls. I labour over each placement, fumbling with the tools. Blocks stick out of the wall, or miss it altogether and pop up on the ground either side of where they're supposed to go. I keep accidentally lobbing my pickaxe across the map instead of chopping. While Sam is a professional, I'm like one of those cowboy builders who turn up on your doorstep offering to resurface your driveway for two hundred quid.

'Daddy, you're slow,' Sam berates. And when I finish a section, I see him counting the blocks and making adjustments.

When all the walls to our grand(ish) entrance hall are completed, we go inside. 'I'll make the door,' I say. 'And you can ...' But I notice that Sam is already adding a roof, then destroying two blocks on each wall to make windows. I'm about to place the door when a pig gambols in and I spend the next five minutes chasing it around the room until it eventually tries to jump out of one of Sam's windows and gets stuck. Sam and I laugh together at the ridiculous sight.

'I *have* caught a pig,' I say. 'We shall eat like kings tonight.'

'Daddy, you do the door,' says Sam as he heads up to the rooftop.

By the time the sun starts to drop toward the horizon, we have completed the first stage of the castle. True, there hasn't been much in the way of cooperation. Sam did most of the work, while I accidentally starred in my own slapstick comedy. But it's a start. Outside, little square stars fill the blackened skies and the silhouettes of trees form sinister shapes in the darkness. We haven't yet made beds, so we can't go to sleep, which would let us fast-forward to the next day. Instead we stand on the roof and watch the vast black clouds pass over the sky.

When the cuboid sun rises again, sending its pixels of light over the blockish panorama, I tell Sam we should explore the area and maybe find a cave or even a village where, apparently, the odd little inhabitants will trade with us.

'I know,' he says. 'We need to find the Crown Jewels and put them in the Tower!'

'How do we do that?'

'We can find some gold, some diamonds and some emeralds – then we can lock them away, like this.'

He grabs the London book and shows me the photo of the Crown Jewels in their glass presentation cases. It seems like an achievable ambition. We dig down a bit and maybe get lucky, or I've heard precious stones are sometimes stored in the villages and temples that dot the landscape. This is basic *Minecraft* – even I can do it.

'OK, let's go. Let's find the Crown Jewels and return them to the Tower!' I say.

So we wander out, through the woodland area and toward the mountains, happy to scour the landscape for now. Whenever we find an apple on the forest floor, Sam shouts, 'Pick it up, we can eat it for health!' – which makes me wonder if he will consider eating them in real life if I try leaving them lying around the house.

Soon we discover a small group of sheep and Sam shouts, 'Let's get them!' But again, we're a little too cack-handed and they disappear into the trees with Sam running after them waving a wooden sword. Seconds later, however, I get lucky when a some-what terrified sheep emerges from the woods right in front of us. Without thinking, and suddenly filled with inexplicable adrenaline and fury, I strike it over and over again with a pickaxe. It's like the shower scene from *Psycho*, if Janet Leigh had been a sheep made out of six white boxes. The poor beast falls backwards then disappears, leaving nothing but a block of woollen thread behind.

'I slaughtered a sheep for *that*?' I say.

Sam rushes out of the trees and picks it up.

'Well done, Daddy!' he says. 'We can use the wool to make beds!'

I feel modestly proud of myself.

And as we play, we become more and more absorbed in the world, until it is seemingly all around us. Somehow, we lose the sense that this is a screen; we are no longer controlling digital characters in a computerised environment. It is *us* peering into the jagged caverns, then hiking across the grassy plains beneath the bright square sun. It feels as though we are free of ourselves.

After two hours, I know we have to quit and do something else. I give Sam a ten-minute warning, and another after five minutes, a preparation tactic I've been reading about. Sudden change is no good. He needs plenty of warning. When I finally save the game and close it, his mood darkens and I can tell a tantrum is beginning to brew, but this time, I head it off, telling him that we're going to the café and that we can talk about our building plans on the way. To my astonishment, he nods and heads off to find his shoes and coat. I shake my head and mouth 'Thank you, *Minecraft*' to myself.

It is busy when we arrive at the café. Everywhere there are couples reading the newspapers over giant buckets of latte as the jukebox churns out soul classics in the background. I feel momentarily jealous of their lazy freedom. Our usual spot is taken by a mum and her son, so we make for a table nearby with a battered leather armchair and a stool. I end up on the stool.

'What shall we work on next?' I ask as we sit down.

'A big mine!' says Sam. 'We need gold, and diamonds and emeralds and redstone!'

The barista comes over with our drinks, setting down the coffee in front of Sam and handing me the frothy milk.

'That's right, isn't it?' he asks Sam, who giggles.

I get out the *Minecraft* book and we flick through it, looking at the detailed descriptions of all the materials available in the game: iron ingots, redstone, lapis lazuli, whatever the hell that is. Occasionally I pretend to misread one of the names and let Sam correct me, allowing him to bask in his growing knowledge of the game. In the background, though, I can hear something going on nearby. One of the staff has taken an order over to our regular table, but now the boy looks distressed. He's about six or seven, with scruffy blond hair and a slim pale face, his Teenage Mutant Ninja Turtle T-shirt covered in paint and other stains. 'It's OK,' says his mum. 'It's the same type of cookie, it's exactly the same type.' But the boy is shaking his head and moaning. Then he is banging on the table, sending coffee sploshing on to a pile of magazines. The other couples start to look up from their papers, whispering to each other.

I glance at the mum. She's maybe in her late twenties, and very slight – the sort of figure men's magazines would call svelte or petite or something equally horrendous. Her auburn hair is streaked with blonde and harassed into a half-hearted ponytail; her dark green lace dress and black thick-rimmed glasses create a studied fifties style. Her facial expression is one of combined exhaustion and determination – a look I recognise immediately. It's probably familiar to all parents, but then I also recognise her son's behaviour. He's autistic, definitely more severe than Sam, but obviously with the same propensity to close off then erupt when something isn't right. I've been there. In fact, I've been on exactly that sofa while it's happened.

I turn back to Sam for a second, but as I do, an Incredible Hulk action figure skims across our table, hitting my cup on the way, sending coffee splashing on to my shirt. Sam looks at me, then looks at the figure on the floor. I bend down, take it in my hand

and get up. OK, I'm freestyling now, not entirely sure of what to do, but – oh, right – I'm walking over toward them anyway. In Sam's case, sometimes an unexpected but friendly intervention can help. I ignore the mum at first and approach the boy slowly.

'Hi there, is this your Hulk? Because I definitely didn't order a superhero today. Maybe he was chasing a bad guy?'

The boy stops banging and looks up at me.

'I thought I'd better bring him back, because he should be guarding your table. I'll put him here. Hulk, you've got to watch this entire area, don't go bounding off again. Honestly, he's so naughty. And where are the rest of his clothes? He must be freezing cold.'

The boy is still staring at me with a look of utter incomprehension, but at least I seem to have distracted him. I turn to his mum.

'Wrong cookie?'

'Well, the right *sort* of cookie,' she says with an instantly noticeable Bristolian accent. 'But it's not the exact cookie he pointed at. Thank you for bringing Hulk back. I'm sorry about your shirt.'

'Oh, this old thing? I've got four more exactly the same. I don't even like it. Who wears gingham any more? I look like a Cath Kidston deckchair.'

The mum smiles. It is a sweet-natured smile, warm and full and unguarded. I have accidentally started a social interaction with a beautiful stranger.

'I'm Isobel,' she says. 'This is Jamie.'

'I'm Alex, this is Sam, he's eight and also likes superheroes.'

The boys eye each other suspiciously.

'Do you live nearby?' I ask.

'Up the road; we've just moved into one of the little flats above the supermarket. It's a bit poky, but it's fine for the two of us. I don't think we're super popular with the neighbours, though.'

'Ah, yeah, that sounds familiar. Is Jamie . . .'

'On the spectrum? Uh-huh. I've known since he was eighteen months old, but it took about four years to get him diagnosed. That was long enough for his dad to get fed up and run away. There you go, story of my life in five seconds. Do you want to bring what's left of your drink over? You obviously don't have to if you're worried about the Hulk.'

But I do grab my coffee and go over, taking the armchair next to the sofa, and pulling up the stool for Sam, which he warily accepts. He goes to pick up the Hulk figure from the table, but Jamie leaps forward from the sofa and snatches it. This, it appears, is not the beginning of a beautiful friendship. For some reason, I tell Isobel about my situation – about Jody and our 'trial separation' that is soon likely to be rebranded without the word 'trial'. I mention our own struggle to get an autism diagnosis, and how we've sort of fallen apart in the process. It feels liberating to be open with someone I don't know, and there is something in her manner that makes it easy. She is unguarded and enthusiastically honest. I find out that her whole family is based in Eastville, famously once the home of Bristol Rovers until they tore the stadium down and built an Ikea ('At least they've kept the same atmosphere of boredom and despair,' she says). Apparently, she has worked in the same vintage clothing store on Park Street since she was eighteen, and is now the co-owner. I tell her I am currently in between dispiriting and unfulfilling careers. All the while, Sam intermittently reads our *Minecraft* book while stealing regular jealous glances at Hulk. Sensing his interest, Jamie walks the figure up and down the table, quietly repeating, 'Jamie and Hulk, Jamie and Hulk.' The boys barely look at each other.

Eventually, Isobel has to go – dinner at her mum's house. We stand up and say awkward goodbyes.

'Maybe we'll see you here again?' says Isobel.

'Yes, I hope so. Say goodbye, Sam.'

He mumbles into the book. Jamie is already away, pushing through the customers queuing at the counter, then running straight over a coffee table, sending newspaper sections flying.

'He's going to be *so* popular here,' she shrugs, and then follows her son outside, seemingly ignoring the judgemental stares that accompany her to the door.

Sam and I wander to the park, talking about our *Minecraft* plans. Whenever I try to change the subject, the conversation dies, so for most of the walk I stay in it, asking questions and letting him ramble on, enjoying his disjointed flow of *Minecraft* memories, plans and observations. He tells me about the Nether, the game's vision of Hell, which exists beneath the normal landscape. When we get to the park, we pretend that the climbing frame is a *Minecraft* house and the slide is a passageway down into a cave. Then we hunt for sheep among the trees as the weak afternoon light fades away. He darts in and out of the bushes, lost in his imagination. The usual hesitation, the fear of other kids or of dogs, seems temporarily absent.

After supper, I have Sam tucked up in bed by 7.30 p.m., with no crying and no breakdowns – from either of us. I read him a story and kiss him goodnight. Is this what being a normal parent feels like? It's pretty strange. As I'm leaving the room he sits up.

'When is Mummy coming back?' he asks.

'Tomorrow evening.'

'I miss Mummy when I can't see her.'

'Me too.'

I'm expecting the worst, but he settles down again.

*

After a bad start, the day has gone pretty well. Actually better than that: it has been fun. Genuine fun. All I have to do is make sure tomorrow is exactly the same. I settle down in front of the television and crack open one of the beers Jody has left for me. Her notes lie unread on the kitchen table.

The positive mood is soured a little when I head upstairs to sleep and discover that Jody has prepared the bed in the spare room for me. I should have predicted this, but it still stings. I am a guest.

Ah well, at least it's not an air mattress.

Chapter 14

Sam is up at 6.25 a.m. on Sunday morning. Something of a lie-in for him. He wanders into my room and climbs on to the bed, walloping the London book down on to my chest.

'They kept a polar bear in the Tower, once upon a time,' he says.

I groan and roll over to face him.

'Good morning, Sam.'

'Maybe they chopped its head off.'

'Can I have five minutes to wake up?'

'Daddy, why did they chop the polar bear's head off?'

'I'm not sure I know what you're talking about. Give me five minutes and then we can get to the bottom of this polar bear mystery, OK, Sammy? Maybe go and get some breakfast.'

'OK.'

I am fully awakened seconds later by the inevitable giant crashing noise from the kitchen.

'Daddy,' says a voice from downstairs. 'Some of the Coco Pops have got out.'

An hour later, I've cleaned up the chocolatey milk lake and

we're labouring through Sam's maths homework with as much enthusiasm as I ever conjured for the subject. Then we move on to spellings, and he struggles with a list of very simple words. I have to let him study it for a long time before he attempts to spell them from memory. A while ago we found out from a classroom assistant that he is often given the same homework as the children in the year below. The school repeats its familiar mantra: 'he is progressing'. I can't help but think of Matt's daughter, Tabitha, with her Harry Potter books. Recently, someone suggested to Jody that he may be dyslexic too – the conditions are often linked, apparently. Another diagnostic battle for us to fight.

When Sam finally spells all the words correctly, after dozens of prompts and restarts, I feel exhausted. But at least we can tick that off the list.

'What shall we do now?' I ask.

'*Minecraft*?' he says simply. And then, without further conversation, we're sprinting up the stairs together, pretending to barge each other out of the way.

'I think we should switch on the monsters,' I say. 'We can get experience points by killing them.'

'But they will get us. I don't like it.'

'It's OK, it's only a game, Sam.'

'Okaaaaay.'

We are extending the castle now, adding two more storeys and building stone staircases to link them together. We start partitioning off rooms, making the floors out of oak planks, and hanging torches to add light. Sam is as meticulous as ever, ensuring a uniform size and shape to every chamber, correcting my many deviations from the plan in his head. Outside, we start to erect a snaking perimeter wall, flattening hills and covering over precipices to make way;

we plan out the four corner towers, so that our castle can start to match the photo of the Tower building in Sam's book. And then night draws in. Outside the small windows we have created, the blue sky becomes orangey red, and then dissolves into blackness.

'Oh no,' says Sam with a mixture of anxiety and excitement. 'Monsters will come!'

'It's fine, don't be silly,' I say, nudging him on the shoulder.

For a while there is nothing, just the sound of cattle mooing in the fields outside, and that plaintive piano music. But then, suddenly, there are noises from somewhere nearby: a weird groaning, growling sound, followed by a guttural yelping. Sam covers his ears and looks away. A zombie appears at the door, its lifeless eyes staring, its chunky arms outstretched. Sam jumps and squeals.

'I'm going out,' I say, revelling in what I see as playful tension.

'Noooo!' he cries. 'The zombie will get you.'

I tease him by moving slowly toward the door, inching closer and closer.

'I want to make friends with the zombie!' I say.

'No, he doesn't like friends!'

'Come in, Zombie, have some cake!'

'No!'

Sam throws down his controller and tries to take mine. For a second we wrestle over it until I notice that the game's night cycle has completed and the sun is rising, sending a warming glow around the castle interior. The zombie – caught outside in the light – bursts into flames.

'My friend!' I wail. 'See, we were *fine*. He's exploded!'

After a lunch of cheese triangles, digestive biscuits and doughnuts, we funnel the sugar rush into an architectural frenzy, completing the four tall towers, carefully gradating the walls to give them a circular appearance. Once again, we lose the sense that we are separated from this world by a screen; we are *in* there, mining stone from our quarries, constructing scaffolding platforms to reach the highest points, looking out over the valley and down to the sea from our battlements. Sam makes a sword, which I tell him he has to name, like the warriors in *Game of Thrones*. He calls it Head Chopper.

As we work, I realise something. Normally, when we play together – in the precious moments he is prepared to concentrate – it is as a shared solitude: I watch or guide or worry about him. Or when we play with building blocks or Lego, I make something that he plays with for a few minutes or simply knocks down. But here, for a few hours, we are working as one – well, as long as I do what I'm supposed to. But that is another positive. In this universe, where the rules are unambiguous, where the logic is clear and unerring, Sam is in control.

But I'm impatient to see more of the world, to begin our quest for the Crown Jewels.

'Come on,' I say. 'Let's go on an expedition. Let's find some gold or diamonds.'

'But we should switch it to Peaceful mode,' says Sam. 'We need armour and torches.'

'Come on, we'll be careful.'

He shrugs and nods, perhaps sensing my frustration, worrying that I'll get fed up and go downstairs. We craft several pickaxes, and then head off toward the mountains, chopping our way through the trees, collecting apples and mushrooms as we walk. We climb a steep slope, jumping from block to block, past pigs and cows balancing precariously on the rugged cliff face. When we reach the top, we're able to look out over the world – a vast expanse of land rolling out toward the distant fog in a patchwork of gaudy colours, like some huge Expressionist landscape.

We walk on, down a rocky pathway, toward what looks like the mouth of a cave. When we step in, I see that it's an immense cavern of stone, leading to a long dark fissure at the far end, like a deep scar in the earth.

'Look!' says Sam. He points to the eastern wall and, amid many of the grey rocks, there are pinkish dots – iron ore. 'We need iron so that we can dig for diamonds!'

As we excitedly chop away with our pickaxes, we also uncover long seams of coal, leading deep into the mountainside. We dig feverishly, comparing our discoveries.

'I have twelve iron ores!'

'I have twenty coals!'

'I think we may find treasure in there,' I say.

I start heading in further, considering crafting some torches, but then we notice that outside, the hue of the sky has changed.

'Night is coming, night is coming!' cries Sam.

'We've got time,' I insist.

But we haven't. The sun drops more quickly than I remember. We should build a hut and wait for morning, but Sam bolts out of the cavern and up the hillside.

'Wait!' I call.

Then we're both running back toward the house, zig-zagging between the trees as the light fades. We look around, trying to spot anything moving amid the hanging leaves. Quickly, it gets difficult to see, the darkness falling around us. Sam rushes off ahead and is swallowed by the black.

'I can't remember how to get back!' I say.

I hear a weird clicking noise, something I've not heard before, something coming at me from the foliage. I'm thinking it's prob-ably another farm animal, a chicken maybe, but then something hits me in the back, and I know immediately that I'm badly hurt.

'Oh no, skeletons!' says Sam. 'They have bows and arrows!'

And then, to the right side, I spot one, hidden behind a silver birch, its pale ghoulish face like some hideous parody of a skull. It fires again, this time catching me in the leg. I am fading fast. Suddenly another figure is nearby. I think it's another monster, but it's Sam re-emerging from the forest at exactly the wrong time.

'Run!' I shout. There is surprising urgency in my voice.

But it's too late. Two more arrows hit home, draining what's left of my strength. The darkness of the forest becomes all-encompassing, there's no hope of escape. I drop to the floor, the food, the iron and everything else I've collected scattered around me. I see Sam lasting only a few seconds longer before being felled by another arrow. Then nothing.

Seconds later, we're awake again, but now we're back at the castle, rejuvenated, yet empty-handed. We know that, in this world, if we can get back to where we died, we can pick up all the stuff we dropped.

'Which way did we go?' I say. 'Which way?'

But in the darkness it's impossible to get our bearings, and soon we hear the low groan of a zombie. We're not going anywhere tonight. We need to get back inside, to safety. The spoils are lost.

Sam buries his face in his hands.

'All our stuff,' he moans. 'All the iron. And my sword that I made. I lost Head Chopper. Daddy, that was your fault!'

'It's OK, we can get some more, it's only iron,' I say. But I know it's no good.

'My stuff, my things!' he says from behind his hands. 'You said it was safe.'

I try to put an arm around him, but he backs away, all the way to the end of the bed, lost in his own disappointment and frustration.

I turn back to the screen and save our game. But it is too late now. Too late again.

We spend the rest of the afternoon in silence downstairs. I make him some toast and let him watch cartoons on TV, which lifts his mood slightly, as it always has done. I almost breathe a sigh of relief when I hear Jody approaching the front door, her key scratching at the lock.

'Mummy!' shouts Sam.

Jody flings open the door almost immediately and hugs Sam warmly, lifting him up into her arms. She looks relaxed and beautiful, her long hair enveloping our son. But when she sees me, something darker flits across her face and she knows I have spotted it.

'How is my boy?' she says.

'We've played *Minecraft*,' says Sam. 'We built a castle, but we got killed by skeletons and it was Daddy's fault.'

I shrug, guiltily accepting the blame.

'I did say I was sorry.'

'What else did you do?' says Jody.

'We went to the park and pretended it was *Minecraft*,' he says. 'I missed you.'

He grasps her as she sits down on the sofa, unwilling to let her go. He seems to be angling himself away from me.

'Was he a good boy, Daddy?' she says.

'Yes, it was fine.'

I decide not to tell her about the minor tantrum. Now she's here, his mood is better, and I don't want to haul it down again.

'How about you? How was the wedding?' I say.

'It was lovely,' she says. Then she turns to Sam, and pulls something from her bag. 'I bought you a new DVD, you can go upstairs and watch it, if you like?'

'Cool!' says Sam, and he is gone.

Immediately, I know that was a deliberate tactic. Something is going on. Jody stands up and walks to the window, her arms crossed. A protective stance.

'OK,' I say. 'Has something happened?'

'Alex, it's been such a weird, difficult couple of months. I . . . Yes, something happened.'

There is an awful silence. I feel a weird sense of disassociation, as though this isn't exactly happening to me, or that it has already happened, centuries ago, and we are having to struggle to recall it. I'm scrambling for some sort of foothold inside a dark cave.

'What?' I manage. 'What happened?'

'Richard was there, from my old university course, and . . .'

I audibly gulp, like a cartoon character, like an exaggerated pantomime of shock.

'You slept with him?'

'No! No. We were on the same table. We got on – it was so easy. And at the end of the night we kissed. Then we went back to our own rooms. I'm sorry. It just happened.'

'Is this . . . are you . . . what are you saying?'

'I don't know.' And she is tearful, which makes it worse, because I know that whatever is happening here is serious. It means something. She has made a decision, or feels that a decision needs to be made.

'Alex, things have been so difficult for so long, and I'm so tired of everything. I thought a break might fix everything – but this situation we're in now, I don't think it's a break. It feels like it might be an ending.'

Her voice is barely audible; it trails off as she lowers her head.

'You have one drunken kiss at a wedding and that's it?' I say.

'It's not only that. But getting away from it – from you – even for a moment, I could see everything differently. Come on, you know how difficult it's been! We were kids when we got together, we barely knew each other, and then we were parents.'

'I knew *you*!' I say, and it erupts with an accusatory force I had not intended.

'Maybe,' she says. 'I'm sorry. I'm sorry.'

I look at her for a few moments, and in that instant, I see the girl I met on that farm, the sunlight framing her face in gold, her arms folded then too, as she leaned against the old fence and wondered to herself about why she was there and where she was going. What if we hadn't got together? How would our lives have played out as separate things? Where would she have gone instead? I feel bereft and responsible. I am embarrassed by the past that I made for us. It has shamed me.

'I'm going to leave,' I say at last. 'Whatever it is you're saying, I'm not ready to hear it.'

I step back toward the door, which is still open, and then walk unsteadily into the welcoming darkness. The chill of the night air hits my face, blanking my expression into something resembling cold acceptance.

Leave me alone, Alex. Leave me alone.

Chapter 15

Once again, I withdraw from the world. I lie in Dan's spare room, sapped of will, as flat and useless as his bloody air mattress. Dan pops his head in now and again to leave cups of tea, chocolate biscuits and pot noodles. He offers to chat, but I turn away from him toward the wall like a sulky teenager. Emma has disappeared to stay with a friend called Posie whose parents own a huge Victorian lodge in Sneyd Park, Bristol's poshest suburb. Jody texts a couple of times, but I delete the messages without reading them. All I do is sleep and think, and then try to get to sleep so that I don't have to think any more. It is not so much sadness as emptiness. I feel like a blank space. I can't lift myself out of it and don't even try.

I am basically a walking Jean-Paul Sartre essay.

When Emma eventually turns up – on the third day of my self-imposed exile – she lets herself into the flat (I guess Dan gave her a key?) and then sighs heavily when she sees me lying on the sofa in a T-shirt and jogging bottoms, watching *Countdown*. I'm expecting either a witty insult or an invitation to the pub. Instead she goes into the kitchen, fills the kettle and switches it on.

'I saw a therapist for a few months in Australia,' she says. 'It was nice, we talked – a lot. Mostly about me, obviously – which is, as you know, my favourite subject. It got a bit boring by the end, but it was definitely helping. And then I moved to a beach commune in Malaysia. You could give that a try. The therapy part, I mean. You wouldn't like Malaysia.'

'Hello to you too,' I reply.

'I'm serious,' she says. 'It might help with stuff. With George.'

'I don't know. It would seem weird, after all this time.'

'Nothing is weird to therapists, that's their job. You've got to loosen up, Alex. And while you're at it, open a window – this place stinks of sad men.'

So she makes me sit down and google therapists. We choose one that meets my criteria (no one too nearby, no hippies), and she hands me the phone. I book an appointment with a kindly sounding woman based in Bath, who apologises that she can't fit me in for a couple of months. At least that gives me time to prepare for my glamorous new life as someone who sees a shrink.

On the fifth day, I wander out into the living room, ensconced in a duvet, and collapse on to the sofa. I consider block-watching some awful sci-fi series but then I spot the Xbox 360 under the TV. I switch it on and idly load up *Minecraft*, not intending to do much, maybe visit one of my saved games, perhaps throw my character down an open mine. But then a message pops up onscreen and tells me that SamCraft04 is online. That's Sam's Xbox name and seeing it sends an electric shock through the dull insulation of my sadness. Almost straight away, I recall how I left on Sunday, the long silence after my foolhardy venture into the game. Will Sam even want me there again? I go to the *Minecraft* main menu and check if any Xbox friends have a shared world open.

And there it is, a single option, but the only one I want. It is Sam and Daddy's World. Sam is playing right now.

I click it and wait as the world loads up, not sure of what to expect or if it'll even work. The screen stays static. It's not going to do anything, I think. And then it does.

Suddenly I am there, in the landscape, in the world I built with Sam a few days before. All around me are birch trees, the woodland floor dotted with yellow flowers. I feel brighter, the most awake I have felt for days. It's like seeing the sunlight after a long illness. But I've no idea where the castle is – or how to find Sam.

As I'm wondering which direction to head in, a line of text pops up on screen: **SamCraft04 has sent you a message**. I bring up the menu and read it: **Dady, put on hedfone**. I scrabble around in the plastic storage boxes near Dan's TV, through piles of leads and controllers, until I find what looks like a pilot's headset, complete with a mouthpiece. I connect it to the controller and put it on.

'Hello?' I say.

At first there's nothing, followed by a few seconds of echoey whirring, then nothing again. But finally, I hear it – faint but clear, like a long-distance phone call – a recognisable voice. My heart swoops.

'Daddy!'

It is the sweetest sound, piercing days of blank grey silence. My son, miles away, but suddenly right here under the same boxy clouds. And he sounds happy to have me here, even after everything. He has let me into his world. I'm so stupidly excited I don't know what to do with myself. He still wants to play with me. I get another chance.

'Sam! Where are you?'

'You have to get your map. Our castle is on there. I am building.'

I delve into my inventory and sure enough I find the map, which shows a mosaic approximation of our shared landscape. The castle we built at the weekend is represented as a large square in the north-east corner.

I walk onwards, winding gingerly between a series of vast chasms, until the land rises in gradients toward the brow of a grassy cliff. From that vantage point, I see the castle that we built, rising tall and grand from the plain. I feel like an exiled king returning to his capital – except there are no crowds of loyal subjects, just a cow hopping down the steps of the hillside. And there is something different about the building now. Two of the exterior walls, once constructed from dull grey cobblestone, are now surfaced with yellow blocks that seem to catch the light of the sun. As I approach, I see Sam, high up on the third wall, methodically adding layers of the new stone brick by brick. Then he spots me and immediately starts to climb down. I reach our perimeter fence, which we made to try to keep the wild wolves away, and burst through the gate as Sam runs up to meet me. There's no hug button. There *should* be a hug button.

'Hi, Sam!' I shout, lost in the moment. 'How are you? What are you doing?!'

'Daddy! I am making the Tower of London colour. It's like the photo. This is sandstone!'

I see it now. The paler colouring is not the only change. He's added a storey, and cut out windows in the correct spaces, so that they sort of match the real building. It must have taken hours.

'It's wonderful,' I say. 'Can I help?'

'Yes! It's *our* castle.'

'Sam, I'm so sorry for Sunday. I'm sorry we lost our things. I keep getting it wrong.'

'It's OK. Mummy said that people lose things on adventures, that's what happens. Do you know, the Tower of London has a place called the Bloody Tower, which is a rude word.'

'I did! So Mummy spoke to you when I left?'

'Yes, I was sad, but Mummy said it was OK. She said adventures are dangerous and that's why they are adventures and not walks.'

Typical Jody – she's always been able to explain the world to Sam, to convert his experiences into the language he uses and understands. This is something I keep forgetting – that in a lot of ways he's a tourist in our world, a baffled traveller with no idea about local quirks or customs. She's his Google Translate. While I stall and flinch and retreat, Jody takes his hand and guides him. I suck. I have to stop sucking.

'Right, let's get this Tower finished!' I say.

I grab my phone and search Google Images for a photo of the building. It's clear we need to reshape and reduce the size of the four corner towers, so I make a start on that, constructing a series of ladders to get to the top of each wall, and then chopping down-ward. It is the most purpose I've had for days. I shake off the duvet and sit upright, focusing fully. There once again is that strange sense of immersion, of moving beyond the screen and into the world. After everything that's happened, it is a kind of escape, like opening the wardrobe and passing into a pixelated version of Narnia – only without the dense religious allegory and talking lion.

While we build and reshape, we talk. At first it is about the task at hand, sharing materials and tools, planning, warning each other to get inside when night starts to fall. But then, very gradually, we broaden out.

'Daddy,' Sam says. 'Do you build houses for work?'

'Almost,' I say. 'I used to work at a sort of shop where we sold houses to people. But I don't do that any more.'

143

'When I am big I want to make houses.'

'You want to be an architect? That's the word for it.'

'Yes, I want to be an artiteck. I will make a castle like this.'

'Good luck with the planning permission.'

It is a joke, but as I say the words, I find that I have a lump in my throat. A realisation hits me. This brief moment of conversation – as fleeting and trivial as it may seem – is perhaps the deepest we've ever had together. *Sam knows what I did for a living.* It's a revelation to me. I'd always assumed he didn't understand, or wasn't interested in anything beyond his own experience. And we've never talked about his future before, or his hopes, or ambitions.

He has ambitions.

We continue to build, swapping out the bricks, smoothing off the towers. He shows me how to construct a furnace where we can convert sand into glass to make proper windows. When we have finished we stand a little distance away and admire our work.

'I think we're ready now,' I say. 'I think it is time we got our swords and our torches and went to look for treasure. We need to find the Crown Jewels and return them to the castle. Who is with me?'

'Huh?' says Sam.

'Will you help me on this epic quest for diamonds, gold and emeralds?'

'Yes,' says Sam.

'We are brave adventurers and nothing can stop us!'

'Yes! Nothing!' I hear some muffled conversation through the headset. 'Mummy says to say goodnight.'

'Ah right, nothing can stop us except bedtime. Good night, Sam.'

'Can we go to London soon? I want to go, I promise.'

'I think so. We'll sort it out. We can see the Tower and lots of other cool buildings. There's somewhere else I can maybe show you too. Somewhere that's important to me and your Aunt Emma.'

'Epic,' says Sam.

And then the mic goes dead, and the world closes. I sit staring at the menu screen for a long time, mulling things over. It feels like my brain is booting up again. I find myself thinking about that movie, *The King's Speech* – about how George VI was able to overcome his stutter by listening to music as he spoke. Maybe this strange blocky game provides Sam with a similar sort of distraction. Maybe *Minecraft* is his music.

Maybe this is the way I stop sucking.

Later that night I get a text from Jody, which this time I read. It is a businesslike reminder that we have our tour around the autism school on Monday. Getting Sam in is a long shot, we both know that. He is high on the spectrum, despite being years behind at school, despite his faltering vocabulary. Last year, we went to a local autism group and the Education Authority adviser told us that there were many children with much more complex needs so it was unlikely we'd get a referral. But we have to try. One thing you learn very early in parenthood is that the health and education systems are a sort of vast and complicated game: if your kid ever needs special help, you have to learn the rules and exploit them. You fight for everything, every test, every consultation, every specialist – you learn the correct terms, you research all the forms and statements and processes you need, and anything you can't get through the system, you pay for if you can. Nothing comes to those who wait.

Dan gets home at eleven. He's been working with yet another hip young creative agency, helping them design an 'offline marketing campaign' (i.e. leaflets) for a trendy new organic fried chicken take-away named Birdhouse. This could perhaps only exist in Bristol.

'You're out of bed,' he says as he slopes in, looking uncharacter-istically exhausted.

'Yeah, I've been playing *Minecraft* with Sam. Online.'

'Welcome to the twenty-first century. How are you feeling?'

'OK. Better. I don't know. I guess my marriage is over.'

'We've been through this. Jody needs some time, that's all.'

'Some time to date Richard?'

Dan is clearly out of his depth here. He pretends to consider the dying embers of my relationship for a second before pulling his MacBook Pro out of a courier bag and flicking it open on the coffee table. Immediately, Photoshop pops up on screen and dominating the display is his half-finished design for a garish advert that declares, 'Birdhouse: for your soul' – a musical reference that will be lost on about 85 per cent of the target clientele. Even worse, the promotional meal on offer – a double-fried chicken burger with sweet potato fries and a large Coke – is called the Chick Beater.

'Dan, is that meal really going to be called the Chick Beater?'

'Yeah, that's what they told me.'

'OK, you've got to tell them not to do that.'

'Why?'

'Because it's wordplay on domestic abuse, for God's sake! How did they ever think that was a good idea? Can you imagine how that'll play out on Twitter? They'll be destroyed.'

'Oh, OK.'

Dan is clearly riled by my unexpected critical input.

'I thought you were wallowing in depression,' he says.

'I was, but I've been playing *Minecraft* and now I'm awake and creatively frustrated.'

'Well, don't take it out on me, dude.'

He snaps the laptop shut and skulks off to his bedroom. I go back to the game and load up a new world. A fresh landscape generates in seconds then fades up on screen – it's an undulating pasture that ends a great distance away in a snowy woodland. It is truly virgin territory, unsullied and unshaped by anything that preceded it. If only everything in life was so easily begun anew.

I'm barely digesting that thought when my phone rings. It's Matt.

'Hey, Alex, how are you?'

'Oh, you know, devastated.'

'Mate, I'm sorry. But look, I have something that might cheer you up. A couple of the lads have dropped out of the game tomorrow – Saints vs Chelsea – do you fancy coming along instead? You can bring Dan, if you like, there are two spare tickets.'

'Hang on, my marriage is falling apart and so you're inviting me to a football match?'

'When you say it like that, it sounds bad.'

At first I think there's nothing I'd like less right now than sitting in a stadium with thirty thousand football fans shouting at each other. But then I haven't seen Matt in a while, and perhaps it would be nice to encounter him in his native environment. And it'll take my mind off things for a bit.

'OK, great,' I find myself saying. 'But I don't think Dan will be coming. Football is not his thing.'

At that moment he flounces out into the room and heads to the kitchen area.

'Dan, do you want to come to the football tomorrow?'

'What is "the football"?' he says.

'I think that's a "no",' I say to Matt.

'No wait, maybe it'll give me some inspiration – being in a completely different place, man. Sure, I'll come.'

And so, fifteen hours later, the three of us are sitting midway up Southampton FC's Itchen Stand, amid a sea of red-and-white

147

striped shirts, as Matt and many thousands of other men proudly belt out 'When the Saints Go Marching In'. It is a cold but bright afternoon, the bronze sunlight painting a portion of the pitch in a sort of transcendental glow. Dan is leafing through the programme, criticising the design and layout, and I'm dwelling on the destruction of my marriage, which Southampton's inevitable capitulation to Chelsea is about to glibly symbolise. When the singing finishes, Matt starts chatting with the fans around us, trading the sort of painfully earnest, over-serious sports analysis that plagues offices and factory floors around the country – and possibly the entire world: 'Player X is on fire at the moment, a true heir to classic player A'; 'Player Y vs Player Z should be an interesting subplot today'; 'They should never have sacked Mourinho'; 'Mourinho was a wanker'; 'You can't spend your way to the Premier League title' . . . It's like being trapped in the *Match of the Day* studio with five thousand Alan Shearer impersonators.

The whistle sounds, the crowd cheers, and then there's fifteen minutes of the ball aimlessly being kicked around as the sides test each other. Matt is leaning forward, hand on chin, like Rodin's *The Thinker* in a stripy bobble hat. Dan heaves a long sigh, fishes about in his bag and pulls out his MacBook Pro, and within seconds he has the screen up and Photoshop open. Matt looks at him, horrified.

'Dan!' he rasps. 'You can't get your bloody laptop out at a football match!'

'What? Why not?'

'Because this is St Mary's Stadium, not fucking Starbucks! Besides, if we score it's going to go flying.'

'I'm no expert on football, dude, but is that likely?'

At that moment, a Chelsea defender heads in from a corner and the small section of away supporters goes wild. All around us, however, there is abject silence. Dan quietly closes his laptop, puts it back into his bag, then stares at me forlornly.

At half-time we dutifully shuffle out to the bar amid a sea of balding men disconsolately shaking their heads and tutting. Dan and I drink our watered-down lagers from plastic pint glasses, while Matt stands in the queue at the burger bar discussing the team's defensive frailties with a massive skinhead. 'I wish they *did* have a Starbucks here,' says Dan.

The second half is an agonising display of cautious attrition football, the two sides barely probing into opposing territory. Even Matt looks distracted, checking his phone and muttering to himself. In the last ten minutes, however, something seems to click for the home side. An equaliser from a cleverly worked free kick garners a raucous response from the crowd. Matt leaps to his feet in celebration, then sits back down and leans across to Dan. 'Unlikely to score, eh?' he goads. Then, in the second minute of injury time, a Chelsea attack breaks down on the edge of the box, the ball spins away wildly, and three Southampton players charge on to it, breaking clear of the midfield. Suddenly, a sense of urgent anticipation spreads through the whole stand. Matt is half sitting, half standing, as though squatting over a toilet. Even Dan is watching. A one-two pass cuts out a defender, the striker is clean on – and then I blink and somehow the ball is in the back of the net. The stand erupts, Matt launches to his feet and punches the air in a terrifyingly unselfconscious act of violent satisfaction.

'Oh God, it's Matt's sex face,' shouts Dan.

Then Matt is hugging us, and the people around us, and the stewards. The hugging is still going on as the final whistle blows. I look out over the crowd, enjoying the atmosphere of celebration; the faces contorted in pleasure because a grown man successfully kicked a ball between two aluminium posts. Then a few rows down, I spot a man and his son, both in replica shirts, the boy about Sam's age – they have an arm around each other, and they are fist-bumping and chatting excitedly. Whatever this match means, to the football club, to the Premier League table, to the ridiculous world of football in general, for them it is a precious memory, it is theirs. They will go home and bore the rest of their family with it – and when the kid goes to bed, his father will sit beside him and they will relive it together. Amid this carnival of victory, as ephemeral as it is, there are probably moments like this going on all over the stand. And this reminds me of what I no longer have, and maybe never did – that easy, natural sense of having each other, of being able to share things, with no complications. Between Sam and me, there were always complications, but now those have multiplied.

'Come on,' says Dan, patting me on the shoulder. 'Let's get back to Bristol; there are too many men and it's freaking me out.'

Chapter 16

When I drive up outside our house on Monday morning, Jody is waiting outside for me in a long woollen coat and scarf; Sam is beside her in bobble hat and school anorak, looking dejected. Clearly, everyone is angry, everyone resents the situation. It is a cold October morning, but the atmosphere between us adds an extra chill.

'I don't want to see the school,' Sam says as he climbs into the back seat and haughtily clamps his seat belt. 'I don't want to, I don't want to.'

'Let's get this finished with,' says Jody as she slams her door.

'Is that your answer to everything now?' I mutter. She shakes her head.

The Avon School for children with autism is on the edge of a leafy suburb, surrounded by a patchwork of small fields. It's a very modern building, almost futuristic in design, with great glass panels forming the entire front entrance. Inside, an atrium-like reception area leads on to a wide white corridor that stretches all the way back to the rear of the building. This time, Sam climbs out of the car on his own, perhaps fascinated by the look of the place, but he is gripping Jody's hand as we approach the desk, repeating the phrase, 'Tighter, Mummy, hold my hand tighter.' It's a clear sign he is anxious. When we're in town and the traffic is noisy, my own hand aches after holding his for any length of time – the grip is never tight enough. The receptionist, a smartly dressed woman who looks more like a bank clerk than a school employee, spots us approaching.

'Ah, Mr and Mrs Rowe? And you must be Sam? Have a seat. Our deputy head will be with you shortly.'

We barely have time to take in the near-silence around us before a tall man in his fifties with greying hair and a smart blue suit appears from an office next to the reception.

'I'm Tristan Foster, the deputy head,' he says as he shakes my hand and then Jody's. He casually crouches right down to Sam.

'Ah hello, Sam,' he says. 'Let's have a look round.'

As we follow, through a set of double doors into the main corridor, he tells us about how the school was set up with a mix of government and charitable funding, and how the environment is carefully planned, with no enclosed spaces, no bottlenecks, no narrow hallways. The walls are kept bare because the colourful art that tends to crowd along every vertical surface in a mainstream school can be too much of a sensory onslaught for some pupils. The class sizes are small, the teachers and assistants are all specialists. The atmosphere is calm and informal, the absolute opposite of what is passing between Jody and me right now. I wonder if the deputy head has noticed the tension.

Sam wanders behind us, clutching at Jody's hand, or her coat. I try to say encouraging things: 'Look, Sam, they're playing with iPads … Look, they have a big television,' but he either stares despondently, or looks away.

As we stroll along, Tristan explains that the children are from all points on the spectrum and some need very close assistance. In one class we see a boy, reading at a desk, flapping his hands continuously either side of his head and moaning quietly. Sam shrinks away. But we also pass a little AV room where some teenagers are making a podcast and when Tristan asks what they're doing, they are polite, funny, seemingly confident. Afterwards, he gives us advice on the application process and the arcane machinations of the local education authority. We try to take it all in, but there is so much to remember. As the visit comes to an end, he turns to us to make one last point.

'We work toward ensuring that all students leave with enough skills to lead independent lives,' he says.

For some reason, the sheer reality of this sentence hits me hard. This is an area we've only ever hedged around in the past – this whole question of what Sam will do when he's older. Now here it is, presented to us in its stark reality. Is a little independence the best he can strive for? To be honest, we can barely imagine even that. I've tried to picture him in a workplace, following instructions, fitting in, understanding the complexities of adult lives, adult relationships. I can't. I just can't. And living alone? Looking after himself? Meeting someone? Right now the idea seems fantastical.

Tristan shakes hands with Jody and me, then once again kneels down to Sam.

'I think you'd like it here,' he says.

But outside, Sam is still quiet and listless. We stand, a forlorn group in the clean concrete driveway, as the automatic door closes behind us.

'What do you think?' I ask Sam.

'Some of the boys were scary. I didn't like it.'

'They had computers and it was nice and quiet,' says Jody.

He looks around, his face contorted in concentration, as though desperately searching for a way to communicate something, some concern too complex for him to put into words.

'But ... I want to be an artiteck,' he says at last. And he walks slowly toward the car.

I look at Jody.

'Well?' I ask her.

'It looks pretty amazing,' she says.

'Yeah. But Sam's picked up on the fact it's different. He knows, doesn't he? He knows that, if he comes here, he's different too.'

We're too wrapped up in our own thoughts and troubles for this to lead anywhere useful. Instead we head back to the car, tailing our son, shivering against the autumn wind.

Later that evening, Sam and I meet in *Minecraft*. We've made stone swords and torches, and found enough iron to forge armour for protection. Now we're heading further out from the castle, gathering food, climbing the rocky inclines and heading into the caves. We find pockets of coal, which we dig out greedily. Sometimes we venture further in, hoping to catch the yellowy glint of gold amid the endless grey blocks beneath the mountains. But there is always a point at which Sam draws back, a depth he won't go beyond.

'There will be spiders and skeletons. I don't like it,' he says.

There's also the one giant cave, east of the castle, which looks like a gaping mouth in the face of a towering cliff. It seems likely to contain an abandoned mine – every *Minecraft* world is riddled with them – and that means treasure. But he will not go near it. Where there are mines, there are monsters.

It's frustrating, but I don't push him. In the outside world, there's always a feeling of having to guide Sam towards normality. Here, I've realised, it doesn't matter. I don't feel the same sense of pressure. He is free to be scared. We can take our time.

So we head north instead, toward a large area of desert, an unending carpet of yellow. We haven't been this way before because it all looked so flat and featureless, but you never know. We bring lots of stone to build a shelter if we need it, and we have made bread and cooked pork chops for energy. We've learned to be prepared.

For a long time, we just walk, past dozens of little cacti that look like green, spiky boxes, past craggy outcrops of dirt and rock. I'm about to suggest to Sam that we head back, that there's nothing out here, when we spot a collection of rectangular shapes on the horizon. We've not seen anything like this before. They don't look like hills or random protrusions of blocks. They look man-made.

'A village!' says Sam.

I've read about these. Every *Minecraft* landscape has them scattered about. They are inhabited by weird characters that aimlessly bumble about the place. As we get closer we see a whole cluster of buildings, quaint and neatly built like Duplo houses. Around them gather the strange occupants, each with the same square head and long nose, all shuffling along in long brown cloaks like some silent monastic order. Sam wanders among them freely.

'I read in my book, if we had emeralds, they would trade with us,' he says. 'Oh, I know: sometimes the blacksmith has gold!'

In a rush, we investigate each building until we find the smithy, a squat building with a trough of lava outside. I burst in with Sam and we find a chest in the corner of the room.

'You open it,' I say, standing back.

He moves forward and wrenches open the wooden box, peering inside.

'Oh, there is no gold,' he says. I feel ridiculously deflated. 'Wait, I see it. There's a diamond! A diamond, Daddy!'

'Grab it!' I say. But then I am suddenly concerned that this is effectively advocating the theft of expensive jewellery.

'We shouldn't usually take things that don't belong to us,' I say sternly. 'However, this is an adventure, and sometimes you have to bend the rules a little. But only a little.'

'Should we leave this saddle behind then?'

'No, take it. And the iron ingots. Leave the apple. No wait, we may need it. Take everything, we'll leave a note to apologise.'

We spend a while opening more chests, finding bread, more iron, some armour; we discover a library lined with bookshelves – and steal all the books. Then we wander into a larger structure, a single room with several small tables. We both realise together that it looks like a classroom.

'Sam, sit down at the back and I'll be the teacher,' I say.

He goes to stand next to one of the wooden desks.

'This is like where I sit in class,' he says. 'It's near the window. But Ben isn't here.'

'Is that the boy who sits next to you?' I ask.

'Yes.'

'Is he your friend?'

'No.'

'Why?'

Usually, this is where Sam would shut down, evading the question, changing the subject or running away. There is a long silence.

'He always hits me under the desk. He tries to make me cry. But no one sees.'

'Have you told the teacher?'

'No.'

'Why not, Sam?'

'No one ever hears me. I want to go away, but I can't.'

Silence.

So that's it, I think. He *is* being picked on – subtly, carefully, the odd jab here and there. Is this what school has always been like for him? The thought makes me queasy. Jody and I often talked about how we'd love to have a hidden camera so that we can see what it's like for him – how he gets on, if the other kids are nice to him, if they care. But sometimes, secretly, I think we're both glad we haven't.

Sam and I stay in another of the village houses for the night, and in the morning raid the vegetable patch for carrots before heading back to the castle. When we get there, we dig down beneath the oak floor in the entrance hall to create a secret chamber. A treasure room. We create a single chest on a glass block and Sam drops the diamond in. After we've climbed out, we bury the entrance and mark it with a birch plank.

'It's safe,' says Sam. 'The monsters can't find it.'

'And neither can the blacksmith. Anyway, I think we've been pretty brave, going all the way out to the village. I think we're ready to go deep into a cave, if we take swords and armour.'

'Yes, OK,' says Sam. 'I think I'm ready.'

'You're a brave boy,' I say. 'People don't think you are, but you are.'

The doorbell rings. When I hop up to check the monitor, I see Clare waiting outside the main entrance, wrapped in a sheepskin coat, anxiously biting at her nails. In all the years I've known her, I don't think we've ever met up without Matt or Jody present. I wonder if this is about Jody and me? Or Jody and Richard? Is there some terrible new angle on what happened at Gemma's wedding?

'Sam, I think I'll have to finish now. I'm sorry, we'll need to start the quest another day.'

'Oh,' he says. I desperately think of a compromise.

'I know, why don't you make a stable for the castle? We have a saddle now, so maybe we can catch a horse?'

'OK. I'll build it next to the wall.'

'Good. Well done. Goodbye, Sam.' I switch off the console, then go through to the hall and press the intercom button.

'Hi, Alex. Sorry to bother you. Do you have five minutes?'

'Sure, I'll buzz you up.'

When she arrives, we make awkward small talk for a few minutes. I tell her about the school we looked at for Sam, my search for a job. She talks about the twins. But things stall when I ask about Matt.

'That's why I'm here,' she says.

Almost instinctively, I head for the kitchen area. It's a very British reaction: this looks as though it's going to be serious, so obviously I need to fill the kettle. Clare sits in the armchair with her coat still on, fidgeting with her phone. I wasn't expecting this to be about Matt. I mean, Matt? All he does is work, sleep, watch sport and play with the kids – like a sort of intelligent Homer Simpson. What could possibly have happened? Unless he's ill? Is Matt ill? Without asking, I pour Clare a mug of tea and take it over with my own. She clasps it with both hands.

'So, what's going on?' I ask.

'Have you spoken to Matt in the last couple of weeks?'

'Not much, the odd text message here and there. We went to the football together.'

'Has he said anything? I know he's your friend, but I need to know, Alex.'

'No. Anything about what? What's going on, Clare?'

She looks at me for a second, as though trying to gauge something in my expression, then looks back at her mug. I take a sip from my own.

'I think he's having an affair.'

I almost spray the room with hot tea.

'What? Matt! Oh, Clare, why would you think that?'

'He went to some software conference in London last month. He was there for three days, staying in a hotel with some of his business colleagues. He goes every year, it's fine. But ever since he got back, he's been acting very strange. He's guarded, he's quiet, he's quite snappy with the kids. The other night, he was watching the football on TV and he flipped out – chucked the remote across the room. It wasn't even Southampton, it was some League Cup game. Then he switched it off. Alex, you know him, he doesn't just switch off the football.'

'Shit.'

'I know! I wondered if he'd said anything to you?'

'No. Definitely not, Clare. I've texted him a few times to tell him about Sam – and about Jody. But he's said nothing.'

'I'm going crazy. I snuck a look at his phone, but there are hardly any texts in his message folder and I've *heard* the phone bleeping. I think he's been deleting them.'

'Clare, you shouldn't—'

'I know, but what else am I supposed to do? Nothing like this has happened before, and after Jody and ...'

She stops, suddenly aware of what she's saying. Her face flushes.

'Jody and Richard?'

'Yes, sorry. I'm sorry.'

'What do you know about that?'

'Only that she met him at the wedding, they had some drinks, one thing led to another. She feels guilty, but nothing much else happened.'

'But you're worried, because if it's *that* easy ...'

'I'm sorry.'

We drink our tea in silence for a while, lost in our own relationship dramas. Outside, I can hear the distant hum of traffic far below, and somewhere, in another flat, someone is playing a Fleetwood Mac song. I wonder what Matt has done, if anything. But mostly, I wonder what Clare knows about Jody. She looks at me for a second, and seems to read where my thoughts are going.

'Look, I don't think it's serious,' she says at last. 'Jody hasn't felt like herself for a long time. Everything she does is for Sam, and you haven't been there for her. I'm sorry, but that's the way it is.'

'I know. I know.'

'Alex, I hate to ask, but will you talk to Matt?'

'Of course. But Clare, our situations – our lives – are totally different. I don't believe Matt would ever do that to you. There are three things in this life he worships: his kids, you, and Southampton Football Club. He's not about to give up on any of that. OK?'

'OK. I'd better go. I've got to pick up Tabitha from her break-dancing class. We've got her bloody fancy dress birthday party to organise too. Is Sam coming?'

I remember Jody mentioning that Sam had been invited. Lots of kids running around dressed in weird outfits shouting at each other? Welcome to Meltdown City, population: Sam.

'We'll see,' I say.

Clare gets up, checks her face in the mirror and then we walk through to the corridor.

'Don't worry about Matt,' I say. 'I'll find out what it is.'

She nods in response and steps into the lift.

'Alex, look. I think Jody is going to meet Richard again this week – for a drink. To sort things out. I don't know. But don't worry, he's a wanker. Hang in there.'

The doors close, and I am standing alone, looking at my reflection in the polished steel.

'You've got to do something,' I say. 'You've got to make something happen.'

Seconds later, the other elevator door opens and out struggles Emma, with a huge backpack and two bags of food shopping. We stare dumbly at each other for a few moments.

'I'm back!' she says. 'Again.'

For some reason, an idea flickers into my head.

'I'm going to take Sam to London,' I say. 'Will you come?'

Chapter 17

Jody is surprisingly fine with the London idea, as is Sam, which is even more of a shock. Two days later, we're driving up to the house at eight in the morning to collect him. Jody comes to the door and hands me a Spider-Man rucksack.

'This has everything he'll need. Sandwiches, water, his headphones, some pens and a pad.'

'OK. How is he?'

'He's excited, but anxious.'

'He'll be fine.'

'He might not be.'

'I know. And if he isn't, we'll deal with it.'

Sam trudges slowly down the steps in his black combat trousers and a huge parka with a fur-lined hood.

'Is London far?' he asks.

'About two hours on the train – it'll be fun!'

'Can I play on your iPad?'

'I'm sure you can. And they have a café on the train so we can buy drinks.'

'Cool!'

Jody looks at me, then out toward the car. Emma waves back at her from the passenger seat.

'What brought this on?' she says.

'He asked if he could go one day,' I say. 'So we're going. Come on, Sam, let's get in the car.'

Jody hugs him, and opens her mouth to say something else, but stops herself. I take his hand and lead him to the car.

'Are you ready for an adventure?' says Emma when he climbs into the back seat.

'I think so, Auntie Emma.'

'Great, but I told you: don't call me Auntie, I'm not seventy.'

We park up at Temple Meads and walk through the bustle of the entrance area to the platforms. The noise of the trains, the people, the crackly announcements, all echo beneath the ornate Victorian roof far above us. I take Sam's ear protectors out and help him put them on.

'Hold my hand,' he says. 'Tighter. Tighter.'

Our train is already here and boarding. We find a table seat and Sam sits next to the window, peering out at the grimy station buildings. Emma drags a copy of *Marie Claire* magazine out of her battered cloth satchel.

'Are you OK?' I say to Sam.

'Are we going to go fast?'

'Yes, quite fast.'

'Do we have seat belts?'

'No, we don't need them.'

'Is that safe?'

'Yes. You don't have to worry.'

He goes back to looking out of the window.

I look at him, my little boy, his darkening blond hair, messy and unkempt, his wide eyes darting from one unfamiliar sight to another, his busy hands grappling with the headphones. As other passengers get on, he turns and watches them closely, intrigued by the weird formality of the situation. Then the doors beep and close, there's a grunt as the wheels start, and we're away, snaking out of the station, into the dull sunlight.

At first, Sam barely moves, his forehead on the window, watching the city pass. But then the novelty fades and he becomes restless, flitting between drawing, playing on my iPad and staring at everyone else in the carriage. He can't sit still, jumping every time the carriage door opens and shuts. 'Are we nearly there yet?' he asks continuously. 'Where is that lady going?' I have made a visual guide to what we'll be doing in the city, like one of Jody's day plans, except my own drawings are truly awful. Trafalgar Square, the Houses of Parliament, the Tower, and finally the museums. We have to go through it several times; Sam repeats the sequence as though reassuring himself. He has brought his London book along, and we study the pictures as the endless fields zoom by. For a while, he sits with Emma and she narrates her way through *Marie Claire*.

'What *is* she wearing? He's fit. I bought a hat like that in Australia. He's going out with her, but she used to be married to him.'

Sam seems genuinely interested, even when she starts testing him on celebrity names. When the train stops at Reading, a group of middle-aged men in rugby shirts get on, holding beer cans and trading loud unfunny banter with each other. Sam scrambles over to me and grabs my arm, and that's where he stays for the rest of the journey.

Paddington station proves a chaotic introduction to London. It is packed and noisy, and the stench of dirt and train engines is thick and inescapable. Vast swathes of passengers gather around the information screens then race each other to the gates, pushing and shoving their way through the squirming masses. Tourists clatter out of the Heathrow Express trains with gigantic garish suitcases the size of fridge freezers. Charity workers pounce on the lost and unwary. I take Sam's hand and follow Emma through the maelstrom and out into the street. He clutches at his headphones as I half lead, half drag him toward a bus.

'If the ravens leave the Tower it will fall over,' he says.

We run up the stairs of the bus and, miraculously, the front seats are free, so we make a dive for them and I put Sam on my lap so he can see out. Unable to take in the sheer scale, the noise, the manic dynamism of the city, Sam sits in utter silence, his mouth drooping open in shock and surprise, his hands gripping the seat, and then me, and then the headphones again – a circle of sensory comfort. Suddenly, I'm terrified that I've made the wrong decision, that he's traumatised, that we should head straight back. I glance at Emma on the seat opposite, but she's buried in her phone, oblivious. We crawl along the Edgware Road, with its shisha lounges and electronics stores, then into Oxford Street, the wide pavements a monstrous swarm of shoppers. We're as far as Regent Street, where endless buses stalk past the grand storefronts, before we talk again.

'Are you OK, Sam?' I ask.

He doesn't reply so I tap on one of the ear cups and he swings around at me.

'Huh?'

I lift up the headset.

'Are you OK? What do you think of London?'

'Everything is happening at once!' he cries. 'I'm scared.'

He tucks himself right into my side, his fingers playing with the buttonholes of my coat.

'It's OK, it's like Bristol but bigger,' I say.

'And it has a lot more creepy guys,' says Emma, tapping away on her phone screen.

*

We get off and wander slowly down to Trafalgar Square, Sam gripping my hand. He seems on the verge of tears, but then he looks up and is astonished to see Nelson's Column towering above us. He immediately wants to sit down on the fountain edge so that he can get the London book out and check the real thing against the photo. I tell him that you used to be able to buy birdseed here to feed the pigeons, but this was banned because they were doing too much poo on everyone. This, I figure, is the sort of historical fact that appeals to all eight-year-olds. Emma takes a picture of Sam and me in front of the fountain. I pretend to push him in and he screams. We walk down to the Houses of Parliament, annoying other pedestrians by holding hands together in a line. Again Sam wants to carefully compare the real site with his book, and is disappointed that the time is different in the photo of Big Ben. 'We're not waiting here for seven hours!' cries Emma. In the end we move on quickly, the bustling crowds too loud and pushy for Sam.

'It's too fast,' he says. 'Everything is so fast.'

We hop on another bus and follow the Thames along, watching the passenger ferries ploughing down the river. At every stop we reach, Sam looks out of the window and asks why people are getting off and where they are going. Emma hands him her phone and shows him our route on Google Maps.

The next stop is the big one. We get off the bus and walk along until we reach the first walls of the Tower. Sam screams and points when he sees it, looming in the fading afternoon light – the building that we have created for ourselves in *Minecraft*.

'The Tower of London!' he shouts, and he grabs Emma's arm in delight.

'Shall we go in?' I say.

At first, he nods enthusiastically, but as we get closer to the entrance, the crowds become denser around us. There are children running around shouting and fighting; a group of tourists gathers in our path, taking photos on their phones. Sam is pushed and prodded out of the way. Very quickly his mood changes.

'I don't like it,' he says softly.

Emma takes his hand.

'You go ahead and see what the queue's like,' she says.

The entrance doorway towers over us, casting a long shadow. I follow the crowd forward, but then turn to make sure the two of them are still together. I quickly spot Emma trying to take a selfie with a beefeater, but I can't see Sam. I stop walking. A sudden thudding panic hits me. I scan the crowds, but he's nowhere. Then I am running back, swirling frantically through the tourists.

'Sam!' I shout. When I get to Emma, I'm already a mess. 'Can you see Sam?' I yell. 'He was supposed to be with you.'

'He can't have gone far,' she says.

We both stand, looking around, trying to pick out a little boy amid the thronging groups of sightseers. I'm trying to formulate a plan when I see a familiar object cast aside on the pathway. It is Sam's ear protectors. I rush over in horror, grabbing them up and shouting again. The terror is suddenly very real.

'Sam!'

Desperate thoughts flash through my skull. Is he walking toward a road? The river? Should I call the police? Has someone taken him? Time drags, the noise fades into an icy pit of dread – the feeling every parent knows: the sick, sinking fear of losing a child. I dimly recall a time this happened before in a supermarket – an agonising ten minutes blindly rushing from aisle to aisle – but that was a shop near our home. This is London. There is no customer services desk.

'Jesus, Emma, you were holding his hand!' I shout.

'I let go for a second,' she says. Her voice is defiant, but I can hear the worry edging in.

'God, you're so fucking irresponsible!'

Then I hear a familiar sound, nearby and never before so welcome. It is Sam crying. I spot him beside the wall with an elderly woman. She is asking him questions and looking around, her face full of concern. I rush over, and at last he sees me. He wriggles away from his helper, running and sobbing. I pick him up and hold him to me.

'I want to go, I want to go!' he's yelling. But I have no answer, I'm in shock, fear is coursing through me, my legs feel like they will give way at any moment. When I look for the woman, she has disappeared into the crowd. And then Emma is with us.

'Oh phew!' she says. 'What am I going to do with you?'

She puts her arm around my waist, but I turn away from her.

'Alex, it's fine, he's here now. It won't happen again.'

I look at her but I don't say anything. My throat is dry, and I don't know what I'll shout at her in the heat of the moment.

'Come on,' she says. 'I've got an idea.'

And with her guiding, we walk away, past the Tower and toward the riverside pathway, then up to Tower Bridge. I'm in a sort of daze, Sam is still sobbing, the ear protectors back on, like some sort of talisman.

'We can cross over here and have a picnic on the other side,' she says. 'That's the best view anyway.'

'OK,' I say. 'OK.'

We head over, pick up coffee and a couple of burritos from a street food van, then find a bench overlooking the Thames. Sam is quiet, but when I hand him his packed lunch of cheese and piccalilli sandwiches and some incredibly strong-smelling pickled onion crisps, he begins to perk up at last.

'It's an adventure,' I tell him quietly. 'Sometimes things like this happen on adventures.'

'That's why it's not only a walk,' he says.

Then we're quiet for a while, watching the pigeons gather nearby, scuttling away as the joggers and commuters pass.

'We've got the windows wrong,' says Sam, looking over the river at the White Tower. It takes me a few moments to work out that he's referring to our *Minecraft* version.

'Yeah, it's tough to make arches when you only have squares,' I say. I turn to Emma. 'We're playing *Minecraft* together online. We've built a replica of the Tower,' I explain.

'You massive nerds,' says Emma.

'I like London, except for getting lost,' says Sam.

'It is my third-favourite city,' says Emma. 'After New York and Tokyo.'

'Why do you live all over the world?' asks Sam. 'Daddy says it's because you are scared.'

'Sam!' I say in mock-horror.

'Your daddy is an amateur psychiatrist.'

'Amateur what?' says Sam.

'Never mind,' she says. 'Look, the fun thing is, when you go travelling, you can be who you want to be. You can invent a new you every day.'

'Like a video game!' says Sam.

'Kind of. And the longer you stay away, the harder it gets to come back. Also, I knew your daddy was very cross with me.'

She smiles and nudges my arm with her elbow. I smile back, despite myself.

'Are you cross with Auntie Emma?' asks Sam, between large mouthfuls of crisps.

'I was. I am. A little. But not much. Only because I miss her. And she went and left me with your grandma – who is bananas.'

'Bananas!' repeats Sam.

'How is Mum?' says Emma.

'You haven't called her?'

'No,' she says. 'Have you?'

'No, not for a while. She doesn't know about Jody and me. Another disaster for her to be wise and stoic about.'

'Don't dwell in the past, my 'ansum,' says Emma, putting on the worst West Country accent I've ever heard. 'The future is the thing you can change.'

'Thanks, Mum,' I say.

'She's right, though. Nothing's over yet. You're a worrier, Alex, and you act like you're sixty-three not thirty-three. But you're not bad. You can be quite likeable when you try.'

'Thanks, can I employ you as my new life coach?'

'Do you have a husband, Auntie Emma?' asks Sam.

'No,' she says, finishing her burrito then screwing up the silvery wrapper. 'Men are scum. Except you.'

'Seriously, what *are* you going to do?' I ask. 'Carry on pinballing around the world all on your own, for ever?'

'Christ, you make it sound so depressing. Maybe. I don't know. Part of me likes the chaos of it. It reminds me that I'm alive.'

'Vietnam did look amazing in your photos. Perhaps *I* should go travelling.'

'You?' laughs Emma. 'Alex, five minutes ago, you shat your pants because you lost your son for two seconds. A jungle would eat you alive – literally.'

We sit and watch the boats pass by for a while. The wind sends rubbish and dead leaves scurrying along the path.

'Auntie Emma,' says Sam. 'Where is Uncle George?'

'Come on,' I say. 'There's one more place I need to go. I can tell you more about George when we get there.'

*

Here is a secret about grief. It's kind of an open secret, because everyone who has experienced it knows it to be true, but here it is anyway. Grief never really goes away. Time doesn't heal. Not fully. After a while – a few months, a few years maybe – grief retreats into the darkest corners of your mind, but it will lurk there indefinitely. It will leak into everything else you do or feel; it will lurch forward when you don't expect it. It will haunt you when you sleep. I still dream about George, two decades after his death. Sometimes, I dream that we're both kids and that nothing has happened. We're playing on our bikes, or exploring a museum – those are the best dreams. Sometimes, though, the facts get confused, and I dream that George suddenly turns up in my current life, but he's still a child. In these dreams I know about the accident, yet it makes sense that he is back again. 'You're OK,' I say, 'you're safe.' And I hug him and I cry – hopeless, unending sobs. Often I wake up convinced that it is real and it takes me a long time in the cruel darkness to work out that it isn't. Time doesn't heal, it cauterises.

Emma and I never discussed anything like this. As teenagers, we were too self-absorbed, trying to form our own identities in the shadow of George's death. And then she went away. In the three or four times she came back home, we acted like distant relations – all polite chat and threadbare in-jokes, skimming over the surface of our lives. If we were appearing in some sort of reality TV series, I would confess to the camera that we haven't 'confronted our issues', or 'dealt with the past' or whatever. I'm not sure we'll ever do that stuff, because a) it's a bit late now and b) we're British. Also, our mum taught us that the future is what we should dwell on, not the past, because the future is something we can change. But I still want to take Emma to that café in London so that we can experience it together again – our last perfect day.

We take the tube to South Kensington. Sam insists we all hold hands again, which makes the escalators challenging. When we emerge on to the street, the light is beginning to fade. It's a five-minute walk, past rows of lavish stucco mansions and ornate red-brick terraces. Then, turning into a small side street, Emma and I suddenly both slow down. We walked along here, many years ago, on a warm spring day. We had our souvenirs from the museums, George and I ran ahead. And there, midway down the street, between two Victorian street lamps, is the Palace Café.

It looks exactly the same; its bright red awning is a little more tattered, but still there. Inside, the chequered black-and-white tiled floor, a long wooden counter, a bookcase jammed with second-hand paperbacks, the walls lined with framed posters showing classic exhibitions from the Victoria and Albert museum. The menu on the rear wall used to be on one of those signs with removable plastic letters, but it's now a large blackboard, the range of coffees and sandwiches handwritten. There are no chairs and tables outside – it's too cold for that today. Sam looks up at us quizzically as we stand and stare.

'Are we going in for a drink? Can I play on the iPad?' he says, confused by the change in mood.

'Sam,' I say. 'We will in a minute, but this place is important to me. We came here a long time ago, with Grandma, and with our brother George. He was a bit older than me, he was very clever and funny. But the day after we were here, he had an accident and he died. I was very sad for a long time, but I have a photo of me and George outside of this café and that—'

'Can we go in and have frothy milk?'

'Yes, in a sec. I wanted to explain this to you, because it's sort of part of the family history. Do you understand? What happened the next day, when my brother died, it was so hard. It is still hard,

172

even now. I think it's maybe why I get so anxious and worried about things sometimes.'

'I'm going to get a table near the window,' Sam says, and he runs ahead, wrenches open the narrow wooden door and disappears into the café. I look at Emma and shrug. She rests her head on my shoulder.

'He's a bit young to get it,' she says.

'I know. He's good on some stuff – identifying fish finger brands with a single taste, recalling passenger airline details, mastering the parental controls on our set-top box to lock everyone else out of watching TV. But he doesn't comprehend this sort of thing. I thought if he saw it, he would click. I don't know if he'll ever understand.'

'Well, I'm glad we came. It's weird to be back, but I'm glad. We've both been running away ever since, haven't we? Just in different directions. Fuck it, let's get a hot chocolate, it's bloody freezing out here.'

Inside, I'd wondered if Sam would ask more questions about George, but instead he sits quietly, looking around the room, sipping his frothy milk, seemingly oblivious. Emma and I try to recall elements of the day – what we were wearing, what we talked about, the things we did; I say that I'm going to call Mum in the week, that I haven't spoken to her in ages.

'Please don't tell her I'm home,' says Emma.

'Why?'

'Because . . . I need to prepare myself. Please don't.'

And for a second, I look into her eyes and see my sister from twenty years ago – gawky and defensive. Suddenly, the confident, carefree world traveller is gone. And sitting here in this café, it's clearer than it has ever been: we both needed to reinvent ourselves when George died. My instinct was to take control of everything, to instil order; hers was to run away, to be somebody else. But no escape plan is infallible – there is always a cost.

When we get outside I notice that one of the lamps is flickering and weak against the descending night.

On the train home, Sam sleeps for most of the journey, slumped against my shoulder. Emma and I say very little, both locked in our own memories, staring aimlessly through the window at the blackness outside. And I think about Sam and what life will be like for him as he gets older. I wonder if he'll ever genuinely know anybody. Do people with autism fall in love? I don't even know that. I don't even know.

I put my arm behind him and pull him closer. His ear protectors slip off into my lap.

Chapter 18

Mum moved back to Cornwall after Emma and I left home. I don't think she ever felt truly settled in Bristol, so me going to university and Emma legging it to the other side of the planet gave her the excuse she needed. She bought a little cottage on the outskirts of Fowey, with views across the estuary. We've travelled down a few times over the years, when Sam was a toddler – we took him for meandering walks through the drizzle in his little red all-weather jumpsuit. He looked like the terrifying dwarf killer in *Don't Look Now*. Mum has travelled up to stay with us in Bristol too, although she and Jody have always been wary of each other, both stubborn and strong-willed, with very firm views that don't always align – especially on parenthood. It has made for some excitingly confrontational weekends. Mum is formidable and outspoken: if she has an opinion, you will listen to it, as countless traffic wardens, teachers, work colleagues, doctors, distant relatives and train conductors can attest. Which is why I'm not looking forward to this phone call.

It's a quiet evening. Dan and Emma are out, there's nothing good on TV, so it seems like now is the right time – or at least a time with no good excuses. I search around the room for Dan's neglected landline phone and dial the number. She answers in one ring.

'Hello, can you wait, I'm watching the end of the news, who is this?'

'Hi, Mum, it's me.'

'Oh, Alex! Hello! How are you? I suppose I can watch the news later.'

'I'm OK, how are you?'

'Alex, I know that tone of voice.'

'What tone of voice?'

Here we go.

'*That* tone of voice. You haven't rung me for months and you sound like a miserable teenager. I don't have to be Miss Marple to know something is wrong.'

'Jody and I have split up,' I blurt out. 'I don't know if it's temporary or not. I'm staying at Dan's.'

'Oh, Alex. What happened? What did you do?'

'What did *I* do? Oh thanks, Mum!' I pause for a second. 'It's more complicated than that. Sam has been really, really challenging, I was working late a lot, we weren't communicating very well.'

'So Jody chucked you out.'

'Something like that.'

'Oh dear. How is Sam?'

'He's OK. We're trying to change his school because we're not happy with how he's getting on. We've seen a couple, but we're not sure. Sam seems to hate them both. I don't know what to do. Oh, and I got made redundant. So that's another thing I've got to sort out.'

'Alex,' she sighs. 'You've always carried the weight of the world on your shoulders.'

If I was playing 'Mum cliché bingo' I'd have my first cross on the card.

We talk for half an hour, managing to bypass the major stuff in favour of family gossip (one of Mum's cousins is in prison for fraud, another has absconded to Norway with his gay lover) and the intense rivalries she has nurtured with some of the other inhabitants of her tiny hamlet, as well as other nearby villages. I mention that I'm picking Sam up from school two days a week and having him all day on Saturdays. I tell her we went to London, that we visited the café. That I wanted to tell Sam about George, but he didn't get it.

'You can't live in the past and neither can he,' she says. Another cross on the bingo card.

Eventually we dawdle to the end of the conversation. If I was expecting any advice or support, it did not seem to be forthcoming.

'How's Emma?' says Mum out of nowhere. I'm silent for a second. Does she know?

'Fine, I think.'

'Ah, she's back. I can tell by your reaction. You can't hide anything from me. I'm like Kylo Ren.'

'Jesus, Mum, you should be a detective. And seriously, you've seen *The Force Awakens*?'

'Yes, Alex, we have cinemas in Cornwall. We even have DVD players. But back to Emma. She doesn't want to speak to me?'

'She thinks we're all mad at her.'

'She's right! I'm sitting here alone in a leaky cottage surrounded by cow pats and farmers, and she's jetting off around the world, having her photo taken with hunky men.'

'Mum.'

'It's true, I've seen it on Facebook.'

'Mum, seriously.'

'Oh, Alex, get her to call me. Or better still, get her to come down. I won't be angry and I won't lecture her. Well, I won't be angry, anyway. And while we're at it, why don't you come and visit? Bring Sam. He'll have forgotten what I look like.'

'OK, we should,' I say, as Dan gets home. He waves from the doorway and holds up a four-pack of Japanese beers. I make a thumbs-up sign.

'Sam is actually getting used to trains now,' I say to Mum. 'I'll need to check everything with Jody first. But we should do that.'

'Yes, you should. And Alex, don't worry so much. You take everything on, you always have. Don't let the world trap you in a corner. George wouldn't have wanted that.'

I honestly don't think she's ever mentioned him in that way before. What George would have wanted . . .

'I've got to go now, son. You take care. Phone me soon with some dates. Give it a week or so, though. Do you remember Mr Davis from down the track? I've got him fixing the roof. I don't know what he's doing up there, but he makes a hell of a noise.'

'Mum, he must be eighty by now.'

'He's seventy-eight and fit as a fiddle. He owes me a favour after he backed his Land Rover over my herbaceous border.'

'Right, OK. I'm going to go now. You take care. Go easy on the poor men of Fowey.'

It's time. We can put it off no longer. It is time to search the big cave for treasure. Sam and I have been getting ready for days. We've gathered enough iron to make swords and armour, we have cooked twenty slabs of beef and twenty loaves of bread, which will cure us if we're attacked. We have one hundred torches to light the way. We're as prepared for this expedition as we're ever going to be.

'We can do this,' I tell Sam as we stare out at the night sky from one of the castle's cross-shaped windows.

'We might find gold,' he says. 'We might find an emerald!'

As soon as the first glimpse of sunlight shows, we're out of the door and away, through the gates and into the plains. Sam is running ahead at first, but as the mountain range and the jagged mouth of the cave draw closer, his pace slows. He doesn't stop, though, he doesn't whine or ask to go back.

'How was school?' I ask, as we duck beneath the trees and up the grassy layers.

'Good,' he says. 'I got a sticker for my maths because I tried super hard.'

'Did you play with anyone at break time?'

'No, I play by myself. But I don't mind. Sometimes the dinner lady comes to talk to me.'

OK, I think, that is heartbreakingly tragic. But he's fine, he's fine.

We jump up the stair-like rocks to the cave mouth, so large and dark that its blackness dwarfs us. I place torches on the walls to light up the interior, revealing the craggy tunnel leading back into the mountain. We walk in slowly, already seeing more veins of coal dotted about in the walls. After a few feet, the narrow passage opens into a small cavern, and when I've placed a few torches I notice a gaping hole in the floor, a deep, angular chasm that drops into complete darkness far below.

'Daddy, there will definitely be spiders down there,' says Sam.

'It's OK. I think we can get down safely,' I say. 'But I'll be careful. I've learned my lesson.'

The edges of the walls have created a sort of staircase, so we're able to walk down for several metres, placing torches as we go, gradually lighting the vortex below us. I relax into the descent, chipping away at stone blocks to make a more navigable series of steps. Sam hops down behind me cautiously.

At last, we're at another little cavern with a series of small passages leading in different directions. We also hear a trickling noise and when I place a torch we see a small stream leading down one of the dark pathways.

'Let's go that way,' says Sam.

'Sure. You're being very brave,' I say. 'It's a bit scary, isn't it? But we can do it together.'

Further down, there's another drop and another passage, but then in the far corner, a few hundred feet ahead, I see something I'm not expecting – an orangey glow, faint, but clear in the darkness. Lava. We're deeper now than we've ever been.

We follow the light to its source, but our way is blocked by a wall of stone, with only one small gap allowing the flickering gleam to leak through from the other side.

'Are you ready?' I ask.

'Uh-oh. Yes!'

I tap at the stone and walk through.

'Oh wow,' says Sam.

We are in a vast chamber, unimaginably large, reaching many storeys above us, and lit by two huge lava falls, cascading down the long flat walls. It is breathtaking, like some gigantic painting of hell, the darkness beyond the fiery liquid seeming to reach into eternity. Below us, the river of lava passes along until a point further down where it meets a pool of water along a jagged line of pitch-black rock.

'Obsidian!' I yell excitedly. I know about this, I've seen it in the guide. It's the hardest substance in *Minecraft*, and the stuff you need to build a portal to the Nether realm.

But I look across at Sam and his character is staring at something else entirely, over the other side of the giant trench, something on the wall. My eyes race over the surface until I see what he's looking at: two pieces of stone dotted with green flecks.

'There is emerald,' he says. 'Emerald for our Crown Jewels!'

'Yes!'

We high-five, jubilantly.

'But how do we get over there?' I ask.

We both look down at the wide flow of boiling rock. If one of us falls in, they'll lose all their items, everything – and the other will be stranded in the cave alone.

'I know, we need to build a bridge,' says Sam.

'But there's no way, there's nothing to anchor the stones to, you'd have to build it as you crossed – it's almost impossible.'

'I can do it,' says Sam.

He walks very close to the edge, mere inches away, until he's leaning over the precipice. Then he carefully places a single piece of stone, jutting out over the drop.

'Can you do that all the way across?' I ask.

'I don't know.'

'I think you can, Sam. You're good at this.'

That's when I hear a familiar squealing sound, faint, but easily recognisable. I whirl around, and further along the walkway to my right, I can make out the unmistakable square red eyes of a spider. But there aren't just two eyes, there are at least six. I take a few tentative steps back toward them and place a torch on the wall. Suddenly it's very clear. Three cave spiders, tumbling over each other in their desperation to reach Sam and me, their giant black bodies a mass of legs and fangs.

'Sam,' I say quietly. 'There are some spiders. Keep building your bridge. I'll deal with them.'

'They'll knock me off into the lava,' he says.

'They won't. Keep building.'

He doesn't reply, but I see him looking once again over the edge of the block. It is infinitesimally slow, but he places the next stone section without falling. I turn to face the spiders. I have a single iron sword – I know that if they leap at me, they could knock me into the lava. I know it's only a game, but the tension, the sense of peril, is palpable. Part of me is distinctly aware that, actually, this has become something more than a game. It is a psychological conundrum that I don't have time to fathom right now because I have to stab three massive spiders.

Sam is on the fourth piece of block, his narrow bridge reaching halfway toward the other side. One step further and he can place a piece on the other side – as long as the spiders don't reach him.

Then they're on me, their weird squeaking cries echoing off the looming cavern walls. I pummel with my sword, not aiming, not looking, just slashing like some sort of psycho killer in a horror movie. One spider falls into the lava, its bulbous body disappearing into fire. But one is still at me, lurching forward, biting me over and over. My health is fading. In the confusion I manage to drop my sword, and have to desperately grab at my pickaxe. Almost dead, I make one final swing, catching the spider on its side. It makes a weird spasmodic jerk, then falls, convulsing wildly, into the lava. There is a moment of relief – then I realise the third has climbed on to the wall, passed over me and is scuttling toward Sam's bridge.

'Oh no!' he says.

'The emerald!' I shout.

He starts to tap at the wall with his pickaxe. The spider creeps on to the bridge. I sprint forward, but I'm too far away. Then I remember I have a bow and arrow. I've never used it, never successfully. But I draw it now as the spider creeps across. Sam is still digging, but finally the emerald block comes loose and he scoops it up. I aim slightly ahead, between Sam and the spider. Sam turns and sees it inches from him.

'Daddy!' he cries.

I fire the arrow. It swoops unseen, unheard, through the cave air. I can barely look. There is a thud. Something has fallen. I hear the hiss of the impact on the molten river below. Slowly I open my eyes. At first I look to where Sam was and I see the hole in the wall where the emerald used to be. But no Sam. No spider.

Oh no, I think, I've knocked them both off.

'Daddy, I've got the treasure!'

And Sam is next to me, jumping up and down in excitement and pride.

'The spider bit me once but I tried to hit him with my axe. I think I got him.'

I hide the bow.

'You did. You definitely did. You got the emerald and you killed the monster.'

'Let's take it back to the castle. We've got a Crown Jewel!'

We clamber back through the caves, leaving torches to mark our route, stopping once in a while to chip iron and coal from the walls. Then we're out into the open air again. It is daytime, the sun almost blinding in the flat blue sky.

'Daddy, we are a team,' says Sam.

'Yes, we are. We're a brave team of adventurers.'

'We need to put the emerald in our chest, with the other Crown Jewel.'

As he runs off toward the castle, I look around once more, back at the mouth of the cave. And for a second I'm certain I see another figure there, a character, not a monster, dressed in an orange suit, looking at me from the ridge. But as I step back they appear to withdraw, swallowed into the darkness.

Chapter 19

The next afternoon it is my turn to pick up Sam from school. I have an extra task to deal with too, something entirely unexpected: he has a friend coming over. It's Olivia, the girl from his nursery, the one who's at the school we like. It feels like a vital social connection. I am nervous about screwing it up, or about him screwing it up. And then I think, what the hell am I worrying about? This is two kids meeting up to play, this is not some sort of royal marriage linking two warring factions.

Approaching the gates, I experience the usual sense of quiet, distant dread, and as parents start to arrive, the sight of them milling and chatting around the entrance completes the familiar tableau that has haunted me all these years. There's always a sense of trepidation too, about how Sam will be, or if a teacher will accompany him out to tell me in hushed tones about some incident in the playground, another 'fifty-fifty' scuffle with another group of boys. As ever, I'm torn between wishing that I could see what happens to him during the day and feeling fortunate that I cannot.

Today, as the bell sounds and the doors open, he is among

the first group to emerge. He runs through the gabble of parents, straight into my arms.

'Are we fetching Olivia? We're playing *Minecraft!*'

'Yes, OK, we're picking her up on the way. How was school?'

'Good.'

'What did you learn?'

'Nothing.'

'Nothing at all?'

'Nah.'

'Brilliant.'

We drive through the agonisingly slow afternoon traffic to St Peter's. Children in unfamiliar uniforms are swarming out of the gates, smiling and laughing, waving various paintings and weird models made out of loo rolls. It's probably my imagination, but they already seem fundamentally nicer than the children at Sam's current school. I park down the road and take Sam with me to the gates. I don't remember what Olivia looks like so I need to rely on him to help me out. I point out the foolhardiness of this endeavour to Jody via text message. Look for the prettiest girl, she replies. Which is not helpful. At least Jody is going to be back home in an hour so she can take charge of this fraught social engagement.

'Olivia!' shouts Sam and runs over to a girl waiting beside the gate. She is slightly taller than him, with long straight black hair and a face of fragile refined beauty. She greets him warmly and starts talking to him. He nods gravely. A woman strides over who I immediately guess is her mother. She is exquisitely dressed in Burberry jacket and skirt, her face, like her daughter's, is beautiful but aloof. She has the easy, confident air of someone with a lot of money.

'Hello, are you Sam's father?' she says. Her voice is clipped and businesslike.

'Yes, hello, I'm Alex.'

'I'm Prudence, Olivia's mother. Olivia is coming to your house, apparently. I spoke to Jody about it yesterday?'

For a second I'm intimidated into silence. Sam has never had a friend home before. Now he appears to have become friends with a family from the society pages of *Tatler*.

'Yes, that's right,' I say. 'Do I need to bring her home after?'

'No, I'll collect her. Will you be providing supper?'

'Um, yes – I mean, Sam doesn't eat much, so it'll probably have to be spaghetti on toast.'

She winces ever so slightly.

'That's fine.'

'Well, great.'

'Olivia was very keen to visit. She's been playing this computer game. *Mindcraft?* He's very good, apparently. Anyway, I gather they're going to play that together.'

'Ah, OK, yes, I know it.'

'Her brother Harry is obsessed with it too,' she says, glancing to a cocky-looking boy behind her. 'So are all his friends. I've no idea about computer games, but it doesn't look like they're shooting terrorists in this one, which is a relief. Anyway, I'll see you later.'

Then she takes Olivia's school bag, grabs her son's hand and strides off down the road, toward an immense, spotlessly white Range Rover. I stand gawping until the car starts and drives away, then disappears behind the curve of terraced houses.

'I'm going to show Olivia how to make a castle,' says Sam.

'Hello, Mr Rowe,' says Olivia. 'Which is your car?'

'It's the embarrassingly awful one over there,' I say. 'Kids, do you want to go to the café first and get some frothy milk?'

They both scream 'yes' and jump around deliriously before running off toward our grubby, battered estate car.

When we get to the café, I swing the door open for them and they slope in, chatting happily (although actually, it is Olivia chatting and Sam nodding). As they meander through to the back area to claim one of the comfy sofas, I head to the counter, where Sam's favourite barista is reading the extensive tea menu to an elderly woman. As she walks slowly away to a nearby table looking thoroughly confused, I give him my order.

'I see you've got an extra guest today,' he says, looking over at Sam. 'Is it his girlfriend?'

I glance over too. They're sitting together, chatting, riffling through the comics and magazines on the table. They look like kids having a regular conversation. But it is not regular for us. I feel as though I could punch the air with pride, like Judd Nelson at the end of *The Breakfast Club*.

'This place seems to bring out the best in him,' I say.

'Ah yes, well, it was nice while it lasted.'

My heart suddenly sinks.

'What do you mean?' I say.

'The owner is selling up. He's met someone – a regular customer, in fact, and they're running off to start a guest house in Italy somewhere. The lease expires in a couple of months, then that's it.'

'Oh no, that's awful,' I say.

'Tell me about it. I liked it here. It's a nice place. A lot of the time it feels like having friends around, rather than working. I'll miss it. Anyway, have a seat. I'll bring your drinks over.'

I see that there are people waiting behind me, so I move away, but the news has shocked me. This was our place, our refuge. I decide not to tell Sam. Not today, not on his big play date. Instead, we sit and enjoy it. Olivia chats endlessly about her day at school – what she did, who she played with, what they said – the sort of information we never get from Sam. Meanwhile, he keeps bringing it back to *Minecraft*.

'I can build with sandstone,' he announces, apropos of nothing.

Then, excitedly remembering something, Olivia stops him by gently putting her hand on his arm. I notice that he doesn't flinch away.

'Oh, my brother told me about a *Minecraft* building competition,' she says. 'It's in a few months – you should definitely enter, Sam. It's at a video game festival in London. Everyone gets four hours to make a model and the best ones win a prize.'

'Can I go?' asks Sam.

I can picture the scene already: a vast exhibition hall filled with noisy teenagers and games consoles and pounding music. If Tabitha's party is likely to be Meltdown City, this will be the tantrum apocalypse.

'I'm not sure. We'll have to see when it is. It'll probably be very loud.'

'London was loud,' he says. 'But I completed it.'

'When we get back, let's make friends with my brother on your Xbox,' says Olivia to Sam. 'Then we can all play in the same *Minecraft* world.'

'Daddy, can we do that?'

'Yes,' I say, grateful to move the conversation along from the competition.

When we get back to the house, they clamber out of the car, then up the stairs. I hear the Xbox being switched on. I get some milk and biscuits from the kitchen and take them up on a tray, hoping to maintain the illusion to Olivia that a) I'm a completely functioning and reliable parent and b) that Sam has friends over all the time and this isn't *in any way* an utter miracle.

In the bedroom, Sam is busy showing Olivia our castle. He's

now added a series of small farm areas where he's growing wheat and carrots. She seems impressed. I set down the snacks and stand watching, but Sam looks back at me with what I detect to be embarrassment. Before I leave, Olivia tells us again about the games festival, and about how Sam should definitely enter the *Minecraft* competition. He nods enthusiastically and it takes me a few seconds to realise that, caught up in the moment, I am nodding in agreement too.

Chapter 20

We start with small talk. It's 7 p.m. on a work night and I'm in a pub in the city centre with Matt. He is here to watch the crucial Champions League match between Manchester United and Porto, whereas I am here to find out if he's having an affair. But I can't let him know that straight away. I've got to work my way there, via some clever conversational back door – or, in our case, via a discussion about United's inability to replace Roy Keane as a combative midfield general. This is the way men get things done.

'So,' I say (and this is about ten minutes into a long analysis of the club's recent history), 'talking about the disappointment that can come from long-term creative stagnation, how are things with you and Clare?'

Matt looks up from his pint.

'Fine, fine. We're gearing up for Tabitha's birthday party. Are you coming along with Sam?'

'Well, we're thinking about it. I'm not sure how he'll be. Is anything else going on with you?'

'Why do you ask?'

'Oh, you've been a little guarded recently. And even at the match, you were on your phone quite a lot, checking texts. I couldn't help but notice.'

Slowly does it, I think to myself. He's going to fend this off, but it's only the opener. We have all night so . . .

'Don't say anything to Clare!' he blurts out in a panicked rush.

Oh shit, he's caved already. He *is* having an affair.

'OK,' I say. 'Don't say anything to Clare about what?'

He takes a moment to collect himself.

'I've got into a bit of trouble. Money trouble.'

'What? How?'

He takes a few deep breaths and watches forlornly as a middle-aged man in a United shirt passes us with a vast tray of pints.

'I've been betting – on football mostly, but also rugby, cricket, motor racing, whatever I'm watching at the time. I do it on my phone.'

'Since when?'

'It started a year ago. I was travelling a lot, visiting developers. I got so bored, sitting in hotel rooms all the time, watching sports channels. When you're a parent you're always going on about wanting a bit of peace and quiet without the kids around and then, when you get it, you have no bloody idea what to do. So I started putting the odd bet on matches to make things more interesting. Then I couldn't watch a game without betting something: first to score, number of goals, number of corners. It sort of escalated. You know you're in trouble when you're sitting in a hotel room in San Francisco at six in the morning putting a hundred pounds on Hartlepool vs Barnet.'

'So . . . are you in debt?'

He makes an incredulous snorting sound. 'You could say that, yeah.'

'Well?'

'About fifteen grand. It was less, but at that office team-building

191

weekend I tried to win it all back in one day. I put down about fifty bets. It was a fucking disaster, Alex.'

'Oh shit.'

He looks down at his lap. At first I think it's out of shame, but then I glance around for his phone. He has it in his hand.

'Wait, you're not betting on this game right now, are you?'

'No! Well, yes.'

I reach over and grab the phone from him.

'Hey!' he yells.

'Seriously, Matt, what the fuck are you thinking?'

'I don't know. Maybe fifty quid on Porto to score first?'

'Matt, I'm serious!'

'Sorry!'

We're quiet for a second. In the background, we hear the whistle for kick-off, and a few half-hearted cheers from a gabble gaggle of United supporters.

'Is the house safe? Can you pay the mortgage?'

'For now, yes. But it's going to be tough. Fuck, it's such a mess.'

'You've got to tell Clare.'

He looks at me, his eyes desperate and red.

'I've tried. But I wonder, if I can pay it back quietly, maybe she doesn't need to know.'

'Matt, she thinks you've been having an affair.'

'What?!'

'She came to see me last week – she thought you'd been playing away. She knows something is wrong. *She's* not the stupid one in this relationship.'

'Shit.'

'You've got to tell her.'

'I'm terrified, Alex. I can't face losing her and the kids. I don't know what I'd do.'

Cheers erupt in the background. Instinctively we both look at the screen. Porto has scored. Matt reflexively turns to his phone.

The next day I take a stroll through the city, still processing the weird conversation with Matt and wondering what I should say to Clare, who has already sent me two texts. I need to be out of the flat, out of that depressing little room. The only positive is that, thanks to a gruelling trip to Ikea, I now have a rickety single bed, rather than an air mattress. I also have a lamp (because you never come away from Ikea with *just* the thing you went in for) and a cheap rug that generates enough static electricity to charge the lamp.

Aimless and bored, I wander the sodden passageways of St Nicholas Market with its fusty, overflowing bookstores and cubby-hole stalls selling drugs paraphernalia and vegan fast food. Then I check my bank balance, which is scarily depleted, but undeterred I head to the music shop on Park Street and buy a couple of vinyl albums to try out on Dan's ridiculously expensive, ridiculously underused turntable. After lunch at a gourmet burger place, I walk down the hill past the vintage clothing store where Isobel works. Then I stop. And almost without thinking, without consciously debating what I'm doing, I back up and walk through the door.

Inside it's a chaotic assault of nostalgia. Clothing rails line the walls, crammed with fifties dresses, letterman jackets and well-worn Levis. The covers of old movie-star magazines paper every surface. A Motown girl group plays over the speaker system. There is a strong smell of incense permeating everything, like a student bedroom.

I see her at the far end of the store, ringing through a purchase on an old sixties cash register and handing a large paper bag over to a customer. She's wearing a pink cardigan over a black dress, her hair styled into a bob. She looks amazing, like she's walked straight out of a David Bailey photoshoot. When she glances over and spots me, I wonder if she's even going to recognise me. But to my surprise, she smiles that same broad, bright smile that lit the café up a fortnight ago.

'Hey,' she says, walking over. 'What brings you in here?'

'I was just passing,' I say, immediately aware of what a boring, stereotypical response that is. Oh my God, I am about to make a complete tit of myself. 'How are things going?'

'Oh fine. My dad has taken Jamie fishing, which is great because what could possibly go wrong when you combine a hyperactive autistic boy with deep water and sharp hooks? Anyway, this place is pretty quiet today, so when the hospital calls I can close up and shoot out. It's nice to see you.'

'And you. So, um, what time do you finish?' It was meant to be a casual question, but I realise as soon as the words trail into the highly fragranced air that it sounds like a proposition.

'Is that an offer?' she says.

'No!' Short pause. She looks disappointed. 'I mean, yes. I mean, I didn't mean it to be, but now I wish it was. Oh God, I don't know, can I go out and come back in again?'

'I get out at six. We can go for a coffee up the road, if you like? I have to be back home by eightish.'

'That's great, let's do that. I'll see you here then. At six. For a coffee.'

I walk out and stand on the corner for a while, feeling weird and disembodied. It's like I've been served an emotional smorgasbord of guilt, elation and terror, and when it doesn't pass, I decide to go up to the museum so that I can calm down in the Ancient Egypt section. This is how I spend the next hour – rationalising everything to myself while surveying the artefacts of a long-dead civilisation. I'm not cheating, I'm not going to cheat, this is a kind of experiment, we're friends, and that's fine. Everything is fine. I mean, obviously it's not. Obviously my marriage is flying apart at the seams, and the woman I love, the woman I spent a decade of my life with, could well be sitting in a wine bar somewhere with a man named Richard. Nothing is fine. But maybe I can tease a strand of happiness out of this mess.

I head back to the store for exactly 5.55 p.m. and hang about outside looking shifty. Ten minutes later, Isobel and a colleague emerge, lock the door and hug each other goodbye. Her friend gives me an askance look and strolls off down Park Street.

'So,' I say, trying to make everything seem as casual as possible. 'Where shall we go?'

'There's a nice coffee shop near the Triangle,' she says. 'Come on.'

We wander up together, a respectable distance between us, swerving between groups of students, our heads down against the wind. The coffee shop is a little independent place, squeezed between a pizza restaurant and a wholefood supermarket. There's been a vague attempt at Parisian chic, which means sepia photos on the walls and a Jacques Brel CD on repeat. The place is full of tired-looking shoppers, except for the window seats which are taken up by a row of twenty-something guys with serious faces and ironic T-shirts, bent over their MacBooks. Dan probably knows them. We order lattes and take a booth by the counter.

'Dad texted me,' says Isobel. 'Apparently Jamie hasn't drowned, which is good, but he *did* get impatient and throw all of the tackle into the canal, so fishing is over for the day. How is Sam?'

'OK, I think. The same old thing. Awful one week, amazing the next. I'm reading all these autism books, trying to work out what starts meltdowns and how to prevent them.'

'Any answers?'

'Yes, don't do anything new or unexpected. Which is easy, obviously, because nothing unexpected ever happens in the world.'

'Jamie trashed the living room last week because *Horrible Histories* was rescheduled by ten minutes. There's not much I can do about that. He is obsessed with the Middle Ages. It used to be Thomas the Tank Engine, now it's torture, siege weaponry and diseases. I had to go into Waterstones last week and ask if they had any children's books on the Black Death.'

'Sam is utterly obsessed with *Minecraft*. If he's not playing it he's reading about it or watching YouTube videos about it. But it's actually fine – it's a calming thing for him, and we play it together a lot, which is great. There's this *Minecraft* modelling competition coming up in London that he wants to go to. I mean, that's big – that's such a huge step for him. But it's a worry just *how* into it he is.'

'That's good, though, it's creative! It's like, Jamie will spend hours playing with his chemistry set making potions. It's the only time he's still. I asked him what he wanted to be when he grows up and he said an alchemist.'

'Is that on the national curriculum?'

This is how it goes for the hour we have together. Wherever the conversation wanders, it continually leads back to our sons and autism, and what a gigantic pain in the ass it can be: the way that every trip out has to be planned and discussed in military detail; the endless questions; the weird hang-ups; the judgemental stares of other parents; the unhelpful suggestions; the long sleepless nights. But we also talk about how hilarious and idiosyncratic our boys are – the way they see the world and how it has shaped the way we see it ourselves; the stuff they say, and how they learn whole sentences from TV shows and parrot them in totally inappropriate contexts. It turns into a version of the scene in *Jaws* where Robert

Shaw and Richard Dreyfus compare scars, only with us it's tantrum horror stories:

'Once Sam got sent home from school for punching a teacher in the groin.'

'Jamie spat food at a dinner lady then wet himself.'

'Sam knocked a TV over in PC World, so I grabbed him and ran away.'

'Jamie threw a tennis racket through my parents' brand-new conservatory window.'

'Let's call it a draw.'

Isobel is sharp and funny. Whatever she's been through raising an autistic child by herself, she is unremittingly positive and optimistic. The cup isn't half-full, it's brimming over. Her eyes sparkle behind those thick-rimmed glasses – I cannot drag my gaze away from them.

'So what do you do apart from work and Jamie?' I ask.

'Well, I told you about the club nights I run? I'm a bit in love with the sixties, you may have noticed. The girl groups, the fashion, the films, the plays. Everything was so exciting and new, there were so many possibilities. Nowadays, we have all these things – all these gadgets – that they couldn't imagine back then, and yet everyone is cynical and lonely.'

'What about Jamie's dad, was he into all that?'

'Ha! No, not at all. I'm not even sure he liked music. We met at college – I was studying fashion, naturally, and he was doing television production. He got a job as a runner in London and disappeared. He's an assistant director or something now.'

'I sort of wonder if Sam will ever … you know … '

'Become an assistant television director and abandon his family?'

'No! I mean, have a relationship.'

'I've thought about it too. I mean, Jamie is pathologically

self-centred, obviously, but I don't know if that's because he's autistic or because he's a man. I'm joking, by the way. I know that he could use a bloke around to learn about man stuff – he needs practical guidance. Unfortunately, I picked an awful teacher.'

'Sam definitely likes girls, but all things considered, he prefers airplane apps and *Minecraft*. I don't know if that'll be different in ten years. People are tiring and complicated to him.'

'I know how he feels. How about you?'

'Huh, you mean me and Jody? I . . .'

'No, I mean you – what do you do? What do you like?'

'God, I don't know. I got swallowed up in work and parenthood for eight years, I sort of lost touch with everything else.'

I look around the room, trying to remember what I'm interested in. The place has quietened down, a few shoppers, the odd office worker. My gaze falls momentarily on a mum and her child sitting near the window; I feel certain I recognise her, but I don't know where from – an old mortgage client perhaps? It won't come to me.

'Well?' says Isobel. 'Are you into *anything*?'

I snap out of it and grab for the first thing that comes into my head.

'Well, erm, I was really into electronic music at university, I blogged about it, I DJ'd, I helped a friend set up a record label – which was a catastrophe and immediately folded. Now, when I look back at that time, it doesn't feel like me. But I bought two records today, so that's a start.'

'Exactly! Hey, you should come to one of my music nights. I'll introduce you to the pub owner – maybe you could put on an event of your own.'

'Ha, I don't think so . . . Oh, I mean, I don't think I can do an event, but I'd love to come to yours.'

'Great, I'll text you the details. Pop by if you fancy. Bring a friend or whatever. It's been nice to chat.'

'Yeah, it has.'

'Goodbye, Alex.'

She gives me a friendly hug and walks up Park Street, toward the grand university building. I start back the other way, replaying our brief physical contact in my head – the slightly coarse feel of her vintage dress, the smell of coconut in her hair.

Chapter 21

Jody phones me about the *Minecraft* competition. Sam has been talking about it as though it is definitely a thing that is happening. Neither of us is convinced.

His love of the game is unquestionable, though. We play online together whenever we can, sometimes for an hour, sometimes a few snatched minutes before Sam's bedtime. I check for his server and when I see he's online, there's a frisson of excitement I probably haven't felt since I was his age, since George and I were settling into some favourite board game. Then we sink straight in, adding fresh architectural features to the castle, claiming new land, watching our kingdom creep outwards with every session. Sometimes we chat, other times we silently focus on our own tasks, happy to be in the world together. In these moments, Sam is assertive enough to give me instructions, telling me to improve the farm enclosures or to go out and hunt for zombies. His confidence is growing – maybe even enough to be tested outside of this sheltered realm.

'How about we take him to Tabitha's party?' I say. 'Let's see how he is with crowds and noise. It's been a while since we tried anything like that.'

And we both inwardly groan, remembering what we have come to know as the Great Ice Cream Vomit Catastrophe that ended his last birthday party appearance. However, it's October half term and after several days of trying to keep Sam entertained while restricting him to only two hours of Xbox a day, I suspect Jody will be more amenable to this sort of experiment. I mean, if we're both there overseeing things, how bad can it be?

'Yeah, it's an idea,' says Jody. 'Good luck.'

And with that, the parental buck is slid very much in my direction.

I pick up Sam early on the morning of the party. He looks slightly wary, but I ask if he wants to do this and he nods slowly. It is clear he has been bribed with iPad time.

'OK, what would you like to dress as?' I ask. 'A pilot? A superhero?'

'Hmmm, a Creeper,' says Sam.

'Oh, OK. Why a Creeper?'

'Because I am like a Creeper!'

'What, because if people get close to you, you explode?'

'Yes!' he yells.

And we both laugh, but I wonder if only one of us is acknowledging the metaphorical truth in that statement. Whatever the case, I know that this option will rule out a quick trip to the giant supermarket up the road for one of its cheap, ready-made costumes. I sigh inwardly. I'm going to have to do crafts. Like a regular parent – with a regular child that enjoys crafts.

'In that case, we have lots to do,' I warn him.

First, we drive into Bristol and spend an hour darting between children's clothes stores, Sam continually asking where we're going and what we're doing. The standard drill. Eventually we find a pair of green pyjama bottoms and a long-sleeved green T-shirt.

'Is this my outfit?' says Sam.

'No, this goes *under* your outfit.'

'Why am I wearing an outfit?'

'Oh God.'

On our way back to Dan's, I stop at a craft shop for paint and a supermarket for cardboard boxes in various shapes and sizes. When we get to the flat, I cover the coffee table with newspaper and lay out scissors, brushes and Sellotape. Together we paint several of the boxes different shades of green. Much to my surprise, Sam manages to put in at least thirty minutes of concerted effort before his attention implodes. However, I discover that if I ask him questions about Creepers, I can keep pulling him back to the task. It's the longest we've ever done anything like this, and for a second I get a sense of what I've missed out on, sitting in that office for nights on end then spending the weekends trying to find ways to escape and relax instead of playing with Sam. There's that old saying: No one's last words have ever been, 'I wish I'd spent more time at work'. I'm feeling pretty smug until Sam takes the mug full of water we've been washing the brushes in and decides to experiment by pouring most of it on to Dan's floor. While Dan and I are frantically mopping it up with some of his unwashed T-shirts, I tell him about the games event and the competition. I wonder if he's been to these things before.

'Are you kidding?' he says. 'That's the Gen X games expo. I go to that one every year. I've already got my tickets. It's wicked.'

I seem to have accidentally unleashed his inner thirteen-year-old.

'Gen X?' I say. 'Does that mean it's going to be crammed with alienated fortysomethings?'

'No, dude. Gen X stands for Generation Xtreme!'

'Of course. Of course it does.'

In the end, the costume consists of one big box for Sam's body, which we cut a hole in so he can jam his head through; then there is one wine box for each of his arms, and two tissue boxes for his feet. I cheated by buying a Creeper boxhead mask online, but this is not bad for a first costume. I put it all on him carefully – I know that with its weight and unfamiliar textures, he'll only be able to put up with it for a little while. I shuffle him toward the full-length mirror in Dan's room. Why the hell does Dan even have a full-length mirror? At least he doesn't have one on the ceiling, I think, before slowly and trepidatiously looking up to check. Anyway, with that mental image banished from my brain, I focus back on Sam, who seems delighted.

'I'm a Creeper!' he yells. 'I'm going to blow you up!'

'No, stay away!' I shout and run off into the corridor. He runs after me – straight into a wall. I turn to see him stagger about comically for a second before collapsing backwards on to the floor. I'm expecting tears, but instead he laughs and struggles to get up. He has mastered slapstick comedy. This afternoon might actually work.

We get to Matt and Clare's before lunch. Even approaching the driveway I can hear the din from inside – the unmistakable sound of overexcited children, off their tiny heads on Haribo and fizzy pop. I press the bell, with Sam hiding slightly behind my leg, and immediately the door is flung open by a tiny Batman. It's Archie.

'Cool outfit!' he barks and then runs off yelling.

We step in. There are bizarrely clothed children everywhere. Two characters from *Frozen* are running up and down the stairs, spilling bowlfuls of cola bottles. Dracula is chasing a robot through the hallway to the sitting room where a group of Minions are endlessly circumnavigating the rug, which is covered in crushed cheese balls. I see Clare in the kitchen dressed as a witch, complete with green face make-up. She is serving cups of cherryade from a plastic cauldron. Sam grabs my hand as we struggle through, stepping over Iron Man, who is slumped on the floor with Robin Hood, playing on a Nintendo 3DS.

'Hi, Clare, great outfit,' I say as she splits gallons of fizzy drink into a series of plastic cups on the work surface.

'God, it's chaos,' she says. 'You'd think five years managing restaurants would have prepared me for this, but it hasn't. Look up there, Alex, there is jelly dripping from the ceiling. I haven't even given them the jelly yet. I thought it was still in the fridge. I do not need this right now.'

She hands out some more cups to a rabble of superheroes, princesses and police officers, who then run out into the garden, leaving a trail of fizzy red liquid in their wake.

'How are you?' I ask.

'Not great. Matt told me everything ... Hi, Sam, amazing costume! Do you want to go and find the others?'

He grips hold of my leg.

'When are we going home?' he pleads as Archie and Tabitha run in.

'You two,' says Clare, 'take Sam in the other room, we're going to play some party games in a minute!'

'Come on,' they yell, and grab his hand. He follows them slowly.

'That stupid, selfish bastard,' she says as she tidies the kitchen, jamming cups into the dishwasher. 'Not Sam, I mean Matt.'

'Ah, yes. He is definitely stupid.'

'How could he?' she hisses. 'He's got a good job, he doesn't need money. Why the hell did he do it?'

'He was away a lot and bored, and it's so easy nowadays – it's like playing a video game.'

'Yes, yes, I've heard all this from him. But I still can't

understand – why didn't he actually play a fucking video game? Why did he have to place us all at risk? And he hid it from me for so long!'

'So what are you going to do?'

'I don't know. I'm too pissed off to even look at him at the moment. He's in the other room, if you want to see him. I'll be through in a minute to do the bloody party games.'

So I go through to the sitting room where the Minions have moved on from wearing out the rug and are now giving each other rides on the reclining armchair. There in the corner is Matt, glumly hunched over a portable CD player, dressed as the world's saddest pirate. There is a pink spotted hanky around his neck, which has come undone, as has his waistcoat. His eyepatch has drooped down to his chin. Even the cuddly parrot Sellotaped to his shoulder looks limp and forlorn. A little girl is intermittently dancing, demanding One Direction songs, and throwing cheese balls at him.

'Hi,' he says. 'I'm a pirate radio DJ.'

'I get that. How are you doing?'

'Not great. Clare isn't speaking to me. The atmosphere is horrendous. I'm scared I'm going to lose them. I'm scared I'll lose everything.'

At this exact moment, the parrot falls off his shoulder.

'You're not going to lose them,' I say, trying to ignore this profound visual metaphor. 'Clare is angry, but she won't chuck you out.'

'She told you that?'

'She didn't have to.'

'It can happen, though, right?'

And he is talking about Jody and me – just as Clare did. It's great that they both hold us up as their worst-case scenario relationship.

'Look, this is different,' I say, with a strong feeling of déjà vu. 'You two are a unit; whatever happens you'll always work it out together. That's how you've managed to have four kids under ten without strangling each other. You two work things out. That's what you do. But you've got to stop betting and get some help. Show her you were a prat but now you have it under control.'

'PARTY GAMES!' yells Clare, prompting a screaming stampede of children, maybe twenty of them, tumbling into the room and fighting for floor space. Sam wanders in after them and grabs my leg. A couple of parents saunter in too, hanging around at the periphery clutching plastic wine glasses and chatting brightly. This all seems fairly normal to them.

'Who wants to play pass the parcel?' shouts Clare.

The suggestion is greeted by a wall of affirmative noise. Sam clamps his hands to his ears, and Clare goes around trying to order the guests into a huge ring, often by picking them up and dumping them in the right place. I attempt to push Sam down into a gap between Spider-Man and a fairy, desperate for him to join in – or at least not completely show me up by sulking in a corner. I get a brief hit of guilt for thinking this, but then, it does get tiring, the disapproving looks of other parents.

'Come on, it's OK, it's only pass the parcel,' I say.

Clare retrieves a large parcel from a cupboard and drops it into Archie's hands.

'Now, you all know what to do – keep passing the parcel until the music stops,' says Clare. 'If you hold it for too long, I'll send my pirate helper to chop off your head with his cutlass. If he hasn't pawned it.'

Matt bows his head joylessly.

As the unidentifiable pop music starts, Archie immediately chucks the parcel across the room, hitting Bella from *Beauty and the Beast* in the face. Several children have already started fighting; the dancing girl is now in the middle of the circle, enthusiastically gyrating. The parcel is retrieved and quickly bounced around the ring, with every child having a surreptitious tug at the bright wrapping paper. When it gets to Sam he grabs it and won't let it go, so Spider-Man grapples him to the floor and the fairy rips it from his fingers. I watch the whole thing open-mouthed. It is like some sort of drug-fuelled prehistoric ritual, a nightmarish clash of repetitive music, gaudy outfits and barely contained violence. A cup of cherry-ade goes flying into Cinderella's lap, prompting her to scream with such ferocity that several other children burst into tears. I look over to Matt and Clare and suddenly they are laughing, her hand on his shoulder, revelling in the chaos. Only *they* could bond over this frenzied menagerie of polyester and E numbers. I feel a tinge of jealousy. Their easy affection, their ability to ride with the punches – whether that's a ruined rug or a debt crisis – is horribly touching.

The music stops, a layer is shed from the package in an explosion of torn paper, and the ritual continues. Sam gradually gets more interested, his eyes glued to the parcel as it makes its wayward route around the circle. But as it is coming his way on the last round, the music stops and Spider-Man makes a successful grab. He whips off the final piece of wrapping to reveal a small Lego kit. Sam tries to grab it, but I quickly intervene. He storms into the kitchen crying. I bring him back, smiling awkwardly at the other adults, who I don't know and don't want to know, but am still apparently prepared to bully my kid in order to appease them.

This is pretty much how it goes for the next hour, through musical chairs (which resembles a sort of Disneyland street riot), musical statues (all over in about twenty-five seconds) and another three rounds of pass the parcel. Sam cries again several more times, and by the end I'm literally praying for it to end, while grimacing questioningly at Matt and Clare, who are too busy going through their collection of *Now* . . . compilation CDs.

When the games are finally over, there's a mass diaspora from the living room into the garden and upstairs.

'Do you want to come up and see our disco lights, Sam?' says Tabitha.

'Come on!' says Archie.

They grab his arms, and before he knows what's happening, they're dragging him out into the hallway and up the stairs. Matt takes the opportunity to put one of his Coldplay CDs on. Clare comes over to me with a glass of wine.

'Here you go,' she says. 'So, how are *you* doing?'

'Hmm, well, let's not go there now, you have enough on your plate.'

'You're doing the right things – helping with Sam, taking charge, being around for him. And she's getting the chance to do something of her own. Have you been to the gallery? It's amazing.'

'Not yet. I should. We're not exactly talking. I don't know what the rules of a trial separation are. I've googled it. That was a mistake. It's usually six months then separate, apparently.'

'Oh, Alex, never google health, relationships or your own name – that's your internet basics.'

'Thanks, Wicked Witch of the Web.'

Suddenly, there's a deafening noise from upstairs – the sound of a CD being switched on at top volume. It's followed by a long cry, some bumps, and then the bang of a door being slammed. A rampage of feet come down the stairs.

'Mummy!' says Tabitha. 'Archie has scared Sam.'

'It was an accident,' whines Archie. 'I put the stereo on too loud.'

I can hear the distant, muted sound of Sam crying.

'Where is he?' I ask.

'He's locked himself in the bathroom,' says Tabitha, sniggering.

'That's not funny,' says Clare.

I pace up the corridor, take the steps three at a time, and walk toward the bathroom. I can hear him clearly now, bawling and banging against porcelain. A fear gurgles up in me, the familiar paralysis. I stand on the landing, hand on the banister, uncertain of what to do. Jody would usually deal with this. Jody should be here. I approach the door and try the handle, it is locked.

'Sam,' I say gently. 'Sam come out, it's OK.'

'No,' he screams. 'I don't like the loud noise!'

'It's stopped now. Come out.'

'No, I don't like it. I want Mummy!'

I rest my head on the door. I can hear him pulling the toilet seat up and crashing it down again. Then there is the sound of objects being swept off a shelf into the bath or basin. I know this pattern and I know it will escalate unless he can be distracted. But while I'm thinking of what to do, something made of glass smashes as it hits the floor, and I snap.

'SAM, STOP IT!' I shout. And I know it's completely the wrong thing to do. Because now there are objects hitting the door – he's scared and I've added to it. I've fucked up.

'Shut up!' he yells. 'Shut up!'.

I'm desperately trying to think of how Jody would calm him down, but I was never there, or if I was I'd walk away angrily and let her cope. I sense that Clare is now behind me, approaching cautiously along the landing.

'I don't know what to do, I'm sorry,' I say. I slump against the wall and sink down in despair. She approaches the door and knocks quietly.

'Sam, it's Clare. Would you like to play on the iPad? I have mine here. It has some good games. *Angry Birds, Candy—*'

The door opens and there is my little boy, in his battered outfit, the Creeper headbox discarded and crushed on the floor. His eyes and face are red, his hair wild. In the bath behind him are dozens of deodorant and shaving foam cans and one smashed bottle of perfume, leaking a heady floral stench into the room. He quietly takes the iPad from Clare's hand, sits down on the floor and starts tapping and swiping at the screen.

Clare turns to me and shrugs.

'It always works on my kids,' she says.

'Sorry about the bathroom. It's autism, you know; sometimes there's nothing you can do to stop it.'

She shakes her head dismissively.

'You do realise other kids do this too? Tabitha has trashed her room several times. It's like living with a drunk rock star. We won't let her have a TV in there in case she chucks it through the window.'

'Well, I'll clear up and replace everything.'

'Oh, I've been meaning to sort out all that stuff for weeks – and the perfume is horrible. Matt's mum bought it for me. Honestly, Sam's done me a huge favour.'

Later, we drive away from the house and I keep glancing at Sam on the passenger seat next to me: his beautiful doleful eyes, his slightly podgy face. For the millionth time I try to imagine how he thinks, and what goes on in that brain of his. I realise that, for his entire life, I've seen autism as a kind of rival; I felt like we were fighting over who got control of him. But maybe it's time we signed a peace treaty. Neither of us is going anywhere, after all.

'You know what?' I say. 'Maybe we should do something else. Have a break. Just me and you.'

He remains quiet beside me, staring out of the window.

'We could, I don't know, go camping or something. Maybe that's it – get out in the countryside. When I was little I used to love camping with Aunt Emma and Grandma. Of course, that was usually in the summer, not the autumn, when it's wet and freezing cold.'

When we get back to the house, Jody opens the door and Sam scuttles through and up the stairs.

'You're back early,' she says. 'How did it go?'

'Not great. There was an incident with a stereo – he had a bit of a meltdown and locked himself in the bathroom. But he's OK now. It's made me think again about that *Minecraft* competition. I'm not sure he's up to it.'

'Don't give up on him,' says Jody. Her voice is conciliatory, but something in me snaps.

'I'm not going to give up on him, he's my son too, for fuck's sake!'

'I didn't mean it like that! What's wrong with you?'

'What do you think? This trial break now looks a lot like a break-up, and I have no idea how to talk to my son or even if he cares that I'm not around any more. So yeah, maybe there is something wrong with me.'

'I tried to talk to you about it, but you walked out – because that's what you always do.'

All at once, I am buzzing with rage. My brain is a swirling vortex of adrenalin. I've no idea what's going on, but I feel cornered and judged.

'I've always tried to do the right thing, that's all I've ever wanted to do! I spent eight years working in that damn office so we could afford a home and everything else we needed.'

'And what was I doing? Looking after our son twenty-four hours a day! You've had a bad afternoon because he had a tantrum at a party? Fuck you, Alex, that's my life!'

She's right. I glance away and watch my breath turn to mist in the cold night air.

'I'm sorry. I don't know what's going on any more. I'm completely lost.'

'I know. I'm lost too.'

And then from upstairs, a little voice.

'Mum, is it bedtime? What time is it?'

'I'd better go back in,' says Jody. 'Look, I think he *should* enter the competition. There's always a chance it'll be a disaster, but what's the worst that could happen?'

'Do you really want me to go there? I have a list, if you want to see it.'

'And we've got to sort this school situation out. I think we need to make a decision this month. I wish *he'd* decide. But all he says is that he doesn't want to go to any school ever.'

'Yeah,' I say. 'I know how he feels.'

Somehow the whole tone has turned around again. Is this what break-ups are like? A series of confusing lurches between confrontation and conciliation?

'Alex, you're doing a good job, picking him up every week. I know it hasn't been easy.'

For a second, it looks as though she is going to reach out to me, to touch my face, or draw me closer, but it doesn't happen and the moment passes. Perhaps it passed a long time ago. Instead, she rubs her hands together and looks down the street. The glow from the living room lends her face a radiant warmth. My heart aches for her.

Chapter 22

'So you're taking Sam camping for a night,' says Jody on the phone the following evening. We were talking about schools again, discussing the events of the previous day, about how every time we think that Sam is moving forward something happens to slam him right back again.

'Um, what? I mean, I suggested it in the car, but I didn't even think he was listening. He was still upset.'

'Well, it turns out he was listening. He already has his backpack by the door.'

'Right.'

'I mean, it's going to be cold, so if you want me to make an excuse for you . . .'

Naturally her assumption is that I'd want to wimp out of it, which infuriates me because I absolutely *do* want to wimp out of it.

'No. No, it's fine. We'll take some duvets and sleep in our jumpers. It'll be fine. I know a great place, honestly, it's pretty much organised.'

When I get off the phone, I grab the iPad and start frantically

213

looking up campsites. I wasn't completely lying to Jody; I know there are dozens of sites in Devon – Mum used to take us as kids. We had this awful, saggy old scout tent that let the damp and everything else in, and would often come back from a wet, windy day on the beach to find slugs crawling around in our sleeping bags. We'd throw them at Emma and send her running screaming over the field. Then Mum would unpack a little gas stove and cook sausages and beans, which we wolfed down under the stars. When it was time to sleep, George always made up terrible ghost stories, which inevitably involved headless horsemen. It was your standard British camping experience.

Perhaps there's a chance I can recapture some of that with Sam. Surely it's impossible *not* to bond when you're stuck in a quagmire several miles from civilisation? This is Sam, mind, so the unpredictability and discomfort of sleeping in a tent for even one night will probably lead to a living hell of fidgety sleeplessness. But when you're camping, that's all part of the fun.

After a while, I find a cheap site near Sidmouth – it claims to be family friendly, which I choose to read as 'won't be a problem if your child cries all night'. There is only one more problem: I don't have a tent and don't want a tent. Right now, I don't actually have a proper home.

'Have you got a tent?' I ask Dan when he arrives home later. He laughs for what seems like several minutes.

'No, but you can take my Porsche if you like,' he says eventually.

'Can I?' I blurt out.

He starts laughing again.

I text Emma, who is still staying at her friend's mansion.

Have you brought a tent back from your travels?

She replies:

No, bro, I always slept with other people ;)

But of course, Matt and Clare have a tent, a gigantic bell tent that fits their whole family, as well as a sort of portable kitchen that I tell them I don't need.

So the next morning, with minimal thought or preparation, I pick Sam up and his backpack and head over to Matt and Clare's. He seems bright and relaxed, a million miles from the kid I left two days ago, curled into a ball at the edge of his bed. This boosts my confidence – although I feel strangely calm. A while ago this endeavour would have sent me into paroxysms of fear and dread, and though I sense the ghost of those familiar tensions, things seem different now. I've decided to think of this as a kind of parenting mission. I figure that if I want to get to know Sam better, in real life rather than a video game, then spending a night in the middle of nowhere may be exactly what we need.

Matt has the tent ready on the driveway for me, together with a stove and a plastic suitcase that folds out into a picnic table with four chairs.

'You're crazy,' he says as I jam the stuff into the back of the car. 'It's going to be freezing tonight.'

'I know. Let's see how it goes.' There's a slight edge in my voice. 'How are things between you and Clare? It seemed to get better at the party.'

'Yeah, it's amazing what utter chaos, pop music and a bit of wine will do for a relationship. But it's still not great. I feel we have to do something. Get some time to talk. It's hard.'

'Tell me about it.'

'Well, good luck,' says Matt, patting me on the shoulder. 'At least the tent is easy to put up.'

Then somehow we're on the road to Devon. I hand Sam a timetable I've drawn up of our day, which lists all the things we'll do. Within twenty minutes we're out of Bristol and past the airport (which Sam wants to stop at; 'Another day,' I tell him). As the road skirts along the Mendip Hills toward the M5, Sam sits beside me in the passenger seat, fiddling constantly with the radio and the heater and asking an assortment of questions, which he repeats on a ten-minute cycle.

'Where are we going?'

'Devon. Have a look at the timetable I made.'

'Are we nearly there?'

'No, because we've only just got in the car.'

'Where is our tent?'

'In the boot. We have to put it up when we get there.'

'When are we going home?'

'Tomorrow, probably. Let's see.'

'OK ... Where are we going?'

Our journey flies by.

After stopping at a supermarket for food, plastic cutlery and everything else I neglected to bring, we arrive at the campsite by lunchtime. It's nothing fancy, a large field at the top of a hill, backing on to a farm. On the southern side, between the trees, we can make out a slither of sea, which looks grey, choppy and cold in the distance. There are five or six other tents dotted about, and between them a group of small children is running around after a football. While I slowly drive off the crumbling concrete track on to the stodgy turf, I mentally run through the five nightmare scenarios I've been compiling on the drive here:

Campsite turns out to be actual swamp. (Seems OK, so can cross this one out.)

Horrendous outdoor eco toilets where you poo in a hole and throw some dirt on afterwards. (I can see a brick building in the far corner of the field, which looks like it may contain standard loos, so not going to panic yet.)

Smug, over-equipped professional camping families. ('Darling, have you see the portable pasta press?')

Unusual nighttime wildlife sounds. ('Daddy, what's that?' 'I don't know, leave everything and get in the car.')

Massive dog on the loose. (No sign yet, but almost inevitable.)

We park up a little way from the other families and I retrieve the bag from the boot, which hopefully contains a tent and not what it feels like – two dead bodies wrapped in a duvet. It is mercifully easy to put up – one central pole, which I fling the canvas over, then a series of ropes to tie it all down. Sam grabs the huge steel mallet and asks if he can hammer the tent pegs in. 'Um, OK,' I say, but as I hold the first one in the ground, I feel like this is the beginning of an episode of *Casualty*. He gets bored after two wild swings, though, and relieved, I finish the job alone. Finally we lay the groundsheet out, then discover that the tent bag also contains two other middle-class camping essentials: some flowery bunting and five metres of solar-powered fairy lights. Sam insists we hang both of them, so when we're finished, the interior looks less like the hardy refuge I had in mind and more like the craft tent at a village fête.

But everything is going well. Everything is calm. We celebrate by heating up some tinned spaghetti on Matt's tiny camping stove and eat it out of plastic bowls, splashing it messily over our clothes and faces. Sam studies the campsite silently.

'Are you OK?' I ask.

'Yes. Do people live in tents?'

'Some people do, but not these people, they're only on holiday. When Grandma took us camping, we had everything: tables, chairs, a cooking stove, we even had a television and a fridge. Grandma took it all very seriously.'

'Where do you live, Daddy?'

'At the moment, I live with my friend Dan.'

'Will you come home soon?'

'I don't know. I think Mummy and me have to talk some more and work things out.'

'What do you need to work out?'

'How much we still like each other. We were getting cross with each other a lot and it was making us sad. But we still love each other. It's complicated.'

'I like home best and *Minecraft* second. I like camping too.'

And as we're talking I think I may as well try something.

'What about school?' I ask.

'I don't like school,' he says.

'I know. What is the worst thing about school?'

Instead of opening up any more, he looks over in the direction of the farm and sees a small herd of cows trudging past the fence.

'Where are the cows going?'

'Maybe to be milked. What is it about school? You were going to say—'

'Can we go and see the cows?'

'We can see them if you tell me what you don't like about school.'

'I don't know. Sometimes I am cross. I am a baddie, like a Creeper. Sometimes I get it wrong and I cry.'

'What? What do you get wrong?'

'Everything.'

Then he's off, running toward the fence, his wellington boots sinking into the soft earth. I put the bowl down and follow him, thinking about what he said. 'Everything.' That's it, I suppose. Everything is hard, everything is a struggle. Most of his time is spent being buffeted from one inexplicable situation to the next. No wonder he loves *Minecraft*, where everything is clear and logical, where the very landscape is malleable to his wishes. Nothing else in his life is like that.

We approach the cows gingerly. A couple of them stop and stare at us. Sam gets closer than I think he will, putting his hand out. I'm about to say, 'be careful', but then one snorts and jerks its head and Sam whips backwards, laughing. Unperturbed, he puts his arm out again, and this time he strokes the cow on its side. It's a surprising moment of bravery.

We stroll along the entire perimeter of the site, past the entrance and then down into a lower clearing. From here, we get a clearer view of the sea, which merges imperceptibly into the slate grey sky. We sit here for a while on an old tree stump. Sam takes hold of my hand.

'The sea looks like it goes on for ever, but it doesn't,' he says. 'At the end there is always an island or a country, but you might not find it. Then you'll sink and drown.'

'Um, thanks for that. Come on, genius, let's find some wooden swords.'

We walk through a copse and pick up a stick each, noisily attacking various trees and bushes, our breath creating a mist around us. There is no other sound apart from the wind rustling through the bare, glistening branches above. It seems like it is only us in the world.

Eventually, we head back to the field and one of the kids we saw earlier, a boy in combat trousers and a parka, runs over and asks if we want to play football. Sam looks down at the ground, silently shaking his head.

'Thank you for asking,' I say.

When we're back at the tent, we sit looking at comics for a while. But then a little boy, maybe two or three, toddles over from another tent with a small *In the Night Garden* football. He throws it toward us. Sam gets up and gently kicks it back, and the boy giggles delightedly.

'Is he bothering you?' shouts a man in cargo shorts and a polo shirt from the other tent.

'No, he's fine,' I say.

The boy rolls the ball to Sam, who sits down and rolls it right back. He's always been good with younger children – patient, protective and indulgent. Perhaps it is a relief to him that they are more vulnerable than he is, or maybe it's because they look at him and see an older boy, not a whiny brat who'll cry if a playground game doesn't go his way. Whatever it is, they sit like this for a long time, passing the ball back and forth as I sit in one of Matt's little camping chairs, reading the newspaper. Actually reading the newspaper.

Later, we pick up our washbags from the car and head to the toilet block. I clean Sam's face and wipe the spaghetti juice from his hair. When we get back, we sit on a blanket and eat crisps and sandwiches and chocolate chip cookies as the sun falls. Soon I can make out the dim glow of lanterns hanging in other tents.

'We can watch the night coming,' I say.

That's what we do for a few minutes, not talking, simply experiencing the unfamiliar space together. It's only late afternoon, but I feel tired after the drive and the stillness is restful. It doesn't last. As everything fades around us, the reality of it all seems to dawn on Sam, who gradually edges closer toward me.

'I'm scared,' he says. 'It's too big out here. I don't like it.'

'It's fine. It's the countryside. It's the same at night as it is in the day.'

'No, it isn't. Can we go back? I want to go home. It's too big, Daddy.'

'What do you mean?'

'I don't like the space. I don't like the feeling. I can't see what's around everywhere. I don't like it.'

And straight away, what he says sounds familiar. I understand what he means. The fear of space, of freedom, of uncertainty – it's how I've been feeling these past three months, cast away from everything that meant something to me. I hadn't thought about this before, how autism is a kind of intense, very centred, version of how we all feel, of the anxieties we all have. The difference is, the rest of us hide it all under layers of denial and social conditioning.

I open the tent hatch and climb in. The fairy lights weakly illuminate the interior.

'Come in, it's quite warm in here,' I say.

'I want to go home!' he shouts.

For a few seconds, I feel the familiar combination of rising dread and panic that overwhelms me whenever a tantrum is building, that sense of helplessness in the face of what is to come. All the parents at our autism group spoke of something similar: your brain frantically searches for something to say or do that will solve everything quickly. All too often, mine comes up way short.

Sam is sitting cross-legged in front of the tent; his face in his hands, rocking slightly. The calm before the perfect storm. But this time, I do have an idea. Kind of.

'I know,' I say. 'If we close our eyes, we can be in *Minecraft*. We're on the Safe setting, so there are no Creepers and no zombies, just the pigs and the cows. Listen, we can hear them. We've built a tent out of, um, sandstone. It's on the top of a very steep hill and in the distance we can see the ocean. We've travelled for many days to get here because we know that out there in the sea is a little island, and on the island is a temple that contains lots and lots of gold. Now the soft music is playing, and look, the sky is going orange and red. Come on, load up the game, come and join me! I want to explore!'

Slowly, he edges back into the tent.

'I'm outside,' he says, putting his hands over his eyes. 'I can see the sun from there.'

And we both see it together. The sun is a glowing hexagon that we watch dipping further toward the horizon. As it falls, the sky darkens in pixelated waves.

'What shall we do?' I ask.

'I'm going to walk down to the sea and find a boat,' says Sam.

We imagine wandering out into the dark field, past the blocky shapes of the other tents. We run and run, looking for caverns and potholes, pointing out the way that the moonlight catches the snow at the top of the distant mountains.

'Come on, down the cliff,' says Sam.

And we step down, from one stone block to another, along the cliff face to the beach. There, on the crunchy sand, we stop and watch as the square moon completes its rise. Within seconds it hangs above us, full and large, dotted with grey and white pixels. Sam walks on toward two boats bobbing at the shoreline.

'Let's sail out.'

I run out after him. He climbs into one craft, and I take the other.

'Can you see any islands?' I ask.

'Yes, a long way away.'

The sea glitters all around as the land recedes behind us into the murky distance. But we're not frightened. We know the rules of this world. At the end of our journey, and not very far away, there will be an island full of treasure. We will find it for sure.

When I open my eyes, I see that Sam – astonishingly – is asleep beside me, his damp stringy hair stuck over his ears, his body still, the slightest twitch of a smile on his face. And I have this strange, shocking moment of clarity: Sam is a human being, separate from me, separate even from Jody. He's not a problem to be solved, a dink in my scheduling, another worrying element of my daily 'to-do' list. He's a person, and somewhere in his head are his own ideas, his own priorities, his own ambitions for the future. It's amazing how easy it has been to overlook all that, amid everything else going on, amid the struggles with autism, the daily battles over schools and food and clothing. He's a person – he wants things, he wants to understand his place in the world. And what I should do is help him.

Sam isn't merely something that's happened to me.

I stroke some hair from his face and lightly kiss his forehead. I take his hand and it flutters for a second, then his fingers close around mine.

Chapter 23

He's wide awake at 6 a.m., the weak sun shining in around the entrance flap. I try to get him to look at a comic, so I can sleep a little longer, but there's no way that's happening.

'Do you want to stay another night?' I ask.

'No. It's too scary,' he says.

I don't know if the *Minecraft* trick will work again, so I decide to quit while I'm ahead.

'OK, how about we do something else?'

'What?'

We walk out to the corner of the campsite where there's mobile reception, albeit weak, and I call Jody.

'Is everything OK?' she asks. 'Did you both survive the night?'

'Yes, we're good. We might stay away another night, is that OK?'

There's a slight pause, I look at the phone to make sure we haven't been disconnected.

'Are you sure?' she says. 'I mean, that's great, if he's OK?'

'Yeah, I have an idea, I think he'll like it.'

'OK then. Well done! Sorry, that sounded patronising.'

'I know what you meant. We'll be back tomorrow afternoon.'

'Thanks, Alex. Good luck!'

I disconnect the call and put my phone in my pocket.

'Right,' I say to Sam. 'I've got a plan – if you're up for it.'

Mum's cottage is off a quiet lane that gradually turns into a narrow track as it winds through the endless fields of east Cornwall. It is the first in a small cluster of ridiculously quaint houses, a chocolate box scene of unspoilt Englishness. Behind them, an overgrown pathway leads to the cliffs, where worn stone steps provide haphazard access to the secluded bay. We first brought Sam here when he was still a baby, but Mum's endless parenting tips drove Jody quietly mad. It turns out that sleepless nights, unsolicited advice and being in the middle of nowhere is not a great mix.

When we pull up outside, I see Mum in the garden wearing a pinafore and sweeping dead leaves from the lawn.

'Well, this is a surprise,' she says as I open the car. Sam leaps out, runs over and hugs her. 'What are you two doing here then?'

'We were camping in Devon. I thought we may as well drive down and say hello.'

She eyes me with what looks like suspicion.

'It's a long way to come to say hello,' she says. And there it is, her astonishing capacity to make me feel like a silly ten-year-old again.

I start to say, 'Well, if it's not convenient . . .' but she waves it away.

'Don't be silly, you're here now. Come on, Sam.'

She takes us through the side door into the kitchen, with its obligatory Aga and dark slate floor. On the windowsill, there are bunches of dried flowers in old tin vases and piles of ancient cookbooks. It's like walking into a photoshoot for *Country Living* magazine.

'I wasn't expecting anyone, so the house is in a bit of a mess,' she says, leading us through into the pristine living room, with its vast spotless sofa and immaculate oak floors. On the mantel above the wood-burning stove there are half a dozen framed photos. I immediately see the one of George and me outside the café in London. There are no photos of Dad.

The house was a wreck when Mum bought it, but she spent years renovating the building and gardens, either doing the work herself, or terrorising local tradesmen. She's alone here a lot of the year – most of the houses around her are second homes, owned by wealthy city workers who turn up during the summer in their spotless four-by-fours. Some of them pay Mum to go and check on the houses while they're away, tidying the gardens, opening windows, making sure the wine refrigerators are set at the right temperature.

She makes us cheese sandwiches for lunch, remembering the piccalilli for Sam. Afterwards she volunteers to take him down to the rock pools, digging about in her shed for a net and a bucket. Although everything has gone OK, I accept the offer with undisguised zeal.

For a while I lounge around reading the newspapers (Mum gets *The Times*, but beggars can't be choosers) and aimlessly browsing the web on my iPad. Then I have a look around, through the kitchen into the dining room, then upstairs, into the neat guest bedroom, with its two plump single beds. Everything is neat and ordered. In an alcove below the stairs I discover a small cupboard, partially hidden behind a row of wellington boots.

Something compels me to open the door.

What I find first are lots of greetings cards, dozens of them, piled up and tied together, most with watery illustrations of flowers. I pick up a stack of them, wondering if they're birthday cards or something, but then I spot that they all have a similar message on the front, in an elaborate handwriting font: 'With sympathy'. I don't want to look inside any of them.

On another shelf there is an old child's shoebox. I pick it up and something rattles inside. Slowly, cautiously, I open it. Inside, there are some photos of George, on a bike, on a beach somewhere, dressed in his school uniform, smiling. Folded among them is an official form, plain and white, the handwritten entries clearly visible through the thin paper. I know that it is his death certificate, I know that here, the accident will be recorded in stark medical terms. Quickly, I put it back in the box, meaning to shut the thing and put it away, but then I see one more object, which first of all looks like an old bracelet, plastic, scratched and dirty. But it isn't. When I get it into the light I see that it is George's digital watch, the one he always wore, its small screen a collage of scuffs and cracks. He saved up for it himself, using his pocket money and extra cash he'd earned by washing the car and doing weeks' worth of other chores around the house. Then one Saturday, Mum took him to Argos to buy it and for days he wouldn't even remove it to have a bath. It became a family joke. 'What's the time, George?' we'd constantly ask him. He was wearing it that day.

I clasp it in both hands and hold it to my face. 'I'm sorry, George,' I say.

Carefully, I put everything back as it was and close the cupboard door, rearranging the boots into their ordered line. I hold the banister for a few seconds, breathing heavily, lost in the past.

It's already getting dark when Mum and Sam return. I see them coming up the pathway – he has a towel wrapped around his waist like a floral skirt and Mum is carrying his trousers.

'I fell in a pool!' he shouts as they burst noisily into the kitchen.

'He's fine,' says Mum. 'He's been very brave.'

'We caught some fish and a big crab. I saw a sea enemy.'

'Anemone,' corrects Mum.

I bend down and put my arms around Sam, but I hold on too long for him and he pushes me away impatiently.

'Daddy, you have to see the rock pools!' he yells.

'I will! I'll put the kettle on for now, though.'

'Go and find a game for us to play,' says Mum. 'They're in the cupboard next to the fire.'

Sam runs off into the living room.

I quietly fill the kettle and fetch the cups. Mum watches me.

'Are you OK?' she says.

'Yeah. I'm fine.'

'Don't tell me – cupboard under the stairs, behind the boots.'

She's like a maternal version of Lieutenant Columbo.

'Yes. I'm sorry.'

She shakes her head.

'I never know where to put that stuff. It was in the attic for years, but I didn't like hiding it away. Here it feels available, but it's not too obvious. I thought you'd find it eventually. We'll talk about it later.'

For the rest of the evening, Sam drags out our old childhood board games and we work through the pile in quick succession. Buckaroo, Mousetrap, Ker-Plunk, all the classics. Somehow Mum has managed to keep them more or less intact, although Operation is missing a funny bone and Junior Scrabble has only seven vowels.

'We'll have to play it in Welsh,' offers Mum.

Then it's time for supper – more spaghetti for Sam, but huge portions of fish and chips from the takeaway in the next village for us. Mum talks to Sam, asking him questions, satisfied with his meagre responses – I wonder if she identifies with him to some extent. Neither of them want to give anything away. Yet when she asks about *Minecraft* he opens up, telling her all the different materials, the mobs, the farmyard animals. He even tells her about

228

the building competition in London, and how he is going to enter. It seems very real and definite to him now. The conversation lasts through a long soapy bath and into bedtime. He's asleep almost immediately. I wonder if this is what it's like with other children, regular children – do they just get into bed and go to sleep? It seems implausible.

It's not long before Mum is opening a bottle of wine and lighting the stove in the living room. We sit quietly for a while, listening to the wood crackle and spit amid the flames.

'So,' she says. 'Jody.'

'Yeah, Jody.'

'What's going on then?'

Her tone is neutral with only the subtlest hint of concern, as though she's asking about a faulty boiler, rather than my disintegrating marriage. But of course, this has been her way since we were children, whether it was dealing with me falling off my bike, or Emma splitting up with a boyfriend, or George.

'I don't know. Obviously we were exhausted all the time. I worked late, she was always at home with Sam, and there was all this tension. We had an argument one Sunday and that was it, I was out. A trial separation.'

I tell her about losing my job, about Jody and the wedding weekend, the possible dates with Richard. As I say the words, it seems like something happening a long way off, to complete strangers.

'What are you going to do about it?' she says finally.

'I don't know. But I'm kind of sorting things out for myself. Sam and I have actually been talking, having fun together. I feel like I'm beginning to understand him. We play *Minecraft* and it's this place where we can be together and nothing's too complicated or fraught. I know I got a lot wrong, I know I have to make changes.'

'You've got to talk to Jody then, work things out. Tell her all of this.'

'I don't know. I think it's too late.'

'Don't tell me about "too late". I know too late when I see it, believe me. This isn't it.'

'So much has happened. I wasn't great for her. In the past I—'

'Ah, here we go. In the past. That's where your head is most of the time. If I can give you one piece of advice, it's to leave that well alone. It's no place to live.'

'Is that how you've coped with everything?'

'I had to cope. What choice did I have? There's never been anything to fall back on. I only ran away once in my life and that was the biggest mistake I ever made – though plenty of good came out of it.'

'But George and everything … I don't know how you got through, how you held us all together.'

She cups her wine glass, then takes a small sip.

'When you're looking after these big houses out here through the winter,' she says, 'it's just too much work to keep the whole building warm. So you choose which rooms you can afford to heat, the rooms you really need to live in, and you close up the rest. You just let them go cold, and you promise yourself that you'll go back to them when spring finally comes. That's how I felt after George died, Alex. Like I had to shut down everything I didn't need or couldn't cope with. Then I waited for any sign of blossom.'

We're quiet again. I think I hear an owl a long way out in the darkness, but it could be the wind whistling through the rickety windows upstairs.

'I'm sorry for not coming to visit more often,' I say.

'Oh stop it! Come more often in the future – it's simple. Bring Jody. Bring that sister of yours. But whatever you do, Alex, you've got to live. You've got to live. That's what Georgie would want. Wherever he is, he's probably been yelling that at you for months.'

We're quiet for a while. Beyond the gentle crackling of the stove, the silence is so complete, it feels palpable, like a heavy mist. The peace is fine, but it would drive me mad after a few days. Eventually we do hear an owl, faint but clear, and it stirs us again.

'Do you ever think about moving somewhere more ... civilised?' I ask.

'Sometimes. I don't know. When you and Emma left home, I wanted to get away from the town and everyone in it. And it's been nice here – so calm. But slowly all the families have moved out and the bankers have bought everything. It's not really a community now, it's like a big holiday village and I'm the caretaker. I don't want to end up murdering everyone with an axe like Jack Nicklaus.'

'That's the golfer, Mum. I think you may mean Jack Nicholson, in *The Shining*.'

'I do have an axe, though. And a typewriter, come to think of it.'

'Should I grab Sam and make a run for it?'

She laughs and shakes her head.

'I'm such a hypocrite – telling you to live your life, to seize the moment. And I'm still hiding out here like an old spinster. Anyway, I think I might head up to bed.'

She gets up, fills my glass with wine and then goes through to the kitchen. I hear her loading the dishwasher. Then she comes to the doorway again.

'Son,' she says. 'I'm going to tell you something, and I'm never going to say it again, because it's always been true and it's never going to stop being true. So get this through that thick head of yours.'

'OK,' I reply.

'You weren't responsible for the accident. Whatever happened between you and George that day, it doesn't matter and never mattered. That boy was always two steps ahead, he never thought about now, it was always "what's happening next?". I saw that in him right from the start – as soon as he could walk he was doing daft things. Remember when we went to Leigh Woods and he climbed that gigantic oak tree and wanted to hang from a branch like Tarzan? You begged him not to and you cried until he came back down. If you hadn't been there, he'd have done it and the branch probably would have snapped. That time he decided he could jump from our old kitchen roof to the shed—'

'I said I'd tell on him, and he didn't do it.'

'Exactly. He was brave and clever but he was so rash, Alex. When I got that call from the school, they said, "Your son has been in a terrible accident." I knew which son it was. I knew it was him. I've tried to tell you this a dozen times over the years. You have got nothing to feel guilty about. *Nothing*.'

And suddenly, my eyes are watery, and my throat is so sore I can barely swallow.

'OK, Mum.'

'Do you understand?'

'Yes.'

'Good. Now stop moping about and sort yourself out.'

Chapter 24

I'm meeting Isobel again. Sort of. She's running another one of her sixties club nights and texted me the details. It's on Thursday at some sort of social club in St Werburghs. I messaged back to say I'd go, but then immediately thought, a) oh God what am I doing, and b) what do people wear at these things? I have three pretty boring suits and a sports bag full of jeans and jumpers – there's nothing that could be considered vintage beyond a Chemical Brothers T-shirt from 1997. I contemplate turning up at Isobel's shop and buying something there, but figure that would look a bit desperate. Instead, I get on eBay and find someone selling a 1960s navy blue Aquascutum suit that looks like it may be roughly my size. I rashly pay the 'buy it now' price of £125, then google 'sixties footwear men', and find a pair of Chelsea boots to go with it. It's a lot of money to stand in a pub looking like a sort of off-duty Austin Powers, waiting for a few snatched moments with a woman I've met exactly twice.

Two mornings later, the suit and shoes both turn up. The trousers are a little short and the waist is tight enough to ensure that

I'll have to hold my breath in all night, but it looks fine. I mean, there's a chance I could pass out, but that's a small price to pay. At least no one I know will be there to see it. Dan has plans, Emma would find it all too hilarious and if I asked Matt then Clare would want to know what was going on and Jody would inevitably find out. I'm not ready for all that. No, this is an experiment, nothing more, I tell myself. I've become so disconnected from what I want, I have to sort of trick the information out of my own brain: 'Surprise, you're on a date, what are you going to do now?'

The club is a prefabricated rectangular hut facing a row of small sad terraced houses. It looks like a large Portakabin, or the type of shelter you'd build on your first night in *Minecraft*.

I am thinking about that game way too much.

As I approach the building, I can see multicoloured disco lights flashing out of the otherwise dark windows, and there is the sound of a Motown song dimly drifting into the damp night air. Outside, a small group of teenagers is smoking and peering in through the open door, looking unimpressed. I go past them, and as I open the second set of doors, a wave of sound and sweaty heat hits me. There are maybe forty people dancing and drinking, most in their late twenties and early thirties, though there's a smattering of much older couples, who clearly remember all this from the first time around. The women are all in authentic dresses, with hair and make-up extravagantly geared to the era. The men, I'm relieved to see, are mostly in suits, though there's a group near the dance floor in jeans and Fred Perry tops. They look like a Blur tribute act.

An old guy sitting at a trestle table next to the entrance shouts, 'Five pounds, please, mate,' as I go in. I scan the room for Isobel and spot her in the far corner talking to the DJ, whose modern CD decks, mixer and laptop seem incongruous amid all the acrylic, beehives and Brylcreem. I head to the bar (staffed by two women who seem to be dressed as sixties air hostesses) and order a pint of weak, flat lager. The Motown track has given way to The Kinks. A group of nine or ten people start throwing angular dance moves in the centre of the room.

This is so not my scene.

It's partly my mum's fault. She hates sixties music, she says it reminds her of the awful dances in her local church hall and being clumsily groped by young farmers. I think it's another example of her refusal to linger in, or even idly think about, the past. I'm still processing this when I feel a tap on my shoulder. I turn around and there is Isobel, beaming at me. She's wearing a black-and-white-checked minidress, and is clearly in her element.

'Hi! Thanks for coming!' she shouts. 'Are you here alone?'

'Yeah, I thought I'd pop by, see what you get up to.' That sounded weird.

'I love your suit,' she says.

'Thank you. It's just something I threw on. Do you know *every-one* here, then?'

'Most of them. I'll introduce you later. Ooh, there's Rachel, I have to go and say hello. I'll be back in a minute!'

And she's off into the crowd, greeting and hugging people, dancing for a few seconds, laughing. I lean against the bar self-consciously, sipping at the lager. I get my phone out, but then feel as though this may be a gigantic faux pas at a vintage event so put it away and instead try to glance casually around the room without making myself look like some sort of predatory barfly. The pop music blends into mod, which becomes psychedelic rock, which oozes into Northern soul. More people start arriving after ten, and the bar is a bustling hot spot of flirting couples. Then I see Isobel heading over again.

'Hey! Sorry, there are loads of people I haven't seen in ages. Are you OK?'

'Yes, I'm fine, I'm enjoying the music,' I lie.

'I'll be back in a second, I promise.'

And then she reaches up, puts a hand behind my neck and leans in to me. The kiss lasts a few seconds, but it is more than a social kiss. I manage to put the pint down on the bar and, not sure of what to do, I lightly hold her waist. My eyes are closed, the music seems to withdraw into the far distance. I don't know what I am thinking. Everything is limited to the contact between us. She draws away, but then kisses me quickly again. When I open my eyes, she is looking at me.

'I'll see you later,' she says into my ear, her breath tickling the side of my face.

And when she walks back into the throng of people, I snap awake, and one certain thought emerges from the sensual thrill of her touch, through the fug of surprise and yearning. This is not right. This is a mistake. I feel a swooping sense of dread in my stomach and suddenly it seems that the whole room, the whole night, is awash with guilt, and I'm sick with it. What the hell am I doing here? I put down the drink I've been nursing for over an hour then half walk, half stagger, toward the exit, pushing impatiently through the dancing couples in their strange antique clothing. I'm close to the first set of double doors when I feel an arm grab me and I'm terrified – actually terrified – that it's Isobel. But it's the doorman.

'There are no returns after ten p.m.,' he warns.

'I'm not coming back,' I say.

And then I'm out into the cold fresh night. I walk quickly away, along the street, around a corner and down toward the main road where I know I'll get a taxi. When I flag one down, the first address

I give to the driver, almost instinctively, is my home – Jody's home, the home we moved into nine years ago when she was pregnant and everything was new and exciting. I quickly give him Dan's address instead and ten minutes later we're pulling up outside the vast apartment complex – this weird antiseptic modern monstrosity, this Death Star of sleek city living. I don't want to be here any more. It takes all my strength to get out of the cab and walk toward the entrance. As I reach for the door, my phone buzzes in my pocket. I pull it out. It's a text from Isabel.

Where are u?

And I think to myself, I don't know. I honestly don't know where I am. But wherever it is, it is not where I am supposed to be.

'Jody,' I say in a whisper. 'I'm so sorry. I'm going to fix things, I promise.'

The next morning, my alarm goes off at 7 a.m. and I am immediately aware that I've barely slept. Instead, I spent vast stretches of the night with my eyes wide open, looking across at the window, playing through old memories in my head. I must have browsed my entire history with Jody, from that first meeting in the orchard, through the blissful early months of our relationship, through to the holiday, the pregnancy, Sam. It's weird how a whole life can be distilled into a series of moments, and how, without thinking, we order those moments into a story that makes sense and seems to mean something. We are endless editors of our own histories. But sometimes we get it wrong. Part of me has felt that breaking up with Jody was inevitable, that we set out upon that path years ago and couldn't escape it. Somewhere around 4.30 a.m., I realised something: that's not true – there has always been a way back. It has to start with me talking to her, telling her that I'm trying to figure things out. I don't have the answers yet, but at least I know there are questions. Or at least, I have to say something *like* that without sounding like a relationship expert on a US daytime chat show.

An hour later, I'm still mulling over exactly what it is I want to say as I'm driving toward our home, edging through the traffic and road-works and swerving cyclists. 'Get out of my way,' I want to shout, 'I'm trying to save my marriage!' But instead I tap on the steering wheel, glaring at the bumper of the car in front, willing it to move.

Off the main road into the suburban sprawl, I wind through the rows of parked cars, past kids running to school, followed by their half-asleep parents. When I get close to our house, I pull into a space on the other side of the street, and then see our front door opening. I know that Sam will soon trudge out in his little grey trousers, prob-ably wearing thin at the knees, and his blue polo shirt, ready to face another unpredictable and baffling day at school.

But it is not Sam who emerges. It is a man I don't recognise. He's wearing a black blazer with dark skinny jeans and a brown tartan scarf. Almost immediately I know who it is. It's Richard. He is smiling broadly, and as he turns back, I see Jody appear at the doorway. They say something, he shrugs and then she leans forward and kisses him. I watch in silence – it is a roaring silence, the loudest I've ever known, it seems to rupture my ear drums and reverberate around the car. She watches him for a second, waves, then heads back in and closes the door. Richard pulls away and drives past in his alpine white BMW. He has been there all night. Maybe he's even staying. Maybe he's living there now.

I sit for a moment, hands still on the wheel, unable to move. I swallow and the sound is deafening. My eyes are dry and I realise I have not blinked. When I do, I feel a bulbous teardrop trickle along my nose then into the corner of my mouth.

Very slowly, I pull out of the space, then I accelerate hard outside the house, and past it, to the end of the street. Then I am driving fast, too fast, past groups of parents and children holding hands, running along, chatting. I screech to a halt at a pelican crossing, and almost jab the horn as an old couple judder across, clutching each other for support. I screech away as soon as it's clear, taking the rat runs and back streets all the way to where I'm going. Matt and Clare's house.

Archie is playing in the garden as I bump on to the driveway.

'Hello, Alex!' he shouts.

I bang on the door and ring the bell.

'All right, all right,' I hear Matt shouting inside.

He opens the door in his ill-fitting Marks and Spencer suit and nasty dotted tie.

'Oh hi, Alex, what are you doing here?'

'Where's Clare?' I say.

'She's in the kitchen, but—'

I push past him, down the hall, through the lounge. Clare is sitting at the table in a dressing gown, the twins next to her in matching high chairs.

'You told me it wasn't serious,' I snarl. My voice is loud enough that both twins jerk upright and stare at me in astonishment. Clare turns round to see me.

'What—'

'Jody and Richard! You said it wasn't serious!'

'I know, I know. What's going on?'

'I've just seen him leaving our house.'

By now, Matt has made it to the kitchen too, followed by Tabitha.

'Alex,' he says quietly, 'I don't know what's going on, but—'

'Your wife fucking knows!' I yell. I don't mean to, but it's like a valve has ruptured and now there's no way to stop it.

239

'Alex,' he says again, but the tone is very different now. 'You can't burst in here and start swearing at Clare. What the hell is going on?'

Now Tabitha is crying, scared by this unexpected tableau of angry adults.

'You told me, you assured me, that nothing was going on, that it was a mistake. Well, that mistake spent the night with my wife in my fucking house.'

'I want you to leave,' says Matt.

He puts his hand on my shoulder, but I thrust it away.

'I mean it!' he says.

Clare rises up out of the chair.

'Alex, I have no idea what you saw, but it's *nothing* to do with me. And whatever Jody has or hasn't said to me, do you think barging in here and yelling at me in front of my children is the way to find out? What the hell is wrong with you?'

There is a moment of quiet. Tabitha puts her arms around her daddy's leg and whimpers softly. One of the twins bangs a plastic spoon on her seat tray.

'You're right, I'm sorry,' I say, and my voice is barely audible.

'Just get out,' says Matt. 'Or believe me, I will throw you out.'

I look at him, confused and astonished, and I know in that moment that I have done terrible harm. This lovable family man, my friend, is so full of protective rage he is almost unrecognisable.

I back away through the house, moving slowly and deliberately, as though in some sort of daze. Halfway through the chaotic sitting room I slip on a discarded comic, but manage to stay upright; Archie sees me and darts upstairs. Then I am outside and I hear the door slam behind me – a shockingly loud final slam – and I'm alone again. I don't dare look back. Instead, I walk to my car, get in and punch the steering wheel, hard, several times. When I see the door opening again, I turn the key, reverse quickly out of the driveway and veer into the road. On the other side of the street, a mum protectively holds her children back, yelling at me and pounding on the boot of the car. My mind instantly flashes back to that driver going too fast outside a school twenty years ago, and the terrible outcome of his thoughtlessness. Because this is the way things work. Eventually, inevitably, everything always ends up back there.

Chapter 25

Dan and I head to a little burrito place around the corner from his current workplace. The only seats available are a couple of ludicrously high stools facing the front window. We climb up on them and for a while we sit in silence, watching the traffic chug along Stokes Croft into the city centre. I try to mentally relive the day, to make some sense of everything that's happened, but it is too much of a tangled mess and all I can do is replay the highlights: Jody's kiss, Matt's anger. I feel the chill of panic, subtle but closing in fast, like some terrifying object caught in my peripheral vision – I cannot bear to look at it head on. The burrito wilts in my hands, its sloppy innards dripping back into the recycled cardboard container. Jody saw him to the door and kissed him goodbye. Where was Sam? Where was my boy? Will they take him from me?

Somewhere at the distant edge of my consciousness, I see Dan despondently prodding at his own meal, similarly lost. I should ask what's wrong, but I am too wrapped up in my own misery. We must be a sight to passers-by. In a minute, one of the staff will tap us on the shoulder and point to a sign that says *Please: no existential breakdowns in the window seats.*

Finally, I do turn to him.

'Are you OK?' I ask. 'Worried about work?'

'Huh? No, not work, something always comes up.'

'What then?'

'Do you think Emma is going to leave again?'

'I'd be surprised if she didn't,' I say. And I understand immediately that this is not what he wanted to hear.

'I wish she wouldn't,' he says, almost to himself.

And finally, about two decades late, it hits me.

'Dan.' I pause as he slowly turns to me. 'Are you in love with my sister?'

He takes a sip from his Diet Coke and stares out the window at the huge Banksy mural over the road.

'Yes, of course,' he says. 'I have been since I met her.'

'Why didn't you tell me?'

'Oh, mate, I tried. But, dude, you did not want to hear it.'

He's right. I've always been too wrapped up in my own drama to notice his. It would have been obvious to anyone else: for the last ten years he's Liked every single photo she's put on Facebook or Instagram; he's asked about her constantly. It was always him encouraging me to call her on Skype. And then she shows up at the flat and he's ecstatic – only for her to keep disappearing again. She always knew how to make an entrance, but she's even better at exits.

The door swings open and a young dad holds it so that his partner can struggle in with a pushchair. She negotiates the clutter of stools around the entrance, smiling and apologising. The dad beams at his daughter in the pushchair. They all head to the counter together, a happy group. Dan and I watch them as they pass, then revert to our cold, unappetising food.

'I'm sorry, Dan.'

'You had plenty on your mind. You still do, by the looks of things.'

'Yeah.'

'That woman? Isobel?'

'No. That was a mistake. I'm not ready to move on. But I think maybe Jody is. I saw Richard leaving her house early this morning.'

'Ah. Have you talked to her? Have you asked her what's going on?'

'Not yet.'

'Why not?'

'Because I don't want to hear the answer.'

'Hmm, I know that feeling.'

I'm eating dinner when I get the call. It's six o'clock, I'm watching the news, dripping noodles on to Dan's varnished oak-style floorboards. I check the caller ID on my phone. It's Jody.

'Hi, Jody. Sorry, I have a mouthful of noodles, hang on.'

But she's not listening.

'Alex, it's Sam.'

She sounds panicked. I slam the bowl down on the coffee table, and then I'm bolt upright on the sofa.

'What is it, what's happened?'

'It's that game, something has happened in that game.'

For a second I relax. It's not an accident. He's not in intensive care. And quickly I'm frustrated and a bit angry – if this is about the bloody game, why is she so upset? Jesus, she scared the life out of me.

'OK, calm down, what's happened? Has it crashed or something? It's fine. He won't—'

'No, it's not that. You know he's been making friends online, with Olivia's brother and his mates? Something happened. I think they've knocked his castle down. Alex, he's lying on the bed catatonic, he won't say anything, he's just staring. Alex, I'm scared.'

'I'm on my way.'

We've heard this sometimes happens. People with autism, when things get too much, far too much, they can switch off. It's a coping mechanism, a way of blocking out the world. Someone at one of our parent meetings said it was like a computer being switched off and rebooted. But it has never happened with Sam. Without even thinking, I'm in the car and on my way.

Time zips past. I remember once when Jody called me at work from Casualty – Sam had fallen off the arm of a chair, head first, on to the cold hard kitchen floor. I was in a mortgage meeting, but I ran out. In these situations, the world compresses around you, until it becomes a tunnel between you and your family. With Sam it has always been accentuated by the fact that he is upset by the slightest scratches, the smallest bumps – he fears pain so acutely. Other boys fall, get up and dust themselves down; for Sam a grazed knee is a major trauma. So to be in hospital, to be bleeding . . .

Then I am in our street and parked. I am at the front door. I am banging on it. Jody answers, looking stressed and confused.

'He's upstairs. I don't know what to do. Should I call a doctor?'

'Let me see.'

Up the steps, into his room. It is utterly silent. The game is on his screen, but all I can see is the mountain range in the distance on the opposite side of the plane from our castle. I look to the bed, and there is Sam, utterly folded into himself, facing the wall. His eyes are open and unmoving, his face is pale. His hands and legs, usually so fidgety and animated, now rigid, locked around his knees. The image drags me somewhere else, a horrifying memory. A boy switched off. I wrench it to the back of my mind.

'Sam? Sam, it's Daddy.'

Nothing, not even a twitch of recognition. For some reason, I put my hand on his forehead, the standard parental routine, I suppose. Check their temperature, get some Calpol. He's cool but not cold. I let my hand stay near his mouth and there's a quiet swell of relief when I feel his breath on my fingers.

'Sam, what happened?'

Jody is at the door now. Her hair tied back, her mascara smudged. She puts her hand on my shoulder, and I take hold of it for a second before self-consciously letting go.

We walk out into the hallway. The small window at the top of the stairs is open. I hear traffic passing in the street outside.

'What shall we do?' she says.

'I think we leave him for a bit, he has to get out of this himself. I'll sit with him, maybe. I can look at the game, see what's happened.'

'I've got missed calls from Olivia's mum. Maybe I can pop round and see if she knows what's happened. Are you sure we shouldn't call the doctor?'

'Let's see. I don't think so.'

'I'm scared.'

'I know.'

I go back into his room and sit on the edge of the bed. I put my hand on his back to let him know I am there, I am physically close, but that is all. I am close. His eyes are motionless as he blinks.

I turn to the game and pick up the controller.

As soon as I swivel around to face the castle, I can see what's happened. The building is all but gone. The perimeter fence mostly stands, but inside there's nothing but the ghostly shell of our construction. Two whole storeys are gone, the lower levels battered and blocky. The towers now resemble skeletal fingers

246

crookedly pointing at the sky. I notice that there are great chasms in the ground around the site. Whoever did this used TNT, the game's explosive blocks. They meant to obliterate it. I feel awful. I feel awful because I wasn't here to prevent it, or at least be with him when he found it. I wasn't here.

'Oh, Sam,' I say. No response. 'Sam, we can build it again. We can do it. You're a great builder.'

Unsure of what to do, I start clearing the ground around the castle, filling in the holes with earth. I realise I need tools, so head into the wreckage to see if the storage chests are still there. They aren't, but some of our stuff is still lying around: pickaxes, food, hoes, a few loaves of bread. Not much left. Not much for weeks of work. Work we did together. Then I remember the Crown Jewels, hidden in our secret chest. I rush through to the other room, and dig frantically at the one different floor tile. The chest is still there, untouched, its contents safe.

I hear the front door open and then quietly shut. Jody tiptoes up the steps to the room.

'I've spoken to Olivia's mum,' she says. 'Apparently, Sam accepted friend requests from Olivia's brother Harry and his friends, and invited them to play. I think Harry left them for a while – they were all being a bit boisterous and they planted some bombs or something. She says they thought it was Harry's castle. He's very upset, apparently. He wants to come over and apologise.'

'I don't think that's a good idea for a while.'

'Olivia is upset too.'

'It's not her fault.'

'Has he said anything?'

'No. I feel totally responsible, Jody. I built this whole thing up as a big project for us and now ... I feel like this is my fault. I was pinning so much on it.'

247

'It's not your fault. He loves this game, it's all he talks about. It's been fine until now. I saw him playing with you online. He loves it.'

We sit in silence on the bed with our son, lost in our thoughts. Here we are in this tiny room with its broken toys and tattered posters, a family together, but somehow a long way apart; whole galaxies apart. I want to say something, but nothing comes, nothing restorative or hopeful or gently funny. Nothing at all.

Then, after half an hour or maybe longer:

'Switch the game off.'

'Huh? Sam?' I say.

'Switch it off,' he repeats.

Jody goes to hug him but he clenches tighter around himself. Momentarily I'm somehow reminded of that scene in *Alien*, where they bring John Hurt back from the alien spaceship with the Facehugger attached to him – and when they try to remove it, the camera focuses on its tail, tightening silently around Hurt's neck. Jody draws her hand away.

'I'll save it,' I say.

'Switch it off,' he says again. 'I don't care. I don't care.'

'But—' I start.

'I don't want it. I don't want to play ever again.'

'But Sam, we can fix it.'

'I don't want to. They came and ruined it and it was mine. People ruin everything.'

We hear a noise downstairs. We wonder if it's Olivia, coming to apologise. But it's Emma.

'Hello?' she shouts up.

'Up here,' calls Jody.

She traipses up the stairs and hovers in the doorway.

'Dan told me something had happened with Sam. I was passing so thought I'd drop in. Is everything OK? Hi, Sam.'

'His game got broken by some other boys,' says Jody.

'Oh no,' says Emma with theatrical horror. Her presence, brash and loud, is almost unbearably intrusive, but it breaks the spell of the afternoon. Sam struggles, unlocking his arms from his legs.

'I never want to play again,' he says.

'Boys are horrible,' agrees Emma. 'Not you, obviously, but most other boys. I stay clear of them as much as I can. They always ruin everything, don't they?'

Sam nods, grimly. But he is in no mood to be jollied along. He sinks back on to the bed and closes his eyes.

'The Crown Jewels are safe,' I tell him.

'I don't care,' is his response.

Later that night, I'm sitting on the cheap single bed in my little spare room in Dan's flat. There's nothing here, nothing of me or my life, just a pile of clothes and a photo, propped up against Dan's computer – the photo of the café, and me and George smiling, the world ahead of us, or so we thought.

But he had no time left, and now I'm here alone again. It's funny how misery takes you straight back, connecting the dots through your life – the memories tumble out like sad photographs from a battered old album. I thought I'd found somewhere safe for Sam and me, but I was wrong. What can I ever do for him when I'm here and he's there? What he needs is stability, and I can't create that for him out of stone blocks and treasure chests that only exist on a screen. I certainly can't create it for him if I have none of my own. Nothing is safe – that is something useful I have learned. It's a lesson every parent wants to hold off for as long as possible. But if you leave it too long, life has a way of illustrating it anyway.

Chapter 26

The only sound is the large clock on the office wall, its loud tick-tock reverberating around the room, underlining the awkward silence between the four of us. On one side of the vast oak desk is the headmaster of Sam's current school, a balding, sombre-looking man in an unnecessarily severe black suit, his remaining hair shaved into a close buzz cut. Next to him, the local education authority's special needs adviser, Jan Parker, a razor-thin, hawkish woman in her sixties, beadily eyeing up Jody and me as we sit together – but also apart – on the other side of the oak expanse.

No one is talking. The headmaster, Mr Jones, has a letter in front of him. We sent it to him last week, or Jody did, giving him notice that we would be sending Sam to a new school. His eyes shift from the single A4 page to us and back again.

'I understand your concerns, but I'm not sure that moving him is the best solution,' he says at last.

'I've been to visit him on several occasions,' continues Jan as she leafs through a large dossier on her lap. 'He is making progress in maths and literacy, he's—'

'He's unhappy,' says Jody.

'Lots of children are unhappy at school,' says Mr Jones, in a weird conciliatory tone that sounds almost like a scoff.

'So that's OK then?' she says.

'No, of course not, I—'

'We're not sure that moving him will prove any more conducive to his well-being. He'll have to fit into a new regime, with new children,' says Jan.

We know that we need to provide a united front, we need to work together. But after everything that's happened, we don't have it in us – we can't even pretend. Instead of me picking up Jody this morning and the two of us walking in together, she texted and said she'd make her own way. We barely spoke as we sat in the reception area, terrified that Sam would come out of a classroom and see us, sparking off some sort of breakdown. And now we're sitting here like naughty children, waiting for their telling-off to end.

'Perhaps the new children won't bully him,' I say. 'Perhaps they'll take that sort of thing more seriously at the Avon School.'

'We've looked into the situation with the other boy,' says Jones, tapping his pen against the table. 'We believe it's been dealt with.'

'And to be honest, it's very unlikely you'll get a place at the Avon School. It's very highly oversubscribed and you'll need a statement on Sam's autism.'

'From you?' says Jody.

'I'll be involved in the process.'

'The process?' I butt in. 'This is a child we're talking about. We're not bringing our car in for an MOT.'

'What about the other school? St Peter's? They have space available,' says Jody.

'But this won't deal with the fundamental issue,' replies Jan. 'He has to learn how to make friends, how to socialise with people his own age. That won't be solved by you moving him around. I think this is a problem that you, as parents, need to step back from. This is something Sam has to find, in an environment that he knows, and where he feels secure.'

Silence.

It feels as though the room is closing in on us, as though the walls themselves want to usher us out and away. I'm so tired of feeling like this – helpless, directionless, buffeted from one seemingly unnavigable crisis to another, like a boat lost way out at sea and now subject to the whims of the crushing waves. But I am beginning to realise something. If I am not the one to help Sam, if this is something I can't do, then I need him to be with people who can.

'So, why don't we stick it out until the end of the year, see how it goes,' says Mr Jones, picking up the letter and symbolically dropping it into a tray of papers on the far right of his desk, as if to say: this meeting is over, you've been told.

Jody shrugs and looks at me; she's biting her lower lip and I know what it means – she's close to tears and trying to hold herself together.

I turn to Mr Jones.

'No, we're not waiting until the end of the year. We're moving him out of this school as soon as we can. You said that sometimes children are unhappy – believe me, we know that. But when we went to see St Peter's, they said that Sam would be happy there. They made it sound like that was the most important thing – the thing they had to get right. As for the other school, we'll fight for it if we have to. If that's what he wants. We'll fight for it. We'll make a bloody fuss. If we can't help him ourselves, we'll get him somewhere that can. *That's* what is going to happen. Goodbye.'

I stand up and, completely unconsciously, I hold my hand out toward Jody – an automatic gesture of unity. For a second, somehow, a part of my brain thinks I'm shepherding Sam over a busy road. Self-consciously, I start to move it away, but surprisingly, Jody takes it and then she is standing too. We walk out of the room as we entered it – in awkward, uncertain silence. The sound of the clock fades as we shut the office door behind us.

'What now?' she says, and I see the glistening in her eyes, followed by a tear, then another.

'Well, we'll see what Sam says and we'll go from there. They can't—'

'No, not Sam this time. Us, Alex. What now for *us*?'

I see the receptionist nearby at her desk, trying to look busy, tapping away at a keyboard, clearly listening in to this juicy drama playing out in front of her. I feel, in that moment, such a helpless nihilistic rage. I want to be out, out of this place, out of this situation.

'I feel like you've made your choice,' I spit, seeing the image of Richard that morning, the kiss.

I start to walk out, determined not to look back.

'You're taking Sam tonight, aren't you?' she cries.

'No, I'm busy.'

I want to say 'Get Richard to do it' but, as reckless as I feel, I can't bring myself to acknowledge him, to confirm his existence in our lives by mentioning him out loud.

'Alex!' she shouts.

But I am gone. So gone. Out of the building, along the side of a classroom, and then into the street. I am running, sprinting, through the alley along the outer edge of the school's small playing field. I used to run home from school like this, almost every day after George died. I'd bolt out as fast as I could and keep going until I was almost sick. I needed to create distance between the accident and me. But sometimes, you can't get enough distance however hard you try. All the things you care about in your life, even the things that hurt, they have a gravitational pull. If you do manage to break free, it's over. You're floating in space. You'll never get back.

'Jody,' I mutter to myself. And as I burst out of the alley, I stop, my hands on my knees like I'm about to retch. I'm on a quiet street, a row of little Victorian houses, identical to the road where I lived with Jody and Sam. I stagger back and sit on a low brick wall surrounding someone's well-maintained garden. I'm not exactly sure where I am.

Later that night, I'm in Dan's living room with the lights off, no one else at home. Almost asleep, a bottle of cheap red wine empty beside me, I jerk forward on the sofa and switch on the Xbox. The screen lights the walls in a weird green hue that makes me feel momentarily queasy. I click on the *Minecraft* icon and sway gently on the sofa as the game loads. To my surprise, when I select 'join' I see Sam and Daddy's World available. It's midnight, he can't possibly be there. He must have left the machine running. I hit the button.

It is early morning but the sky is a flat grey, and the rain is pouring down. Beyond the sound of the rain, I hear only the baying of nearby cattle – for some reason there's no music. I walk over the plain toward the castle, half hoping, half expecting to find it whole again. But no, it is still a ruin, the remaining stones black against the storm.

Then I notice a shape, a few hundred yards ahead, where the farm used to be. I walk forward, slowly at first, thinking it could be a zombie or some other monster. But it's not moving, and when I am closer still, I know what it is. It's Sam. Utterly motionless, facing what's left of the castle. He looks like some destitute lord after a bitter siege, surveying his ancestral home, now wrecked and lost.

I know that Sam can't be playing, surely not, but I pick up the headset anyway and plug it in.

'Sam?' I say.

But the figure is perfectly still, its gaze locked toward the fallen towers.

I turn away quickly, realising that somehow I am frightened by this wraith-like vision.

And that's when I see it.

A figure in orange withdrawing into a copse of birch trees, barely visible beyond the sheets of incessant rain. Instinctively, I give chase, leaping up on to a narrow ridge of blocks, skirting the trees, chopping away at leaves and branches, ducking and leaping over obstacles. As I reach clearer land, the rain seems to be easing off, the deafening roar becoming quieter. But as I make it through the last few trees and the world opens up, I see nothing but a lunar wasteland of rock, leading down to the edge of a large lake. Whoever it was could easily have doubled back through the woods, or veered off toward the mountain range. If there was ever anybody there at all. My head nods involuntarily forward, the wine and exhaustion blurring my vision. I think about heading back to Sam, but I cannot face that lonely shape, even as the sun shines and a bright blue tint edges across the sky.

I close my eyes and when I open them with a start, I'm somewhere else in the world and I don't know how I got there. I try to get up off the sofa but fall backwards. There are specks of red wine on my T-shirt and the corners of my mouth are dry and crusted.

I switch the machine off and curl up on the overstuffed cushions. My phone rings then beeps – a missed call from Mum, the third this week.

I can't face anyone right now.

Chapter 27

The next Saturday, Jody is at some gallery event for the afternoon. Unable to conjure an excuse and heavy with guilt, I tell her that of course I can have Sam. She brings him over to Dan's after lunch, and tells me I need to get him to Olivia's for 4 p.m. They have a 'play date'. He's brought a backpack filled with books and action figures, but he looks tired and cautious as Jody hugs him and nudges him toward me. It has the feel of a tense hostage exchange. I watch her drive off and then gently pull Sam through the automatic doors into the apartment building, out of the numbing cold. I kiss him on the top of his head, his messy hair smelling faintly of Johnson's Baby Bath.

Emma and Dan are at the Old Ship, so we're in the flat alone. For a while we sit together on the sofa, looking through his books; I find the London one, but he skips past the photo of the Tower of London. Then I suggest that we load up Flight Track and watch planes flying overhead. For a second he's enthused, leaping off the sofa and running to the window – but then we see that the sky is a thick broth of grey and black cloud. I try to make up a story with the action figures, but my mind is wandering: is Jody with Richard now? When is she going to tell me? I feel like I'm in some sort of limbo, caught between two planes of existence – my old life with Jody and Sam, and whatever is coming next.

'What do you want to do now?' I ask. 'Hey, maybe we could put on *Minecraft*, get some practice in for the competition? It's not too late.'

'No, I'm not doing it!' he yells. I decide it's probably best not to push it.

'What else then?'

'I don't know. Where is Auntie Emma?'

'She's at the pub.'

'Where is the pub?'

'It's down the road.'

'What is she doing?'

'Probably getting drunk with Dan.'

'Can we go and see Auntie Emma and Dan?'

And for some reason that seems like an acceptable plan.

The Old Ship is relatively busy as we bundle in through the narrow, battered old door – and by busy I mean some of the tables have people sitting at them. There is an old couple leafing through the *Daily Mail* and a small group of workmen in high-visibility vests, clearly on a break from the latest building site down the road. I see Sid at his usual table, the chessboard out, the half-pint of Guinness at his side. Then there's Dan and Emma in a corner near the window, empty pint glasses and crisp packets littering their table. They are slumped in toward each other. I put my arm around Sam and wonder if this was such a sensible idea after all.

'Sam!' shouts Emma. She struggles to her feet and runs over. Sam ducks in toward me but she swoops at him, clasping him around his waist and kissing his forehead, leaving a visible lipstick mark. He buries his head in my chest, but he's smiling. Dan is standing up now, motioning toward me.

'Drink?' he asks.

'Two Cokes,' I say.

As Dan heads to the bar, I see one of the workmen, thickset but amiable-looking, trudging over to Sid, pint glass in hand.

'I'll give you a game,' he says, sloshing his glass down on to the table.

But, as ever, Sid lurches away, then bows his head and shakes it slowly. The workman shrugs, picks his glass up and looks at his colleague, mouthing 'nutter' and twirling his finger at his temple. Emma takes Sam back to the table and settles him down on the seat next to her. I take the rickety wooden stool opposite them, sitting down cautiously.

'So what are you two talking about?' I ask.

'Oh, you know,' says Emma, wafting her drink around with the carefree manner of someone who has very much parted company with sobriety. 'Old times ...'

'Uh-oh,' I say.

'Uh-oh, uh-oh,' repeats Sam.

When Dan delivers the drinks he brings another three bags of crisps, which he clumsily splits open and lays out on the table in the traditional pub manner. Sam immediately grabs a huge handful.

'Hey,' I say. 'We're sharing!'

'It's OK,' says Dan.

I try to start a conversation with Emma about her current life plans but it's clear I'm not going to get any sense out of her, so instead I glare at the grubby TV in the corner, showing the football scores. It makes me wonder about Matt and Clare and how they're getting on. In the background I hear Dan trying to strike up a conversation with Sam. This should be good.

'Hey, Sam, so what are you into at the moment? Do you still like planes?'

Sam nods self-consciously, his mouth still full of crisps.

'Do you like computers?'

He nods again.

'Do you think you'll be a programmer when you grow up?'

'A pilot or an artiteck,' says Sam. 'What job is it that you do?'

I look up, fascinated that somehow Sam is asking a question, unprompted and seemingly interested. I have clearly been doing this wrong for eight years – it seems I needed to have been slightly drunk the whole time.

'I design things on my computer. I design websites and posters and magazines. Sometimes I make music too. I make things on a big screen.'

'Like building,' says Sam. 'But with flat shapes.'

'Yeah,' says Dan. 'Shapes and colours. The important things are knowing which shapes are best together and which colours are best together.'

'If you put them together wrong, it's sad to look at,' says Sam.

Dan sits forward.

'Exactly!' he says. 'Design is about creating a response in someone. If you use the shapes and colours in a certain way, you can make them feel different things – it almost doesn't matter what the words are or what the photos on the page are showing.'

'Words aren't more important than shapes, words are just shapes too.'

'Sometimes I look out the window at the city, and it's all ... it hasn't been properly designed. It's a mess.'

'People are shapes and colours. They don't know it, but they are.'

'That's it! That's it exactly! Everything is about design. Every person – the way they dress, the way they talk – is a kind of layout.'

'Some people are a messy layout!'

And with that, they both start laughing. Emma and I stare at them, and then at each other.

'What the hell was that all about?' she says.

Dan puts up his hand and Sam eagerly high-fives him.

Behind us, the workman who wanted to play chess is now at the CD jukebox, eyeing up the dated selection of tracks. He puts in some money and taps out a couple of selections. He's returning to his seat when Frank Sinatra's 'My Way' begins to play.

'Hey, I didn't choose this,' he says to the landlord.

'Yeah, all the discs fell out when I was fixing it a couple of years ago, mate – it's a lucky dip now. Like pressing shuffle.'

The workmen all look at each other with barely concealed smirks. They'll be telling everyone to avoid this weird little place when they get back to the site.

As the first verse of the song starts, Dan decides to sing along in a ridiculous baritone.

'Regrets, I've had a few ...'

Sam puts his hands over his ears and Emma quickly does the same – followed by Dan himself, much to Sam's amusement.

'I have three regrets,' slurs Dan. Emma, almost imperceptibly, glances up. 'I regret asking for an N64 for Christmas in 1996 instead of a PlayStation; I regret not going to university – art college was for wankers; and I regret that time I saw a pristine copy of Radiohead's *Drill* EP in a charity shop for 50p and I didn't buy it. That's all.'

He lifts his pint and takes a long drink.

'Alex?' he says.

'What?'

'Regrets?'

I do not want to get into this now, on a Saturday afternoon, with Sam beside me and everyone else sloshed.

'Oh God, Dan, how long have you got?'

'Until closing time, I guess.'

'Then we don't have time. Emma?'

She sways as she's thinking. Sam gets up and wanders toward the gambling machine near Sid. I'm focused on what she's about to say.

'Well, there's the whole *Lion King* drama.' She shrugs. 'The week George died, Mum was supposed to take me to the cinema to see it. All my friends had been already, everyone was talking about it. I wanted to be part of that. But we never went. I couldn't let it go, I don't know why. I got so angry with Mum. I regret being horrible and spoiled. I *still* haven't seen it.'

She suddenly jerks up, as though aware that she's said too much, and laughs self-consciously.

'And ... um ... ' she says, in a brighter tone. 'Oh, I really regret not going to South America – Brazil, Argentina, Peru. I wanted to, but somehow I didn't make it. I ought to, I ought to go.'

She slaps her hand down on the table then picks up her phone, theatrically.

'I'm going to search for flights,' she declares. 'Fuck it.'

'Seriously?' says Dan, his voice faltering.

Behind his eyes, there is something that has never been there before – dread. Real dread, flickering into existence and then expertly subdued. He smiles and cradles his pint, seemingly examining the contents of the glass. I look at Emma's phone and see a missed call. I know the number. It's Mum's. Before I can point it out, Emma has brought up the web browser and she's tapping 'flights to Brazil' into the search engine.

That's when I notice something happening at the other side

of the room, something quite unbelievable. I need someone else to look over as well, to confirm it's actually happening. I glare at Dan, who switches his attention from Emma to me, and I gesture toward the other corner of the pub. He turns around slowly and his mouth drops.

Sam is sitting with Sid and they are playing chess.

The duo are perfectly silent, Sid looking down at the table, Sam out of the small window at his side. They make their moves quickly and quietly, taking it in turns to study the board.

We're not the only ones who have noticed. The barman is standing with a pint glass and a tea towel in his hand, motionless, dumbly watching. And now, at last, there's something I notice about Sid – while he's thinking, he taps at his ear in a constant, almost rhythmic motion. And duh, I know what this is, I know what's going on, I'm kind of amazed I never realised it before. He's autistic. Of course he is. That tapping – I've been reading about the way that people on the autism spectrum often self-stimulate, flapping their arms, making repetitive vocal sounds, or touching their faces. I'd just always associated autism with children. How stupid. This poor man, he's probably been stigmatised his whole life. And to think, Jody and I were pissed off that it took the education authority two years to diagnose Sam. No one ever diagnosed this guy.

'Ah,' says Dan, at last. 'He wants people to play with, but he doesn't want them to talk.'

'I can sympathise with that,' says Emma.

The game only lasts for about five minutes. Sid is far too good. Within twenty moves he has taken Sam's rooks, a knight and the queen. Eventually, Sam lays down his king, then, still in silence, the two of them set the pieces back to their start positions. Sam gets up and walks over, grabs a handful of crisps and sits back down with us. Dan and I are still staring at him.

'What?' he says, his mouth full, his voice muffled. '*What?*'

'OK,' I say. 'Let's go and see Olivia.'

On the walk back to the flat, the wind behind us, nudging us along the slick wet pavement, Sam is bright and chatty. He seems more upbeat than I've seen him since the whole *Minecraft* apocalypse.

'Is Auntie Emma going on a plane again?'

'It looks like it.'

'Can I go?'

'No.'

'Why not?'

'Because she's not coming back.'

'Why is she going?'

'She gets frustrated here, I think.'

'Do you get frustrated here?'

'Ha, sometimes.'

'Are you going on a plane?'

'No.'

'Why?'

'Because I have you and Mummy, and I'd miss you.'

He thinks about this as we turn on to Dan's street and see the weirdly artificial apartment complexes set back from the road, each with its own neatly rectangular parking zone. It strikes me that the developers have simply replaced one industrial estate with another, but these new warehouses store humans rather than goods. I suddenly feel like I need to get out of here as soon as possible.

'Why did Emma come back?' says Sam.

It takes me a while to jolt out of my mode of thinking and register his question.

'What do you mean?'

'If she likes to go on planes and be in new places, why did she come back?'

'I don't know. I thought maybe she wanted to see Grandma, but that's not it. I suppose she came back to find something out, and now she knows the answer, she can go.'

'I don't understand what that means.'

'Neither do I, Sam.'

We reach Dan's building, walk down to the car park and climb into our old estate car, an embarrassing anomaly beside the shining BMWs, Audis, Mini Coopers, and Dan's gleaming Porsche. It is the same story when we pull up at Olivia's, behind the family Range Rover, which towers above us as we climb out. I can't help but notice their car doesn't have mildew growing around the windows.

As soon as Sam rings the doorbell, Olivia is there, swinging open the door to greet him.

'Sam,' she screams. 'Come up!'

They disappear into the house and, unsure of the correct etiquette, I amble up the short path to the vast wooden door and peek in.

'Hi,' says Prudence from the hallway, looking as authoritarian as ever, in a dark green tweed blazer and polo-neck jumper. 'Come in!'

Begrudgingly, I walk into the hallway, past the wide staircase and an oak sideboard, which, in our house, would be covered in keys, unopened mail and unwashed mugs, but here is spotlessly tidy, with two very expensive-looking vases. The floor is varnished oak. The walls are painted in a classic Farrow & Ball olive.

'Would you like some tea?' asks Prudence.

I definitely don't. I want to leave as quickly as possible without breaking anything, spilling anything or, worse, having to make small talk with her husband, a Cambridge-educated classical composer who, according to Jody, looks like Doc Brown from *Back to the Future*, only more eccentric. I hear some running around upstairs, then the sound of children jumping on a bed.

'I'm OK,' I say. 'I'd better get off, if that's all right?'

'Yes, I'm sure that's fine,' she says, with what I read as relief. 'Sorry, it's a bit chaotic here – we've had the builders in, extending the kitchen at the back. Such a mess.'

I look around, and then through the hallway to the kitchen. There is absolutely no evidence of builders or mess.

Just then I hear Sam shout, 'NO, I DON'T WANT TO,' and then there is a loud, high-pitched scream. I look at Prudence and she looks at me, her face a grotesque mask of alarm. I turn to head up the stairs, but she pushes by and is bounding up the steps. At the top is Olivia's brother, Harry.

'Sam threw a controller at Olivia!' he shouts.

Then Olivia sheepishly walks out of one room, her hand on her head. When she removes it, there is blood streaking her dark, neatly combed hair.

'It's OK, Mummy,' she says quietly.

'Olivia!' cries Prudence.

'Sam!' I shout.

He is inside a bedroom – Olivia's, judging by the dolls littering the floor and a poster of One Direction on the wall. At the end of the large iron bed is a flat-screen TV and on the screen is *Minecraft*. Sam is on the bed, curled up in a ball, his head hidden behind protective arms.

'Sam, what the hell did you do?'

'She wanted me to play *Minecraft*, but I don't want to, I don't want to! Because HE broke my castle! And it is not my place any more.'

I'm not listening. I grab him off the bed, he tries to cling on to the sheets but I rip them from his hand.

'Come and say sorry.'

I yank him out of the room, and see Olivia and her mum in the bathroom. Prudence is holding a wet cloth to her daughter's head, stroking her hair.

'I'm so sorry,' I say. 'Is she OK?'

'She has a nasty cut,' replies Prudence in an almost childishly accusatory tone.

'Say sorry,' I demand from Sam.

But he is limp and dejected and has begun to sob.

'OK, maybe I should take him home,' I say.

'No,' says Olivia. 'It was an accident. He didn't mean to hit me. No, Mummy.'

But Prudence looks up with barely contained protective fury.

'I think that would be best,' she spits.

'Come on,' I say. And partly I know I should be protective too. He threw the controller out of frustration, I expect, he wouldn't have meant to hit her. But I'm stressed, angry and embarrassed – and pumped full of gurgling adrenalin. That familiar blinding maelstrom of emotions. The same old scene.

And now I take his arm and go, half guiding, half dragging him down the stairs behind me. We're through the door and on to the street. 'YOU MESS UP EVERYTHING! FUCK!' I shout horribly, forcefully. The cold hits me, but I'm barely aware – I zone in on the car. I fling open the passenger door and cram him in, then slam it and storm to the other side. When I get in, still furious, still filled with malice, I look across at him, ready to unleash yet more fury. But instead, everything stops. I see him struggling with the seat belt, his hands shaking as they pull at the jammed material. And my heart breaks. I'm engulfed with guilt. It crashes in through my senses like floodwater.

'I wanted one visit that didn't end like this,' I say quietly, mostly to myself. 'Just one. Do you understand, Sam?'

'I'm hungry,' he says.

'I know, but do you understand why Daddy gets so upset?'

'Where's Mummy?'

'I don't know, Sam. I don't know.'

When we get to Dan's, I park up and as soon as the engine is off, I turn and touch Sam on the shoulder. Sometimes he flinches when I do that but this time he lifts his arm and puts his hand on mine.

'I'm sorry,' I say. 'I'm sorry I shouted and said a naughty word.'

'You said the F word. I think that's the naughtiest. It is naughtier than poo or wee.'

'I know, I know. I'm sorry. I love you, Sam.'

We sit in the car a moment longer.

'I'm hungry,' he says.

Chapter 28

That night, Sam stays with me at Dan's. I make him a little bed on the floor next to mine, using cushions and sleeping bags and duvets. For a while, I lie down with him and we look at the flight app, tracing the paths of random planes across the globe.

'Hey, your entry ticket has arrived for the *Minecraft* tournament,' I tell him. 'Do you want to see it?'

It is a pathetically hopeful gambit – a last-ditch attempt to ignite any sort of interest. He shakes his head and goes back to the app.

'The maximum passenger capacity for a Boeing 747 is six hundred and sixty people,' he says.

Maybe this isn't the right time. Maybe it is over.

The next morning I drive him back home, where I get to indulge in another crushingly awkward wordless exchange with Jody. Eventually I suspect, these handovers will evolve into the sort of exchanges you see in Hollywood spy movies – we'll be meeting in underground car parks or remote country estates.

'Do you have the child?'

'Yes, are you alone?'

'Yes.'

'Have you brought the money in unmarked non-sequential bills?'

Instead of heading straight back to the flat, I decide to take a drive through the quiet morning streets. I head over the vast Bedminster Bridge roundabout with its confusing mass of lanes and exits, and follow the river, past Temple Meads station to Totterdown. There's a pub here that Dan and I used to go to, with strip lighting and lino on the floors, but a brilliant jukebox filled with old punk and reggae singles. It's all flats now. It makes me think of the café – our café – probably soon to meet a similar fate, subsumed into the unquenchable property boom.

It's amazing how little control we have over our own lives, when you think about it. In theory, I could keep driving, back into the city, then up the M32, the M5, the M6. I could be in Scotland by the evening. But obviously that won't happen. Family, responsibilities, fear, the awful reality of service station food. The easiest thing is to accept your role as a passenger, staring out of the window at the rolling scenery. The years pass like traffic.

I decide to head back toward Bedminster, through the snaking Victorian streets, the cars parked densely on either side so that you have to crawl along, praying that you don't meet a vehicle coming the other way. I feel I need to take decisive action on something. Anything. I glance at my phone on the seat beside me and see another missed call from Mum. I realise that this is it. I need to get her and Emma together. I need to invite her up to Bristol, get them in a room, get them to talk to each other – sort out whatever it is. Once and for all. Maybe that's something I can fix, if nothing else.

Back at the flat, I find Emma lounging on the sofa, an iPad on her lap, music blaring from Dan's Bluetooth speakers. As soon as she sees me, she launches herself at the remote control and turns the noise right down, and then off. On the floor are piles of her clothes, seemingly sorted into type: skirts, jeans, tops, dresses. She looks as though she has been caught doing something she shouldn't.

'Hi, Alex,' she says. 'How are you? What have you been up to?'

'I took Sam home and then went for a bit of a drive,' I say, trying to gauge her mood.

'Oh nice,' she says.

There is such a strange atmosphere. I hear the buzz of the fridge, the distant sound of a television in another flat somewhere above us.

'I was thinking,' I say. 'Maybe I could get Mum to come up to Bristol, perhaps in the New Year – put her in a nice hotel, show her round the city again. It would give you two time to talk, maybe?'

'Oh,' she says.

'What?'

'Alex . . .'

We hear the front door open and close. It is Dan, dressed in a huge parka and skinny jeans, with a plastic bag full of breakfast supplies.

'You're just in time, dude,' he says. 'Bacon butties and tea.'

But I'm not listening.

'What, Emma?' I say. 'What is it?'

Dan stands uselessly in the entrance to the sitting room, quickly understanding that he has walked into something unusual.

'I've booked a flight to Rio,' she says. 'I'm leaving in three weeks. Then I'm going on to Peru, then into Mexico. Then I don't know.'

'You're leaving?' says Dan, his voice almost childlike in its uncomprehending shock.

'Yes,' she says. 'Sorry, I should have said. I don't feel like I belong here.'

'Because you've given it all of three months,' I say.

'Alex . . .'

'What the hell, Emma?' I say.

Dan puts the plastic bag down on to the kitchen work surface and slowly takes off his coat. He looks around the room as though he has lost something and then walks out.

'What about Mum?' I say. 'Don't you think you should at least see her?'

'Why, Alex?'

'Why? Because you've barely spoken to her for eight years! Liking her fucking photographs on Facebook doesn't count!'

'I know! I know that! But I can't face her.'

She swivels around on the sofa and looks away from me, out of the window. Another escape. I move forward, standing right next to her now.

'Emma, what the hell is going on? Why won't you speak to her? Why won't you see her?'

Suddenly, she turns right back to me, her face has reddened, there is a flash of anger or hurt in her eyes.

'Because something happened to me, Alex!' She takes a moment to calm herself, to regain her casual composure, before beginning again. 'Last year I met this guy. It was a fling, nothing serious. But we took a stupid risk and, of course, my period was late – and then it was *really* late. I took a pregnancy test, and I was like, shit, what now? I was in a sort of daze for two weeks, I didn't know what to think or do . . . But the decision was made for me in the end. I had a miscarriage. It should have been a huge relief. I mean, I was living in a beach hut, for God's sake. I went to hospital and they checked me out and I told them it was for the best and I was fine. But then I went home and cried for two days. All I wanted was Mum. I wanted my mum to look after me. It made me think about everything she'd been through, and I felt so awful for leaving, so selfish. I had no idea. I had no idea about anything. I had to come home, to see her, to apologise for disappearing and making things harder. But now I'm here, I can't face it.'

'Why not? She'll understand. She won't be cross with you for not coming home more.'

'Oh, Alex, it's not that.'

'What is it then? Why is it so hard?'

'Because I know what will happen. Awkward chit-chat and skirting around everything, like we've done for twenty fucking years! I want her to talk to me! But nobody talks about anything in this family, or what's bloody left of it.'

With that, she gets up and marches toward the front door, just as Dan is emerging along the hallway. It's obvious he's heard everything. Stuck in her path, his expression is one of horror and surprise, as though he's just been wrongly identified in a police line-up. He doesn't know whether to move or stop her; his mouth goes through the motions of speaking but nothing comes out. Instead, he steps aside wordlessly as she passes – and then she turns back.

'No one says anything!' she cries.

She shakes her head and rips open the door, thrusting it shut behind her with such force that the whole building seems to quake.

Dan and I stand motionless, staring at each other, goggle-eyed.

'She had a miscarriage,' I say, shaking my head. 'She's had this whole life we know nothing about.'

I sink down on to the sofa again. Dan comes over and slumps next to me. We sit like this for a long time.

'I should have told her how I felt … how I feel,' he says. 'I'm such a twat. I wrote her a letter before she first went away. I sat up all night and wrote her a letter on my computer, asking her not

272

to go. All the stuff I couldn't tell her to her face. I didn't want her to laugh at me. So I poured out my heart into that letter – I even spellchecked it. Then I printed it out, put it in an envelope, stuck a stamp on the front. But I didn't send it. I thought that, beside everything else going on in her life, this wasn't important. What right did I have to tell her how I felt? What did it matter? It's the same thing now.'

I turn to him slowly.

'It mattered, you idiot,' I tell him. 'It still does. If there's anyone who can get through to her it's you. Jesus, we've got to stop being passengers in this life. We've got to – I don't know – we've got to drag the driver out, punch him in the face and steal the car.'

He thinks about this for a second, then puts his arm around my shoulder.

'I shouldn't have let you play *Grand Theft Auto*,' he says.

Chapter 29

It is already dark when I pick up Sam from school. We don't say much on the way home – robbed of *Minecraft*, I'm back to the old conversational gambits: 'How was your day?' 'Did anything happen?' 'Was everyone kind?' – all ignored or batted back at me. I know that Sam reacts to our moods, becoming edgy and more aloof, even when he doesn't understand what's going on – especially when he doesn't understand what's going on. Sometimes, since Sam's diagnosis, I have wondered if *I'm* on the spectrum – maybe that's why I've never been able to deal with George, or anything else for that matter. When we reach the house we trudge upstairs to his room and sit on the bed, glum and separate.

But I realise, quite suddenly, that I'm not prepared to go backwards. I won't settle for this. All the hours we spent together in that game, sharing the same adventure, they meant something. They changed us. I know something about him now, something true and important. He's clever and creative and resourceful. We've both come too far to slip back into the old routines.

So I pick the Xbox controller up off the floor and switch the console on. Maybe I can't get Sam interested in another building project, but I figure that if I play right in front of him, he will be possessive enough about his things that he'll take some interest.

The game loads up. I find Sam and Daddy's World on the menu and select it. As the hard drive whirrs inside the machine, I recall the day we created this file, this whole universe – how excited and connected we were. I look up but his head is hidden behind the large hardback book, so I turn to the screen, a new determination growing in me.

Everything is deceptively calm. The piano music, slow and deliberate, sets its peaceful tone. The sun is up, and along the ridge of the hills I see sheep gathering in clusters. In front of me is the wreck of the castle, looking more pathetic than ever, the jagged foundations almost lost amid the grass like some ancient ruined abbey. I could try to construct it again, but it would take many hours and the building itself is so obviously not the point. What else? What else can I try?

And then, as I'm walking down to the base of the front wall to check the old treasure chest, a message pops up on screen. Olivia has joined the game. I can't see her at first, but then she wanders over from a clump of damaged trees. I'm not wearing the headphones so her voice is clear and loud through the television speaker.

'Sam?'

I look over to him again, allowing myself a small spark of hope, but again, there is no response. I shrug and turn back.

'No,' I say. 'It's Sam's dad. Hi, Olivia.'

'Oh, hi.'

She walks past me to the ruin and looks up, then across as though carrying out an informal survey.

'Is Sam with you?' she asks.

'Yes, but he's reading a book.'

'We've been waiting for him for ages.'

'Oh, that's a shame. He doesn't want to play any more, I'm afraid.'

'We want to say sorry.'

'I know, that's very kind of you, Olivia. He knows it's not your fault. But I'll tell him.'

'No,' she says. 'We don't want to tell him, we want to show him.'

And then I see another name pop up on screen, a boy's name. Sure enough, I see him walking up from the same place that Olivia arrived. He is in a curious outfit, like a superhero costume. He glances at me, nods, then walks purposefully over to Olivia. I hear some chatter, it sounds slightly distant as though a conversation is being held far away, and not for my ears.

'This is my brother, Harry,' says Olivia finally.

Harry walks away, back past me, toward the mountains, pickaxe in hand. Olivia, meanwhile, is picking up the remnants of the fences that used to form our farm enclosures.

'What are you doing?' I ask.

'Tidying,' she says. 'Hang on.'

More voices, very quiet, a long way off. The conversation is ethereal, almost ghostly. I wonder if she's talking to her mum or dad, or maybe she's bored and getting ready to leave. Harry is nowhere to be seen. Tired and frustrated, I'm about to switch off, when two messages pop up on screen: **BatBOY03 has entered the game. PoTTer45 has entered the game.** And then two more names, possibly three, that flash up and disappear too quickly. I walk back, away from the building, unsure of what to do or what's happening. They can't be back to do more damage, surely? What's the point? And then I see them, heading out through the trees, a small band of brightly dressed characters, like something out of a Disney animation, all carrying axes, some heading toward the mountains, most to the beach at the other side of the castle.

'What's going on?' I ask.

There is no reply. Sam is still buried in his book, though I notice the pages aren't turning. He's heard the notifications; he knows there are several children here now. I feel an anger rising. How could they? I reach for my phone, intending to call Olivia's parents and ask why the hell they're not watching their kids.

But then there they are, walking back from the sheer rock face, and back from the water's edge. There is a pause as they assemble. The music lifts gently, then swells into a beautiful rush of strings.

'Right,' says Olivia's brother. 'Let's work.'

A flurry of activity. They move out across the wrecked building in all directions, a perfectly synchronised party.

A construction crew.

The blocks begin to appear in neat rows, tracing the original lines of the old building. The same combination of cobble and sandstone, layer upon layer, quick, yet artful and accurate. The characters leap up on to the walls and add block upon block, a weird hive of insect builders, almost silent, but also symbiotic, perfectly in tune.

'Sam,' I say quietly.

And beneath them, out front, Olivia is rebuilding the farm, laying down the fences, adding the gates, the enclosures all the exact same size, the correct dimensions, the dimensions Sam so painstakingly decided and adhered to.

'Sam.'

Between the walls now are the beginnings of oak floors, emanating out from different points, fanning across the strengthening skeleton of the building. There are no windows yet, but the builders are guessing where they should be and leaving spaces.

'I'm not sure what shape the windows are,' says one voice.

'Leave them for now,' says another. 'Sam will know.'

It is this mention of his name, from the other boy, that finally secures Sam's attention. He lays his book down on the bed and squints at the screen, at first unable to comprehend what's happening. He shuffles closer to the television, and rubs his eyes.

The towers are clear now. Each of them, at every corner. Rising up slightly higher than the main roof. They're not quite right, a block too narrow, but close enough – close enough to understand the intention.

'They're rebuilding it,' I say. 'They're fixing everything.'

'Sam?' calls Harry. 'Sam, are you there?'

I offer the headset to him. He lifts his hand and sheepishly takes it, putting the mouthpiece to his face.

'It's … it's not quite right,' he says. 'The tower is eight across. It's eight.'

'Sorry. Jay, the towers are eight across, you prat.'

Instantly, one character is back on the towers adding the blocks, reshaping. Outside, Olivia is already working on the stable, building its rough stone walls. Without saying anything, Sam gently takes the controller from me and gets close to the screen. He wanders to Olivia.

'I can't remember …' she says.

'Ten across, eight high,' he says. 'I'll help.'

And damn it, I'm grinning, I'm grinning like a kid as I watch him take to the wall and then help craft it. The music builds again, soaring up, resonant and stirring – and I bite my lip. I put my hand on Sam's shoulder and watch as he builds, totally engrossed already. And the other children build around him, and the castle rises into the blank blue sky.

278

'We need your help,' someone says to Sam.

'I know where the windows went,' he says. 'I can show you.'

'Yes please. Yes please, Sam.'

And then he is up on the battlements, directing the builders. The windows need to be crosses, three to each floor. Within an hour – maybe more, I don't know – it is almost complete: the castle we built and rebuilt together. One of the boys has begun planting wheat. Soon they'll be able to use it to round up cattle and sheep. The farm will be alive again.

Alive.

Sam laughs and chats. His words are sometimes scrambled, sometimes half-lost, half-repeated. But no one corrects him. They understand. They came here to right a wrong, but now, it is clear, they are learning too. Sam builds a furnace and starts smelting glass; he shows them the hidden chest; he tells them that we can put up pictures and build a library with an enchantment table at its centre, which will give their weapons and armour magical powers. Then they can use redstone to make proper sliding doors and hidden rooms. He's read about it all, you see, in the books and magazines that litter his floor, in the *Minecraft* guide I bought long ago.

When they're finished, the children stand back and admire the building. It is better now, with stone walls beneath the wooden fences to give them height, and a grand new arched doorway. Inside, they've made four-poster beds, chandeliers and large fire-places. For a while, they chat about future projects, like a bunch of old architecture bores.

'We have a plan,' someone says. 'Have you heard of the Ender Dragon?'

'Yes!' says Sam, excited and thrilled. 'He lives at the end of the game. It is very hard to get to him. He lives in a big cave.'

'We're going to defeat him. Do you want to come?' says Olivia. 'You have to come, you're the best player.'

'Yes, please come, Sam.'

'We'll need bows and arrows,' he says slowly. 'We'll need diamonds and lots of iron to make armour.'

'Yes,' says a chorus of voices. 'Yes.'

Caught up in the excitement, the childlike buzz of adventure, I nudge Sam gently.

'Go on, we can do this, Sam. I've read up about the Nether, about getting the right ingredients, about following the Ender Pearl to the end. I can mine for the obsidian we need and you . . .'

He puts his hand gently on my knee. At first I think he is about to agree, to let me in, but I realise, in an almost shocking moment of incredulity, that it is a conciliatory gesture.

'It's OK, Daddy. It's OK, thank you.'

'Let's have a meeting in the great hall,' says Olivia.

'Oh yeah!' says another voice.

And with that, the children tumble from their rest, racing through the building, up a new flight of smooth stone stairs, into a room lit by rows of flaming torches. But I feel like I am far away, like the door has closed. Sam is gabbling into the headset, alone with his clan of helpers, his new army. I get up off the bed slowly, and I pause, waiting, waiting for him to say 'don't go, I need you'. Because I remember, I cannot help but remember, that I sat with him night after night, and we built this castle together, and sometimes I would lie in his bed next to him and we would read the *Minecraft* book together and plan our escapades.

When Matt and I used to talk about parenthood, he would say that as your children grow up, they move away from you so seamlessly, so quietly, so gradually, that you barely notice it happening, and then they are themselves and don't rely on you any more. Jody and I were never sure how much that would happen for Sam.

But within this world that we made, as the night draws in at last, I get to see it happening. It is so weird and sudden, like a child's fingers trailing from your grasp and then they're free and there is air between you. And that is the way it is; it is what you hope for and what you hope you can cope with. You have to let go.

I remember once, Mum took George and me to a big adventure playground, I'm not sure where – maybe we were visiting relatives. Mum sat on a bench and read a magazine, and George ran off to a climbing frame, with me following as usual. We swung back and forth along the monkey bars. One of us would try to hang on for as long as they could while the other pulled their legs. We kept falling off, lying together in a cramped heap, laughing. Then we decided to play hide and seek, so I hung from the bars with my eyes closed, counting, as George ran off.

When I opened them again, I was startled to see that there were three bigger boys surrounding me. They had very short hair, like skinheads, I thought, and their podgy faces closed in on me with dark intent. Almost immediately, one punched me in the stomach and I fell to the ground, which made them all laugh. Then another geared up to kick me and I put my head in my hands and curled up into a ball. The kick never came. Instead, I heard a noise, a sort of slapping sound, and when I looked up George was hitting the boy who punched me. My brother looked terrifying – his face contorted in rage. He was hitting and hitting, spit was bubbling between his snarling lips. The other boys ran away, leaving their friend to his beating, but then Mum looked up from the bench she was sitting on and saw George laying into his cowering victim.

'Stop it!' she shouted. 'Stop it now!'

And when George looked to her, the last boy took his chance and limped away, snivelling.

For ten minutes, Mum shouted at George, she yelled that children shouldn't try to deal with things like that without an adult. But as she bawled and berated, I sidled up to my brother, as close as I could, and behind our backs I took his hand. We looked at each other and suddenly we knew – we knew something very important. She was our mum, and we loved her, and we understood that we would always listen to her. But there would be times, times like this, when we would have to work things out alone.

And now I realise something else – something so obvious I almost laugh. The reason she was so upset was because she knew it too.

Chapter 30

Days later, and still feeling a little pushed out by Sam's new-found independence ('So you're feeling sad because Sam is playing a video game with other kids?' asked Dan incredulously, 'What is *wrong* with you?'), I take him to the café after school. The sky is a cold mass of white, the odd speck of frost swirling in the air. We walk hand in hand, winding through the other parents and children chatting about the school day. I decide to ask about his, expecting the usual short response.

'How was school, Sam?'

'OK. Ben hit my leg with a ruler. But I told the teacher. I told on him, and the teacher moved him. Gracie sits next to me instead.'

'That's good. That was a good thing to do. Well done.'

'I have friends now. Like Olivia. I know what friends do. They are nice.'

'That's right. Friends are nice.'

'When we are at the café, can I have frothy milk?'

'Yes, of course, but did anything else happen at school? Did you have any good lessons?'

'I know how to make a door lever that works.'

'Is that school or *Minecraft*?'

'*Minecraft*.'

'OK, that doesn't count. Well done anyway.'

Small steps, I tell myself. Small steps.

When we reach the familiar building, we see that a *To Let* sign has already been hung on the wall above the heavy glass door. A few parents are sitting with children in school uniforms; there's the guy in the scarf and corduroy jacket who's always here; a young couple sitting in silence, focused intently on their smartphone screens. Sam's favourite barista is behind the counter, whacking the coffee machine like an unreliable TV set. He sees us and smiles, waving at Sam.

'The usual?' he asks.

Sam nods gleefully. 'I can make a door lever,' he says.

As we walk through to the back of the room, I suddenly see a familiar face and judder to a halt for a second. It is Isobel, sitting in one of the knackered armchairs, with Jamie lying face-first on the coffee table in front of her, pushing a toy car along the floor. Oh God, I think, this is awkward. I get a flashback to that night at the community centre: the excitement, the kiss, me legging it out of the door like an idiot. I feel myself flush with embarrassment, but just as I'm considering making a swift exit, Sam yanks me by my arm and points.

'Look, Daddy, it's your friend,' he yells.

Isobel looks up and, without missing a beat, smiles at us both and waves us over. I feel like the proverbial rabbit in the head-lights – a particularly cowardly rabbit that hopped out of a date and never explained why. But somehow I manage to guiltily shuffle in her direction, while Sam clambers on to the table alongside Jamie. She is wearing another beautiful vintage dress, this time with a voluminous skirt in a shimmering deep blue.

'Hi,' she says in a genuinely friendly tone. 'How are you?'

'I'm OK,' I say in a cautious drawl as I sit in the chair opposite.

I'm not sure how to play the situation, or even what the situation is. Are we going to pretend nothing happened? Does she even remember?

'I haven't heard from you since the music night,' she says.

Ah yes, she remembers.

'No,' I reply. 'I, erm, I'm sorry.'

I look across cautiously at Sam, but he's busy trying to prise a toy car out of Jamie's fists. Her eyes follow the direction of my gaze and when I look back at her, I see an indulgent smirk play across her lips.

'It's fine,' she says quietly. 'I understand. It was a bit fast, wasn't it?'

In my head, I'm telling myself, 'Don't say "It's not you, it's me", don't say "It's not you, it's me".'

'It's not you, it's me,' I say. Damn it. 'I mean, sorry, that's such a cliché.'

Sam and Jamie are now rolling on the floor in what could either be a friendly embrace or a vicious physical struggle, but I'm trying to ignore them. When they tumble near me, I lift my feet so they can roll straight under, unimpeded.

'You could have got back to me, though,' she admonishes. 'I felt pretty silly.'

'I know. I was embarrassed. And sort of amazed and grateful and confused. That is a combination of feelings I've not had for a while.'

'Let's be friends,' she says. 'We'll chalk it up to experience.'

'You're being very good about this. I'm such an idiot.'

'Yes, you are. But my son seems to like yours, so let's be adults.'

The barista comes over with our drinks and Sam gets up from the floor, leaping on to the sofa next to me in anticipation of his milk and cake.

'Here you go, monsieur,' the barista says, placing Sam's drink in front of him. 'This may be your last milk with us, I suppose?'

'Are you closing soon?' I ask.

'This is the last week. They haven't managed to lease it yet, but we're going anyway.'

'It's such a shame,' I say.

'Yeah, this is a nice place. You get to know everyone. You see relationships start, families growing up. You see kids playing and . . .'

He looks over to Jamie and Sam.

'. . . smacking each other in the head with action figures. That's all part of it. This isn't like some trendy coffee bar in the city where people rush in, order a skinny mochaccino and storm out again. We've got people who spend all day here. There aren't many places you can do that any more.'

'Have you not thought about taking it over yourself? You're pretty good,' I say.

'Ha, no. I'm only working here while I finish my PhD. I'm out of here when that's done. By then, this place will have been converted into luxury flats like everything else.'

'No, don't say that,' cries Isobel. 'This is the only place Jamie will come and actually relax.'

Jamie is jumping up and down on an armchair, throwing chess pieces at the window.

'Hey, maybe one of you should do it,' says the barista. 'You're here more than the rest of the staff.'

'Yes, that's a great idea,' says Isobel, but turning to me. '*You* totally should!'

'What? No! I don't know anything about running a café. I'd blow up the coffee machine.'

'They're pretty indestructible,' says the barista. 'Running a café is pretty straightforward, according to the owner of this place – as long as you like very long unsociable hours and crying over budget sheets.'

'Hmm, that does sound like my kind of thing,' I say.

'Honestly,' says Isobel. 'This area needs a good café. All those big chains are moving in, and if it's not them, it's those achingly cool places where you need a degree in coffee to order anything – and then they look at you funny if you ask for sugar. Or biscuits to dunk in it.'

'Well, I don't know . . .'

'What do you think?' says the barista to Sam. 'Could Daddy run a coffee shop?'

'Yes!' says Sam. 'We could have an Xbox and everyone could play. But me first.'

'You *see*,' says Isobel. 'That's a business plan. I mean, I know about retail, I could give you a hand. When I first took on the clothes shop I had this big pros and cons list, and the cons *far* outweighed the pros – I had to start another piece of paper! But then I imagined this roomful of beautiful vintage dresses, an old rock 'n' roll single playing on the gramophone, movie posters on the walls. I had such a longing for the place. It's hard work, but I would have regretted it for ever if I hadn't done it.'

'But that's it. You had a passion and you went for it. I'm not sure I have that in me.'

'Oh, you do,' she says. 'No one who lacks passion can kiss like that.'

I feel myself going beetroot red, and instinctively glance around, checking for Sam.

'It's OK,' she says. 'He's over on the far table with Jamie, sword-fighting with rolled-up newspapers.'

'Right,' I say. 'I'm sorry again.'

'Look, forget it, you silly arse. The point is, you have it in you. You know how important this place is to Sam, to Jamie, to me. People need somewhere to go that isn't home or work or owned by a massive corporation that wants to process them like cattle. You understand that. You'd make people feel welcome. People need to feel welcome – especially weirdos like us. All you need is a bit of help, someone with experience in the catering trade.'

And despite myself, I think: Clare. Clare was in catering. But straight away I banish the idea, partly because this whole line of conversation is ridiculous, and partly because Matt and Clare are still not talking to me. That's another broken relationship I have to try to patch up somehow. That's pretty much my full-time job at the moment.

So I chat to Isobel as the boys wheel and chase around us. I tell her about *Minecraft* and the tournament; about how we were going to enter but now we probably won't, even though Sam's castle is fixed, even though he seems to love the game again. I've broached the subject with him a couple of times, but he shrugs it off. Isobel talks about the shop and the club nights. Somehow we allow our shared escapade to fade into the background. But the thought of my lips on hers stays with me throughout the afternoon. Mixed in with the memory is the dull ache of guilt. Even though I know about Jody and Richard, I feel utterly unexcused, and I know why that is. It's because I am nowhere near letting go.

We sit in silence for a few minutes, watching Sam and Jamie, sprawled on the floor, crashing two toy cars into each other over and over again with increasing ferocity until finally it explodes into violence and they are hitting each other. The mood has tipped.

'OK, OK, boys,' I say. 'Sam, I think we should take you home to Mummy now.'

'Yes, come on, Jamie,' says Isobel. 'Don't ruin another afternoon by getting us arrested for assault with a deadly Hot Wheels truck.'

We all stand together and I head to the counter to pay the bill.

'Go on, rent the café,' says the barista.

'We can live here,' says Sam.

'You two!' I groan.

Halfway home, I remember the appointment I made with the therapist all those weeks ago. It's tomorrow. At that moment, Sam looks up at me, his brow furrowed, as though trying to read my thoughts, his expression serious and enquiring.

'Daddy, what *are* you doing? I think you are stuck.'

'What do you mean?'

'Sometimes I am stuck on a thought and I can't get off it, not for a long time. It stays and stays. Are you stuck on a thought?'

I stop walking.

'Hey,' I say. 'Yes, I think you're right. You're totally right. I *am* stuck on a thought. Well, I'm stuck on a lot of thoughts. Wow, you're pretty smart.'

And it comes out as shock and surprise, which I suppose it is. The glimpses into Sam's interior life are so rare and fleeting that, when they come, I treasure them like jewels. I'm so stupidly moved, I crouch down in front of him.

'Thank you for thinking about me,' I say. 'Thank you, Sam.'

He quickly looks away, his eyes scouring the pavement, avoiding both my gaze and my gratitude. I gently ruffle his hair, but he leans back and away. It's all too real now, this casual conversation. He did not know it would lead to this. This emotion.

I give up and struggle to my feet, taking his hand and walking on, thinking it is all over, this little window of intimacy. But when we stop at a road, he slips his hand out of mine for a second, then softly pats me on the back.

'My daddy,' he says.

And the moment is so perfect, I feel like the stars will fall upon us.

Chapter 31

The Assembly Centre takes up two Georgian houses on a leafy street behind Bath's Royal Crescent. It's here that my therapist has what she describes on the phone to me as a 'non-threatening and very cosy consulting room', so for some reason I am expecting beanbags and a lava lamp. I'm here rather than in Bristol because I didn't want anyone I know to see me emerging from a clinic and asking what is wrong with me. This is not a conversation I'm ready to have with myself, let alone anyone else. Fortunately, discretion does seem to be a key concern at the Assembly Centre. The small brass plaque next to the door is the only clue as to what people come here for, and when I try to peer in through one of the large sash windows, the lace curtains inside are closed so I can only make out an expensive-looking chesterfield sofa. I don't know what I expect to see – perhaps someone lying on a couch with a man resembling Sigmund Freud sitting behind them making notes on a clipboard.

I push the door open, and inside the large waiting room is empty apart from the sofa against one wall and above it, a large Victorian painting of the Bath skyline. The polished oak floorboards creak loudly as I walk in, and as though on cue, a woman emerges from a doorway opposite, dressed casually in a black polo-neck jumper and tartan skirt. She's in her late forties, maybe, very smart and confident, her blonde hair greying slightly.

'Alex?' she asks.

'Yes,' I stutter.

'I'm Jennifer, nice to meet you. Did you find us OK? Great, come this way.'

We walk through the door into a corridor, the walls lined with smaller paintings of Bath scenes. Her room is at the end. It's small but airy and welcoming, like a little study, with two armchairs (not beanbags, sadly), a bookcase, and a window overlooking a tiny courtyard garden.

'Sit down,' she says.

Suddenly this all feels very real. I am actually having therapy. I am sitting here with a therapist and she is about to ask me questions about my mother. Do I have to fill out some sort of personality test? What do I do?

'OK,' says Jennifer, sitting down in the seat opposite, a small hardback notebook in her hand. 'This is a getting to know each other session. I'll ask you a few questions, you can ask me some. If we're both happy, we can have a think and maybe book in another appointment. Is that OK?'

'Yes. Yes, that sounds good. Thank you.'

She starts by asking how things are for me right now and what made me decide to come. I give her a concise history of the last five months; the increasing exhaustion, worry and frustration that led Jody and me to part. She wants to know about my background, my relationships, my family. At first my answers are short and uncertain, the sound of my voice is weird and shaky – the idea of simply unloading all of this in such a strange environment is bizarre. But her questions are gentle and positive, so that it gradually becomes something very close to natural. And then we get to Sam.

'For the longest time, I didn't want to hear about autism,' I say. 'I felt like it was an excuse, a label. I thought his speech was slow because he had ear infections and couldn't hear us. I thought he was just anxious and shy. I didn't want to face it. I didn't want to face anything.'

'How do you feel about it now?'

'I feel like there's a dividing line between him and the world. It's not huge, but it's there – it's like we all speak in impenetrable regional accents and he has to struggle to understand and fit in. I don't know how much he takes on board. But then sometimes he surprises me – he says something funny or shows a fragment of affection. It takes my breath away.'

'Do you talk to him, though? Do you ask him how he feels?'

'I try. Not much, but I try. And that makes me think, well, if it's a struggle for his own dad, what's it like with other people? What's it like at school? He must be so alone. There's this old guy at our local pub, I'm sure he's autistic too. He sits at a table by himself and no one knows how to talk to him. I worry that's Sam's future. I mean, they say he's "high functioning", which makes him sound like a computer, or a top-of-the-range fridge-freezer, but compared to other kids his age, he's so far behind. Sorry, this is all Jody and I have talked about for the last few years – that and me working late.'

'Do you think you stayed at work so that you wouldn't have to worry about Sam, so you wouldn't have to face that?'

'I don't know. That would be awful, wouldn't it?'

She shakes her head. 'We all have ways to protect ourselves.'

Then we head backwards, to childhood, and to George; making the gentlest of ripples on that vast reservoir of grief. Ninety minutes later – though it seems like barely half an hour – we're done and the session ends. She writes quietly for a few seconds and then looks up.

'Well, I think we can work together, if you're happy?' she says.

'Yes, if that's OK? I wasn't sure what this would be like, but it was fine. It went very quickly.'

I realise this makes it sound like I've had a minor dental operation.

'Good,' says Jennifer, standing up and closing her book. 'Let's make an appointment. Also, I have some homework for you. Before you come in next time, I want you to be spontaneous, I want you to do a few things that are out of character. You talked about parenthood, but I want *you* to be childish. At least once. Then we'll talk about that. OK?'

'OK,' I say.

Outside, as I'm walking through Bath's wide city streets toward the railway station, I actually feel physically lighter. It's like coming out of the gym, except I'm not wearing jogging bottoms and don't smell like a sweaty locker room. I've told this stranger more than I've told anyone else in years, she knows as much about me as Jody – more perhaps. Why have I never done this before?

But I know why. There was always something in the way, some darkness that I had to hold back. But the darkness always comes, whatever you do. Eventually, you have to turn around and face it.

When I get back to Bristol, I head toward Dan's but then he texts me and asks if I can meet him at the Old Ship. Therapy and then a pint seems like a reasonable proposition these days.

'I have this idea,' he says, when I sit down next to him.

We're slumped in the corner area as usual, trying to ignore a guy in a tasselled leather jacket quietly headbutting the fruit machine. Sid is at his table, glancing over toward us occasionally, but then looking away.

'OK,' I reply. 'Are you going to tell me what it is?'

'It's about Emma.'

'Oh.'

'I mean, it's all too late, but ... you know it's her birthday on Wednesday, right?'

'Of course,' I lie.

'Well, there's something I want to do for her, but I need your help.'

Wow, this day is full of surprises.

'Sure,' I say. 'What do you want me to do?'

He won't give me the details but says it involves subterfuge and a nice café so of course I tell him I will help. As we're about to get up and head out, I see that Sid has wandered over in our direction.

'Is your lad about?' he says. He's not looking at me or Dan but at a place on the floor, a few yards away from us both.

'No,' I say, trying to hide the note of surprise. 'He's probably at home playing video games.'

'Good little chess player,' he says.

'Yeah, I think he gets it from his mum. I'm sure he'd like to come back and play, though, if you'd like?'

He nods distractedly.

'A good little player,' he says again.

'I'll tell him. His name is Sam, by the way.'

'Sam,' he repeats. 'Sam is a good player.'

As he makes his way back to his table, I exchange looks with Dan and we leave. I know how difficult it was for Sid to come over to us – I now recognise it in Sam, that struggle to meet the world halfway. But the world always wants more, and Sam is trying, stretching out over the chasm to reach Olivia and the others. I need to learn from him now. I need to be strong enough to reconnect with the world.

Chapter 32

The next day, Matt calls me, sounding subdued and cautious.

'Alex, are you free this weekend?' he asks, before I've even had a chance to apologise for that whole bursting-into-his-house-and-shouting-at-everyone thing.

'I think so. Matt, look I'm—'

'It's just that, well, Clare and I need some time to sort things out. We were thinking about going away. We can take the twins, but we wondered if you'd be willing to come over and sort of look after the other two. From Saturday morning to Sunday afternoon. If you're not busy.'

I go through the mental permutations. I owe them, of course, and I've babysat for Tabitha and Archie before, although mostly after they've been put in bed, or for an hour here and there. Never for a day, let alone a weekend.

Matt seems to read my train of thought.

'Look, I know babysitting is not your thing at all. But we completely trust you, the kids like you. Plus, we're desperate,' says Matt.

It turns out they have already tried everyone else they know: Jody (away at an arts festival in Exeter), parents, neighbours, very distant relations, a guy who came round to ask if they wanted Sky TV – I think Matt was joking about that one. But no one was available. They have no other choice.

'All the standard parenting rules are out of the window,' continues Matt. 'Whatever will make this easier for you. The kids can watch movies, play video games and eat crisps for two days, we don't care. We'll deal with the fallout when we get back.'

'Well, I've got Sam on Saturday ...'

'Bring him,' says Matt. 'Bring whoever you want. I'll stock the fridge with beer – you can either drink it yourself or give it to the kids.'

A few months ago I would have immediately made some excuse. The thought of looking after Sam alone would have been terrifying enough, but three kids? For a whole weekend? Madness. I'd have ended up lying in the garage in the foetal position as the kids descended into *Lord of the Flies*-style anarchy. But then Tabitha is precocious enough to look after herself, and Archie is several times less challenging than Sam was at his age. I can also hear the voice of Jennifer in my head, like some sort of feminine Ben Kenobi: 'Be spontaneous, trust your feelings, say yes to life.' It doesn't seem so crazy. It seems like something I could do for a friend.

'OK,' I say. 'OK, I'm in.'

When I call Jody to ask if it's OK to take Sam along, she sounds surprised as I describe Matt's solemn tone.

'It's weird because I met Clare yesterday,' she says. 'According to her, they sorted everything out. She's taken control of the joint bank account, he's given her his credit cards. She sounded fine about it all. They actually sat down and talked it all through. A bit like adults.'

'Oh,' I say, choosing to temporarily ignore Jody's barbed closer. 'Maybe they've had a relapse?'

*

So on Saturday morning, I go to collect Sam and wait patiently as he makes several attempts to get the Velcro straps on his trainers to exactly the right tightness. Then I manage to get him into the car and we head off. On the way, he asks a series of questions about why we are going to live at Matt and Clare's, and where he will sleep and how exactly we'll be spending the next thirty-two hours.

'I don't know, we're going to have to be flexible,' I say.

'What does "flexible" mean?' says Sam.

I briefly appreciate the irony of this question.

'It means we have to see how things go and not make too many plans.'

'I don't like that.'

'I know, but sometimes you don't know what's going to happen so you have to make it up as you go along.'

He thinks about this for a second.

'When I am grown up I will definitely plan everything very well,' he says.

'Well, sometimes life just throws stuff at you.'

'I will duck.'

When we reach the house, I see that Matt is already outside, leaning into his silver Audi estate, loading the twins into their car seats. He spots me and waves frantically, seemingly both surprised and thrilled that I've actually turned up.

'Hi,' I say, getting out of my car, which looks particularly shabby on the driveway next to his. 'Sorry I'm a bit late.'

'Hi!' he says. 'Thanks so much! How are you? The kids are upstairs watching *Adventure Time*. They've had breakfast. The good news is, Clare's mum can look after the twins. Officially children-free for thirty hours. We've got to head off, I'm afraid. Long drive to the Cotswolds. We're staying in the pub in Burford where I proposed. Come on, Clare!'

Clare bursts out of the front door carrying a small suitcase which she hurls into the boot. I gear up to apologise.

'Hi, Alex, thank you for this!'

'Hey, Clare. Look, I'm so sorry about that day. I should never have come round.'

She looks at me indulgently, then puts her hand on my arm.

'There's a note for you on the table. Thank you, Alex.'

Then she disappears into the car.

Sam and I stand dazed in the driveway as Matt closes the boot with a loud thunk, then scuttles into the car and bangs the door shut behind him. The Audi engine roars into life, and the car backs out of the drive on to the road. The tyres actually screech as it accelerates away. I remember what Jody said on the phone and suddenly realise they haven't had a weekend alone together since the twins were born. I've been set up.

'Oh, I get it,' I mutter to myself. 'Make-up sex.'

'What's make-up sex?' asks a small familiar voice from beside me. Somehow, Tabitha has crept out of the house and is now standing on the driveway, watching the car disappear up the road.

'Um, never mind,' I say. 'What are you and your brother up to?'

With that, Archie tumbles out of the house and runs in a circle around us.

'We're watching cartoons!' he yells. 'We're allowed to play *Minecraft* later!'

I look at Sam, and he takes my hand.

'They are scary and loud,' he says.

'They're excited, that's all. Do you want to watch cartoons? I'll come up in a minute.'

'OK.'

We head into the house, and Sam cautiously follows the other two up the staircase, which is as usual booby-trapped with toy cars, skates and Lego blocks. Matt has clearly tidied up, though, because some of the steps are actually visible beneath the brightly coloured detritus.

In the living room, they've left me a selection of newspapers, a bottle of wine and the note from Clare. It says:

Do whatever you need to, lots of food in the fridge freezer, the kids can survive on chicken nuggets for several days. Don't bother bathing them. Bedtime usually 7 p.m.-ish. Call if there are any problems. Oh, and I forgive you.

And that's that. This is clearly my penance. Now all I have to do is survive.

Like any responsible adult, I let them watch cartoons for two hours, then I make everyone sandwiches and crisps and call them down. We eat sitting around the coffee table in the lounge. Tabitha insists on sitting next to Sam, chatting away to him, asking questions and then not caring when his responses are a grunt or a shake of his head. But he's smiling and I can tell he's enjoying the attention. Archie mutters quietly, pulling his sandwiches apart and slapping them all over his face.

'Alex, is it true you don't live with Jody now?' asks Tabitha.

Her tone is polite and indifferent, as though she's merely enquired about my favourite colour. I wonder if she's overheard Matt and Clare talking. I look at Sam, wondering if he's taking this in.

'Yes, it is,' I say carefully.

'Mummy says you were under a lot of pressure.'

Now I see that Sam is watching us, but his expression is impassive. This is more than he's ever asked about what's going on, and

I'm still not sure how much he gets it. But I need to tread carefully. You hear all the time about kids blaming themselves when their parents split up. I wonder if that thought has ever entered his head?

'We had some big problems to deal with,' I say at last. 'And then we fell out. So we thought it was better to have some time apart.'

Again, I look at Sam, but he has moved his attention to his bowl of crisps, carefully studying the unfamiliar crockery. I wait for him to ask something, but he's silent and unreadable.

'Mummy shouted at Daddy because he did a fart,' says Archie.

The kids burst out laughing and I'm grateful for the diversion. A few minutes later, text number one comes in from Clare, checking everything's OK and letting me know that the pub is lovely. I text back and ask if the shed in the garden is *supposed* to be on fire.

After lunch, it's time for *Minecraft* on Matt's brand-new Xbox One. I scrupulously check everyone's hands for sticky sandwich gunk before they're allowed to touch the controllers; I know that'll upset Matt, who has left a special pack of wipes by the side of the TV for this very scenario. Tabitha clearly knows the game and takes control of the menu screens, while Archie hits the buttons experimentally. We start a new survival map and the display splits into four quarters, so we all get our own little view. It is a chaotic hour of building and exploring. Together we manage to construct a bizarre interconnected settlement with multiple oddly shaped extensions constructed from cobblestone, wooden planks and dirt. It looks like the set of a *Mad Max* movie. Tabitha and Sam add a swimming pool with a diving board and I try to create a rollercoaster out of mine cart rails, but Archie smashes it up with a pickaxe. It's noisy and fun, and when I tell everyone it's time to switch off, I placate them by suggesting we build a *Minecraft* house in the dining room. I drag in a clothes horse and a variety of sheets and duvets; Sam and Tabitha work together to construct a roof over the table, using clothes pegs to clip it into place. I get immersed in the whole process, raiding the cupboards in the garage for lanterns, making a crafting table out of a cardboard box. I help Tabitha find her play kitchen so it can double as a furnace.

'We have to leave a space to get in,' shouts Tabitha.

'No, we have to make a door or zombies and skeletons will attack us,' replies Sam.

He's holding his own in the conversation, chatting through plans, answering questions. They turn the clothes horse into a tower, and Sam puts a stool inside so he can see over the top.

'I can see a lot of sheep around, we can make beds,' he says.

'I want to kill the Ender Dragon,' says Tabitha.

'We need ob … obsidian to make a portal. I know how to do it.'

'You're good at *Minecraft*, Sam.'

I put the oven on and then get Tabitha to choose a book, which I read to them all, sitting underneath the dining table in our *Minecraft* den. Sam shuffles over as I start, resting his head on my knee. The easy unselfconsciousness of this little act is so surprising I have to stop and smile at him. I remember reading to him as a toddler, working through book after book as he lay in my arms. He loved rhymes and repeated phrases, he would try to learn them, but they'd come out all garbled and nonsensical. Eventually, he lost the patience to sit and listen. Instead, he'd writhe away from me; it was all too much. We kept the books anyway. Sometimes I'd go up to his room and read them to him as he slept.

When the food is done, we stay undercover, eating fistfuls of chicken nuggets and cod goujons, all smothered in tomato ketchup. Tabitha gets Sam to try a nugget but he starts to retch and then manages to sick it back up into my cupped hands, much to Archie's delight. Instead of freaking out, Sam laughs with the other two while I simply crawl from under the table with my fists full of semi-digested junk food and deposit it in the kitchen bin. We talk about what we want to be when we grow up.

'I want to be an actor or a computer programmer,' says Tabitha.

'I want to be Batman,' says Archie.

'Architect!' adds Sam.

'What is your job?' says Tabitha to me, once again exhibiting her incredible ability to get to the very heart of the matter.

'I don't have one at the minute,' I say. 'But I am thinking of buying a café. What do you think of that?'

Saying that aloud, as if it's something that is actually happening, gives me a surprising whoosh of happiness.

'Could we come and eat all your cakes?' asks Tabitha.

'Of course. What do you think, Sam?' I ask.

'Yes,' he shouts. 'You will say, "Hello, sir, what drink do you want, sit down please!"'

He says this in a weird 'grown-up' voice, which amuses the others.

'So you think it's a good idea?' I ask, trying to get something useful out of him. He nods enthusiastically.

'I could come after school and see you,' he replies, but he is enjoying his little audience too much to be serious, and reverts to his bizarre voice, which I'm only now realising is an impression of me. 'Hello, Sam, you want cakes? Sit down please. Who's next? Shut up, everybody. Who wants frothy milk?'

The others are giggling helplessly. It's going to be a long afternoon.

Much later, I take them upstairs into Tabitha's room, where there's a bed ready for Sam and Archie on the floor. We make up a story together, a sprawling epic involving witches, superheroes, the

Tower of London and mining for magical diamonds. Text number two comes in from Clare. I text back that everything is fine and that we're having an all-night *Saw* movie marathon. I sit with the children until they're almost asleep.

I go to kiss Sam goodnight and he looks at me briefly.

'Will you really have a café?' he asks.

'Maybe. We'll see. I don't know if I can do it.'

'I think you can,' he says. 'I think you can do it.'

'You're not going to do that voice again, are you?'

They're all up at 6 a.m., rampaging around the house in various states of fancy dress. I am awoken by Sam, bursting into the guest bedroom wearing an Iron Man mask and vampire cloak. I look at my watch. I have at least eight more hours. For a second I think about Jody and what's happening with us. I wonder where she is – who she is with – and what the next stage is going to be. I think about Isobel and what that means. But Sam is grabbing at my arm, pulling me away. So we head downstairs, and with Tabitha and Archie we turn the kitchen into an apocalyptic wasteland of spilled breakfast cereal, jammy handprints and pools of milk.

'Right,' I say, against all my better judgement: 'Shall we go to the park?'

It takes an hour to get everyone dressed, then I put them in the car and drive through the silent streets, Sam beside me, the other two in the back, sitting in the car seats Matt left for me. I park up and they're all away, running through the gate toward the swings. I do the usual sweep of the area, looking out for dogs and older groups of kids. But Sam isn't lurking at my side, he is away with the other two.

'The climbing frame is our castle,' he shouts.

'I'm the queen,' says Tabitha.

And I can sit and watch, like other parents do. Sam doesn't look for me or even acknowledge me, he doesn't go through the familiar tics and routines – he is somewhere else, somewhere I guess other kids take for granted.

Matt and Clare get back at 2 p.m. The kids have had lunch, and are upstairs watching a film.

'Have they actually been down yet?' asks Matt.

'Jesus, what's happened in here?' says Clare from the dining room.

'That's now a *Minecraft* map,' I tell her. 'Brace yourself for the kitchen.'

'Well,' she says as she comes back in. 'It looks like you guys have had fun. Thanks so much, Alex.'

'Am I off the hook now?' I ask.

'Only when you've paid the cleaning bill,' she says.

'Actually, I have something stupid to ask.'

'Go on.'

'You know the café I take Sam to? The current owner isn't renewing the lease. I had this crazy idea – to take it over. It's mad, I know, but . . .'

'I don't think it's mad.'

'Well, thank you. But I don't know anything about running something like that.'

'Ah,' she says. 'I can see where this is going.'

'I just thought – I've made an appointment to go and view it. Would you consider coming along? Having a look?'

'Sure. It's been years since I was in the race, though.'

'I know. But it would be amazing to have you there. I mean, it would be amazing to have your help with the whole thing.'

She stands looking at me for a moment, as though weighing up how serious I am: if I'm worth the investment or having some sort of early mid-life crisis.

'One thing at a time,' she says. 'Let's see the place first.'

In the car on the way back to Jody's house, Sam is quiet beside me.

'Did you have a good time?' I say.

'Yes!' he says. 'You were funny, Daddy. I liked making the *Minecraft* den.'

'I did too.'

'Daddy?'

'Yes?'

'I do want to do the competition again.'

'You do?'

'Yes.'

'Definitely?'

'Definitely.'

And I think, actually, this weekend hasn't been hard, it hasn't been worrying – all I needed was to let go a bit. Maybe being a good parent is about improvisation and spontaneity; maybe it's about genuinely being *with* your kid.

Sometimes, though, it is also about being able to catch sick in your hands.

Chapter 33

'Can we talk?'

My question hangs between us as Jody moves aside to let Sam bolt past, into the house and up the stairs to his bedroom.

'Sure,' she replies.

I notice as I follow her in that she's wearing one of my old T-shirts, now threadbare and pockmarked with little holes. Her black jeans have large tears at the knees and her hair is tied back with a grubby red scrunchy. It's either wash day or she doesn't give a shit because she's not seeing Richard. The thought of that guy ignites a small firework of anger in my mind, but I don't want to go there. I want this to be OK.

'How is the gallery?' I ask.

'Good,' she says. 'I'm taking on more of the curation and planning, meeting artists, all that stuff. It's fascinating. I love it. How about you?'

I tell her about the café and my hare-brained scheme. She doesn't visibly recoil from the insanity of it, which I take as a good sign.

I look around the room – at all our books piled up in every corner and crevice, the coffee table lost under a sea of comics and magazines. It feels like the place I left behind. My face hasn't been scribbled out of all the family photos cluttered on the mantelpiece. There is no huge portrait of Richard above the fireplace. I hear the Xbox switch on upstairs and the familiar music. He's getting in some practice for the competition.

'So everything went well at Matt and Clare's?'

'Yeah, it was fun, actually.'

'I can see that, Clare texted me a photo of the den you all made.'

'Wow, that was quick.'

'She's pretty impressed.'

Jody wanders through to the kitchen and I follow. She fills the kettle and plugs it in, grabbing two mugs from the cupboard, the same cupboard they've always been in. She doesn't ask if I want tea or coffee, she knows the answer – it's after 2 p.m., so always tea. Preferably with a ginger biscuit. And then, as if on cue, she pulls a packet from the cookie jar on the counter.

'You remembered,' I joke.

'I never forget a biscuit.'

We smile, but we both know we're leading up to something. This is the preliminary chat, a way of testing the space, working out the mood. Somebody has to step in and move this up a gear.

'I'm, um, I'm seeing a therapist,' I say. 'She seems nice, quite maternal – very unlike my own mother in that respect. I wasn't sure about the whole thing, but I'm going to give it a shot.'

'Good,' says Jody, and her response is enthusiastic and genuine. 'That's good news.'

'We'll see,' I say. 'How about you, what's been happening away from work?'

'Oh, not much. I've been thinking a lot about this whole school thing with Sam, worrying about what's best for him. I got letters through from both places this week; they need to have an answer.'

'Were you going to tell me?' I ask. 'Am I still involved in this decision?'

I can feel a low gurgle of adrenalin. I form an image in my head, the merest glimpse – of Richard picking up Sam from school.

'I'm telling you about it now, aren't I?'

I don't answer. The kettle starts to boil and Jody switches it off with a thud, yanks it from the base and slops hot water into our cups and all over the work surface. She pushes past me, takes a carton of milk from the fridge and splashes that on too.

'Honestly, are you sure you're still interested in *us*?' she says. Instead of looking at me, she's furiously scrubbing the worktop with a cloth. 'Lottie saw you with that woman in the café a couple of weeks ago.'

Oh right, I think, that *was* a mum from school. And suddenly, in barely a second, the roles have flipped and now I'm the accused – I wasn't prepared for this. I have no strategy ready. I feel a cold panic flushing down through my spine like icy water. In an instant, worst-case scenarios start playing out before my eyes. I could lose Jody for good. I could lose Sam.

I decide to play it cool – but then I completely don't.

'Oh, Isobel?' I blurt out. 'She has an autistic son too. We got talking, then we met again, the two of us. Then I went to a sixties club that she runs and it was a fiasco – we kissed, but I knew straight away that it was a horrible mistake. Then I ran away ... These are good ginger biscuits. Very spicy.'

She looks at me, then takes her tea and sits down at our tiny dining table.

'You ran away?' she says.

'Yes, it's true. I've still got it.'

She considers this while dunking a biscuit into her tea and seemingly assessing me.

'Richard was a bloody nightmare,' she says simply. 'He manages some sort of arts organisation in London. I guess after a few glasses of Prosecco that seemed impressive. But I met him again after the wedding and I realised he's this horrible guy – arrogant, pretentious and he talks continuously. I never got a word in, he just talked at me. You know those men? You ask them how they're doing and they say something like "Well, that's a long story and it starts in Peterborough in 2004 . . ." And you know you're going to be listening to this bullshit for the next half an hour.'

I feel a giant rush of relief. Clare was right, he *is* a wanker. But then I remember the morning, the kiss. Jody seems to read and understand my thought process, as she has always done throughout our marriage.

'The last time I saw him, he turned up here early in the morning on his way back to London. He wanted to offer me a job in his office, as his PA or something.'

'What did you do?' I ask.

'Well, Alex, you know what I did because you were parked twenty yards down the road. I kissed him goodbye.'

'You saw me?'

'Maybe,' she said. 'Or maybe half an hour later I got a call from an incredibly angry Clare telling me you'd turned up at their place yelling about seeing me with Richard. She also told me not to be such a prat, by the way.'

'Right,' I say. 'I always liked Clare.' My brain is spiralling, it feels like we're having this conversation on a rollercoaster. I grip on to the work surface, the mug shaking in my other hand. 'So what now?'

'I don't know,' she replies. 'I'm sorry. Let's see how it goes – for a little while longer. We've both got things to sort out in our own lives.'

'Well, how about we meet for coffee?' I say. 'There are some nice places near where I used to work. Or we could meet near you. Or somewhere in between?'

'Yes, sure. I'd like that.'

'Great! We could talk about the schools.'

'Or maybe about us for a change?'

When I finish the tea, I decide I should leave on this ambiguous yet faintly positive note. For the first time in ages, there isn't that overwhelming compulsion to get out as soon as humanly possible, but I'm also worried that, if we talk for longer, I could easily put a gargantuan foot in it. I shout goodbye to Sam, then walk with Jody to the door. It feels natural, as though I'm only leaving for the weekend. We make vague plans, there is a hug. When the door closes behind me, the world seems, if not full of possibilities, then at least a little less blatantly malevolent. It's a start, anyway. And that's where life seems to be at the moment: full of starts, instead of endings.

Chapter 34

Outside the old café, the rain is falling hard. Deep pools are already collecting on the uneven pavement and every time a car passes, it sends up a great muddy tidal wave, so I have to step far back, almost against the crumbling brick wall. The windows are boarded now and on the other side of the glass door there's a pile of unopened mail and free local newspapers spilling across the floor. All the furniture is gone; the wooden counter and a couple of broken armchairs are all that remain. It is so weird and so sad to see it, this sanctuary away from home for Sam and me.

Now I'm here with a forlorn plan, devised on a whim, to try and take the place over. I feel almost guilty having asked Clare along. She's a real parent, with a real family and real problems, she doesn't need to be sucked into my fantasy of running a café. But she's coming anyway. At least, she said she's coming. When I check my watch I realise that both she and the estate agent are ten minutes late. As I look out along the road, blinking the rainwater away, I see a brightly coloured Corsa parking a few hundred metres away – and I know exactly what sort of person drives a car like that. Sure enough, out pops a young man in a grey suit, clutching an over-sized golf umbrella and a clipboard. He may as well be bellowing 'Yes, I'm an estate agent' into a megaphone. Then, as he gets closer, I realise with a slight sense of horror that I recognise him.

'Hi, Daryl,' I say.

'Oh, hi, mate! How are you?' he replies with an awkward smile.

After making a great histrionic show of looking all around me and back along the road, like some hammy provincial pantomime actor, he finally twigs.

'Oh, *you're* the client?'

I nod slowly and shrug my shoulders.

'It's been a weird few months,' I tell him.

We look at each other silently.

'Well ...' he sighs, putting down his umbrella, almost getting his head trapped in its garish, collapsing expanse.

Then, just as I'm worried that things can't get any more awkward and uncomfortable, Clare arrives, pushing a double pushchair, the two tiny occupants enclosed in a vast bubble of transparent plastic.

'Sorry I'm late,' she cries.

'This is my friend Clare,' I say. 'Clare, this is my old colleague Daryl.'

'Good morning,' he replies, slowly regaining his professional demeanour. 'Yeah, mate, I left Stonewicks a month ago. It all went a bit pear-shaped after the merger. I'm doing commercial lets now. It's a bit more dynamic.'

He leers horribly at Clare, twirling the café keys around on his finger. Inevitably, they fly off into the road and he's almost decapitated by a bus when he goes to retrieve them.

'So you're thinking of getting into the café trade then?' he says, pretending nothing has happened. 'It's a good time. Vibrant area,

313

lots of young people moving in, prime position ... Shall I cut the bullshit and get us inside before we drown?'

He fumbles with the lock, then has to shoulder-barge the door to get it open, sending the postal pile spraying across the dull wooden floor.

'Thanks for coming,' I say to Clare.

'I'm happy to, it's exciting,' she says.

'How are things at home?'

'Better. I'm still angry at Matt, but at least since that weekend he's stopped skulking around like a wounded dog, which made me even more cross. I mean, this was never going to end our marriage, but it'll take a long time for me to trust him. I've had everything moved into the joint account so I can monitor it. I feel as though I'm treating him like a naughty schoolboy, but it's not tense any more, which is good. It was affecting Grace and Amelie too. They pick up on these things, don't they?'

'I don't know, I never know.'

'Right,' she says. 'It's different with Sam. I'm sorry.'

'Come on, let's see what you think of this place, business partner.'

We struggle to guide the vast tank-like pushchair into the café, and when I'm inside, the faint smell of coffee and furniture polish is immediately familiar. This is, after all, where we spent so many weekends, first as a family, then just me and Sam, slouching in the comfy armchairs and sofas among all the other families, happy to simulate relaxation and contentment for a few precious minutes. Without its plump, tattered furniture the room looks bigger, colder, and as I wander through I'm dimly aware of Daryl beside me, going through the features, automatically parroting his mindless spiel.

'There's plenty of potential to stamp your own tastes on to the interior,' he drones. 'You could go American diner, that's popular, or we had a place in Clifton that's become one of them Tokyo kitten bars – you know, cats walking around everywhere; have a cuppa and a stroke. It was closed down by environmental health for two weeks, mind: the little bastards keep shitting everywhere. Wouldn't recommend it.'

Clare has ventured behind the counter and into the kitchen area next door; the twins sit quietly in their pushchair, looking around the room, wide-eyed and docile. I get a brief image of us running this place: the walls repainted, the floor sanded. No garish local art on the walls, no loud music, no kittens, maybe a few board games, some books – a room for people to relax and feel safe and comfortable. The thought of it gives me a tingle of excitement.

'Well, the kitchen looks fine,' says Clare, coming back into the main room. 'I mean, there's nothing in there right now, but there is plenty of space, it's not damp, there are loads of sockets, and it's all health and safety compliant, as far as I remember. It's nice, Alex.'

Daryl looks at me expectantly.

'How much do you think it will cost to fit it all out?' I ask Clare.

'Well, you need a complete overhaul of fixtures and fittings, coffee machine, chilled display cabinet if you're selling food, dishwasher, microwave, furniture, carpentry, plumbing, electrics, then all your cutlery, alarms, fire extinguishers ... Fifteen grand, to be on the safe side.'

'You'll need to find three months' rent in advance,' adds Daryl. 'But the rent is good for this area ... honestly. And it's not exactly the centre of Bristol, so they know they won't be getting Costa Coffee here.'

His voice is different, for a second. It is strangely ... human. I realise with a start that he is actually telling the truth.

'I mean, I'd love to help, I'd love to invest but ... ' Clare tails off for a second. 'Well, that's not an option now.'

I looked at my bank balance before coming out; it's not up to that. Paying the mortgage on the house and rent to Dan has eaten away at the redundancy package.

'You could look into a business loan,' says Daryl, instinctively picking up on my train of thought. 'That'll help.'

We all stand in silence for a few seconds, looking around at the vast bare room.

'Well, I've got to go,' says Clare at last. 'I need to get these two home for lunch. But Alex, I'd be happy to help. I mean, everything has to fit in around these two, but I'm here. Shout if you need me.'

'Thanks, I will,' I say.

She nods and heads over to the pushchair. The twins smile and bob up and down excitedly. She clips the rain cover back on and I rush over to help, then hold the door open.

'Clare. Thank you,' I say. 'And, I'm truly sorry. About bursting in and swearing at your family. I'm ashamed of what I did.'

'It's fine. I'm always bursting in and swearing at my family, they're used to it.'

As she gets the pushchair through the door, into the endless rain and whining traffic, she turns back.

'Alex, I think this would be good for you. I could see you here, serving lattes and cookies.'

'Yeah, maybe. I have no experience, though, it's crazy. I can't even bake cookies.'

'No, it's not – and I would handle all that. The important thing is to create an atmosphere. Everyone's getting bored of all those identikit coffee chains, they want something personal. And you care about people, Alex. That comes across. Even when you're being a prat. You know what Jody said to me once? "I'm proud to be with him." It wasn't because you're good-looking, because obviously you're not. It's more that ... people like you. God knows why. That's why it's so sad, you and Jody. That's why you have to fix it. Then you can open this café and destroy Starbucks.'

I can feel something stinging at my eyes. Perhaps it's the smell of furniture polish. We say goodbye and I close the door behind her. Daryl is tapping something into his mobile phone.

'Can I have another look around?'

'Sure, mate, go ahead.'

And I leave him and walk toward the rear of the room, to where Sam and I used to sit. I can see the marks on the floor where the sofa was. I sit down there, cross-legged. Sometimes, when he was very small, I carried him in and plonked him on the sofa, and called over my order, and we would look at the colour supplements together. I'd make up stories to connect the photos. Sometimes, a lot of the time, he'd get bored after ten minutes, or it would be too noisy and he'd cry. But coming in and sitting with him, even for a few minutes, sharing the buzz of a Saturday lunchtime, or the peace of a Sunday afternoon, it was magical in a way. It was restorative. A week of struggles and tears and arguments and worry, diminished by a quarter of an hour with a coffee and a sofa and some people all around us.

I could do this, I could make this feel like that again, for other people. I would like to try. I just need to somehow find a lot of money.

'You OK?' says Daryl, wandering over. 'Only I have this next place to show off.'

'Yeah, I'm fine,' I say, struggling to my feet.

'What do you reckon?' he says.

'I'm interested, but ...'

'Money?'

I nod.

'Go and see your bank, mate. Look up some old rich relatives.

I'll go easy on the sales patter with the other clients, I won't push this one too hard. Don't tell anyone, though, I've got a rep to protect.'

I have this strange urge to hug him, but fortunately I resist.

'Thanks, Daryl,' is all I say. And then we leave. He jams the door shut behind us, then sprints up the road to his Corsa. For a while, I stand outside, daunted but strangely happy. For a split second, a connective tissue of memory takes me back, a long way back, to a café in London, somewhere else that has become a safe space, if only in hindsight. I see the two boys outside, the sister and the mother, tucking into cakes and fizzy pop, the sun glinting through the glass, almost blinding. Somehow, through the sharp cold rain, I can feel its warmth on my face.

Overcome for a moment, I put a hand on the brick wall, as though to steady myself. Then I look up at the sign, or the place where the sign once was. And I already know what I would call this place, if it were mine.

Chapter 35

It turns out that I am the bait.

Dan calls me to say that Mission: Emma is on. Tonight. I ask him not to call it Mission: Emma, but he's not listening. All he'll say is that I've got to call her and get her to meet me at The Box, a little arts centre at the end of the Stokes Croft road, beneath the towering student accommodation blocks. It has a nice café with a live DJ, the sort of vibe I'd expect from Dan. I imagine him standing there, ready to deliver an armful of roses and a thirty-minute hard house set.

'But Dan,' I protest, 'I'm looking after Sam this afternoon – I'm off any minute to collect him from school.'

'Bring him,' says Dan. 'It's fine.'

So later, when I meet Sam at the school gates (well, about fifty metres from the school gates, but I'm getting closer every time) I casually mention that Dan is setting up a sort of nice surprise for Emma, and he might need our help.

'Is it like a game?' he says.

'Kind of. I don't know. But we'll at least be able to get a mug of frothy milk out of it.'

'Yes! Let's help Dan.'

On the way to the car, I call Emma, but I get flustered, not sure of how much I should say, or indeed, why the hell I'd want to meet her in that part of town.

'Hey, Emma, it's Dan ... I mean Alex. It's Alex here. Happy birthday! How are you?'

'Erm, fine,' she says. 'How are you? You sound a bit stressed. Is this about Mum? Is she OK?'

'No. I mean, yes, but no, this isn't about Mum. I'm in town this evening with ... Sam. I'm showing Sam around. You know, seeing the city.'

'I thought we were helping Dan,' says Sam.

'Shhhhhh,' I respond.

Then I'm back to Emma:

'I wondered, did you want to meet up for a quick birthday coffee? And Sam would love to see you before his tournament. For luck. If you're not busy?'

This is ridiculous.

'That's fine,' she says. 'I'm at my friend Pacha's. We're planning our trips. Where will you be?'

'Well, meet us at five o'clock at The Box? Our treat.'

'The Box? OK, see you then.'

I hang up on the call and quickly text Dan the agreed message: Game on

His reply is almost instant. Thank U!!!

In the car, crawling slowly through Bedminster and then into the city centre, Sam has more questions.

'Where are we going?'

'To a café called The Box.'

'Why is it a box?'

'It's just a name. How are you getting on? How is your building going?'

He has a little shoulder bag with him, which we've filled with sandwiches, a *Minecraft* book, some Lego and a feather he found yesterday in the park that he wants to show to Emma. He takes it out and runs it softly over the back of his hand.

'Daddy, why are we going to the box?'

'We're going to meet Auntie Emma, and maybe Dan too. Remember? I'm helping him with a plan. He wants to talk to Auntie Emma, but he's a bit scared so he needs our help.'

I know this is blowing his mind, so I put the radio on in the hope it'll distract him. It doesn't. After a long forensic analysis of the situation, we mercifully arrive at the expensive multistorey car park near Cabot Circus shopping centre, and begin the walk up the hill to the arts centre. Sam clasps my hand as we stroll, but he doesn't ask for my grip to be tighter, tighter – instead he chats. He tells me about *Minecraft* and then very carefully explains something specific: he and Olivia made a beacon that shines a shaft of white light into the sky.

'The light points all the way up to heaven,' he says. 'I think that is where people go afterwards, when we're not allowed to see them any more. It is nice.'

I wonder if he knows what that means, or if he's simply repeating something Olivia said to him. Before I can ask, he has moved on. He wants to know more about Emma and her travel plans, and what specific airline she is using. As we get closer, he stops talking, and I wonder what Dan is doing, what he has planned, and why this place, more than any other, was the right location. Will Emma even care? She's going away again in less than a week, for who knows how long. What can he say to her in a small arts centre canteen that he could not say in, for example, the Old Ship on fish and chips night? But then, he is new to romantic gestures. Oh God, this could be horrible. And now I've brought Sam into it.

By the time we get to The Box, Emma is already waiting for us in the café. She has a latte and an iPad, sitting there in a raggedy sweatshirt and jeans, her short hair messy, her face lit up slightly by the screen. When she sees us, she smiles broadly and waves us over. Sam runs toward her, stops short of her open arms, but then accepts her hug.

'Auntie Emma, I found a feather,' he says.

'Oh lovely, can you show me? Hi, Alex.'

'Hey, happy birthday,' I say, looking around for any sign of Dan. The canteen is small and quiet, its stark interior all bare concrete and glass. There's a small group of students at a table in the far corner, noisily comparing photos on their smartphones, and a middle-aged woman wearing a Sonic Youth T-shirt, reading a battered copy of *Vanity Fair*. All regulars, I expect. None of them are Dan. Or even Dan in disguise. Shit. Where is he? Emma and Sam are looking at her iPad screen, chatting about flights and airplanes. I nod intermittently as I scan the room. When Emma heads off to the bathroom, I check my phone, but there are no messages from Dan. Is it Mission: Abandoned?

Then I see him. He's standing by an interior doorway wearing a sky-blue fitted suit and a crisp white shirt – like a playboy super-model on a night out in San Marino. He beckons me over.

'Hey, Dan,' I say. 'Are we all set?'

'Yeah,' he says. 'How do I look?'

'Like you're in a Dolce and Gabbana magazine advert.'

'Right. Is that good?'

'Sure, why not. Are you OK?'

'Fine, yeah. Where's Emma?'

'She's gone to the bathroom.'

'OK, yeah. So, when she gets back, can you bring her over here?'

'Sure. Are you certain you're all right?'

'I'm a bit nervous.'

'It'll be fine. It's only Emma, you dummy. I'll bring her over. You get yourself ready.'

He takes a few breaths. And as I walk off, the background music fades and I hear him say to himself:

'OK, go.'

When I get to the table, I see Emma, strolling back from the bathroom. Here goes nothing.

'Erm, so, Emma,' I say. 'I've spotted a friend over there. Come and meet him.'

She looks at me sort of agog. Sam is still swiping the iPad screen, oblivious.

'Come on, I want to introduce you.'

'Okaaaaay,' she says slowly.

Dan has disappeared through the doorway. I take Sam by the hand and pick up Emma's iPad. She looks at me and I walk toward the door with her following idly behind. There are two staff members behind the café counter who look at Emma and whisper something to each other. We get to the doorway and I push it open slightly. There is a corridor, then a double door, which is ajar, leading into a large dark room. I've never been here before, I've no idea where I'm going, but I lead Emma through.

'Where are we going?' she complains. 'You're being extremely weird.'

'I know,' I say. 'Just follow me.'

She looks about ready to turn and bolt, but then Dan appears in the double doors, smiling that smile of his.

'What is going ON?' squeals Emma.

'Hi, Emma,' he says. 'I've sort of got a birthday surprise for you. Um, I hope you don't mind, I didn't want you to go without knowing something. But first, come this way.

'What are you doing, you prat?' she says. But he holds out his hand and she walks forward and takes it, then they both go through the door. I have to follow, I have to see what he has done. As soon as I peek inside, I understand.

It's the cinema room. I forgot this place has one. It's small, but unlike the rest of the building it is plushly decorated in red velvet. Little ruffled curtains run along the side walls, like in those classic thirties movie theatres, and the seats are plump and wide.

There is no one else here.

Dan leads Emma to two seats right in the centre of the auditorium and sits her down, picking up a huge box of popcorn from the floor beside him and balancing it on their laps.

'Ha, are we watching a film?' she says. 'Dan, what are we watching? Why is no one else here?'

'I hired the whole room – I kind of know the owners. Anyway, Emma, um, here's the thing. When we were going out, all those years ago, I was completely in love with you. I was utterly besotted. You may not have noticed. And then you decided to go away, and I understood, I honestly did. I thought I would get over you eventually. But, Emma, I didn't. I didn't and I don't think I will. So when you came back, I couldn't believe it, I couldn't believe how lucky I was. I should have told you straight away, but I thought it was all in the past for you. Now that you're going again, it doesn't matter. I've got nothing to lose. So I wanted to tell you: wherever you are in the world, whatever you do . . . you *are* the world to me.'

There is a brief silence. 'You're not going to sing, are you?' says Emma.

'Yes, I've got a whole jazz band behind the curtain, I've just got to cue them in.'

'Oh God.'

'I'm kidding. Look, I don't care if you're in Brazil or Vietnam or Thailand or the Isle of Man ... I'll be thinking about you. I can't help it. I always have, I always will. If you ever need anything, anything at all, I'll be here. Does that sound creepy? It didn't sound creepy in my head, but now I'm not sure. Anyway, before you go, I wanted to give you something. It's silly, but I think you'll understand.'

Then he raises his arm. And somewhere his signal is noticed, because the curtains open on the screen, and then we see a logo, and the familiar musical refrain of 'When You Wish Upon a Star' begins.

And the movie starts. And of course, *of course*, it's *The Lion King*.

'What is it?' whispers Sam. 'What is happening?'

He nudges past me and looks into the room.

'A movie? Can we watch? Is it scary? Where are my ear defenders?'

'No, we're not watching, Sam, it's for Emma and Dan. We need to leave them alone now.'

I usher him out, but for a second I glance back through the closing door, and I see that Emma's shoulders are hunched and shaking slightly; I see Dan put a hand on her shoulder, his face a shroud of concern. But with sudden abandon, she turns to him and flings her arms around his neck, and kisses his mouth. Then he is holding her too, their faces lit by the rising sun on the screen. The bucket begins to slip and then it falls to the floor. The popcorn scatters like confetti.

Those two. Charming, beautiful but, oh God, so dumb. It took them half a lifetime to get here – now they're making out in a Disney movie.

I think about the kids they were and all that's happened since, and how tentative and fragile happiness is. It's so easy to miss. Sometimes it passes without you seeing it. But sometimes, if you're incredibly lucky and patient, it will come around again.

'What's going on?' says Sam. 'Can I still play on the iPad?'

I don't answer.

'Daddy? You're crying.'

Chapter 36

On the drive to Matt and Clare's, I'm trying to weigh everything up. Jody, Sam, school, work: so many mental balls to juggle – and these aren't ping-pong balls; they're bowling balls. Filled with cement. This morning, to get things off to an exciting start, I went to see a small business adviser about the café. With the dour down-beat compassion of a funeral director, he explained all the risks involved in setting up a retail catering business, the failure rate, the long hours, the strain on relationships. He then handed me some forms about government grants and a blank five-year business plan and told me to think it over. It was the motivational equivalent of listening to a Smiths album before going on a first date.

It's Clare that answers the door.

'Come in,' she says. 'How was the meeting?'

'Hmm, OK,' I lie. And as I walk in, I almost skid straight over on a stray roller skate.

'Yes, be careful – the cleaner has taken the year off,' she says.

Inside is the usual chaos. Archie, Tabitha and several of their friends are running about dressed in a visually challenging mix of fancy dress outfits – a vampire cape here, a space helmet there, like some kind of weird avant garde show at Paris Fashion Week. In the kitchen, Matt is fussing over the hob where four bubbling pans are gushing steam into the already foggy microclimate.

'So?' says Clare as she clears a pile of picture books off the sofa for us to sit down.

'I don't know, Clare. I mean, it looks like I could get a start-up loan and I have some savings, but the whole thing is so risky. It's a huge upfront investment and then – well, I'm completely new to this. And neither of us can afford to put in a lot of money.'

Despite myself, I glance through at Matt, who was about to walk in, but then slowly backtracks into the kitchen.

'But I *do* have experience,' says Clare. 'And I know you can do this. It's a small venue and it was obviously popular. We're not looking to set up a giant new coffee house in the middle of town.'

'I know, but, to be honest . . .'

I look down, away from her, toward the floor and what looks like half a banana mashed into the rug.

'I don't have a lot of faith in myself,' I say at last. 'I mean, things haven't been working out for me, I don't know if you've noticed.'

'Join the club,' says Clare, but her tone is conciliatory rather than dismissive. 'I certainly didn't see twins and gambling debts on the horizon two years ago. We were trundling along quite well, I thought. Nice house, nice car, nice area, nice schools. But life has a way of shaking you about and slapping you in the face. Then kicking you in the balls. Then—'

'OK, OK, I get the general idea.'

'You lost your brother, but you survived and you made a beautiful family. Five months ago, Sam was terrified of noise and crowds, now he's competing in a video game tournament. You can do this, Alex. I think you *have* to do this.'

'Thank you,' I say. But it's all I can say. And just as I'm about to get emotional, Tabitha runs in screaming, followed by her brother, who's wielding a plastic sword and a laser gun.

'There is no such thing as stability any more,' says Clare as the parade passes. 'I mean, the pace of life, the uncertainty of everything. You've got to hang on somehow, haven't you? You work out what matters and go with that.'

We sit quietly for a few seconds, listening to the sound of Matt serving up pasta in the kitchen.

'Clare,' I say softly. 'Have you been reading those motivational posts on Facebook again?'

For the rest of the week, I spend hours hunched in front of my laptop building a spreadsheet of costs, the things I'd need for the café: rent, furniture, equipment, staff. In the evenings I pop in and see Jody and Sam – but mostly Sam. As the tournament approaches we let him play more; he's meeting Olivia online almost every evening. Mostly they practise building, trying new things, making simple little machines with pistons and batteries. But with his other friends they're also closing in on the Ender Dragon. They have scoured the landscape, slaying monsters, collecting the treasures they need to locate the mythical end portal. Hidden deep beneath the surface of the world, this is *Minecraft*'s final location.

There, the dragon awaits.

Chapter 37

It's the day before the *Minecraft* competition. I've planned a route into London on Google Maps and I've arranged to meet Dan at the entrance so he can chaperone us in. Later today, I'm heading over to the house so I can see how Sam's training is going. Yes, training. We're taking this very seriously. It's madness. Clare was right: a few months ago, he would have been terrified to attend something like this. I've seen photos on the website of previous events – a huge hangar crammed with teenagers playing games on massive screens in near-total darkness. I can only imagine the noise. Part of me still thinks when we get there, he'll grip my arm and ask to be taken home straight away. Then we can get on with things and chalk it up to experience, like everything else that ends this way. But part of me thinks he won't.

I sit at Dan's little table, looking out over the city. I have slipped into the habit of imagining each building as a *Minecraft* model, and I wonder if Sam and I could make the Clifton Suspension Bridge, or the Wills Memorial Building, or at least the weird Cheese Lane Shot Tower. Open but unread in my hands is a book entitled *How to Run Your Own Coffee Shop*, which had good reviews on Amazon. I keep trying to start it, but I am dragged away by other thoughts. The crowd of parents, the sound of screeching tyres. Don't let him through, keep him away. The images flood in whenever I think about moving on with my life, starting something new. Decisions George never got to make.

But something is different now. Maybe it's the therapy, maybe it's this sudden sense of purpose around everything – Sam, me, Jody – I can't be sure. But in the past, whenever I thought of George, I'd admonish myself if I did not continually return to that day. Guilt obliterated everything. This morning, however, I've drifted further back, dwelling on little moments of us together: kicking a football around in the park on a sunny afternoon, play-fighting in front of the television, lying on our beds after school, reading comics for hours. I realise I'm smiling. I'm not certain I remember George's voice, but I can conjure up his laugh, a staccato giggle filled with mischief.

And this brings me to Sam, and the spark I have seen in him these past few months. It was doubtless always there, but I was too blinkered to see it – too caught up in the 'problem' of Sam. Now I understand that his view of the world is completely different to mine; it is full of patterns and surprises and beauties that I don't see and can't comprehend. When he was a toddler, we had this weekend routine. I would put him in his pushchair and take him to this particular bench, set on a small scrap of land near one of the main roads snaking through Bedminster. There we would sit together for an hour, sometimes longer, and he would point at the cars, vans and buses and ask, 'Where going, Daddy?' and I would make up a destination. In the distance, we could see a row of colourful houses, way up on the hill; I would point at each one in turn and he'd say 'blue, yellow, red, blue'. The colour he gave rarely actually matched the house, but that wasn't the point. I loved those moments of calm and togetherness. I thought it was only a silly game, an exercise in comforting repetition. I was wrong. It was his attempt to understand and compartmentalise the world, to read the mad flurry of activity around him. He needed systems, however fragile, to process what was happening. Because the city wasn't background noise to him, he couldn't just tune it out – the world was an endless assault on his senses. He desperately needed to make sense of it.

Now it seems that everything is becoming clearer, like sunlight streaming across an unfamiliar landscape. He's not a problem, he's brilliant. He's my beautiful son. He's funny and smart and full of curiosity, and he links things together in weird but brilliant ways. His imagination is a gigantic furnace that sculpts meaning out of this mess of noise. Why didn't I see that? Most annoyingly, while I've struggled to understand everything, clever kids like Olivia and Tabitha got Sam right away. All along, I thought it was him, wilfully trapped in his own world. But it was me.

My phone buzzes and it's a text from Emma, wherever she is:

> I've got a missed call from Mum, have you spoken
> to her?

I get to the house in the late morning, parking down the road and stepping out into the familiar street. The sky is a mass of cloud, lending a weird, flint-like greyness to the day, but there's a warm glow from the twinkling lights of a Christmas tree in the sitting room window, and from Sam's bedroom above there are brief coloured flashes. He's playing *Minecraft*. When I ring the doorbell, Jody opens the door and gives me a hug.

'How are you doing?' she says. 'The big day is coming.'

I nod. 'What are we doing?'

When I get in, I see that the front room is tidy, the books are all stuffed into the shelves instead of piling up on the floor and tables, and there are dozens of Christmas cards hanging from long pieces of twine draped along the walls. There's even a new coffee table with space underneath for a box of toys and comics. Jody has placed large church candles along the windowsill, and an actual fire is crackling gently in the fireplace, giving the room a cosy evening feel on this dull, dark day.

'Wow, this looks beautiful,' I say.

'Thank you. I've got more time – things aren't as crazy at the gallery, and Sam is . . . well, Sam has actual friends! Olivia and her brother come around and they all read computer game magazines, and talk about *Minecraft*, of course, but also Lego and *Adventure Time* and lots of other things I don't understand. He still struggles to keep up with them, and he listens much more than he talks, but they don't seem to mind. It makes me think, he must have been so lonely, and he had no way of telling us.'

'Have you talked to him about school?'

'I'm not pushing it at the moment – he's got so much to think about with the competition. But we do need to let them know next week. I don't want another year at that school. I feel like he's finally moving forward. Not great big strides, but little steps.'

We're standing together now, in the tidy room, a metre apart. The orange glow from the fire reflects in her hair and on her skin. It's in her eyes and her smile. I feel for a second as though the two of us have always been here together and always will be. She puts her hand gently on my arm.

'Go up and see him.'

As I climb the stairs, I hear the music first, as always. That piano sound, gentle, almost meandering, beckoning you to explore the world, to take your time. I push the door open, and Sam is on his bed surrounded by books and magazines; a little reading lamp providing the only light beyond the small LCD display.

'Make some torches to light up areas at night,' he says when he sees me. 'Monsters will avoid the areas around these torches.'

'Hi, Sam. What are you up to?'

'I'm building. I have a wall now. A big wall that goes round the Tower of London, like in the photo.'

Sure enough, beyond the building that we made together all those weeks ago is a vast wall, constructed with an artful mix of plain and cobblestone. There are narrow windows along its perimeter and a couple of entry gates teased into blocky arches.

'Do you want to go on an adventure?' he says.

I pick up the controller and we are in the world together again.

There is warmth from the sun; the sense of a breeze rustling the ragged leafy squares that make up the canopy of the nearby woodland glade. We wander along, away from the castle and deeper into the wood.

'I will make a railway track,' says Sam. 'It will go from the castle to the village. I will go on a cart when I need to steal more carrots.'

'That's a good idea,' I say.

We pass a trench leading into a network of caves and tunnels, somewhere to explore on another day. There is a deep pool amid the birch trees with a small island in the middle. For some reason it reminds me of the island we imagined at the campsite, the one that I took Sam to when he was scared and couldn't sleep. It feels almost real now. As night begins to close in, I expect Sam to panic, but instead he draws a sword.

'It is made of iron and has an enchantment. It is very strong.'

'OK, but maybe we should head back, we don't want to get completely lost.'

Grudgingly, he follows as I turn, the trees now becoming grey in the dying light.

'We've had some fun here, haven't we?' I say.

'Yes. Thank you, Daddy.'

With the castle wall in sight, I hear something familiar, and not too far away. The clanking sound of bones. Very quickly, there is the swoosh of an arrow, and then another.

'A skeleton,' says Sam.

I dive beneath the trees, chopping at the undergrowth with my axe as I run. I look for Sam, but he's disappeared amid the darkened branches. I can't tell where the archer is, but its weird bone-jangling sounds are so close. Then I see it, white under the pale moon, its bow drawn. It is between me and the castle gate.

'I'm stuck!' I shout. It hits me with two arrows in quick succession. I almost feel the energy, the life force, ebbing away. Is this the way the adventure ends? Within sight of our building, but too far away to make it?

But no, in a sudden rush of sound and colour, Sam bursts out of the forest, his sword raised. The skeleton turns, but it is too slow. Sam swings the blade and it connects with a crunch, sending the monster jerking backwards.

'Go!' says Sam, but as he hits it again, the sword shatters, and now he must run too.

I rush forward, with only half a heart of health left, inches from the safety of the gate entrance. The skeleton has turned to me again, lining up another arrow. When I hear a whoosh, I brace for the life-sapping damage, and hear the sound of an arrow making impact. But I'm still alive.

When I turn, I see Sam, now armed with a bow, standing beside his fallen enemy.

'I swapped weapons in time! I saved you.'

'That was amazing, Sam!'

When we look back at the skeleton we realise it has dropped some loot, a single gleaming object, lying amid the grass and flowers. When we approach, we see what it is: a golden helmet.

'The last Crown Jewel,' says Sam.

'We did it,' I say. 'We completed our quest.'

He walks ahead and I walk behind him, through the gates and toward the imposing tower. Inside, the main hall has been utterly transformed: I see paintings lining the walls, which are now constructed with oak panels interspersed with grand stone columns.

'Follow me,' he says.

And we ascend the low sweeping staircases together, up to the next storey, where a long corridor leads to several smaller chambers. I wander from room to room like a visitor at some lavish National Trust property, inspecting every detail, peeking through the windows at the scenery beyond. He takes me to a small spiral staircase that leads out on to the battlements and we walk to the edge together, so close we're almost holding hands. Under the looming polygonal clouds, we stand silently, gazing beyond the wall to the mountains in the distance. From the paddock below, we hear the horses and cows, but nothing else. We're blissfully alone in the universe.

'Sam, are you ready for tomorrow, do you think?'

'What's tomorrow?'

'The competition, at the video game event.'

'Oh yes. I have to build something good. That is my job. Olivia is coming to watch.'

'You know there will be a lot of people?'

'They have computers there, so I don't need to bring my own console.'

'Do you remember going to London? With me and Auntie Emma?'

'We saw the Tower! But I did get lost and I was scared.'

He steps down from the battlement and wanders off toward the staircase again, and I follow.

'But you think you'll be all right at the event? If we put on your ear defenders maybe?'

'Yes. I won't be sad.'

'It's fine if you are though, Sam. No matter what happens, it's OK to be sad. Everyone gets sad sometimes.'

'Do you?'

'Yes, of course.'

'What about?'

'Sometimes he's sad about his brother,' says Jody.

We both look around and she's there, standing in the doorway with a mug of tea and a glass of milk. 'His brother George died when he was little. That makes Daddy a bit sad. But we'll look after him.'

Sam doesn't look away from the screen.

'Sometimes wolves try to get in to eat the pigs and the sheep,' he says. 'I have to not leave the gates open. Daddy, don't leave the gates open if you come in.'

'I won't.'

'If you give the cows some wheat they will fall in love with each other.'

'Right. That makes sense.'

I look up at Jody and she makes a sympathetic shrugging gesture. I smile and kiss Sam on the side of his head. He doesn't move away.

'Can I join you?' says Jody.

'You mean . . . in the game?'

'Yes, Sam showed me how to play.'

She picks up another controller, sits beside us and hits the Start button. A third character appears on screen. A character in an orange jumpsuit. It takes me a few seconds to twig.

'That was you!' I say. 'You were the one in orange.'

'I wanted to see what you guys were up to. At first, I watched Sam playing, then I felt like being part of it. But I didn't want you to think I was interfering, so I hid.'

'Mummy told me not to tell you,' says Sam.

'You stalked us in *Minecraft*?' I say with mock horror.

'Not very well. But yes. I'm sorry.'

'Don't be. I'm glad it was you. Next time, let's all build something together.'

'We can start something new,' says Sam.

'OK, but I want you to know that if we get to the competition and you don't want to do it, that's fine,' I say. 'We can go and have ice cream instead.'

Sam sighs heavily.

'No, I will do it. Olivia says I can obviously win because I know how to make flashing lights.'

'Well, that's that then,' says Jody. 'We're going to London.'

'You're coming?' I ask.

'Of course! I wouldn't miss this. We'll all go together. It'll be an adventure.'

Later, Jody and I head downstairs, and I look around at the house again and take in its changes – changes that have happened without me.

'So the therapist,' says Jody. 'Have you talked about us?'

I hesitate a second.

'I'm sorry,' she blusters. 'I know it's all confidential. It's rude of me to ask.'

338

'No, no, it's fine,' I say. 'Yeah, we've talked about it.'

'And? Oh, I'm sorry!'

'It's fine! It's early days – I've only had two sessions. But I told her about, you know, work and money and Sam and how it all got complicated and exhausting. And, well, it turns out I've maybe done a lot of the wrong things for the right reasons.'

Jody goes to say something, but I stop her.

'I know, I know. You were right. I took everything on and I didn't need to. I should have been here more; and even when I *was* here I was always somewhere else. I wish I'd worked this out sooner.'

'You always have been a bit slow,' she says.

And we are very close to each other now. I feel her breath on my face. She leans in and I do too. Her perfume rises like heat. Our eyes close. I wonder if this is happening.

Then suddenly, the embers crackle loudly on the fire and it breaks us out of the spell. An old possibility that seemed real again edges backwards away from us.

'Well, I'd better go.'

A look passes across her face that I can't read.

'Yes,' she says, flicking a curl away from her eyes. But neither of us moves. From the doorway behind me, there's the slight chill of the December air, the sounds of the street, the low hum of cars far away and all around us. We're looking at each other.

'How long do you think you'll stay at Dan's?' Jody asks.

'I don't know,' I say. 'It's like the school thing, and the café, and . . . us. A decision needs to be made.'

'Yeah, it does,' she says.

A car horn, a long way away. A slight breeze ruffles the curtains.

'So, I was thinking,' she says. 'I mean, if you want to, I was wondering if . . . '

'Yes?'

Jody laughs self-consciously and looks away from me. The air between us seems charged; it sparkles like glitter.

'I was thinking . . .'

I feel the phone buzzing in my hand, and almost as a gesture to break the tension, I glance at the screen. I'm sure it's going to be Dan, wondering where I am. But then I look at the words, and that's not it. That's not it at all.

'Are you OK?' says Jody. 'You look like you've seen a ghost.'

'It's from Mum,' I reply. 'She's in hospital.'

Chapter 38

I did not want to see George. I remember that.

Mum asked me, she said that it was my choice. I could go in and say goodbye if I wanted – one last time. He was in a little room in the mortuary, lying there alone, on a metal gurney. But I shook my head and looked down at my feet. It wasn't about grief – I was scared. I didn't know what he'd look like, I'd never seen a dead body before. I was worried there would be blood and horror. When Mum took my hand and led me away, I felt ashamed.

I don't know how I feel about that decision now – perhaps my therapist will tell me, in time. But I know that my view of hospitals is entirely shaped by that day and its aftermath. They are places of darkness and catastrophe. People you love don't come out.

I phone Mum back immediately.

'Hello?' she says. Her voice is slightly shaky but her old force and confidence are there.

'Mum, it's me.'

'Yes, I know, your name comes up on the screen, dear.'

'What's happened? Are you OK?'

'I had a bit of a fall last night. I was changing the light bulb on the upstairs landing, for one of those new eco bulbs, you know the ones. They're very expensive, aren't they?'

'Yes. But Mum, what happened?'

'Well, the stool gave way and I fell off. I knocked myself a little bit unconscious and broke my wrist. I'd have been lying there all night, but Mrs Ferris from up the lane came over to ask if I could look after her dog for a few hours – she plays bridge on Thursday nights. I never get an invite. Anyway, when I didn't answer, she came upstairs, nosy cow, and found me. She brought me to the minor injuries unit and they made me stay in overnight. I did try to call. How are you, anyway?'

This is typical Mum. Don't mind me, I'm just in hospital with concussion and broken bones, nothing to see here, move along. But the guilt throbs at the back of my head – because I never checked my phone messages, I was too tied up in everything else going on.

'A nurse is here, can you speak to her?'

'Yes, of course.'

I hear the phone being passed over.

'Mr Rowe?' asks an officious voice.

'Yes. Is Mum OK?'

'We think so. She has suffered a Colles fracture in her wrist, it's quite common in older people when they fall, so we realigned that this morning. However, we were also worried that she may have been dizzy before she fell, so we have run some tests. It could be nothing, but ... well, it could be a sign of something else, like diabetes or a transient ischaemic attack.'

'A what?'

'A transient ischaemic attack. A mini stroke.'

There are a few seconds of silence. I can hear my mum in the

342

background protesting the use of the phrase 'older people'. I hear what sounds like the nurse moving further away.

'A stroke?' I repeat. Jody puts her hand on my arm.

'We don't know,' says the nurse. 'We've done some tests, we'll have a better idea later on. It might be nothing at all. She'll definitely need some help for a few days because of that wrist, though. Is your father at home?'

'No. No, he's long gone.'

That is a weird way of putting it.

'Well, can you or another relative stay with her for a day or so?'

'Yes . . . I-I'll be there as soon as I can. Goodbye.'

I look at Jody and try not to betray the fear rising from deep inside me. Then I hear a voice from the stairs.

'What has happened to Grandma?'

Sam has come down and is now standing on the last step, the controller still in his hand.

'It's OK,' says Jody, rushing to him. 'Grandma has had a fall and she's in hospital, but she's OK.'

'I'll drive down,' I say. 'If I head off now I'll be there by fourish.'

'Would you like me to come with you?' says Jody. 'Clare and Matt can look after Sam. I will. If you need me?'

I nod silently, unable to meet her kindness with actual words.

'I want to come too. I want to see Grandma,' says Sam.

'What about the competition?' I say to both of them.

There's a pause.

'Emma and Dan can take him,' says Jody.

'I want to see Grandma!'

'Oh shit. Emma,' I say. 'I've got to tell her.'

When she answers the phone her voice is thick and blurry.

'Hello? Alex? Ugh, I'm in bed. I have a hangover.'

'Emma, Mum is in hospital. She's had a fall and broken her

wrist, but they're also doing some tests on her – they think she may have had some sort of mini stroke.'

I hear someone grumbling incoherently in the background, obviously still asleep. I know it's Dan, but I don't have time to interrogate her about their rekindled romance.

'Emma, I'm heading down to see her. I wanted you to know what was going on.'

'I'll come,' she says. 'I'm coming too.'

I hear her scrabbling around, obviously looking for clothes.

'What? Are you sure?'

'Yes. Shit. Yes. I should have gone to see her weeks ago. Oh dammit, Mum. Can you pick me up? Please, Alex, I have to come.'

I put my hand over the phone and look at Jody. She's already heard and nods her head.

'OK,' I say. 'Be ready in ten minutes.'

I look down at Sam and wonder how much of this he is actually taking in. It's the same old question. If we get to Mum's, will he understand that we've missed the competition? If she is ill, will he understand that? I kneel down beside him.

'Sam, your auntie wants to come too, but Dan could take you to the video game festival. You can still do it.'

'No, I want to come with you and Mummy. I want to see Grandma. I don't want her to go away.'

'She's not going anywhere, she's had an accident, that's all.'

'I want to come. I don't care!'

'We can do the competition next year,' says Jody. At first, I assume she's talking to Sam, but then I see that actually she's looking at me. 'Let's all go and see Grandma, OK?'

We charge around the house, stuffing clothes and toiletries into a suitcase. Everything is moving so fast it's hard to process the whirl of emotions. But deep down I know that there's one thing I can identify beneath the worry and confusion. It is disappointment. Disappointment for Sam, but also myself. I wanted him to prove something at that silly contest – and I didn't realise how important that was to me.

Eventually, we're crammed into the car, heading through Bristol's outlying suburbs and then on to the M5. Beside Sam in the back seat is an extremely hungover Emma, clutching a huge thermos flask of coffee to her chest and whimpering pitifully. Her and Dan went clubbing last night, rolling back to his flat at 3 a.m. Sam is watching her with a degree of morbid fascination.

'Will she be sick?' he asks.

'Nooooooo,' groans Emma.

'What are you going to say to Mum?' I ask.

'I don't know,' she says. 'I can't tell her about you know what. It's not the right time, is it?'

'OK.'

'I mean, this is about her, not me.'

'I know.'

'I'm just going to play it totally cool.'

'OK. But don't tell her about Sam's *Minecraft* competition. I don't want her to think we're missing anything to look after her. OK?'

'Fine. Whatever, I'm going to sleep.'

For the rest of the journey, all I am thinking is a stroke. A *stroke*. Sure, she seems OK now, but where would that lead? Would there be another? The possibilities and ramifications shoot through my brain. I always took it for granted that Mum was there, Mum was indestructible. It was the only certainty I ever had. Now what?

Now what?

'Do you want me to drive?' asks Jody.

'I'm fine. I'm fine.'

Four hours later, we're pulling into the car park of a small community hospital. With its modern brick buildings, neatly positioned around a small neat lawn, it looks like a retirement home, and it's just as deathly quiet. We clamber out of the car, Emma leaning against the door for several seconds, breathing heavily. Sam runs off and jumps on to a bench near the lawn. Jody is already walking toward the entrance, taking control, putting her hand out for Sam as she passes. We all follow.

As soon as the doors open, the familiar hospital smell hits us – that exquisite combination of disinfectant and boiled vegetables, an immediate reminder of all the times you've visited before. An olfactory gut-punch of memories. Behind the counter there's a receptionist, and a very young nurse reading through some notes attached to a clipboard. She looks tired and harassed. I tell them who we are and the nurse leads us along a bright corridor lined with children's paintings and through some double doors into a small ward. Two of the beds are empty; one has a very old woman wearing what looks like a Victorian nightdress. She is sitting up and talking to an even older man, who is slouched on a plastic chair and bent over toward her, seemingly dozing. Then in the far right corner, I see Mum, already wearing her coat, a bag on her lap, sitting bolt upright at the end of her bed. She has a thick cast on her arm and hand.

Suddenly, I'm hit by an all-too-familiar feeling. Perhaps it's tiredness, perhaps it's all the worry, but more likely it's a memory, lodged in the back of my consciousness, of a similar moment years ago. Mum waiting in the hospital, alone and confused. A voice explaining there was nothing they could do. Do you want to say goodbye?

346

Grief wrenches at me like a hidden current beneath the surface of a dark deep ocean.

The nurse looks at me and her expression becomes one of concern.

'Your mum had a bit of an eventful day yesterday.' She smiles.

'The tests?' I say.

'The consultant will explain everything.' And with that, she's gone. The consultant will explain? What does that mean? Is that good or bad? Why couldn't she say? That's bad. It has to be bad.

Our little group clatters toward Mum's bed – and she waves, tutting and shrugging her shoulders at the lunacy of having to be here.

'Hello, son!' she says. 'They won't let me go until the consultant has been round. It's like Colditz, except the food isn't as good. How are you? Hello, Jody, hello, Sam. Ah, hello, Emma. What a pleasant surprise. Is this what it takes to get you to visit me? I should have thought of it sooner!'

'Hi,' says Emma, giving Mum an awkward stooped hug.

We stand around, not really knowing what to say next. Sat there on the bed, somehow separate from this fidgeting group, Mum's resolve melts and she looks old, pale and scared.

'I'd very much like to go home,' she says.

Her eyes dart around the room, taking in the dull green walls, the bleeping medical machinery, the bustling nurses. I know that the terror she communicates has nothing to do with her own accident, it's the one that haunts us all.

A middle-aged man in a crisp white shirt strides over, his sleeves rolled up, his glasses perched on the end of his nose. It could only be the consultant.

'Mr Rowe?'

'Yes,' I reply. And my voice is as quiet and reverential as a child's.

'We have your mother's test results.'

You see these moments take place in television dramas. The big revelation. The patient in front of the desk, or on a ward, worried, tense. The long dramatic pause, the camera panning into their face to drink in every last emotion. But when these things happen in real life, these moments of utter dread and uncertainty, they play out so differently, almost as anticlimaxes. There is no swell of music, no choreographed emotion. Just a man in a crisp white shirt preparing to tell you the absolute worst. And then you have to deal with it, and the camera doesn't cut away. It never cuts away. I feel someone tug at my arm and assume it's Sam, but when I turn slightly, I see that it's Emma.

The consultant idly flips through some more papers.

'She's fine,' he says. 'It was a light concussion.'

The whole room is suddenly lighter, like a blast of pure oxygen has been pumped in. I feel giddy. Emma audibly breathes out.

'But the dizziness?' I ask.

'Well, what she didn't tell the doctors last night was that she'd had half a bottle of wine with her neighbour in the afternoon,' he says. 'That was what caused the dizziness.'

'Mum,' I say. 'You were pissed?'

'No, I was not!' she says. 'We were having a pleasant lunch. Now can I please get out of here?'

When she gets up, she wobbles slightly, so I rush forward and grab her elbow.

'Steady!' I say.

I look over to Emma for some support, but to my surprise, I see that she's crying.

'I'm sorry, Mum,' she suddenly and surprisingly wails. 'I'm so sorry!'

And then she sort of stumbles forward and grabs Mum in a bear hug, almost sending them both falling on to the bed. Jody and I look at each other with a mixture of surprise and amusement.

'What's going on?' asks Sam.

'I can't be sure,' I reply. 'But I think Aunt Emma is sorry.'

The drive to Mum's is an uncomfortable crush of unspoken tensions. The whole Rowe family together again, packed into a knackered old estate car; and then Jody and Sam wedged in too. It's a Venn diagram of simmering regrets and uncertainties. We stop for fish and chips on the way, and by the time we pull into Mum's gravel driveway it is utterly dark, a half moon weakly lighting the trees around her cottage in a blueish glow.

Inside, Emma helps Mum get some plates and we spread out the paper packages full of steaming hot chips and battered fish on the table. Luckily Jody has brought cheese and piccalilli sandwiches for Sam, and he eats them quietly, watching the awkward family dynamics cranking back into life.

As we sit around the table, Mum asks Emma some tentative questions about her travels, and then my sister is off, providing a detailed account of her ten years flying from country to country, cherry-picking anecdotes suitable for both her mother and nephew. Some of it we've all heard before on her previous visits home, but no one stops her, because it is a relief to listen after a hard, worrying day, and not to have to add anything. Then she moves on to her return, her half-hearted attempt to give Britain another go, then her plans for the future – which may or may not include my best friend.

'You're going out with Dan again?' Mum splutters.

'Yes,' says Emma. 'Why, what's wrong with Dan?'

'Oh, nothing at all. But that poor boy moped around for a year after you left. I hope you're not going to do that to him again.'

Emma looks at me, but says nothing.

So Mum talks instead. She brings Emma up to date with her own life in Cornwall; she asks Jody about the gallery and me about the café.

'And what are you up to, Sam?' she says.

'Nothing,' he replies.

'What do you like?'

'*Minecraft* and planes and not school. Are you better now?'

Mum laughs but I'm worried he's going to bring up the competition.

'I'm fine,' she says. 'But I'm not getting any younger. I'm thinking of selling this place, maybe moving a little closer to Bristol again. We'll see.'

'Really?' I say. 'I mean, I think that would make sense.'

'Only if you don't mind. It doesn't mean you have to stay in the area.'

'No, I will,' I say.

'He has to,' says Jody. 'We're here.'

We look at each other and I remember that she was about to say something, before I got the text from Mum. I don't want to guess, though. I don't want to get my hopes up.

'And you'll have your café by then,' says Mum.

'Well, we'll see. It's very expensive and risky. I'd need about twenty grand to even get it going. I'm ... well, a little short of that figure right now.'

'But you want to do it?'

'Yeah. It's exciting, you know? The idea of it. That place feels like a part of our lives, doesn't it, Sam?'

He nods silently.

'Well,' says Mum. 'You've got to try. George would want you to – he'd say, give it a go, what's the worst that could happen?'

Sam is about to say something, but doesn't.

'Right,' says Mum. 'I'll do the washing up.'

'You have a broken wrist, I'll do it,' says Emma.

'My God,' says Mum. 'She *has* changed.'

'Actually, there's something I need to tell you. Something that happened to me. I need to tell you and I need to say sorry about running away. But I don't want to do it all in front of an audience.'

I expect Mum to make some sort of smart comment, but she looks at Emma and senses that this has taken courage and that it's serious. She puts her arm around my sister and guides her into the kitchen. The door shuts behind them.

Later, we are making up beds: Jody and Sam in the spare room, me in the little box room next door, Emma downstairs on the sofa.

'What's the plan then?' says Emma, as we roll out her sleeping bag.

I can hear Mum in the kitchen, and Jody helping Sam brush his teeth in the bathroom upstairs.

'We all stay tomorrow, see how she is. Your flight is on Sunday evening, isn't it? You could get the train? Or can Dan take you?'

'I'll worry about that. What about the competition?'

'Oh, it's OK. I can't leave you with Mum by yourself, that's not fair. We'll go next year. To be honest, I'm not sure he would have gone through with it anyway. This is a good excuse not to put him in that situation.'

She nods, but she looks unconvinced.

'Good night then,' she says.

Chapter 39

There is a light tap on my bedroom door. Then a louder more insistent bang.

'What? What is it?' I slur.

'It's me,' says Emma.

I check my phone. It's 7 a.m. My first thought is that something has happened to Mum.

'Is everything OK?' I say.

'Yes,' she says. 'But there's been a change of plan.'

Then I see Sam looking around the door – he's fully clothed and has a *Minecraft* book under his arm. Jody is with him.

'We've had a chat,' says Emma. 'You're going to that competition.'

'What?' I say.

'Mum is OK. I'll stay here with her today, and get the train on Sunday. There's no point in you missing it. But you have to leave now. I'll explain everything to her when she wakes up. It's fine. Get up now and go.'

'But—'

'Alex, it's fine. Get Sam to that tournament. Jody, you tell him.'

Jody looks around the door.

'Alex, she's been on at me since six o'clock. I think we're going to have to do what she says.'

Sam walks into the room.

'Come on, Daddy.'

'OK,' I say, scrambling up out of bed. 'Let's do this. Where are my boxer shorts?'

And then we're in the car, heading out toward London. Jody is in the front with me, Sam in the back studying his *Minecraft* book. The competition starts at 1 p.m. It's going to take us five hours to get into London. It's going to be tight. If there's traffic, we won't make it.

No one says very much. We're lost in our own thoughts, our own trepidations. I want to ask Jody about that conversation back at our house. Was she going to ask me to come home? I want to tell her that I feel so much better about things, that I know where I was going wrong, being so distant, keeping everything to myself. I know that there was something perhaps always between us, and that the roots of it led back, a long way back, to a cold afternoon and a terrible accident. My therapist talked about survivor's guilt – the feeling that I somehow caused it, or that it should have been me. Guilt has loomed over me like a thick canopy of thorns.

We're into Somerset when my phone starts buzzing, so I pull it out of my pocket and lob it at Jody.

'It's Dan,' she says.

'Shit, we're supposed to be meeting him at the event – about half an hour ago.'

'Does he know what's been happening?'

'Only if Emma has told him.'

'Then I'm guessing no?'

She answers the call and puts it on speakerphone.

'Hello?' I shout.

'Hey there,' says Dan. 'Where are you all? You know the competition starts in two hours?'

'Um, yeah, we had a minor diversion. We're running a bit late.'

'There are a lot of people here, dude. Sam needs to sign in to enter. Do you want me to sort that out?'

'Yes!'

'OK, but guys, get a move on. Is Emma with you? She disappeared yesterday and she's not replying to my texts.'

'Um, not quite,' I say.

And while I'm navigating the dual carriageway traffic, Jody explains what's been happening, and how Emma is now in Cornwall looking after her mother.

'You'd think she might have told me that,' says Dan.

Three hours in and we're on the A303, zooming through Wiltshire, muddy fields and farmland extending endlessly around us, pockmarked by anonymous villages. I weave in and out of trucks and MPVs, glancing at the clock every few seconds as it ticks toward 1 p.m. I look in the rear-view mirror and I see Sam, quiet and alone. His world is always separate, this much I understand. But I now know that it is accessible. It's just weird that I found it out through a video game. If we make it in time, we are going to play that game with a hundred other people. Despite all I've learned, I have no idea how he is going to react.

The M3 passes in a blur of identikit suburbs and fleeting stretches of woodland, but as we approach London, the traffic gets heavier, and we begin to slow. Jody opens the satnav app on her phone and it says we're maybe forty minutes away. The M25 is in sight when Dan rings again.

'Um, guys, they're starting in twenty minutes. I'm holding Sam a space, but I don't think they'll wait.'

'Are we there yet?' asks Sam.

'Nearly,' I say. 'Dan, can you stall it somehow?'

'Um, how?' he says.

'I don't know! Tell them we're only coming for the competition!'

'I've told them. They sort of shrugged.'

I jam my foot down and accelerate past a row of coaches, almost catching the wing mirror of a BMW in the fast lane – the driver beeps and shouts something unintelligible.

'That man is cross,' says Sam.

'Come on, Dan, you can think of something.'

The motorway looks hopelessly clogged, but I manage to swerve in and out of the vans and buses, Jody gripping on to the dashboard, Sam jerking left and right. We're on the periphery of London surrounded by the endless grimy patchwork of industrial estates and densely packed houses. In the distance, clusters of sixties tower blocks rise like gravestones. Sam stares out of the window, fascinated.

There is a jam as we're coming off the motorway, a snaking queue of cars lining up to enter the road we're aiming for. Sam leans forward and stares at Jody's phone screen.

'There's another way,' he says. 'That road and that road.'

'Can we go that way?' says Jody to me.

'What the hell, let's try it,' I reply.

We screech across two lanes, careering off on to a side road. Dan calls.

'I've bought you about fifteen minutes,' he says.

'How?' asks Jody.

'I may have asked my friend Jay to hack their network and bring the server down. It's fine, it's only a little hack. They'll figure it out.'

Then finally we see the convention centre: a hangar-like edifice in the distance, nestling amid a weird hinterland of hypermodern office buildings and surrounded by hundreds of acres of car park. It looks like some sort of sinister military complex.

'Are we there?' asks Sam.

'Yes, almost,' I say.

Driving into the labyrinthine parking areas, we begin to see vast groups of teenagers and twenty-somethings walking toward the venue. Most are in jeans and hoodies, but there are also small groups dressed as martial arts warriors and zombies, shivering against the bitter cold.

A series of apathetic staff in hi-vis jackets guide us to a parking space. We all emerge from the car, stretching our legs, watching the ragtag procession of gamers. Over the entrance is a huge sign that says GEN X GAMES CON, flanked by large adverts for games I haven't heard of, featuring space marines and muscular guys with machine guns. Sam grabs my hand as a giggling group dressed as stormtroopers jogs past.

'Come on, we've got to go,' I say, pulling Sam behind me.

We join the weird crowd as it snakes in toward the venue and into the imposing entrance hall lined with snack bars, cloakrooms and merchandise stalls. There are masses of people, queuing for food, waiting to get into the exhibition halls, hanging around playing on handheld games consoles, shouting and laughing.

'They are noisy,' he says. 'I don't like it.'

He stops dead in his tracks and looks down, refusing to budge. It is something I'm familiar with from a thousand school runs, a thousand frustrating mornings spent haranguing and bargaining with him – until I get angry enough to pick him up and carry him.

But not today.

Instead, I kneel down, low enough that he can see me amid the tumult.

'Sam,' I say. 'It's OK. It's OK to be scared. But Mummy and I are here, and I have your ear protectors. We need to pretend this is a game, that we have to work out a way to get through all these people – like a spy. Remember in London? You did it in the end, didn't you?'

'I conquered my fear.' He nods.

'You can do it again. This is how things are – we conquer our fears together, OK?'

'OK.'

He stands still for a moment, gently tapping his head with the palm of his hand, mulling things over. I know now I have to give him this time to process things quietly. I clasp the ear defenders in my jacket pocket and look around for the entry gates that lead to the show floor. When he's ready, he takes my hand and pulls me forward.

'This way,' I say confidently.

'Well played,' whispers Jody to me as we set off again.

We file as fast as we can through security, into a giant corridor leading to the row of halls. This is when the noise hits us – a scattershot bassline of ear-bleeding electronic sounds, sending shockwaves through the polished stone floors. And inside it is chaos.

As far as the eye can see, through the almost pitch-darkness of the hangar, there are dozens of stands devoted to different game publishers. Hundreds of gigantic monitors are arranged into rows, each blaring out video game footage, each surrounded by a gaggle of people staring intently at the flashing, mesmerising visuals, laughing, high-fiving each other. Hundreds of competing sound systems blaring out dance music, rock guitars and shoot-'em-up explosion effects create an utter aural barrage, a strobe-lit blast chamber. We stop and stare, bumped and pushed from all sides by crowds desperate to get to the latest game releases. I look down at Sam and see that he's saying something, but there's no way I can hear. I bend down to him.

'Pardon?' I shout.

His response is incomprehensible.

'PARDON?'

'HEADPHONES, DADDY, HEADPHONES.'

I grab for the ear defenders and put them on his head; he grasps at them desperately. I check the map on the back of the programme that was thrust into my hand as we passed through the entrance. Jody points at the *Minecraft* area on the diagram and then at a far corner of the hall. We make our move, wading between teens in game T-shirts and staff dressed as Pac-Man and Sonic the Hedgehog. I see a sign for *Minecraft*, in the game's distinct stony font, and push through.

Finally, we're standing in front of a large area, separated from the main hall by high screens, decorated with large cardboard cut-outs of Steve, Creepers and zombies. Sam smiles up at us. We're going to make it.

Inside, the atmosphere is suddenly very different and somehow quieter. There are rows of desks, each with its own monitor and chair, like a school computer room. Around the perimeter are big boxes painted to look like *Minecraft* blocks and piled up into little huts; there is an area carpeted with fake grass and scattered with beanbags. In one corner a large model of a spider appears to be climbing over one of the wall panels, its torch-like eyes flashing. Worried it'll scare Sam, I try to shield it from view, but he spots it behind me.

'It's OK, it's not real,' I say.

'Spiders won't attack you during the day – unless you attack them,' he replies.

The gamers here are noticeably younger. At each desk there's a tousle-haired tween, most of them in *Minecraft*-branded tops, tapping away at keyboards or gripping joypads, staring intently at their screens – and at *Minecraft*. For the first time since we got out of the car, I feel like this is something I recognise and can relate to. I know what they're doing. I look down at Sam, who has let go of my hand at last and is surveying the landscape, his eyes moving from screen to screen.

It looks like each row is playing a different *Minecraft* mini-game, with players fighting each other as they explore. They shout and laugh, maintaining a continuous commentary on what's happening like the YouTubers they all watch.

'I've got a diamond sword!'

'I need a pickaxe!'

'I'm hiding in a cave, leave me alone.'

'I've found a treasure chest.'

The language of the game, its materials and conventions are utterly familiar to them all. It is their natural habitat. They are like Sam.

I find a woman in a green *Minecraft* top with STAFF written on the back, leaning down speaking to one of the players.

'We're here for the building competition,' I say.

'Ooh, is this Sam? We've been waiting for you. Your friend Dan is holding your desk. I'll show you over.'

We follow her through to a much larger area with the monitors now on long trestle tables, with room for maybe a hundred players. There are already plenty here, idly working on buildings, or running around landscapes. I finally spot Dan, sitting at a desk, a Nintendo 3DS in his hands, tapping away at the buttons. He's wearing a *Call of Duty* T-shirt and a *Tomb Raider* cap, and he's surrounded by bags filled with posters and more T-shirts.

'Oh God,' I mutter. 'He's gone totally native.'

When he sees us he leaps up and high-fives Sam, before slapping me on the back.

'Finally,' he says. 'The servers are all up again, they're ready to go right now!'

'Thank you,' I tell him.

'What for?'

'Oh, you know, being here, helping us out, bringing down the festival's entire online infrastructure.'

'Oh, it's nothing.'

Sam takes his seat, and I realise he's between two girls roughly his age, both utterly engrossed in their own games. He sits down awkwardly, and clutches his satchel to his chest. I'm surprised he's made it this far, but now, the reality of being here, staying in this bewildering environment may be the moment it becomes too much, too real. But I've planned ahead.

'I've brought some of your toys to decorate the desk,' I say.

And then I notice Jody is also going through her own bag and producing a handful of action figures and models.

'Great minds,' she says.

'I brought Hulk and an airplane.'

'I have Batman, a Lego car and a photo of us three at the seaside,' she says.

'Ah yes, of course.'

We arrange all of his stuff around the monitor. And that's when we realise that this is the PC version of the game, not the Xbox version we have played on. They're sort of the same, but the controls and menus are different. But Sam grabs the mouse and loads up a map.

'I did not know he could use a PC,' says Jody.

'Olivia's brother has one,' says Sam. 'It's easy.'

'Remember that time when he was four, and he set up the cable TV system to record every episode of *Octonauts*? He learned by watching us. He also learned our smartphone passwords.'

'And the combination lock on my mountain bike,' says Jody.

'He tried to wheel it behind the bushes at the back of the garden because he was afraid you'd fall off it.'

'Yes! I remember all that. I'm surprised you do. It's nice.'

'I've started remembering a lot of good stuff again,' I say.

'Me too,' she replies.

A staff member gets us connected to the network.

'Are you OK?' I ask.

'I am overcoming my fear,' Sam says.

It seems like a lifetime ago that we first created Sam and Daddy's World together; that space we shared while apart. That connection between us. While everything else was chaos in our lives, we had somewhere that we could escape to and explore – a place that had logic and rules and definite borders. We knew where we were. We were safe and we could make anything we wanted. Being here suddenly brings it all into sharp, almost overwhelming focus.

As he sets himself up, I step back next to Dan, who seems to read my mind.

'We made it,' he says, then he puts an arm across my shoulder in a sort of matey side hug.

'Yeah, it's such a big thing for Sam. I can't believe we're actually here.'

'I can,' he says. 'I knew you'd do it, I knew you'd make it all OK.'

'I haven't done anything,' I say.

'That's what you always think. And you're always wrong. Have you no idea how much I rely on you? Ever since we moved in next door it's been the same. You fixed my bike, you told me what computer to buy, you didn't beat the shit out of me when I started dating your sister. I knew you'd get Sam here. You'll always get him where he needs to be.'

'Wow,' I say. 'What brought all that on, you soppy bastard?'

'I don't know ... we'll see.'

Then we look at each other, both thinking the same thing, that silent 'are we going to hug or not?' negotiation that male friends are cursed to endure. But then we do hug, much to Jody's obvious surprise. I want to say I hope we'll always be friends – instead it comes out as 'I hope we'll always be together.' But he knows what I mean, because, well, that *is* what I mean. I turned up at his flat with nothing, a broken figure, and his easy generosity brought me back. It took months, and he never once asked when I would be leaving. To be honest, I'm not sure if he ever would have.

Then it's all too much for us both and, spotting an empty sofa nearby, Dan runs for it, collapsing into its abundantly stuffed green cushions. Beside him is a row of parents, some staring around looking awestruck, others with blank expressions, reading magazines or checking their phones, as though sitting in a GP waiting room. As though nothing amazing was happening.

Sam is running around the virtual landscape, chasing the farm animals, then racing between the trees, getting the hang of the controls. The girl on his left is maybe ten or eleven, in a Creeper sweatshirt and thick glasses, her long hair in two pigtails. She's pointing at Sam's screen and saying something. He can't hear so she carefully lifts one of the ear cups; I almost flinch, worried about his reaction – I don't want him to strike out in fear or anger. But he listens intently and nods. This is another thing I'm learning: give him credit.

At the front of the room, a staff member steps on to a small stage, holding a microphone.

'Hello, everyone, the creative building competition is about to start. Anyone wanting to take part, can you all stop your games and load up Creative mode. We'll come round and check your names. Then we'll give you the theme of this year's competition and you'll have four hours to build your creation!'

I lift Sam's headset off and relay the message to him.

'Do you want me to stay with you?' I ask.

'No,' he says. 'I can see Mummy on the sofa. Will you sit on the sofa all the time?'

'Yes, we'll be there. Are you going to be OK?'

'Yes. Everything is OK. Daddy, what do I have to make?'

'They're going to tell you, Sam. They'll give you an idea, then you make something that is like that idea.'

'Can I make a castle?'

'I think it depends on the theme.'

'What's a theme?'

I kneel down next to him and put my hand on his.

'Sam, it doesn't matter – just make what you want; make something cool. You're good at this, you can make anything you want. Have fun.'

'But I want to win.'

'I know, and that's great. But don't worry. If you get upset, look over to me and I'll come, Sam. I'll come and get you.'

I stand back as a young guy with a clipboard approaches. He checks Sam's screen, then asks for his name. There is excited preparation as more kids race over to take part, clambering up on to the chairs, plugging in their laptops and games machines. There are maybe seventy of them now, chatting, fist-bumping; some are in their early twenties, looking quiet and confident. I wonder about walking past and accidentally yanking out their power cables. Instead I head over to the sofa, where Jody edges up to give me space.

'Is he OK?' she asks.

But before I can answer there's a loud squeal from the speaker system.

'OK, is everyone ready?' yells the announcer.

There's a muted drone of 'yes' from the assembled gamers.

'That's not good enough – ARE YOU READY?' she shouts.

'YES!' comes the reaction.

Sam, visibly shaken, takes off his ear protectors and looks around. The girl next to him says something and points to the stage. He puts the protectors on his lap.

'OK, the theme for this year's GEN-X *Minecraft* building competition is ...'

A dramatic pause. The kids at the screens all look up at her, mouths open, hands poised above keyboards and controllers. Everyone has been told to load the game in Flat mode, where there's no scenery at all, so I see dozens of screens with these flat empty worlds, ready for a spark of divine creativity; waiting for genesis.

'The theme is "The most important building in London". GO!'

There is a sudden flurry of activity and chatter as seventy gamers all open their crafting inventories at once and start scrolling through building materials. Some open another window on their screens and start googling 'London buildings', others begin to build almost immediately. I get a sudden jolt of excitement and confidence. Sam has been studying London buildings – he's already made the Tower of London and he can do it again. I see him look over to me, but I can't read the expression on his face, and now there are staff patrolling the area, trying to create a sort of cordon around the entrants. I give him an OK signal through the patrolling bodies and smile encouragingly. He's still looking at me and Jody has noticed now. He's staring, almost. I know the expression: he's thinking. I wonder if he's about to ask if he can go. But slowly, subtly, his face forms back into a smile, and his eyes return to the screen.

Then he starts to build.

Chapter 40

As Sam builds I catch something out of the corner of my eye, a familiar figure, near the entrance to the *Minecraft* zone, searching. It is Emma, looking confused and flustered. For a second I think she's abandoned Mum at home, but then I see – with some relief – that she's there too. Dan spots them and starts extravagantly waving, then seems to stop and think. He turns back to Jody and me.

'Oh God, do you think Emma has told her about us?'

I look at Jody and then we both look back at him. We nod simultaneously.

'Right,' he says.

Emma bounds over and hugs Dan. I wind through the groups of kids watching the *Minecraft* modellers to meet Mum.

'Hey, are you OK? I'm sorry we left, Emma totally made us do it.'

'I'm fine,' she says, taking hold of my arms. 'You should have told me about this, I wouldn't want Sam to miss it! Where is he?'

I point him out, through the mass of screens. It looks like he is getting the hang of the mouse and keyboard. He is utterly absorbed. He is happy.

'Look at him,' she says. 'He's doing it!'

'I know! He's made friends with the girl next to him.'

I feel like I could explode with pride. It is a strange and unfamiliar thing.

'I'm so glad you're here,' I say. 'I'm so glad you get to see this.'

Emma wrenches Dan over toward us. He trails behind like a sheepish schoolboy.

'Hello, Mrs Rowe,' he says.

'Well, hello, Dan,' says Mum, clearly relishing the meeting. 'I hear you're after my daughter again. Are you going to make an honest woman of her this time?'

'Erm,' he says. Even amid the din and darkness of the hall, his embarrassment is palpable.

'Mum!' exclaims Emma.

'I'm kidding. It's lovely to see you again, Dan. And Emma's right, you *are* a hunk.'

'MUM!' exclaims Emma again, in what will surely go down as the most mortifying exchange of her adult life.

'Come on, let's sit back down and watch the action,' I say. 'And by action I mean seventy kids sitting at computers in a massive dark room.'

And so, amid the constant reverberating noise from the main hall and the darkness alleviated only by blinding spotlights, I sit with my wife, my mum, my sister and my best friend, watching my son building something on a computer screen. Except with the tumult of staff and judges, the kids running around, the bustling parents, it's hard to make out what he's actually doing. So we sit together on the long over-stuffed sofa, shouting inane comments into each other's ears, occasionally sending someone out for over-priced cups of stagnant, muddy coffee that tastes like it has been made with unfiltered Thames water.

'If you do open a coffee shop,' shouts Jody, 'make sure you get their recipe!'

Mum is reading a magazine, Emma and Dan go into the main exhibition to play games. When they return, Emma is wearing a matching *Call of Duty* T-shirt. I sit forward, shifting my head left to right, trying to see what's on Sam's screen.

And somehow, my mind wanders to other waiting rooms, at other times. The last time I sat with Mum like this – waiting, watching, silent – well, it does not bear thinking about, but the memory lurks anyway, daring me to shut it out. Jody and I, meanwhile, have sat in countless surgeries and hospitals waiting for test results for Sam. Getting his hearing checked several times, then his motor skills, then his memory functions. So many tests, most coming back inconclusive because he wouldn't cooperate with the little exercises he was set. We've been waiting for Sam, in one way or another, for a decade. I look toward Jody and try to catch her eye, but she too is now dipping and rising in her seat, attempting to catch a peek at Sam's screen.

'I can't see what he's doing,' she says to no one. 'His screen looks blank.'

This worries me. What if he's sitting there doing nothing, confused about the whole thing? What if he suddenly can't make it work? But I see the mouse in his hand and his finger tapping the buttons thoughtfully – he's doing something. In some ways, I know that it's enough for me. It's amazing that he's here, amid this bizarre maelstrom of screens and action. He's here, like the others.

But at the same time not like them at all. This is what makes me so proud and so awestruck. He's got here on his own terms, combatting his own uncertainties. His grasp of our world is delicate and fleeting. It is often terrifying to him. But he has somehow constructed within himself the strength to be here. I think of the boy playing alone in the park, ever watchful of threats, and me wishing he could be like the gangs of other children, confident, running amok together. I don't want that at all now. Sam is himself; he can build his own world. It won't be like mine, there will be more systems – a lot more plans and timetables. I don't need to worry about it, I need to understand it.

'Are you OK?' says Jody.

'Yeah, I'm thinking. It's weird the way we learn things sometimes. All those nights, Sam and I sat playing the game online – we were both alone, but also sort of together, I mean actually together, in a way we hadn't been before.'

'I know,' says Jody, still staring beyond me to Sam's desk. 'I was there, remember?'

'One hour left!' shouts a man into the microphone.

As he leaves the stage, Jody rises to her feet and waves someone over. I look to where she's gesturing and see Prudence with Olivia and Harry. They bundle through the rabble of despondent parents.

'Hi,' yells Olivia, 'Sam said you'd be here!'

Jody and Prudence embrace with practised detachment, but when I get up to greet her, we perform the awkward middle-class air kiss; I try to stop at one but she goes in for the second, so that we end up in a half headbutt, half snog – another nightmarish social faux pas for the collection. As if the afternoon could get any more strange and unsettling.

'We came last year, the kids love it,' shouts Prudence, pretending that whatever just happened didn't just happen. 'They wanted to come and see Sam.'

'Where is he?' yells Olivia. I point over to him.

'What's he making?' asks Harry.

'I don't know, I can't see. The theme is the most important building in London.'

'He could make the Tower!' says Olivia, clapping her hands in excitement.

But who knows? Who knows what he's thinking. I picture his brain as something entirely segmented, the thoughts and feelings categorised and stored separately, like an old post office sorting room. Nothing must disturb the balance and order, but everything he experiences pummels the system with new information, new content, and he can't file it quickly enough. How on earth is he even here?

Mum is still reading; Jody is now chatting loudly with Prudence. Emma and Dan are back with plastic glasses of flat beer. The time ticks on. The competitors stare impassively at their screens like airport flight controllers. Underneath everything the sound of dance music and gunfire thuds like a quickening heartbeat.

'Ten minutes!'

I manage to glimpse a few of the screens. I see something that looks like Buckingham Palace, a couple of unidentifiable skyscrapers, an attempt at the Gherkin which looks extraordinarily phallic. The complexity of the challenge suddenly hits me. Reconstruct an identifiable landmark, a marvel of architecture, in four hours, with giant building blocks? What were they thinking? Will Sam even remember what we saw in London and in his book? Will he get London mixed up with Bristol? Will the crowds part, revealing his screen, and a chunky, childish model of the SS *Great Britain*? Suddenly guilt mixes in with trepidation – that old familiar friend. What have I set him up for?

'That's it, put down your mice,' someone on stage shouts. 'The competition is over! Please leave your computers so that the judges can come round.'

Sam gets up and wanders over, spotting Olivia and waving. Jody is up first, grasping him to her.

'Well done, Sam, I'm so proud of you!'

'What did you make?' shout Olivia and her brother, almost in unison.

'It's a secret,' he says. And he reaches out a hand, and places it in mine.

As the judges pass from screen to screen, I see them chat and make notes, and the weirdness of it hits me again. They're taking it very seriously, like Crufts or the Turner Prize. Behind the stage, a huge projector screen switches on, showing the GEN-X logo and the words '*Minecraft* builder of the year'. Engineers fiddle with a spaghetti-like flow of cables from the rear of the screen to a stack of servers and computers at its side. There's a buzz of activity as competitors and their friends and relatives discuss what they made. I stand there, looking around, blinking, uncertain. Dan slips a cup of beer into my hand and slaps me on the back. Jody takes my arm in hers.

'You did it,' she says. 'You got him here.'

'Do you think he made anything?'

'I don't know. I don't care. Look at him.'

And together, we glance across, and see him standing now with Olivia and Harry watching a *Minecraft* 'Hunger Games' tournament going on, pointing and laughing. He is showing off for Olivia, gesturing extravagantly at the screens, relishing her attention. It's OK. It's OK now, whatever.

And then a man dressed as Steve walks on to the stage, in dark blue trousers and a sky blue top, flanked by two other staff in Creeper-head boxes. The crowd cheers and there's a small surge forward at the front as people start to gather expectantly. This is it.

'The quality of entries was very high this year. We had a lot of amazing work, so let's have a round of applause for all the entries.'

There is a polite smatter of clapping and the odd whistle.

'But we can only have one winner, and this was a very special model indeed. Shall we tell you who's won?'

Cries of 'yes' from the crowd. One bored parent nearby yells 'Get on with it' and a few others laugh. I feel a rising tension, my stomach doing weird cartwheels.

'And the winner of this year's *Minecraft* building competition is ...'

A long theatrical pause. I watch Sam, his face slightly bored, slightly bewildered.

'Hannah James! Hannah has built a spectacular version of Big Ben and the Houses of Parliament. Come to the stage, Hannah.'

A teenager who looks about fifteen, with spiky black hair and a green-and-black striped jumper, bounds on to the stage, waving at a group of friends nearby. Then, on the large screen, footage of her model appears. It is indeed an impressive recreation of the Parliament building, capturing its stately gothic grandeur, its rows of small windows. I look at Jody and she shrugs. My heart sinks through the floor. Sam has wandered over now, standing between us, watching Hannah being interviewed on stage, but not, seemingly, with much interest. I desperately think of what to say to him, how to placate him, wondering if he'll even get that the event is over.

As I'm mulling this over, I barely hear the words coming from the stage.

'But we're not quite finished,' says the announcer. 'There was one more model ... we're not too sure what the building is, or why it's important, but we all liked it a lot. So we've decided to award a special commendation.'

There's a faint murmur from the audience. Several parents shush their kids and look back toward the stage.

I glance down and realise I am holding Jody's hand. Sam is

standing with Mum, examining her bandaged wrist. Olivia and her brother are sitting cross-legged on the floor, looking through their vast bags of freebies gathered from the various stands in the main exhibition. The lights catch my eyes and dazzle me a little. Jody grips tighter. Time seems to drag out. Children flit past in slow motion.

'So can we please invite Sam Rowe on to the stage.'

I don't hear it. Or at least my brain doesn't register it. There is a sort of silence, a whine, like faint tinnitus, then Jody has Sam in her arms, and Mum is hugging him too. Dan has his arm around my neck and he's shouting something. And then the noise breaks in.

The music, the crowds, the miracle of being here at all.

'Mummy?' says Sam. Jody looks at me and then the stage. The announcer is waiting, his hand cupped to his eyes, scanning the floor.

'Sam?' he says.

'Do you want to go up?' says Jody. 'You don't have to, I can tell them.'

He backs up a little toward me. Olivia is on her feet. She rushes over and hugs him. He looks bewildered. I feel him grab my leg.

'Daddy, you come with me.'

I nod dumbly. He puts the ear defenders on. And we walk forward. I try to make some sort of facial signal to the staff that will somehow magically indicate that he's autistic, that I don't know if he'll actually get on stage. But they're all beckoning him up. There is a polite ripple of applause. It sounds like rain.

Then we're at the front, and somehow he climbs slowly on to the platform. As the announcer is about to go over, I frantically gesture him to me. He's barely in his twenties, bouncy and enthusiastic. He comes over.

'He's autistic,' I shout. 'My son's autistic. This may be too much.'

He nods and moves away from me, then quickly talks to the others. After a few moments, I see him switch off the mic and gently kneel down next to Sam. He says something that I don't catch, and Sam nods. He's looking down at the floor, but he's smiling. Then the announcer switches the mic back.

'Let's look at Sam's model,' he says.

But I am looking at Sam, trying to read his expression, desperate to see that he's all right. This is him on stage, in front of hundreds of people, so far from his comfort zone he might as well be on another planet. And so far away from me, from us. But then, I suppose, he always was.

Around me, people are muttering and studying the model being projected above them, pointing and questioning. At last, I take a few pensive steps back and I look up at the massive screen. It takes a few seconds to sink in, to connect, but in a burst of recognition, I get it. I know in my heart; I know what he's built.

'Oh, Sam,' I whisper. 'Oh, my boy.'

I feel a hand on my shoulder, and it's Jody, I put my arms around her.

'How did he know? How did he understand?' I say.

'Because you talked to him about it,' she says. 'Because of the photo you take everywhere. He has always understood, you dummy.'

On the screen, twenty feet high and modelled in beautiful, intricate detail, is the Palace Café in Kensington. George's café.

There is the red awning, the glass front, the little wooden door. Either side are the two street lamps, glowing brightly; one is even flickering – as it had done, that day with Sam and Emma. Inside are the bookcase, the black-and-white square tiles, and some paintings dotting the walls. Sam has even built the houses either side, and the road in front. He has left his player character outside of the café, just like in the photo, and next to him there is a beacon, projecting a shaft of white light into the sky, and it breaks me into smithereens.

Then I can't see any more, because my eyes are full of tears and they keep coming and coming.

'Now, Sam,' says a voice somewhere at the very edge of my awareness. 'Can you explain what this building is? Don't worry if you can't.'

There is a long silence. Sam stands on the stage, looking around the audience, trying to find us. Jody waves and I look up. When he sees us, he waves too. Then he slowly and carefully takes off the ear protectors.

'It is the café,' he says.

'Go on.'

'The café my daddy went to. He was with his brother. They had a nice time.'

'It's a café in London?'

'Yes. But after ... some days after, Daddy's brother died. My daddy has a photo of the café and he carries it with him. He'll show you, if you like.'

'Is that why it's important?'

'Yes, because Daddy always remembers it. It makes him sad and happy. Some buildings are important because they are big, but some are important because they have memories in them. This is where my daddy's brother lives, I think.'

'That must have been very hard for your daddy?'

'It is hard but Daddy kept going. When I am scared, he and mummy say to me ...'

He looks around for me, and I wave. When he spots me, across the dark and the mass of people, he looks right at me – not down or to the side. Right at me. As he never has before. And when he says the words I know he'll say, I mouth them back to him.

'Life is an adventure, not a walk. That's why it's difficult.'

It feels like my heart will burst; a vast firework display of pride and love. I turn to say something to Jody but I can't, I can't find any words.

That's why it's difficult – because life is extraordinary and it means something, and those things are costly. You have to be patient and prepared and strong. For a long time on this adventure I was stupid – I saw Sam as an obstacle, something I'd have to work around. But that was wrong. Sam was the guide. Sam was always my guide.

He turns to the announcer.

'Please can I go and see my mummy and daddy now?'

'Yes, of course. Well done, Sam.'

Sam walks from the stage, taking care on the steps down. Applause begins again, quiet at first but growing. He looks around, the groups part to let him pass, someone points to us, he runs, and when I bend down to meet him, my arms open and he jumps into them.

'I made it for you,' he says.

'I know.'

'I almost won.'

'You did. You did win.'

We are engulfed by whooping and cheers, but all I can see or feel is my son.

Chapter 41

Heathrow, Sunday morning. Last night, after the excitement died down, we decided to get a hotel near the airport so we could see Emma off. Now we form a tired, ragtag group around my sister in the vast Terminal 5 departure lounge. Around us, travellers scuttle to check-in gates, pushing trolleys loaded with piles of chunky plastic cases. Children, bleary-eyed and confused, dawdle along behind their parents, trying to take in the unfamiliar noise and sights of it all. Airports are always a weird mix of excitement and fear, even for those who aren't going anywhere.

'I hate long goodbyes,' protests Emma, as we all stand around her, unsure what to do. In her immense hoodie and tracksuit bottoms she could either be flying to Rio or taking a pilates class. Mum is fussing, reunited with her daughter for the briefest time and now determined to pack in as much care as she can.

'Do you have moisturiser for the flight? And wet wipes?' she asks. 'Do you have those special socks – you know, to prevent, what is it? Toxic shock syndrome?'

'I think you're aiming for deep vein thrombosis, Mum,' says

Emma. 'And I've been on a lot of flights, I know what I'm doing. But thank you.'

Sam is a little distance away at the windows, looking up at the sky, watching aircraft thundering over. This morning he has talked us through the *Minecraft* competition several times. He started when he woke up and kept going throughout breakfast and then on the drive over, as though trying to make sense of it all. Otherwise, he is weirdly calm and dislocated – we have perhaps overloaded him with love and pride for the last twenty-four hours.

This is what I'm thinking when Dan theatrically clears his throat and says in a trembling voice: 'Emma, can I have a word?'

With that he leads her away from the rest of us, and out of the revolving doors. We all watch in quiet puzzlement as we see him talking to her, showing her a piece of paper. Then she nods, and the nod quickly becomes a hug, and Dan momentarily lifts her off her feet.

'What are they doing?' asks Sam.

'I have no idea,' I reply.

'I do,' says Jody.

They come back holding hands, looking stupidly excited.

'Well,' says Dan. 'I'm going too.'

And he holds up what is obviously an incredibly expensive and foolishly romantic last-minute plane ticket to Rio.

'He bought it online yesterday,' says Emma. 'He was waiting for the right time to tell me – apparently the right time was two hours before departure.'

There is a fair bit of squealing, laughter and more hugging, but no one apart from Sam and me is at all shocked or surprised. We stand together watching the weird show unfold.

'I don't know what's going on,' says Sam.

'Me neither,' I say.

'You take care of this young man,' Mum says to Emma.

'I will. I'm sorry, Mum. I'll stay in touch, I promise. Properly this time.'

'I know. I might come out and meet you somewhere, you never know.'

'Do it,' says Emma.

While Mum continues her checklist with Emma, I take Dan slightly to one side.

'How are you?' I ask.

'Yeah, good. I mean, apart from everything being batshit crazy. This time last week I had a job and a flat, now I'm on my way to Brazil.'

'You *had* a flat?'

'I'm going to sell it, Alex. I don't know how long we'll be away, and I don't want the hassle of renting it out. I want to start from scratch. I'm sorry, man. It'll take a few months to go through, obviously. But that's all you'll need.'

'All I'll need for what?'

'To sort things out with Jody, yeah?'

'Right.'

'I mean it, you dumb shit. Jody will give you another shot. You've got to take it.'

'I hope so. I will.'

'And give that café a go. You can do it. As Darth Vader said, it is your destiny.'

'Hmm, well, destiny is going to need to provide some capital.'

He gives me a curious lopsided smile and slaps me on the back.

'Your lack of faith disturbs me,' he says.

I go over and hug Emma, and she whispers exactly the same advice into my ear – go back home, open the coffee shop, live a little. Sam runs over too and for the first time he embraces Emma unselfconsciously.

'Now I have to find out where to get the plane,' she says. 'Sam?'

'Your gate is S48,' he says. 'It is a fifteen-minute walk.'

'Thank you,' she says.

There are no tears, no last-minute changes of heart or desperate pleas to stay or rethink. We're not like that as a family. We've been through a lot, after all. Emma's departure is – I think we have all come to realise – inevitable. Sure, I didn't realise she'd drag my best friend along with her, but it's fine, I'll cope. We'll always have the Old Ship Inn, we'll always have Sid. Actually, Sam and I are going in for a quiet drink this afternoon – I've promised that he can play chess, and perhaps it will become a regular thing. Safety and friendship are important, but for some people they are harder to attain. We should help when we can.

As our two travellers saunter off toward the security gates, we stand in silence and watch them until they disappear beyond the checkout counters. I feel a hand on my shoulder and it is Jody's.

'Are you OK?' she says.

'Yeah. I mean, she stole my best mate, but yeah.'

'Shall we go home?'

I put my hand on hers and her skin feels as familiar as my own. When I move closer to her, when we kiss, it is somehow both thrilling and familiar. For the briefest of moments, everything else dissolves away. The voices around us fade to a murmur, the jet planes tread silently across the sky above. There is only this, the thing I once lost, the connection forged in a cider orchard one summer a long time ago. I swear to myself that, if we do manage to get it back together, I will never take this intimacy for granted again.

Then I think we both have the same thought, because, together, we look around to find Sam – and he's there, pointing out the departures board to Mum, reading out the airlines, the cities, telling her the flight times. She listens patiently, holding his hand.

Tighter, I hear him saying. Slightly tighter. Tighter still. And I understand now, that this isn't him being fussy and annoying: his grip on the world is more fragile than ours – he doesn't trust it as much. We need to prove to him that we won't let go. And if we do that, he'll be fine.

'OK,' I say, snapping out of this reverie, 'let's find the car.'

Mum nods and playfully hauls Sam toward us. I hope I can convince her to move, if not to Bristol, then at least somewhere close by. Apart from anything else, there is clear babysitting potential here.

And as we trudge back toward the exit, I look over my shoulder toward the security area, and I'm sure I glimpse Dan and Emma passing through the gates to the other side, their arms around each other. I wonder when I will see them again, and how different everything will be when I do.

Chapter 42

The first day of term, the first day at a new school – the school Sam has chosen, with our support. Once, I would have been terrified by this, I would have done anything to escape. Instead, I'm parking up outside our home, at 7 a.m. in the morning, and I'm rushing to the door. I want to be a part of it.

Christmas was quiet, but happier than I could have expected a few short weeks ago. I stayed over the night before; Jody and I sat up late wrapping dozens of *Minecraft* books, toys and Lego sets for Sam, then we spent Christmas day together as a family. I stayed again a few nights later, and somehow that became a whole weekend. I'm still in the spare room; we are moving cautiously. We want to play it safe. We are learning, as a family, to handle things together, and to listen to each other.

When I press the bell, Sam answers almost immediately, his new uniform untucked and already dishevelled.

'We've lost my new shoes!' he shouts.

'I can help.'

I walk in as Jody flies past, up the stairs, a cup of coffee in her hand, the contents sloshing over the wooden steps. The radio is blaring, there are toys and pyjamas and towels everywhere.

'Hi, he hasn't had breakfast,' she says without stopping. 'We can't find his shoes!'

'Can I show you my pictures?' says Sam. 'I have drawn a Creeper fighting Spider-Man.'

'I'd love to see them. But let's find those shoes first. Come on, quickly. It's a quest.'

We run through the living room, flinging cushions and blankets and toys out of the way. I pretend to be Hulk as I lift the sofa for him to peer under; he laughs when I put it down on my foot. In the kitchen, we crawl under the table, flicking stray cornflakes and Cheerios at each other, becoming wedged between the chair legs. He is getting tall. He's growing up.

When we eventually haul ourselves out, there is Jody, standing above us, with mock impatience, holding the shoes.

'They were in the laundry basket,' she says simply and hands them over. 'With some books and action figures.'

Sam makes a long 'ahhhhh' sound in recognition.

'Laundry basket?' I say.

'I was playing. It was my treasure chest,' he says.

Jody is preparing for a new exhibition, the gallery's biggest. The artist uses video game graphics projected on to the walls to make these immersive digital tapestries. She understood the appeal as soon as she saw them – because of Sam, because of how he discovered and built a world around himself. As she gathers all her notes and papers, I straighten out Sam's uniform, tucking in his shirt, helping him to put on the jumper. The static makes his hair stand on end, much to our amusement.

'You're going to a new school,' I say.

'I know.'

'How are you feeling?'

'A little bit scared. The scariest airport is Gibraltar because the runway is very short and the plane might fall off the end.'

'OK. That does sound scary.'

When we eventually leave the house, we leave as a family, a regular family, chatting and busy and not shouting or sick with nerves.

Then we're at the school entrance, on a bitterly cold morning. Sam becomes quiet as he watches the other children file past him. A new gaggle of parents surrounds us, and though I feel the familiar tinge of fear approaching the gates, we press on.

Now we are here, we're hoping we all made the right decision. Hoping he'll be accepted. We need this. It feels like we're building a momentum toward something better.

'Are you OK?' I say to Sam, ruffling his hair.

'Yes,' he says.

'And this is the right school, do you think?' adds Jody.

'I think so,' he says.

When you start out as a parent, you have these big ambitions for your child: success, popularity, brilliance. But as life goes on, sometimes that scales back to something much more profound. Happiness. That's what we want for Sam. There were times it felt extraordinarily out of reach, like a distant star. It took a video game, of all things, to show us how close it was, and how tangible. Sam told us which school would make him happy and we believed him.

Our boy shivers as he surveys the schoolyard, the children playing in their little groups, the parents watching anxiously, or chatting between themselves. I'm not sure what he is looking for, but it feels like he is summoning the courage to make those last steps forward, over the threshold. For a few seconds it seems as though he'll need a gentle nudge from us. We brought this decision to him, this fork in his journey. Maybe we need to give him one last push.

But then he spots her, running toward him through the crowd, waving her new school bag.

Olivia.

'Sam!' she cries, and unselfconsciously wraps her arms around him. 'You're coming to my school?'

'Yes,' he says, proud and embarrassed, a sheepish smile on his face.

Yes. St Peter's, the school Jody and I drove to, months ago, barely able to talk to each other, and then Miss Denton told us that he would be happy there, and even in the midst of our own misery we understood that there was something in the promise that rang true. Perhaps we communicated that to Sam more clearly than we thought. Perhaps he came to the decision on his own. Perhaps it was Olivia, his friend, his ally, who helped him. Then from behind her, Harry and his friends gather around welcoming Sam, patting him on the back. Then somehow, before we are ready, they are guiding him through the gate and he is going. And I feel Jody tense up beside me.

'Oh,' she says quietly.

I put my arm on her shoulder – a gesture that once again feels natural.

'It's OK,' I say. 'This is good, this is a good sign.'

But then, as the rabble of kids walks down the path toward the school doors, a flurry of over-sized backpacks and winter coats, Sam suddenly breaks out and runs back; back into our arms.

'Goodbye, Mummy, goodbye, Daddy. Will you pick me up from school?'

'Yes, of course,' says Jody.

'Daddy too?'

'Yes,' I say.

Then he walks slowly to the doors and the others pull him through.

'Shall we get a coffee?' I say.

'Yes,' replies Jody. 'I've got some time, I think. Where are we going?'

And as we wander to the car, I ponder exactly how to answer that question.

When I go back to the flat later that morning, I open the door and the stillness and silence hit me like a wave. Without Dan, the stark modern design of this place just feels cold and austere. I suddenly recall the moment I turned up all those months ago, a sports bag in my hand and nothing else, and nowhere else to be. I was in shock. I thought that it was the end of the world. But it wasn't. I wander through to the guest bedroom, where my things are still scattered about, and that awful air mattress is slumped in a corner, a reminder of my first weeks here, staring up at the ceiling, trying to map out a constellation of my fears and woes. What I couldn't see then, but what seems obvious to me now, is that I was lost in my grief and sadness. I saw fear everywhere, and I backed away from everything – including Jody, including Sam. I couldn't imagine the future.

It took my son to bring me back, and it took being apart to make that happen. It's weird how life works out. I'd always thought there was a barrier around him, that there was no way in. I couldn't see a way of developing an understanding, a point of contact. I didn't realise we would have to build it together and that he would show me how.

I walk through the narrow corridor, into the living room with its giant television and the console unplugged beneath it. And there on the coffee table, now creased and well-thumbed, is the *Minecraft* guide I bought as an afterthought. Guiltily, I concede to myself that the autism books I also picked up that day have been skimmed, but barely read at all. In the end, they were hardly needed.

On my way out of the building, I check Dan's cubbyhole for post. A couple of bills, a local paper, and something else. A letter addressed to me, in handwriting I sort of recognise but haven't seen in a while. It is only as I'm opening it that I remember: it's Dan's.

Dear Alex

Happy New Year from Rio! I'm hoping that you had a good Christmas and that you're making a go of it with Jody. If not, for God's sake, Alex, do I have to come back there and sort you out?

Anyway, before I left, I sold my car (I'm sorry, I know you loved it) and then a lot of big pay cheques came in at once. The flat will go for double what I paid for it. So I've enclosed something for you. It is not only a gift, it is an investment. Please see the instruction on the back – and then follow it. It's what George would want.

Be brave.

Your friend

Dan

I look inside the envelope and fish out a slip of paper – it takes me a few moments to recognise that it is a cheque. I didn't know people still used cheques, least of all Dan. That is the first thing that hits me. The second is that it is a cheque made out to me – for £20,000. I feel my lungs emptying of breath, my head swirls slightly. Dan, you crazy bastard. I flip it over.

And on the other side, written in large letters, is the message I sort of knew I'd find. I understand immediately why it's there, and what I now have to do – for me, for Jody, for Sam, for the future. It is two simple words.

Ok, GO.

Acknowledgements

It turns out that writing a book is really hard. In fact, for me, it would have been impossible without a lot of help. I just wanted to say thank you to a few of the people who were there when I needed them.

For example, there was a lot of practical guidance along the way. Jake Mattock gave me useful information about estate agents, and Liz Andrew essentially told me how to set up a coffee shop. I also had long conversations about autism and parenthood with Brigid and Adam Moss, and John Harris and Ginny Luckhurst. Thank you for your time and for sharing your own experiences with me. Thank you Adam Clarke (aka Wizard Keen) for your invaluable *Minecraft* modelling advice, and thank you Josh Ling for your information about *Minecraft* competitions.

I would also like to thank my colleagues at the *Guardian*, who were so good about me taking last-minute month-long sabbaticals to write this book. Thank you Jemima Kiss and Jonathan Haynes; thank you Alex Hern and Samuel Gibbs (who I accidentally named my lead characters after); thank you also to Stuart Dredge, Hannah Jane Parkinson and Shiona Tregaskis.

Of course, this book really, *really* couldn't have happened without the creator of *Minecraft*, Markus 'Notch' Persson, and the whole team at Mojang. Thank you for making this incredible game and enriching so many lives. I would especially like to thank Paddy Burns and 4J Studios, who made the Xbox 360 version of *Minecraft*, which is the one I first discovered and the one I shared with my own sons. Super special thanks go to Roger Carpenter at Microsoft, who took the time to show me the game during a very crowded preview event in San Francisco and has stayed in touch ever since. I'd like you to know, Paddy and Roger, that you changed the lives of my family for the better.

I want to say thank you to all my friends and colleagues in the games industry. João Diniz Sanches shared an office with me during the writing process and put up with me regularly interrupting his work to ask ridiculous questions or just to dramatically moan and whinge and bang my head on the desk. Simon Parkin, Christian Donlan and Will Porter are just wonderful. Also thanks to Ann Scantlebury, Simon Byron and Ste Curran on the radio show *One Life Left* and Ellie Gibson and Helen Thorn, who present the brilliant Scummy Mummies podcast – both let me appear on their shows to talk about the book while I was writing it. Thanks too, Ellie, for the white wine, quality television and convenient accommodation.

My unending thanks and admiration go to my editor Ed Wood, who first approached me about this book, then approached me again when I ignored his email, then guided me through this entire process with incredible warmth, patience and enthusiasm. He has been amazing, and I will be for ever in his debt.

I would like to thank my mum and my sisters, Catherine (also my medical consultant) and Nina. I wish my dad was here to see this happening. I wish he was here full stop.

Finally, my eternal love and gratitude go to my sons Zac and Albie, and to my wife Morag, who read this book throughout the process, who provided brilliant feedback and who came up with some of the best scenes. Morag is the greatest, really, and that's all.

Now read on for the beginning of
Keith Stuart's next book

Days of Wonder

Chapter One

Tom

There is such a thing as magic. That was what I always believed. I don't mean Abracadabra-type magic; I don't mean pulling rabbits out of hats or sawing people in half (and then putting them back together: otherwise it's not magic, it's just basically murder). I don't really mean fairy tale magic, either, with its princesses and witches and frogs that turn into handsome guys – although maybe we'll come to that. I just mean the idea that incredible things are possible, and that they can be conjured into existence through will, effort and love.

I especially believed in the magic of theatre: the transformation that happens when any space becomes a stage. Okay, so I *had* to believe in that, because I owned a theatre – well, I ran one. Technically the council actually owned it. Look, that's not important right now. The important thing is, I believed in magic, and I believed magic could change things. That's how it started. That's how we got through everything in the way we did.

So this is a story about magic, and therefore I should start somewhere magical. Or *kind of* magical. Look, it'll make sense, trust me. I suppose I really ought to begin with Hannah's diagnosis, but screw that, we're not going there, not yet. We'll begin two weeks later, on Hannah's fifth birthday – because, ha ha, this is what life is like sometimes: you're planning for a big day and then suddenly – pow – have some shocking news, no go on I insist. Of course, I didn't explain things fully to Hannah, how could I? But Hannah was already wise, wiser than me – wise enough to look into my eyes and understand the essence of what the doctors had told me, and what was coming. We stood at the bus stop outside the hospital, the cold sun glinting off the scratched plexiglass shelter. I tried hard to swallow, but it felt like I had a bowling ball in my throat. She looked up at me.

'It's okay,' she said. 'It's okay.'

And she put out her tiny fist for me to bump. I bumped it.

Anyway.

Anyway.

Where was I?

So yeah, I thought, I have to do something special for her birthday – something to take us out of this place. I asked her what she wanted, and she shrugged and said, 'I just want to play Lego with my friend Jay.' So that's what we did.

But I had something else set up. She had this book she absolutely loved; a fairy tale collection that had been handed down through my mum's family. It was incredibly ancient, so had none of the neurotic delicacy of a modern translation: kids died in the forest, dwarfs were eaten by witches, wolves butchered woodcutters – just horrible stuff. Hannah adored it. Whenever we got to the end of a story, she'd always say, 'But fairies aren't real, are they?' and I'd tell her they definitely were, but that only special people got to see them. It was just a little joke, a little routine to end the day. But on that night, the night of her fifth birthday, she asked as usual, only this time I said to her, 'Look out of the window later and you may be lucky.' She laughed at me dismissively, and buried her head in the duvet until I got up to go. But I knew she was curious, because she was *always* curious.

So I kissed her on top of her head, her curly hair bedraggled and knotty because neither of us were any good at combing it; then I walked out of the room, closing the door behind me – except I left a gap, just enough to peek through. And sure enough, when she thought I was gone, she pulled back the duvet and crept toward the window. Outside, the night was almost completely black, the stars obscured behind a layer of cold distant cloud. Our house backs onto a field and during the day, we'd sometimes see horse riders pass by, following the bridleway up to the woods. But at night, there was nothing but darkness and then the distant twinkling lights from the next town miles away.

I could see that Hannah was now on tiptoes at the window, her small body silhouetted against the darkness outside. Suddenly, her head flicked to the right. From behind the tall hedge at the rear of our neighbour's garden there was a curious glow, orange and warm, like a bonfire – except there was no crackling, just the sound of very gentle music, almost lost in the buffeting wind. Then, indistinct at first but gradually louder, there were voices too. They were singing.

I heard Hannah take a sharp intake of breath, and then she rubbed furiously at her eyes with the sleeve of her Buzz Lightyear pyjamas before staring out again. She didn't move away, she didn't shrink from the window – she stayed still, as though entranced, as though connected to whatever was happening outside. Then, as the music got louder, she somehow stirred from her reverie.

'Daddy!' she shouted. But there was no fear in her voice, it was not even shock or surprise. It was delight.

'Daddy,' she said again. 'I can see them, I can see them!'

'See what?' I said. And I was bounding into the bedroom,

pretending that I had no idea what was going on. She grabbed my hand and dragged me to the window.

'The fairies,' she said. 'There are fairies here!'

And right enough, dancing along the bridle path at the end of the garden, holding lanterns and waving and smiling as they passed, was a line of beautiful figures in luminous white dresses and giant fluttering wings. Hannah watched, at first transfixed, then banging on the window, waving back delightedly. It was the first time in a week I'd seen her forget herself and everything else. If only for an instant, it wiped away the darkness of the proceeding days. The figures danced and sang and waved, the light from the lanterns forming a halo around them.

I'll let you into a little secret. Technically, they weren't fairies. If you listened carefully you would recognise that the music was not some enchanting lullaby or mystical ballad – it was '2 Become 1' by the Spice Girls, playing on a ghetto blaster. The thing is, when you manage a theatre, one of the perks of the job is twenty-four-hour access to enthusiastic amateur actors, who respond positively to the request 'will you come and dance past our house on Sunday night dressed in glowing leotards?' And yes, we also had a reasonably stocked props department.

So I'd had this silly whim, a daft way to lighten the darkness. And it worked. Eventually, Hannah bolted from the window and made for the stairs, determined to see the show up close. But by the time she got to the back door, the fairies were gone (as we had arranged), scarpering into the alley a few houses down. I still don't know if she believed they were real or knew it was a show, but when I caught her up, she was standing in the open doorway, the breeze blowing her hair around her shoulders. She glanced up at me, then grabbed my hand.

'Again,' she said. 'Again.'

I suppose it was clear from that point that Hannah would be a sucker for escapism, for wonder – it was in her genes after all. As for me, I knew I had a way, however trivial and momentary, to distract her from what had happened, and what was to come. I could arrange something like this every year, for every birthday, if that's what she wanted. And she did.

So that's what happened And then the years passed, faster than I could ever have imagined, and there I was, three months before her sixteenth birthday, wondering if there was time to put on just one more show for her. It felt important – as though a little part of the future depended on it. I was a big believer in the magic of the theatre, you see. Did I mention that?

Chapter Two

Hannah

Don't die on stage. Don't even think about it. I'm completely fucking serious.

This is the rip-roaring motivational speech drifting through my head as I walk out beneath the theatre's glaring spotlights for the first time; for the first proper time, at least. As an actor.

I've been here before, of course, lots of times. When your dad is a theatre manager, you quite literally grow up on the stage – which sounds incredibly glamorous until you learn that this particular stage is in a small market town in Somerset, and not, say, New York. I am also making my debut for the local drama group, not for the RSC, and while we're being totally honest and self-deprecating here, the play isn't *Hamlet* or *The Doll's House*, or anything else I've been pretending to read for GCSE Drama. The play is a 'bawdy farce', written in the seventies by some guy I've never heard of – my dad calls it *Carry On Being a Sexist Prick*, but that's not its actual name. Anyway, this sort of thing goes down well with audiences here, so we're stuck with it. This is a small theatre and the usual fare is stand-up comedians, tribute bands and children's plays performed on Saturday afternoons in front of aggressively uninterested four-year-olds, so this is comparatively high-brow stuff. Sally, the drama club creative director, has at least adapted the script for the modern era – which has basically meant taking out the racist jokes. The sexist ones have stayed in, though, because apparently they're fine as long as we perform them with irony. I have learned a lot about what adults consider acceptable since joining the drama club last year. I don't get out much so I have to take my life lessons where I find them – even if that means performing in a 'bawdy farce' in my dad's theatre.

When it's my time to come on stage, things are already in full swing. The set is a seventies suburban living room, complete with a lime green sofa, shag pile carpet and a bamboo coffee table. Ted is putting in a brilliant performance in the lead role as a neurotic and flustered accountant, staring retirement in the face and having to deal with a moribund home life. It was genius casting by Sally, because he is, in real life, a neurotic and flustered accountant staring retirement in the face and having to deal with a moribund home life. Natasha is playing his wife, a role she is at least twenty years too young for. Dora, our props lady (and head of refreshments), found her a grey wig in a costume hire store, but Margaret – the drama club's oldest, wisest and rudest member – said it makes Natasha look like a French harlot. She's wearing it anyway – despite, or perhaps because, of that. I had to look up 'harlot' on Google and it is now my favourite word.

So that's the scene I am stepping into: a neurotic middle-class couple in seventies Britain, about to host a dinner party for the new neighbours, who seem extremely posh and respectable. But then the hosts' drunken teenage daughter comes home from a party and they have to hide her in the understairs cupboard.

401

That's me, by the way. I'm the drunken schoolgirl and I am wearing a garish flowery dress made out of polyester and static electricity.

It's while I'm trying to flatten out the skirt that Sally nods at me from the side of the stage and I realise my cue is coming; there is the sound effect of a doorbell, and then I'm on, out into the open auditorium in front of rows of people who have paid actual money to be entertained.

Oh shit, here we go then.

The first thing I notice is that the air has this weird crackle to it, a kind of all-enveloping tension that seems to tingle all over my skin – it's either the anticipation of the crowd or the static from this polyester fire hazard I'm wearing, I'm not sure which. I try to block it out and concentrate on what I'm doing, which is giggling and shrugging apologetically when my parents ask what the heck is wrong with me. Then I stagger past Natasha, whose wig has sort of slipped over her right eye at a jaunty angle. Then I prat-fall onto the dessert trolley. I hear some actual laughs from the audience, which is such a relief because I have zero personal experience of alcohol. In drama, we're learning about the theatre practitioner Constantin Stanislavski and he said that all the best acting comes from the 'emotional memory' of the performer – you have to call on things you've experienced. However, the only emotional memory I have of alcohol is seeing my dad fall off a pub bench at his fortieth birthday party and cracking his stupid head open. So I did what everyone does nowadays – I learned from watching YouTube videos. Can I just advise you that typing 'drunken teenage girls' into a search engine yields some highly interesting and useful results, but ninety percent of them are not safe for work.

So now I'm safely on stage, collapsed across the ugly furniture; and Ted and Natasha are splashing me in the face with vase water to try and sober me up – and the audience is chuckling along. It's fun, it's actually going well.

Then out of the corner of my eye, I spot Dad – or Tom as he is known to everyone else – watching me from the side of the stage. He is wearing his usual outfit of black jeans, shirt, tie and blazer. His hair is all spiky, and the gel glistens in the light. My friends say he looks like an aging popstar. I don't know if that's a good thing or not. They seem to like him anyway. He's not like other dads, they say, because he's always in a good mood, he isn't obsessed with sport and he actually listens to them when they talk. These are apparently rare commodities in fatherhood, which seems weird and sad to me. Anyway, his face is the familiar mix of deranged pride and encouragement that I have become accustomed to.

He used to bring me here when I was a toddler, when he first got the job as manager. He'd lift me up onto the stage and act out stories for me. He practically taught me to read sitting up here, a single spotlight on us, working our way through the syllabus of books that every burgeoning thespian is drawn to: *Swish of the Curtain, Ballet Shoes, The Town in Bloom*. Those were the best days. Even when he was working, he'd pick me up from school and bring me straight to the theatre. He'd be sat with some touring company planning their show, while I ran about the place, prancing across the stage or legging it along the aisles of the auditorium, yelling and singing. Then, for my birthdays, we started to write these little plays together, and we'd put them on with the drama group, for all our families and friends. It became a sort of tradition. It meant so much to me when I was younger.

Of course I was desperate to be in a actual real play, but Dad always told me that I'd have to be really good before he'd consider it. 'We can't let people believe there is nepotism in the arts,' he always says. 'The critics will tear us apart like wild dogs.' I seriously doubt the theatre reviewer at the local paper – the only critic who ever comes to Dad's productions – would be capable of tearing anything apart, let alone a person – being as she's a gentle seventy-year-old woman with a penchant for Noël Coward. But Dad has always been adamant.

So when they'd decided on this particular play, and it had a part for a fifteen-year-old girl, I literally begged him for the part. I thought it was hopeless, to be honest. This year already, he refused to let me play Cecily in *The Importance of Being Earnest*. He said there were some dangerous stunts – I've read that play three times and I know for a fact that Wilde doesn't do stunts. Then he rejected my brilliant idea for a modern-day production of *Macbeth*, where the whole cast would be teenage girls, except for the witches who would be men. I said to Dad, 'It's all about sex and rivalry on social media and the witches are internet trolls.' He didn't go for it. He always had some excuse. I know it's because he worries about me and not because he thinks I'll be crap at acting and bring shame and disrepute on his theatrical empire. Ideally, he'd like to keep me locked up in a small room and never let me out. No, wait, that sounds weird. Ideally he'd like to roll me up in bubble wrap and … oh God, whatever, you get the idea. Anyway, when I started drama GCSE I think he finally realised I was being serious, and that it was technically *all his fault anyway*.

After a whole skit about a soufflé that hasn't risen (which some-how segues into a really gross mother-in-law joke) we get to the part where Ted has to drag me to the understairs cupboard at the rear of the stage. This is no shoddy piece of sub-Ikea furniture, by the way; it was purpose-built by Kamil, the drama club's props manager, who teaches a woodwork diploma at the local college and takes the theatre very seriously. With perhaps slightly too much pride, he worked on it for weeks then unveiled to us an actual wooden staircase, complete with actual cupboard, all built on casters for easy deployment. It's so solidly constructed that you could conceivably throw it off a cliff and it would still be in one piece at the bottom. Which is probably more than could be said for the person locked inside.

Sorry, I get a bit dark sometimes. Especially when I am being hauled across a stage. It's sort of weird to be manhandled in front of a roomful of laughing people, but Ted is very professional and also extremely careful not to hold me anywhere that could conceivably get him arrested.

'Are you okay?' he whispers as he shoves me in the box. His thin, slightly haggard grey face is a mask of concern and his glasses are slipping off the end of his nose, as always. I nod imperceptibly. Seemingly assured, he tries to slam the door shut, but my arm is still sticking out, so he lifts it in and tries again. Cue general hilarity. Thanks, Ted.

Now I have to sit here for twenty minutes, which is not great as I'm slightly claustrophobic, and under these lights, it gets really hot. Heat and darkness and no air ... not a great combination for someone with my health issues. I try to ignore my rapidly increasing heart rate. Deep breaths. Deep breaths. This is the theatre and the show must go on, even when you're locked in a box that is rapidly turning into an oven. I hear Sally and Shaun enter the stage as the neighbours, and I know they're hilariously overdressed in ridiculous Oxfam approximations of upper-middle-class seventies casual wear.

It turns out in the play that the neighbours think they have been invited to a swinging party, rather than a polite dinner soirée. As soon as Ted and French-harlot Natasha leave the stage to 'fetch the crudités', Sally and Shaun discuss whether this is some sort of code and then start removing their clothes. The audience is really into it, guffawing unselfconsciously. Inevitably, the local vicar arrives, played by James, who is twenty-seven, quite fit, and also the most devout atheist I've ever met. He finds the semi-naked couple in the living room and then passes out on the sofa – spontaneous applause follows. Natasha shouts, 'I'll get you a stiff drink, this is not what it seems', and then opens the cupboard door, at which point I sprawl out, swearing loudly. The vicar tries to help me up, but I fall on top of him (my favourite part of the play) and we sprawl together on the stage floor unable to extricate ourselves from each other. Natasha drags me up, almost yanking my arm out of its socket, and James crawls out through the door.

Our big finale has my parents chasing me around a table, as the embarrassed neighbours get dressed. I lollop about the stage as Natasha and Ted grab at me while also berating their guests, and then they finally restrain me, dumping me on a chair at the dining table. As two police officers turn up, responding to reports of a possible orgy or violent murder, I end up passing out at the dining table, my face in a strawberry Pavlova. The generously constructed stunt dessert fills my nose and eyes with squirty cream – which would be fine if it hadn't gone rancid under the lights. Whatever, the audience is in pieces and I'm going to get an Olivier Award.

When the play is over, there is a genuinely rapturous applause. I bound to the front of the stage with the other cast members, taking Ted and Natasha's hands and swinging them extravagantly. I am euphoric; I feel like a proper part of this bizarre little team. Later, at the pub, if Dad lets me come, we'll probably relive every line, every audience reaction, as the drama club always does after a performance, whether it is good, like this, or bad, like their ill-advised attempt to stage *Equus* at a local horse and pony show.

With the spotlights lower now, I look into the crowds of people, hoping to spot my friends Jenna and Daisy, or perhaps my drama teacher Mrs Gibb, who said she would come. But all the faces are sort of similar and hard to make out beyond the clapping hands. Ted is hugging me and so is Natasha, and they pat me on the back, and then Natasha is very close and saying something, and I have to grasp her arm and lean in to hear it. 'Are you okay, Hannah,' she's saying again. 'Are you okay?' I want to say, 'Of course I'm okay, I'm a STAR'. But then I realise I can't really feel my legs, and a swirling black fog has gathered at the edges of my vision. I stagger backwards a bit.

'I'd quite like a glass of water,' I say, but actually nothing comes out, and the world is a woozy carousel of blurred shapes.

From a long distance away, I feel a hand on my arm, and another on my back, but it seems as though I am falling through them, and down, and further down. Suddenly, I worry that the audience can see what's happening. Oh God, how mortifying. Maybe they'll think it's part of the show? Like a sort of comedy encore. Then I have a strange hallucinogenic vision of Dad standing at my graveside delivering a eulogy: 'She died as she lived – like Tommy Cooper.'

And that's how I know something really is very wrong because that's just fucking weird.

Finally, I manage to say, 'Oh, this is so bloody typical.' Because this is not the first time I've done this, not by a long way.

The theatre lights look like stars above me. They swim about in the darkness. Then there is absolutely nothing.

Connect with
Keith Stuart

On Twitter 🐦 @keefstuart

WIN AN EARLY COPY OF HIS NEW BOOK

Sign up online for a chance to win
an early copy of *Days of Wonder*, and receive
news about Keith's new publications:

www.boymadeofblocks.com